GINGERSNAPS

GINGERSNAPS

DELORYS WELCH-TYSON

One World
Ballantine Books
New York

A One World Book
Published by The Ballantine Publishing Group

Grateful acknowledgment is made to Helen Chu-Lapiroff for permission to reprint
ˏthe poem "Legend of the Sleeping Princess."

http://www.randomhouse.com

Library of Congress Cataloging-in-Publication Data
Welch-Tyson, Delorys.
    Gingersnaps / Delorys Welch-Tyson. — 1st ed.
       p.   cm.
    ISBN 0-345-42245-7 (alk. paper)
    I. Title.
PS3573.E45445G5   1998
813'.54—DC21   98-21211
                                        CIP

Text design by Cathy Cahill Towle

Manufactured in the United States of America

First Edition: October 1998

10   9   8   7   6   5   4   3   2   1

Dedicated to
my brothers, Henry, Jr., Johnnie, and Connie

In memory of
my cousin Cedric

Gingersnaps:
Spicy, hard, brown cookies

PROLOGUE

Once upon a time—way back sometime during the volatile, mean-spirited, and divisive nineties, which actually were fallout years following the high-living, self-absorbed bullshit eighties—at a bus stop on the corner of Seventh Avenue and Fifty-seventh Street stood a young, handsome, and apparently exhausted black man wearing a colorful down-filled jacket and a pair of Levi's.

He stood in a pool of moonlight, relaxed and unsuspecting. It was a bit past midnight.

The shops in the area were closed and their gates were down. The streets were empty of the usual hand-flailing, loquacious New Yorkers, and the only sound that could be heard was the rhythmic thumping of Geraldo's helicopter taking him home to his family across the river.

The young man had been digging into his pocket searching for exact change or a token for the bus when a van drove up to the curb directly in front of him. He frowned and squinted as he tried to read the words stenciled on the side of the van.

SOCIETY OF THE SISTERHOOD, it read. He wondered what it was all about as he made sure that he had retrieved the token he needed from his jacket pocket.

Suddenly he felt two sets of hands shoving him from behind toward the truck. They were strong hands; they had locked him in, in such a way that he couldn't even turn to see who they belonged to. He thought that he was about to get mugged, right there on a major New York City thoroughfare, and cursed himself for violating the number one rule of the young black man's survival—never let your guard down.

"Look, if you want my wallet, you can have it!" he yelled as they pushed him further toward the back of the van. He noticed, just before the door opened, that the license plate read "S.O.S."

That's exactly what he wanted to shout out—but to whom?

He was suddenly thrown onto the bare and dirty floor; then someone he still couldn't see pulled a blinding hood over his head.

He realized that this was going to be something a whole lot bigger than a New York mugging. It was *really* serious!

What the young man didn't know was that he was just another one of a long series of innocent victims that the S.O.S. kidnapped on the night of the full moon every single month for the previous ten years.

He decided that instead of screaming, he'd be better off remaining silent in order to listen and perhaps ascertain his fate.

He began to feel light-headed, then dizzy, and smelled an unfamiliar, sour odor penetrating through the hood pulled over his head. Just before he lost consciousness his brain flashed and he wondered what his friends would say about him after he was gone.

The night sky was a festive blanket of starry pins of light. In contrast, below was a quite alarming and peculiar gathering—chillingly familiar in some way.

Deep in an otherwise silent, thickly wild, and verdant forest was a beautiful black hoot owl with huge yellow eyes, screeching and jumping up and down on one of the branches of her pine tree as she watched, wide-eyed, the thirty-foot cross blazing with fire. Okay . . . it wasn't *really* an isolated forest. It was actually way past midnight, smack in the middle of Sheep Meadow in New York's Central Park.

Six hooded figures stood in a circle around the lone black man. The fire from the cross reflected upon the sinewy curves of his naked chest. His only garment was a pair of Levi's jeans—as his jacket, shirt, socks, and shoes had been taken away. A rope hung from the owl's tree; at its end was a noose, firmly tied to the man's neck.

The image of the hooded figures became clearer in the firelight. These were *not* six hooded white Klansmen, but six black *women*, all standing with their hands on their hips and wearing ugly expressions around their mouths!

The owl swooped down from her tree and flew in the faces of the women. The high-strung, light-skinned chick—a shock of braids peeking nastily from under her hooded crown—struck out at the owl and yelled, "This is not your business, you rodent-eating buzzard!"

The owl flew away.

Then a petite cocoa-skinned, green-eyed member of the group approached the man. She slapped him hard on the face and shrieked, "Niggah, you have never held yourself accountable for your actions. So now, we're taking you out in this life. Maybe you'll fare better the next time around!"

"What have I ever promised you bitches that I didn't deliver?" the man yelled over the noise of the thundering fire, confusion mixed with conviction.

"Bitches?" they all screamed in an outraged response, moving in closer to him.

"Let's string him up, girlfriends!" bellowed the light-brown-skinned, big-busted sister. She balled her hands into fists.

"Fry the muthafucker!" yelled the deep-brown-skinned big-legged empress of the group.

"You mean I don't even get a fair trial before you all execute me?" asked the man, with the arrogance of a martyr.

"No way, José. We've had enough of you men's bullshit!" thundered the empress smugly.

"You got *that* right!" snorted the sister with the sable-colored face, who was holding the other end of the rope, her eyes glistening with unbridled ecstasy.

The beautiful black hoot owl returned to rest on the victim's shoulder. The man's image became clearer, illuminated now by the increasingly larger fire.

The brother didn't look the least bit frightened; in fact, his full brown lips spread into a wide, perfectly white toothy smile. His eyes, sparkling in the firelight, reflected an amused irony. He looked at the panicking owl and chuckled. "Aw, bird, don't panic. If it ain't been one kind of folks stringing up the brothers, it's been another. Everybody trying to find themselves an 'escape' goat in order to justify the mess they're living."

"That's it, girls. Let's string him up!" shrieked a fine brown sister.

The moment was swift and final. The brother didn't even make a sound.

The owl cried out in despair.

Ms. Green Eyes ripped off her hood and looked at her watch in the fire-light. "Damn, girls, it's late! Let's get out of here. I've got to pick up little PJ from the baby-sitter's—with his two-year-old evil self. I don't know *what* to do with him anymore. He's more and more like that tired daddy of his every day."

"I hear *that*, girlfriend," sighed one of the sisters, heaving her heavy breasts forward and sucking her teeth—a sign of empathy and annoyance.

They all left swiftly for the van, cackling gleefully into the night. . . .

"Honey, wake up, honey, and come to bed," he had said, placing his hands on his wife's shoulders. She wasn't exactly sure where she was at that moment.

Then she remembered.

"What *time* is it?" she asked, trying to focus on the face of her watch.

"It's two A.M., and it's time for you to get away from that computer and continue to work on your novel tomorrow."

"You didn't sneak a peek while I was asleep, did you?" she asked, eyeing him suspiciously.

"I swear I didn't. You know I promised you that I'd wait until you were ready for me to see."

He had understood. How *well* he understood. After all, he was a writer himself. She had been working on her first novel over the last year and a half and didn't want anyone to read any of it until it was completed.

She saved her latest entry, turned off the computer, and got up from her chair. They turned off all the lights downstairs and went up to bed.

SNAP ONE

CHAPTER ONE

"*A*nd the nominees are . . ."

Aletha leaned back and slowly rotated her head, feigning a stiff neck, at the same time sliding her eyes—heavily lashed for the occasion—discreetly about the huge auditorium. It was a controlled and practiced act of self-conscious discretion, as she did not want to appear so wide-eyed and childishly starstruck, especially after all these years.

Famous and infamous faces were everywhere!

Elegantly and not so elegantly clad in other famous people's haute couture, these show business folks were trying to mask their quite natural and inborn lust for public accolades with bogus airs of insouciance.

"It's all pretty political, you know . . . doesn't mean a thing," most of them had said at one time or another—usually after having *lost*, Aletha thought, smirking to herself.

Aletha returned her gaze to the stage. She looked up at the podium with rapt attention, her large, black eyes swiftly frisking the two celebrities. One of them was about to announce *her* name along with the others on the list of the very best of the season. The long, dark, tall one—a veteran of the industry—with what looked like silver dust elegantly sprinkled around his temples, clad in a fabulous-looking Brioni tuxedo, used to star in her teenage, erotic fantasies. Now, there he was in person, about to acknowledge her, from those full, plum-colored, juicy lips, acknowledge her as one of the contenders. The female copresenter, a dowager queen of a daytime soap opera, was wearing an inadequate little frock. It looked like something that Bill Blass might have penciled up during his off-hours. The recent face-lift was a bit too obvious as well—girlfriend was looking a little Chinese tonight, Aletha mused, giggling.

"What are you laughing about, Aletha?" her escort asked, lightly touching the hand that had been resting on her lap.

"Shh, Reggie," she snapped, placing the index finger of one hand over her lips and slapping his hand away with the other.

Even though she was one of the famous ones, too, she still found herself on those occasions pinching the tight flesh of her forearm from time to time in order to confirm the reality of her situation.

"... *The Victoria Stone Show,* Bob Dennison and Kathy Myerson, producers ..."

A large wad of mucus knotted up in Aletha's throat. She wanted to cough but had to seize control, because only hours ago she had slithered into the too-tight Azzedine Alaia number she was wearing, and she had no intention of bursting out of it for all of America to witness. The gossip columnists would have a field day . . . but then, they probably already were. They always managed to come up with *something*—even in a vacuum. She had to remind herself, though, that those same vultures were the very people who had helped to make her who she was—rich, famous, powerful, and a familiar presence in more houses than Lemon-Fresh Joy.

"... *The Dabney Wilkins Show,* Maxine Tyler, producer," Ms. Dowager Queen continued.

Reggie, her friend and lover for over five years, reached over and reassuringly held her hand. Aletha gently removed her hand from his and placed it on his cheek and adoringly stroked the smooth, tan flesh. He jerked his head away from her in response.

He hated it when she did that. Especially in public. He had told her time and again that those cheek-rubbing scenarios made him feel like a prize pony.

Aletha's brow furrowed for a moment, and she pursed her lips as she was about to register her displeasure with Reggie. She was hurt and annoyed that he had pulled his body away from her, but she had a much more important issue to think about at that moment.

"... and *The Aletha Brown Show,* Veronica McPheerson, producer," Juicy Plum lips added *finally!*

Aletha glanced quickly around the auditorium to see who was looking at her—with envy she was sure—then her eyes locked with Geraldo's.

He winked.

She looked away from him, her chin raised to a point just below smug, and she relished the fact that he was not among the list of nominees for the first time in who knew how many years and *she* was. Of course, *he* had won the damned thing zillions of times, and she had yet to get the award despite being nominated five damned times in a row. She had no doubts that this year would be the year of *The Aletha Brown Show*. She looked over at her producer, Veronica, who was sitting next to her escort, Derrick, whose arm was supportively draped around her shoulders.

Aletha grabbed Reggie's arm then awkwardly and comically ducked her head beneath it and placed it around *her* shoulders. Reggie looked at her with an amused smile and left his arm there.

It was a far cry better than cheek rubbing.

Aletha slipped her stockinged feet back into her Charles Jourdan pumps as she positioned herself to get up to accept her award. Her acceptance speech also pushed forth readying itself in her brain.

"The envelope, please."

At that instant, something Aletha couldn't see caused the soap star to stumble to the floor. The envelope then flew from her hand and landed across the stage. Juicy Plum Lips went over to help the actress up and to regain her composure, and then he had to walk a mile and a half—or so it seemed to Aletha—to recover the envelope.

"Damn! What's *wrong* with the old broad anyway? What's she got? Some kind of joint disease in the old knees or something? Some people just don't know when to step down! She should just retire. Look at her!"

"Aletha, calm down!"

"And the winner is . . . ," Juicy Plum Lips began as Aletha leaned the heel of her hand into Reggie's thigh as a support to get up, negotiating as elegantly as she could around her constricting gown.

"Ouch! Aletha, be careful! What are you doing?" Reggie whispered, grabbing her hand and trying to ease her back into her seat.

"*. . . The Victoria Stone Show!*"

Thunderous applause and Aletha's own anger exploded in her head. That nitwit hussy Victoria Stone with all those fistfighting guests had won the statue, Aletha raged to herself.

Tears threatened to leap from her eyes.

She glanced over at Reggie, who had a look of alarm on his face as he noticed that hers was now fixed in a contorted portrait of outraged disbelief.

"Are you okay, Aletha?" he whispered, taking her hand in his and raising it to his lips to kiss it.

She snatched her hand away.

Silence.

She couldn't believe it! Her fifth loss in five years. She didn't care how many people said that it was all purely political.

It didn't matter that she was as rich as milk chocolate, or that she had a gorgeous man who loved her. Aletha Brown wanted that statue!

"*The Victoria Stone Show,* my ass," Aletha hissed, loud enough for her producer and a couple of others to hear. "Who in the hell is she sleeping with?"

"Shh! Aletha, look, you know you are fabulous. You're still in prime time, baby," Reggie soothed. If he couldn't massage her damaged ego by the end of the ceremony, he knew he'd have one big, high-drama, angst-filled evening—perhaps week—even month—ahead of him. "Look, your show has a lot more integrity than that Victoria Stone's, honey," Reggie lied, trying to pacify her.

"You've got that right, Reg."

She looked around and caught Geraldo's eye.

He winked, again.

She turned away, sucked her teeth, and crossed her legs. Her right foot hit the seat in front of her, breaking the heel of her expensive Charles Jourdans.

"Damn! Look what you've made me do, Reggie," she hissed, needing at that moment to blame the person closest to her for anything and everything.

Reggie knew it was going to be a long night.

His eyes fell on her full breasts, which were swelling with indignation. At that instant he smiled to himself, thinking that just maybe when they got back to her place he'd tear that tantalizingly tight gown from her body and mollify her with some ardent and libidinous gymnastics.

Months passed.

The windows of Aletha's spacious New York City bedroom were frosted with ice. On the fireplace mantel was the gaping space where the statue had been intended to reside. She had every intention of leaving that space there, ready and welcoming for the day that her statue finally found its way home.

While staring at the empty space, tangled in her musk-scented linen sheets, her ire rose as she focused her attention again on her lover's most recent grievance.

"What do you mean, I'm too manipulative and pushy? What are you trying to say, Reggie, baby?" Aletha started to get angry, but as usual, his reassuring touch melted her into that same cozy, blithe submission that only *he* had been gifted enough to induce. Sometimes his harsh criticisms hurt her, but she reminded herself that he was the only man she had ever known who knew exactly how to calm her impetuous spirit. She knew that he said those things because he simply wanted her to become a better person.

Aletha surrendered to his sumptuous oral embrace.

A faint moan rose from the depths of her chest as she lightly rested her strong, dark legs on his smooth, muscular, golden brown shoulders, pointing her toes toward the ceiling.

"Ohh, Reg ... I ... love ... you. . . ." gasped Aletha, her hips rocking gently beneath him, expressing a familiar all-consuming yearning.

Her gorgeous lover looked up at her, his greenish hazel eyes merging with her deep brown ones, and responded with a fervent sincerity, "You know I love you, too, Aletha." He let his full, moist lips linger on her thigh.

A dulcet cadence of soft, steadily escalating rhythmic sounds filled the room for a long while.

"Go, open your present, Reggie," she sighed breathlessly, as their sensual symphony concluded. Momentarily satiated, she snuggled in his arms. Her lips grazed in the soft down of his chest hair, savoring the moist salty-sweet aftertaste of their lovemaking. She reached up and caressed his thick, curly hair with her long possessive fingers.

Aletha Brown certainly knows how to trash a mood, Reggie thought, a familiar charge of vexation shooting through his body.

"I thought I just *did*," he responded provocatively, pulling her warm body gently back underneath his strong hard one, entering her again with a commanding thrust. He guided his moist lips across her chest, leaving a glistening trail on her full, firm breasts, and then bounded abruptly from her bed.

Reggie's got a sadistic streak, she thought at that moment, startled by the curious gesture. Her body began to ache for more, but she remembered that he had told her that she should try to put a governor on her insatiable passions.

He said that they were intimidating.

He was probably right. Reggie was *always* right. That was why she had fallen irrevocably in love with him. A woman in her position rarely met people who could be so openly candid with her. Most were nothing but groveling hangers-on, more than happy to immerse her in unsolicited bootlick flattery and yes-ma'am platitudes, hoping she might feel obligated to offer them *something*, money most likely or perhaps a glamorous, high-paying job.

She watched Reggie reluctantly tear open the gift-wrapped package on her dresser. She smiled in anticipation and said, "You know, baby, I'm really *not* materialistic, as you say—just rich! Why shouldn't I share my wealth with the people I love? When you start making your big bucks I'm sure you'll do the same kinds of things for me, right?"

"Umm-hmm . . . ," he answered, distracted by the exquisite leather-bound book she had given him for an occasion he couldn't recall. Pre-Christmas, maybe?

He had told her time and time again to stop buying all these presents for him. He couldn't afford yet to give her all the things he knew she liked, but Aletha persisted. Reggie had become convinced that the woman didn't think that men had any feelings at all.

Reginald Pinkney was no gigolo!

He loved her—more than he knew how to express—which was probably why he found himself pulled into this manipulative madness.

In fact, he adored her.

He couldn't believe it, way back then, when the glamorous and famous Miss Aletha Brown had shown a serious interest in him—a mere neophyte and much younger writer. Nevertheless, he had always been strongly attracted to forceful, high-powered, older women. Those women knew exactly what they wanted and were direct in their approach to achieving their goals. Most of the men that he knew were intimidated by that sort of woman, but Reggie felt more comfortable with them than with those scheming, behind-the-scenes, undercover, self-centered Jezebels, who smiled in your face, picked your pockets, and then complained to their vindictive girlfriends about the games the brothers were playing.

Besides, Reggie had found that women like Aletha were also powerfully present and utterly rewarding in the bedroom—and anywhere else they chose to be.

Aletha could be so direct sometimes, though—words shooting out of her mouth like loose cannonballs—that a lesser man would find his member retreating in horror into the lower intestinal tract in response to her.

Lately, though, he had become aware—because he knew her well—that the marriage issue was causing her already-aggressive personality to take on a weird bend. She had eased up on the gift giving for a while, but now it picked up again and she'd started creating her own holidays in order to justify her actions.

What was so important about marriage anyway? She was rich, beautiful, independent. And she had him anyway. He just wasn't ready for marriage yet, because he knew that Aletha would want the nuptials immediately followed by the onslaught of a brood of offspring. He was definitely not ready for fatherhood!

Aletha had known that he would love the book. Her brother, Marshall, had brought it—*The Illustrated Diaries of Casanova*—back from France on one of his business trips. When she saw those fabulous watercolors inside, she knew it would be the perfect gift for Reggie. She had paid Marshall a handsome price for it knowing that her brother had probably bought it to give *his* own lover—whoever she was. Reggie liked art, especially paintings, and she wanted him to know that she understood the kinds of things that he needed for inspiration.

"*The Illustrated Diaries of Casanova,* Aletha? Is *that* what you think I am?" He chuckled, a hint of resentment catching in his throat. He turned and threw a caustic glance of disappointment at her.

She was devastated.

"No . . . no, Reggie . . . it's the—"

"How much did you pay for this anyway, Aletha?" He asked, his back still to her, leaning over the book as if it was as intriguing and valuable as *she*.

She was jealous of the book now and wanted to take it back, because he used to look only at her like that. Now he was looking with lust at an inanimate object.

As Reggie reflected on the previous year, he realized that he was beginning to feel more as if he was servicing her than loving her. It wasn't his fault, as far as he could make out. The dilemma was that he didn't know how to explain it in words that would not cause her to get all upset and start freaking out.

He was no fucking gigolo!

Also, another daunting situation had begun to take place over recent years.

He thought that he had slowly gotten sucked into the swill of some kind of sibling rivalry between Aletha and her sister, Desiree. It also seemed to have been initiated by Aletha, not her sister, who was apparently completely absorbed in her life up in Connecticut with her husband, David. But Desiree's husband was a writer, too. Each of the last three times that one of David's books had come out, Aletha would start canceling dates with him and weird shit like that. Leaving messages on the answering machine, asking him if he had seen the man on this or that panel or interview show.

What did a man do with shit like that? Didn't she realize that he had enough problems with folks thinking that he was only with Aletha Brown for her money? The last thing he needed was for her to go around measuring his achievements against another man's. A *white* man's at that!

She had become even more dominating and high-handed.

Like a rich, manipulative white man.

He laughed at this revelation. Food for a future novel, he thought, smiling to himself.

"What are you smiling about, Reggie? What's so funny?" she asked him with an insecure tremble in her voice.

"*You,* Aletha!"

Nope. He wasn't going to allow her to manipulate him and turn him into a submissive, faceless white *woman* right out of a John Cheever novel or some such pitiful muck. No way!

"Thank you, Aletha. The book is great. I love it," he said dryly.

After a long moment, he jumped back into bed with her and kissed her *everywhere*, from the hairline of her forehead to the tips of her toes.

Aletha reveled in his reassurances.

"Reggie, baby, why don't you just take a couple of days off and go down to the Bahamas with me? It could be real fun, don't you think? We could get away someplace where no one would know who I am."

"You know I have these deadlines, Aletha. I wish you would stop asking me to run off with you on one of your frivolous jaunts. I just don't have the time," he said gently, running his fingers through her thick, long, bushy hair.

Aletha was well aware of the difficulty that he and many other men would have had going out in public with a nationally famous woman, but in the Bahamas most people had never even heard of Aletha Brown. She had tried not to nag him about the fact that, since the awards ceremony, he never went out to public places with her anymore. She couldn't understand why he wouldn't jump at the chance to spend a romantic few days on a secluded beach with her.

Perhaps his insecurities ran deeper than she knew. She'd just have to become more sensitive to his ego. She curled her body into his and nestled her face into his soft hairy armpit, inhaling the warm masculine scent of his flesh. She kissed him there.

Aletha Brown was who she was, professionally, and that would never change—if she could help it. But she was determined to create a fulfilling personal life for herself, despite it all.

"Gorgeous lady . . . ," he began, jumping out of bed again, this time in order to put on his clothing.

She always loved it when he called her that.

"Yes, Reggie?"

He stood in front of her in such a way that allowed her big, brown, desperately searching eyes to absorb the sight of his compelling physical gifts.

Was it her imagination, or was the balance of power tilting in another direction in this relationship?

It was probably just her imagination, she thought, quickly sweeping a nagging discomfort from her mind.

He stood completely dressed leaning over her. The sunlight that streamed through the window onto her bed spotlighted her complete and vulnerable nakedness. It made Aletha shudder and quickly bury herself beneath the covers.

He bent over and kissed her on the *nose*!

He straightened up, stepped back, and stared at her, frowning.

Those hazel eyes of his squinted in the afternoon sunlight as if there was a wall of smoke separating the two of them, frighteningly distorting their view of one another.

Reggie was exhausted in more ways than one. He needed a break, which had nothing to do with running off to the Islands with Aletha. Reginald was not the sort of man to drag his problems along with him.

The vibe she picked up from Reggie at that instant caused her to imagine a humongous, cold butcher with a dull blade stabbing her through the heart—twice.

"I gotta go," he said, grabbing his book and his leather overcoat from

Aletha's closet. He then swaggered like a caramel-dipped cowboy out her bedroom door.

As he headed toward the door to leave the apartment, Aletha's fox terrier ran from the kitchen, where he'd been taking his afternoon nap, in order to see Reggie out. He stood up on his hind legs and, after a friendly bark, grabbed the left sleeve of Reggie's coat. All a part of their usual routine.

"See ya later, Sparky." Reggie smiled and petted the dog on the head.

"I'll talk to you later, baby," Aletha yelled out from her bedroom.

Silence.

CHAPTER TWO

Although it seemed to Reggie as if he'd been listening to the rantings for hours, he glanced at his watch and realized only ten minutes had passed. His neck had begun to cramp up, so he switched the phone receiver, which had been sandwiched between his left ear and his left shoulder, to his other side.

This is becoming just too damned much! Reggie grumbled silently to himself. He leaned over to pick up the remote control and began aimlessly clicking through the channels of the set directly in front of him. He stopped momentarily on the image of Aletha, who was sympathetically embracing one of her simpering guests on the panel of the day's program.

He quickly clicked off the television.

Despite the fact that Aletha had been out of town in the Bahamas for the past couple of days, it seemed to him that she had left behind this image of herself in his TV set in order to spy on him.

He was beginning to crack under all this pressure: the pressures of newspaper deadlines, Aletha's unspoken demands for a marriage proposal, and now *this* unrelenting shit being hissed at him through the receiver of his phone.

Reggie chose the tone and content of his response carefully. "Yes, I *am* listening to you, Mother. As I told you before, I refuse to discuss with you my relationship with Aletha. I am *not* wasting my time, as you say, *and* Aletha Brown is *not* a menopausal old woman. No, I'm not going to tell you how old she is. Go look it up in the tabloids!

"No, I do not feel that I'm speaking to you with a disrespectful tone. I just wish you'd stay out of my business. I am a full-grown thirty-two-year-old man, Mother! No, at this time I can't possibly tell you when I'll be down in D.C. to visit you. I'll let you know.

"What? *Grandchildren?* Look, I've gotta go. Bye." He clicked off the phone and threw it across the room, where it landed on one of the silly art deco armchairs that Aletha had bought him. He stared ruefully at the papers that now lay scattered across the floor and the phone that pointed at him accusingly.

He picked up from the coffee table a book that Aletha had recently given him and opened it. He sprawled his body out on the couch, then with a sigh of exasperation, placed the open book over his face and closed his eyes.

Reginald Pinkney's women were suffocating him.

How did he get into all of this, he wondered, turning over onto his stomach, knocking the book onto the floor.

With his mother, he understood the problem.

When his father dropped dead from a heart attack at the absurdly premature age of forty, Reggie was only twelve years old. It was hard enough dealing with the rage he felt over losing his father, but having his mother cling to him like a life raft threatening to float away, made his life all the more difficult.

He had wanted to get away from Atlanta and go east to prep school, as they'd planned before his father keeled over and left them, but he didn't. His mother had made him feel that he would be abandoning her to a life of lonesome mourning.

When he finally went off to college in New Haven, Connecticut, his mother quickly sold her house and moved to nearby Ridgefield. When he graduated and got his job at *The Post* in Washington, D.C., his mother sold her house in Ridgefield and moved to Chevy Chase, Maryland, just outside the city, where she quickly began scrutinizing his dates and making derogatory comments about his preference for older women.

Reggie laughed at the fond memories of life as a single, young black man in the female-laden "Chocolate City," as he got up to make a cup of coffee. He needed a kick to keep him awake so he could work late into the evening and meet his deadlines.

As he rummaged through the kitchen drawers looking for the filters, he realized he had run out. Aletha had forgotten to bring him a box when she came over last.

Damn! What was he going to do?

He went over to the refrigerator and reached in to get a bottle of soda.

"Shit, diet!" He had told Aletha that he hated the taste of the stuff. Why did she *do* that? Why did she insist on bringing him things that he didn't want?

He looked in the cabinet over the sink for a glass and stared instead at the rows of canned goods and jars of spaghetti sauce.

Aletha's short Haitian maid was always rearranging things in his kitchen, always putting things on lower shelves where they were easier for *her* to reach. Once a month, Reggie had to explain the difference between *clean* and *rearrange*.

Reggie unscrewed the cap of the diet soda and took a swig, his mind snapping back to his old life in the "Chocolate City." He had often felt like a sultan with a harem back in those days.

Then, when the paper sent him to New York to do an interview with Aletha Brown, everything changed. Reginald Pinkney instantly fell in love with Miss Aletha. So, to his mother's apparent horror and dismay, he quit his job, took the money his father had left for him in a trust, and moved to New York to be close to his new lover, to work on his novel, and to write freelance.

He told his mother to stay put, and so far she had. Luckily for him, since she felt that his relationship with Aletha was outrageously inappropriate, she had chosen to stay down in Maryland away from his "scandalous lifestyle," as she called it. He and Aletha have been together for over five years.

He left the kitchen, taking the bottle of soda with him, wondering what he was going to do about dinner.

He figured he'd better order out, since he had to spend most of the evening at his computer.

While shuffling through the wicker basket full of take-out menus next to his couch, newly alphabetized by cuisine—Aletha's magic touch—Reggie tried once again to figure out why he had allowed his relationship with the woman to become so oppressive.

He had been thinking of speaking to a psychologist, but Aletha had always said that black people didn't need shrinks. Pretty ironic considering the fact that Aletha's sister was a quite successful one and a sizable proportion of her patients were black.

He had to do *something*, he knew, because things had really been getting out of hand.

At that moment Reggie realized what he had to do. He had to be more of a man and lay down some hard, nonnegotiable ground rules for their relationship. No more trying to reason with the woman. He was going to take control—be the boss. Having been surrounded by lackeys for most of her adult life, she obviously had a tendency, from time to time, to mistake him for one of them. Well, that was going to stop. It was going to be a new day. And if Miss Aletha could obey the new rules and handle the way he decided to set up their lives, then he would marry her. She would have to agree to wait a couple of more years for them to start a family once she got that ring on her finger. Being married would assuredly relieve some of the pressures he'd been under and probably create the kind of environment in which he could complete his novel.

Yep! When she got back from the Bahamas, he'd sit her down for a serious talk, and then he'd pop the question as he well knew she had wanted him to do for some time.

Just as he selected the menu from a Chinese restaurant his phone rang.

"Yeah, Reginald Pinkney's residence."

He smiled into the receiver, as he realized it was his foxy redheaded, long-legged agent on the line.

"What's up, hon?" He glanced over at his pleasing refection in the full-length mirror in the corner and ran his hand through his hair.

"Of course, I'd love to have dinner with you. Yeah. Okay then, see you at Gleason's at eight o'clock."

He dropped the take-out menu back in the basket and looked over at the mirror again.

At that moment Aletha's angry image seemed to spread beyond the boundary of the mirror's frame, larger than life.

"Damn! It's *only* dinner."

Suddenly embarrassed at the realization that he'd slipped back for a moment, he stared back into the mirror, his face hardened into a mask of righteous indignation, and said, irrefutably, "You'd better understand that *I'm* the man in this relationship . . . not *you*, Aletha baby!"

He unbuttoned his shirt and headed toward the bathroom and a shower.

CHAPTER THREE

"*B*rother, let me tell you," Jim, the chauffeur, was saying to another driver who was standing next to him in the arrivals terminal at La Guardia. "I have been motoring celebrities around for over twenty years now, and I can swear to you that the black ones are bigger pains in the ass than the white ones." His eyes searched the airline terminal crowd for Aletha. "Just a bunch of prima donnas, divas, and slave drivers." He chuckled.

"But, *Aletha Brown,* man. I can't believe it. What's *she* like? What a fox!" the young driver declared, his eyes following those of Aletha's chauffeur, hoping that he'd soon spot her.

"Yeah, she is, but she's just like all the others—high-handed and—oh, *there* she is." He nodded his head in her direction.

She seemed raging mad, not exactly the mode he had expected her to be in, considering the fact that she had just spent the last few days in the sunny Caribbean. As she approached, he noticed a slash of red dripping all over the front of her mink coat.

"Whoa . . . what happened, Miss Brown?" he asked, looking with disbelief at the damage.

"Those bitches don't know who they're dealing with, Jim. I should have had them arrested for assault and battery." She grabbed his arm and pulled him along, casting nervous glances over her shoulder. "Let's get the hell out of here before I *really* get evil!"

"May I have your autograph please, Miss Brown?" asked the young driver, all agog, thrusting a piece of paper in front of her face.

"I don't have a pencil." She brushed past the spellbound fan, leaving him in the dust as she led Jim to the exit.

It had started snowing, so Jim opened the umbrella he was carrying and led Aletha to the awaiting sleek white stretch limo.

"Want to tell me what happened, Miss Brown? Is there anything I can do?"

"Lesbians! Some crazed lesbians with a huge paint roller came up and—"

"*Lesbians?* Why would lesbians want to—"

"Okay. *Feminists,* then!" She glided into the backseat and brushed icy white crystals from her ten-year-old Blackglama mink.

Jim got into the car, shifted into drive, and trying to suppress a convulsion of laughter, said, "I think you mean that some of those *animal-rights people* targeted you for—"

"Whatever! Who do they think they *are*? Don't they know who I *am*?"

They were off the exit ramp when the chauffeur prudently suggested, "I can take your fur to the cleaners. They'll make it just like new again."

"That's not the point, Jim."

She removed her coat and threw it on the floor in front of her. Aletha had to admit that at that moment it *did* resemble a wounded animal lying at her feet.

As she stared at the coat she recalled the day, back in the early eighties, when the Blackglama people contacted her asking her to pose for a full-page spread for their outrageously expensive "What Becomes a Legend Most" campaign. At twenty-seven years old she had become a legend, along with Liza, Diana, Lena, Shirley, and a host of others asked to promote the company's sumptuous furs. They had each been rewarded with a complimentary coat. Considering the outrageous amount of money they had spent on this campaign, she suspected that they had had a premonition about the coming censure of animal fur.

Over the past few years, she'd been criticized by her public for wearing the thing, but Aletha Brown's conscience was undisturbed. The mink was the only fur she had ever owned, and she hadn't actually *bought* it. Besides, she had suffered some abominably cold winter days, and those lush animal pelts had kept her from freezing to death. Animal rights? What about *human* rights? What organization was working to support her right to be warm?

"You know, Jim, my big sister Desiree said—"

"What did your sister say . . . *sister*?" He grinned into the rearview mirror.

"She said that this concern over animal rights didn't start until after racial integration."

"How's that, Miss Brown?"

"Desiree said that for all of history, people wore animal fur in cold climates in order to keep warm. She said that for years white Americans lived over in their parts of town, strutting about in their minks, sables, raccoons, and the like, while the black folks uptown spent their Saturday nights and Sunday sermons draped snugly in their stone martins, foxes, beavers, and the like, and no one ever said a word about the poor defenseless animals back in those days."

"That's the *truth*, isn't it." The chauffeur chuckled.

"Desiree said—and she is a famous psychologist so she *knows*—that as soon as blacks and whites started living in and frequenting the same places together then the need to denounce fur coats suddenly became urgent. She said that one look at fudge-colored folks in fur caused an upsurge of humanitarian impulses to leap into the hearts of white folks."

Aletha leaned back and kicked off her bright red Italian leather pumps from her aching feet.

"Your *sister* said that, did she, Miss Brown?" the chauffeur said, smiling through his doubt and checking her reaction through the rearview mirror.

"Umm-hmm. That's right," Aletha responded tightly, rolling her eyes at the wry implication in his voice.

"Damn!" she gasped as she noticed that some of the red paint had splashed onto her brand-new cream-colored silk Chanel pantsuit. This perfectly tailored, excessively pricey garment had caught her eye while she was shopping in Nassau, and she had decided to indulge herself. Shit! Something had *told* her that she shouldn't have worn this outfit, especially on this particular day. Despite the fact that the suit was rather lightweight and that it was cold in New York, she just couldn't wait to wear it.

"Well, I guess that's just how the white folks operate, Miss Brown."

"Well, I don't care what *they* say. I do not live in the sunny climes of Africa and I . . . am . . . *cold*!" she said conclusively. "Just *look* at this weather," she groaned, looking out at the snowfall that had become heavier by the minute.

"It *is* the second week in December, Miss Brown," the chauffeur responded as he slowed down in the heavily backed-up traffic on the turnpike. "It's kind of a nice way to bring in the Christmas season, don't you think? Haven't had a white Christmas in *years*."

"Humph. Yeah, *real* nostalgic," she sighed.

Leaning back into the warm, plush upholstery, she brought up one leg, then the other to massage her sturdy calves and stretch her sore and tired tootsies.

Black women were always suffering from feet that hurt, she thought to herself; it must be because they were always stuffing their feet into shoes made for high-arched white women.

"Tell me something, Jim, do you find that your feet annoy you more often than not?"

"Oh yeah, Miss Brown. It's hard to get a good fit even when you're a man. It's a black thing, ya know," he said smoothly as he winked at her from the rearview mirror.

"Well, then why on earth don't one of you brothers come up with a line of shoes designed specifically for black folks, huh?"

Jim looked at her briefly with covert annoyance.

"Why don't you do a show on it, sister?" he volleyed back sarcastically.

She sucked her teeth, rolled her eyes, and added, a bit peeved, "Do a show on it. Do a show on it! I'm tired of hearing that crap whenever I try to have a meaningful discussion with someone on an issue."

"Lighten up, Miss Brown. Didn't a few days on the beach take the edge off?"

"No!"

"By the way, where do you want me to drop you off?"

"Since you apparently forgot to do it, Jim, first I've got to pick up Sparky from the boarders."

"I didn't forget. You didn't give me any instructions on the matter."

"Whatever. We've got to pick up Sparky. Poor Sparky! All cooped up in that kennel with all those strange dogs." Aletha sighed, abruptly shutting the translucent panel that divided the front and back seats of the car. She leaned her head back to look at the snowfall outside.

Aletha could hardly see a thing through the curtain of white crystals, but she hypnotically watched each individual snowflake with its intricate pattern dance gracefully to the ground.

The snowfall made her reflect back on her childhood. Aletha's full, wide, vermilion lips spread into a faraway and nostalgic smile. She remembered how she used to love cutting out snowflake patterns from Kleenex tissues, using her mother's tiny nail scissors. Big brother Marshall and big sister Desiree would help her, their baby sister, place the little creations all over the family Christmas tree. They were feather-pretty—just like those falling against the tinted window of her limo—and certainly preferable, in her opinion, to that itchy, bullshit angel hair with which her parents loved to cover the tree.

Maybe she'd make some this year and bring them to her parents' house when she saw them in a couple of weeks for their Christmas dinner party. They would be sure to bring back familial memories of more pleasant, simpler times.

She curled up in the backseat and resumed massaging her legs. "Do a show on it, my *ass*."

Aletha had fulfilled her childhood dream of having her own television talk show. As a young girl, she had sat glued to the TV set for the couple of hours a week that her parents allowed. Instead of the standard cartoons and Disney flicks that mesmerized most of the children of her generation, Aletha loved watching a well-dressed host or hostess interview prominent politicians on fascinating issues or glamorous celebrities who would reveal their secrets to success. She had absorbed herself in precocious fantasies about what life would be like meeting and socializing with all those fabulous people—people who were far more fascinating and exciting than the folks that surrounded her and her family in their rather mundane Manhattan neighborhood.

"You know, Jim," Aletha began, lowering the panel again to talk.

"Miss Brown?"

"When I first moved up here from Miami, in the eighties, all the talk shows seemed to have been trying to take the high road. There was basically only Phil, Geraldo, and Oprah, back in those days. The shows were about *real* issues back then. Important issues. Not all this mess about 'I Married My Daddy's Sister.' "

" 'And We Raised Her Other Brother's Love Child!' " Jim added with a hearty, knowing chuckle.

"Yeah, or 'I Was a Man about Town, Now I'm a Lady of the Evening.' "

"I think I missed *that* one, Miss Brown!"

"Oh, you did, did you? Well, what about the one about 'The Women We Love and Why We Beat Them.' "

"Oh, I preferred the one called 'The Women We Love to Beat and the Women Who Love Them.' "

Aletha and Jim were caught up in laughter, when she abruptly stopped, her eyes having fallen on the tabloid newspaper that Jim had placed earlier on the seat beside her.

"You know, Jim," Aletha said soberly, leaning back and running her fingers through her thick hair, "it seems that every sucker with some major dysfunction now takes the opportunity to showcase America's most dirty laundry for all the world to see."

"Miss Brown, I used to think that all those folks were actors on those shows."

"No, brother, they are *for real*."

"It's a shame, isn't it? There's a talk show on every channel, it seems, every hour, and you never even see the same people twice on those panels—so they say."

Aletha shot Jim an amused look, thinking how funny it was that most of the viewers of those shows try to deny religiously watching them.

"I could never have imagined that so many people had so many of those weird problems," he continued, shaking his head solemnly. "I used to think that those producers went scouting up in those Blue Ridge Mountain hamlets or out in the backcountry Alabama towns, looking for certain kinds of folks."

"They do, Jim."

"You don't say."

"Those are just the kinds of people who'd be willing to sell out their entire families, reveal personal betrayals and other sordid family details on national television. And all for the bargain-basement price of a hotel room, a meal, and a bus ticket back to the woods from which they came."

"Well, lately, Miss Brown, don't you think the shows have been calming down a bit? I haven't seen as much fussing and hollering as I did before."

"It *looks* that way, but let me tell you, Jim. There seems to still be something insidious lurking beneath the surface that I just can't put my finger on.

"Damn," she blurted out, reaching over for the tabloid newspaper. "It's just no damned fun anymore."

The front-page headline jumped out and hissed at her with the venom of the nation's steadily mounting envious rage: DUSKY TALK SHOW EMPRESS TO COLONIZE THE CARIBBEAN! The caption under her picture read: "Chat queen plops down seven million for island paradise!"

Aletha believed that she could feel her blood pressure soar as she stared with breathless horror at the photo they had chosen of her. She could certainly feel the blood pounding in her temples, the slow grind of her teeth.

"Did you see this picture, Jim? Where on earth did they get this thing, making me look like the image of Little Black Sambo?"

"Miss Brown, this is what you get for being a pretty little black woman, making too much money, honey. You're rich, thin, and have twenty-four-hours-a-day, three-hundred-sixty-five-days-a-year *color*, too." Jim laughed, glancing at her angry face through the rearview mirror. "I'm surprised you're not used to all this by now."

"Nobody ever gets used to being mocked, especially for no reason at all. Those asses can take a flying leap. I'm going to find a new media gig or opt for early retirement and make room for someone who thinks they deserve this insanity," she groused, shutting the panel again and leaning back into her seat.

She was becoming increasingly annoyed at the love/hate relationship that the public had with the celebrity persona of Miss Aletha Brown. Maybe she was just hitting the hump of her late thirties, and she didn't have the energy anymore nor the sense of humor.

Aletha had been contemplating a change for some time now. Having only a few months left on her contract, she'd been thinking about getting out of show business altogether. Her sister, Dr. Desiree Simon, had turned down her very lucrative offer to be the show's resident shrink. She had explained time and time again to Aletha that being attached to a TV talk show would be, to her, something like volunteering to be the victim in one of Stephen King's horror movies.

Desiree appeared to be the only person Aletha knew who could calmly and firmly resist the lure of show business.

She had to admit that she had always been more than a bit jealous of her older sister. Aletha had always tried to do things either to impress Desiree or to gain her approval. Yet somehow Desiree, unwittingly she was sure, always made Aletha feel classlessly materialistic, shallow, misguided—just plain out of it.

"The highbrow hussy," Aletha muttered, shredding the newspaper with her long, gloved fingers and then tossing it onto the floor, on top of the coat.

Nevertheless, what troubled Aletha most at that time was that she hadn't decided yet what she would do if and when she retired. She'd been in the business ever since she graduated from college almost two decades ago. Maybe, she thought, she should marry Reggie and move to the house she had just bought for them in the Bahamas and have a couple of kids. Money would certainly be no problem.

She had made a fortune and had invested well. They could move to the Islands, and instead of that silly walk-up he insisted on living in, Reggie could finish his novel in the beauty of the Caribbean—away from the stress of the city and the silliness of white folks.

Maybe she'd also auction off this coat. Despite animal rights, she knew that there'd be hundreds—maybe even thousands—of buyers clamoring for it. Probably end up selling it to some hypocrite for ten times its actual worth.

Yes, she decided definitively, she and Reginald Pinkney *would* get married.

Aletha Brown Pinkney. Mrs. Reginald Pinkney.

She smiled to herself at the sound of the name, then reached over to pick up her large Louis Vuitton handbag, which held everything she had needed for a few days in Nassau: some toiletries, a tube of bright red lipstick by Iman, a small jar of red nail polish, her wallet with some credit cards, a pair of clear plastic high-heeled mules, a pair of thongs, a tiny canary yellow sundress, and her metallic gold string bikini. She took out the photos of the little Bahamian hacienda she had just bought, and the deed—her *dowry*.

Yes! She was going to demand that Reggie marry her today, she decided in that instant. Why should she wait for *him* to ask? They'd been together for over five years. Why wait any longer? Aletha Brown had never in her life waited for anyone or anything. That's how she got where she was today—by seizing the power. She smirked triumphantly as she leaned toward the bar and opened it.

Yep, there was the Dom Perignon.

She decided that she'd take it up to the apartment, and if Reggie was there, she'd show him the pictures of the new house she had just bought them, and then give him an ultimatum. Actually it really couldn't be an ultimatum because she had no idea what she'd do if he refused. She didn't have another man, nor did she have any intention of letting this one get away.

He couldn't refuse her anyway. Reggie had always done exactly what she had asked of him in the past.

They would celebrate over some ice-cold champagne, and . . .

It had been only a couple of days, but she had missed Reggie.

She curled up her petite body in the backseat to take a nap.

Mmm, she thought as she began to doze off to sleep. I can see it now in all the papers: HOTSHOT TV HOST ALETHA RETIRES TO ISLAND RETREAT!

She would hire the best decorators and make a dream house she could show off to all her enemies, past and present, on one of those lifestyles-of-the-rich-and-famous shows. She would flaunt her gorgeous tropical estate, handsome writer husband, and her two gorgeous children, Marley and Khadijah (of course, she'd already named them years ago, long before she knew who the father would be) for all the world to see.

Demons created from childhood memories were the forces that had molded Aletha into the quintessential American Dream she was today—in spades, no pun intended. She laughed at the thought.

Even after all these years, she could still vividly hear the piercing taunts of self-hatred that the evil, brown, project-dwelling skeezer children had hurled mercilessly at the sisters: "Brillo head, Brillo head, big lips, bubble lips, think you're somethin', you ain't nothin'." Those mostly fatherless waifs were unrelenting in their jealous torture—all because she and Desiree were pretty, petite, dark-skinned girls, whose thick, long wavy hair was in contrast to the short, greasy, processed locks of the tormentors. The Brown girls wore beautiful clothes and were straight-A students with a gainfully employed father at home, curious liabilities that rendered them pariahs among certain groups of African American youth. Plus, the Brown family didn't live in the projects, but in the predominantly Jewish, middle-income co-op housing complex on the other side of the avenue.

There were a few other black children like themselves at school, but not enough to shield them from the aggressive anger of the majority. The pecking order of the few other middle-class black kids had turned out to be defined by skin tone. Since most of them were a subtle variation of light tans, again the Brown girls found themselves excluded, since they were both dark-skinned like the majority of the poorer children who shunned them.

Those mean, black sugar babies used to steal their coats and jackets, throw spitballs into their lush, bushy, unprocessed manes, and challenge them to an after-school fight almost every week, it seemed.

"Fight! Fight!" big, Amazon-like adolescents used to chant, surrounding them menacingly as she and her sister tried to make their way home from school.

Whenever Aletha and Desiree came home all scratched and bloody, hair sticking out wildly from their heads—some little skeezer was always trying to rip out a clump of hair—instead of the proverbial "What do the *other* guys look like?" Mom would yell, "What on earth did you two *do* to the others that would make them beat you up like that?"

How could their mother not have been aware of the hostile climate they had to contend with day after day, right in their own small neighborhood, Aletha had wondered bitterly. Why couldn't she have stopped this, especially since she and their father had known, or were at least acquainted with, the parents of most of those bonehead children?

Pops would reprimand Mom by saying, "Look at these girls. I told you that you shouldn't buy their clothes at Saks while all the other colored children get their rags from Alexander's bargain basement. The other children are acting out their jealousy. You just too seditty for this neighborhood."

"We are not common people," Mom would sniff, time after time.

Needless to say, Aletha and Desiree were each other's only ally in this matter.

Of course, back in those days, Aletha and Desiree had no idea that the little skeezers were jealous of them. She and her sister had been convinced that there was something wrong with themselves in some way. They used to beg their mother to straighten their hair with those hot combs that the other black children's parents used. But their mother, being more progressive about those things back then, had refused. Back in those days, blacks who exposed, unaltered, their naturally frizzy hair to the world were an embarrassment to the Negro community, as it was called in those days. Aletha had despised the beautiful clothes they wore that set them apart from the other kids. The others used to ridicule her sister Desiree's interest in art over playground games. They used to mock Aletha's crisp manner of speech and her far-flung vocabulary—which was not *that* far-flung at all, actually—that their mother had encouraged. It was all a nightmare, which in later years she had come to understand were manifestations of African American tribal behavior and attitudes.

Ghettoisms.

Aletha had been convinced that ghettoisms were the black achieving child's greatest challenge to overcome. Greater than the racism inflicted by the majority population—which she learned to take for granted or anticipate at a young age. She had discovered that it is far more painful to experience rejection from people of one's own group than from outsiders.

Nevertheless, the pressure to conform to a group's lowest common denominator has contributed to the self-inflicted oppression of a nation of black geniuses, especially those who fell outside of the more traditional areas of basketball playing, blues singing, and tap dancing.

Aletha sighed into the sweet-smelling upholstery of her limo, calming the familiar flame of anger that had again risen in her chest.

She laughed to herself as she recalled one particular afternoon following yet another school yard confrontation. Desiree had walked briskly into their apartment and rushed past their mother without even the slightest greeting. Aletha had heard her sister slam down her books, then slam the door to the bedroom they shared behind her. Aletha was always afraid to go near Desiree when she was in one of her angry moods. Normally Desiree was a rather mellow child, but every now and then she would flare up, scaring the hell out of everyone in the house.

Well, after a few minutes, Aletha tiptoed into the room to check the climate. Desiree was kneeling in front of her twin bed, laying out what seemed like tiny strings or threads on the chenille bedspread.

"D-Desiree, whatcha d-doing?" Aletha had stammered in a whispered voice, noticing a sinister look on her sister's normally placid, shiny, voluptuously sculptured face. "What is that on your bed?"

"Shh, Aletha." Desiree glanced over at her sister, motioning her to come closer—a surprising development since her pink side of the room was usually off limits. Aletha looked at her own curtains and bedspread, done up in beige and white and then to Desiree's side, which was always in some shade of red. Years before, Desiree had also drawn a line down the middle of the room separating their areas and had forbidden Aletha to cross over that border into her frontier except when summoned.

Desiree always insisted on clear-cut boundaries even though they had been forced to share a room. She always resented the fact that although she was the oldest of the three, she had to share her room with her baby sister, when their brother Marshall—the middle child—had been granted the luxury of a room of his own.

Aletha noticed that Desiree was pulling string or some kind of fiber from little, dark fuzzy balls.

"It's hair, Aletha," Desiree snickered.

"*Hair? Whose* hair, Desiree?"

Aletha's heart pounded.

"You *know* whose hair, lamebrain. You were right there, whipping those jerks with your books when I ripped this mess from their big ole scalps."

"Why would you keep all that hair, though?" Aletha started to whine in panic. "What are you going to do with—"

"Shut up, before Mom hears us," Desiree snapped, then pointed at the clumps and strands. "You see, there are people who can *do* stuff with this. Weird stuff. Like make people break out in boils or grow horns. I heard Mom talk about it with one of her friends on the telephone."

"*What* friends on the telephone? What are you *talking* about?"

"I'm taking this stuff to the voodoo lady."

"Oooooh, Desiree, I'm going to *tell* Mom. What's a voodoo lady, anyway?" she asked, suddenly shaking with terror, remembering a late-night horror movie she had seen one Saturday evening. "You don't know any voodoo ladies. They have snakes and things."

Desiree jumped up, grabbed Aletha by the shoulders, shook her, and hissed, "Stop talking so loud. You *do* want those jerks to stop bothering us, don't you?"

"B-but—b-but—"

"What are you two *doing* in there? It's awfully *quiet* back there, Desiree," their mother yelled from the kitchen.

"Homework, Mom," they both yelled back at the same time.

Aletha had no idea if Desiree had actually gone to a voodoo lady, nor had she ever cared to find out.

After a time, the more overt hostility directed at them died down. Desiree eventually went off to study at the artsy-fartsy High School of Music and Art, making new, exotic artsy-fartsy friends. Aletha would sometimes tag along with her sister and her pals, but being a shier child, she mostly kept to herself, studying. When her parents sent Aletha to the elite, predominantly Waspy

Brearley School, the black children in the neighborhood, thankfully, simply canceled out her presence by looking right through her. Attendance at those schools rendered the sisters invisible to the little skeezers and finally gave them some peace of mind and body.

"And that's how the *black* folks operated," Aletha murmured.

The anger resulting from this ostracism propelled the Brown sisters from the mediocrity of the neighborhood to successful lives of achievement. Aletha later chose to attend the bourgeois Howard University in Washington, D.C., because after four years at Brearley she figured she'd like a "black experience" for a while. Desiree had chosen to go to Columbia University in New York. They were both enjoying now, despite Aletha's burnout, lucrative and satisfying careers. Desiree had her successful practice in Manhattan, and Aletha had become a popular talk show host.

Aletha had managed to snag Reggie, too.

Yes, dark, small, Brillo-headed, flat-footed Aletha got Reginald Pinkney. She got tall, copper-colored, curly-haired, green-eyed, Ivy League Reggie! Exactly the kind of man who, at her predominantly black college, hardly ever acknowledged her existence as a desirable woman. Instead, they chose light-skinned or often white-looking black girls. Even the so-called middle-class black men in her professional world seemed to suffer from those same inclinations. Sometimes Aletha believed that many of these fair-skinned colored wives and girlfriends were actually white women passing as black in order to land a handsome, well-off brother and to fend off the oftentimes hostile repercussions of an interracial relationship in a racist society. She couldn't blame the bitches one bit, though. Aletha might have done the same herself if she were white and had wanted some of the fine, affluent brothers she had been attracted to over the years.

Despite her dark complexion and full features, she'd managed somehow to attract and hold on to her fabulous Reggie. Someday he was going to be a bestselling author; Aletha Brown would see to it!

"Bubble lips. Brillo head." The words throbbed in Aletha's head.

When her new lifestyle would be featured on the rich-and-famous show, she was sure that all the derisive baby witches from her childhood would be watching as they padded around their pathetic, little middle-class—if they were lucky—dwellings, wearing dirty house shoes, and pausing only long enough from their gnawing on neck bones to feed their fatherless rug rats lunch from twelve-ounce cans of pork and beans!

"Miss Brown, I'll be right back." They had arrived at the boarder's. Jim left the car quickly to fetch Aletha's dog.

The Brown children were never allowed to have pets when they were growing up, she recalled, staring at the entrance to the building where other pet owners were leaving and entering with their four-legged friends. Their strict father had felt that it was unsanitary to have pets in a New York City apartment. Aletha thought that was extremely cruel, because there were so many animals living in the city who were orphans. She used to go and visit the Bide-a-Wee home for abandoned animals when she was little, just so she could reassure those poor animals that there were plenty of little kids who would love to take care of them, but had mean old parents. She had vowed that she would always have an adopted pet when she grew up.

And she always had. Her Jack Russell terrier, Rover, whom she adopted after she landed her show in Miami, had lived a long time. Over twelve years! He died a couple of years after she relocated to New York. She was certain that he could have lived longer but had expired from loneliness—he missed all of his friendly and outgoing Southern doggie friends—and from the shock of the aggressive winters in New York.

Jim opened the door, and Sparky, Aletha's two-year-old fox terrier, bounded onto her lap, licking her all over the face.

"Sorry I had to leave you, Sparks, but them's the breaks." She laughed, rubbing his head as he settled down resting his head on her lap. "Soon you're going to have beautiful grounds to explore on a lovely tropical island."

Jim got into the car and asked, "Want me to drop you off at home now, Miss Brown?"

"Yes, I've got to get out of these clothes."

"Yes, ma'am," he said, heading back downtown a few short blocks to deliver them to her apartment building.

It *was* difficult keeping a dog in the city, Aletha thought, looking at her happy and scrappy little terrier, but obviously not impossible. She and Sparky had a great relationship. They were best friends, and *he* adored Reggie, too.

When she retired and moved to her new house in the Islands, she planned to have zillions of pets—a menagerie of animal friends! Birds, doggie pals for Sparks, and some sweet long-haired kitties.

The chauffeur eased the limo up to the canopied entrance of Aletha's luxuriously sterile Upper East Side apartment building. He slammed down on the brakes, jolting Aletha from both her seat and her semiconscious thoughts. Sparky's quick reflexes kept him from tumbling with his owner, the claws of his paws digging into the leather of the backseat.

"What the *hell*?" she shouted, lifting herself back to her seat and brushing herself off, then sliding the partition down to assess the situation.

Sparky let out a stream of angry yelps in Aletha's defense.

"Oh, I'm so sorry, Miss Brown." Jim smirked, leaning over so that Aletha was unable to see the expression on his face. "I thought that cab was trying to push in front of me," he lied.

After squeezing her feet back into her pumps, Aletha threw the mink over her shoulders as the doorman opened the door of the car.

"Jim, wait here until I see if Reg . . . uh, Mr. Pinkney is upstairs. If he is, I'll have the doorman tell you what time to pick us up."

"Yes, ma'am." He hesitated, not knowing what else to say.

As Aletha stepped out of the car and under the doorman George's proffered umbrella, she glanced back at the chauffeur. Something about his expression, at that moment, caused a sharp chill of apprehension to shoot up and down her spine.

She slammed the door.

With the champagne and her handbag in one hand, she grabbed hold of George's arm with the other and rushed into the welcoming warmth of the lobby.

"Good day, Miss Brown. Did you have a good trip?" he asked, giving her his dutiful, doorman smile.

"Yeah, George," she grunted. His obsequious behavior, although appropriate, thought Aletha, had become highly irritating.

Everything had been annoying her lately. She definitely needed to retire . . . or at least take a nice *long* vacation somewhere. A few days in Nassau looking at houses couldn't exactly be called a vacation.

If Reggie wasn't at the apartment, she'd go down to his place and surprise him. She knew he didn't expect her until the day after tomorrow.

"Wait until he sees the pictures of the house. He'll be blown away," she imagined, as she and her dog brushed abruptly past the doorman to the private elevator to her penthouse. Aletha had begun to realize that she no longer felt warm and satiated when Reggie left her bed to return to his world. She kicked off her shoes in the carpeted foyer as she ran into the apartment to see if Reggie was there. No, she no longer felt sexy and lovingly possessed the way she used to. Perhaps she had opened herself too much. Aletha had chalked up some of their problems to their age difference, his being only thirty-two years old to her thirty-seven. Perhaps she should never have given him the key to her apartment to use whenever he wanted.

Of course, she had the key to *his* apartment, although he had never exactly *given* it to her and she had never dared to ask him. She had just stolen it out of his jacket pocket during one of her office Christmas parties and had one of her assistants run over to the locksmith to make a copy of the key to Reggie's dingy, little walk-up.

Okay, it really wasn't dingy. His place was quite quaint, especially with the good pieces of furniture she had bought him over the years. It was just that she could never understand why he would choose to live like a bohemian in Greenwich Village when she had offered that they live together in her beautiful penthouse.

He had banally responded that he "needed his own space."

As she sat primly on her own plush, white velvet couch, she surveyed her living room. It was orderly, structured, and had clean modern lines, even down to her collection of slick geometric paintings by Bernie Casey, Xenobia Smith, Milton Young, and Daniel Johnson—African American painters who spoke to her need for reassurance. They were artists who could soothe her anxious and driven spirit with their structured works of uncomplicated patterns of colors and images. It was not as if she knew all *that* much about art. That was Reggie's department. She only knew that she needed to come home to order and harmony at the end of her chaotic days.

She jolted back to the present. Why was she just *sitting* there, when it was obvious that Reggie was at *his* place?

Not only was she impatient to pop the question to him, but she was horny as hell.

She rushed into her master bedroom to change.

Aletha threw her coat onto her oversize art deco chaise longue. The royal blue chair sat in the center of the room creating an exclamation point among the rest of the furniture, which was Early American and covered or upholstered in white, cream, and tan. She just loved exclamation points!

Peeling off her paint-spotted silk suit, she dropped it to the floor and looked into the mirror that covered the bedroom walls floor to ceiling, pondering what she would wear to Reggie's apartment. Her eyes involuntarily ricocheted over to the fireplace and the empty space that still taunted her.

"Ahh, pish!" she muttered to herself, fanning her hand at the space, then turning back to scrutinize her reflection in her mirrors.

She was pleased with her body. The reflection rewarded her with the image of a smooth, tight form with nice subtly sculptured muscles molded by hard and diligent workouts with her personal trainer. She ran her fingers through her hair, fluffed it out, and smiled slyly at herself as she decided on the perfect outfit to wear to Reggie's place.

Aletha went over to her bureau and pulled out a tiny red lace tasseled bra with its matching lace string bikini panties. Then going into her walk-in closet, she found her thigh-high red leather spike-heeled boots.

That was all she was going to wear under her red down coat!

She looked around the room, trying to recall where she had left what she called her "New York City Handbag of Essentials" then remembered that it was on the bathroom vanity.

Standing on the thick black carpeting in her bathroom, a narcissist's paradise like her bedroom, decorated with wall-to-wall mirrors, black glass, marble counters, and gold accents, she carefully cleaned the makeup from her face. Reggie preferred her face naked.

Aletha slipped her daisy-covered shower cap over her hair and then stepped into a steamy shower in order to freshen up.

She would have a small intimate wedding, she thought, soaping up, which meant that she would definitely wait until she retired. She didn't want any news people, star stalkers, or lackeys hanging about on the most important day of her life. Maybe she and Reggie would go on a cruise and be married by a ship's captain. That would certainly be romantic. The ceremony would take place before they set sail, and she would have her sister, her brother-in-law, David, her brother, Marshall, her parents, and Reggie's mother present. After the vows, some champagne, and wedding cake, the family would all leave, and she and Reggie would sail off to their new home.

But she'd have to discuss this with Reggie; he might have some ideas of his own about what flavor the cake should be.

Quickly toweling dry, she lotioned her body into a silky luster with some Biotherm Moisture Creme that her brother, Marshall, had brought her from one of his stays in Monte Carlo, then spritzed on some Fendi perfume. She slinked into her itsy-bitsy garments and tugged on tall hooker boots. Reaching into her jewelry box on the vanity, she pulled out her eight-strand pearl choker from Mikimoto's and clasped it around her neck. Aletha smiled at her reflection in the mirrors again. The white pearl necklace was the perfect touch—another one of those exclamation points that she just *adored*.

Looking about the room, she checked to see if there was any indication that Reggie had spent any time at her place while she was away. She had told him that she had a surprise waiting for him in the den, and she had hoped that he would come up and look for it.

Looking at Reggie's toothbrush hanging next to hers, she reached over and felt the bristles. They weren't even moist. A sting of disappointment pricked her when she noticed that the toothpaste cap was firmly in place and that the toilet seat had remained exactly as she had left it. He had obviously not bothered to come over.

Aletha strutted from the bathroom in her four-inch heels to the den to survey the room and the work the decorators had finally completed before she left for the Bahamas. She smiled with approval at the results. The decorators had transformed one of the rooms into Aletha's idea of a chic masculine refuge. They covered the walls in knotty pine paneling. Scattered about the shiny parquet floor were three faux zebra skin rugs. Rubber plants were strategically sprouting throughout the room. Aletha had selected substantial deep green leather chairs and sofas and had purchased an enormous mahogany desk inlaid also with green leather. An elaborate installation of bookcases and shelving were in place for Reggie's TV, stereo, CDs, computer, books, and other work material. Over the fireplace hung a twelfth-century Moroccan Berber saber that she had purchased from her brother, Marshall, and above that was a huge moose head. Actually, it wasn't a *real* moose head. She had commissioned an artist in SoHo to make one up in papier-mâché.

Everything was perfect! Men *liked* this sort of thing, Aletha thought to herself smugly.

She turned on her heel, closed the door to the den, and returned to her bathroom to retrieve her New York City Handbag of Essentials and went back to her bedroom.

"Come on, Sparky! Let's put on your raincoat." She put on her own red down coat, then grabbed Sparky's from the hook behind her bedroom door.

Sparky started barking urgently.

Aletha stood back, crinkling her brow trying to figure out what he was trying to tell her.

"Oh. You want to eat something, is that it?" she deciphered, then headed toward the kitchen.

Aletha took a half-empty can of dog food from the refrigerator and spooned some into his empty bowl.

Sparky looked at the ground meat, sniffed indignantly, and whined.

"Okay, okay, *forget* the dog food," Aletha sighed impatiently, reaching back into the refrigerator to retrieve some leftover slices of roast beef. "What a food snob, you are, dog," Aletha said, watching her terrier scarf up the expensive meat.

"Are you ready to go now?" she asked when he had finished, bending over toward him with his rain gear.

Sparky gingerly stepped into his bright yellow slicker with its pointed hood and then ran ahead of her to the door. With champagne, her handbag with the photos, and the deed to her dowry in hand, Aletha quickly left the apartment with Sparky trotting at her heels.

They swept through the lobby to the exit, and the doorman held the umbrella over Aletha as he opened the door to the limo. He slammed it shut and fought his way back to the lobby as the winds from the snowstorm picked up with a vengeance.

"To Mr. Pinkney's place, Jim. Then you can go wherever you wish to go," she commanded, trying to relax again in the backseat.

Jim cleared his throat, thinking that the last thing a woman should do was to just drop in on a man after cutting her trip short . . . that is, unless she was looking for dirt. Jim doubted that Aletha would find anything unsavory going on at Reggie's place, but experience told him that she should go back home and get some rest.

"Look at this snowstorm. Mr. Pinkney, I'm sure, doesn't expect you back yet, so—"

"*You* work for *me*, Jim, not the other way around. Now let's *go*."

"As you wish," he mumbled, maneuvering the car into the snow-covered avenue.

Like most career-oriented women of her generation, Aletha had just waited too long to put her personal life in order. They had all thought that their money and success exerted some kind of gravitational pull, attracting proposals from the kinds of handsome, successful men they had all dreamed that their lofty status would bring into their orbits.

No such luck, Aletha thought. There had been a few stray comets—brief, pleasurable flashes in the sky—then whoosh . . . gone! "See ya in eighty-seven years, babe!" Of course, there were always the pimps, wimps, and star-humpers lurking about. God, what a circus it had been!

Until Reggie.

She ran from the car through the muffling blankets of snowfall and into the entrance of Reggie's brownstone building. She briefly thought about buzzing his apartment, but her intuition told her to surprise him, so she used her key. She bounded, two steps at a time, up to his third-floor walk-up apartment, Sparky eagerly springing ahead of her.

Aletha could hear Beethoven's Fifth booming from under his door. How could he listen to his music so loud like that, in such a small apartment? Didn't his neighbors freak out or something? Probably not, since this was Greenwich Village. Most of his neighbors were probably too absorbed in drug-induced stupors to even notice, she supposed.

She stalked into the living room and walked over to his computer. One of his weekly columns for *The City Voice* was still on the screen. Aletha yelled out over the music, "Hey, Reg, it's *me*, baby," as she ran toward the bedroom.

A female-sounding shriek exploded from the bedroom.

"Sparky! What are *you* doing here?" Reggie's astonished voice roared from the bedroom, almost simultaneously.

A shocked and outraged Reginald Pinkney yelled something to the effect of, "Woman, what the *hell* do you think? . . ."

An outlandish picture of rage and indignation—the surreal image of Reggie in his unclothed splendor trying unsuccessfully to block her view of the bedroom and the bare-assed, naturally redheaded, familiar-looking white woman with the frightened hard-boiled-egg eyes, screaming as Sparky, having cornered the bitch, lunged, snapped, and growled in his yellow hooded raincoat—became firmly etched in her mind . . . *forever*! After all, Sparky was a fox terrier and had simply done what had come naturally—harass a fox out of its hiding place.

It felt as though four thousand layers of betrayal and humiliation detonated in her brain!

How *dare* Reggie do this to her! And in the extravagantly expensive Porthault sheets that she'd bought for him, too, no less!

An absinthe wave of fury swept over her.

Aletha's scream of devastation could have resurrected the entire population of a necropolis. She took her pistol out of her New York City Handbag of Essentials and aimed . . . somewhere, at someone, splashing a crimson abstract canvas before her eyes.

There was nothing but a black hole of memory after that. The next thing she knew, she was at the desk in the den of her apartment, absently and hypnotically rubbing bloodstains from the photos of her new hacienda. Her hands trembled uncontrollably once she realized that she had no idea what had actually happened or how she had gotten back to her apartment.

Yet she was all alone, and the phone kept ringing, ringing, ringing. . . . And Sparky was barking, barking, barking—quaking in terror at her feet at the bizarre scene he had recently witnessed.

Aletha looked up at the wall over the fireplace and could have sworn that that stupid moose head was glaring down at her flagrantly ridiculing her predicament.

A glance at the clock told her it was eight o'clock at night. She'd lost all track of time and the events that had transpired since she had gotten off that plane at La Guardia Airport. She knew, with terrifying dread, that in a split second, she had lost control and had done *something* unspeakable that would change the course of her life.

She also realized that she was losing her mind.

She licked away the tears that were spilling onto her lips and dialed her sister's number.

It barely rang once; Desiree's nervous voice came on the line.

"Sister . . . this is A-A-Aletha . . . Desiree . . . I'm in *trouble*, girl."

"I know, Aletha. Everything is going to be all right. I've talked to Reggie."

"Reg . . . ? B-but, I—"

"I know. He's okay, you know? *Everyone* is okay, Aletha."

"But, my *show* . . . the newspapers . . . the *police*!"

"Listen to me, Aletha. Things seem to be under control, okay? But this is what you are going to do. I'm sending a car for you. It will meet you at the side door of your apartment building. You know where I mean, don't you?"

Silence.

"Aletha . . . are you *there*? . . . are you okay?"

"Yeah . . . yeah . . ."

"Okay. The car will bring you here to Connecticut. You'll stay with David and me tonight. You'll get some sleep, and we'll talk about all of this tomorrow. As I said, it seems as though everything is under control. Just pack some toilet articles and that stupid handbag of New York City essentials and come on up here. And, Aletha? Don't worry, nobody's said a thing to Mom or Dad."

"Will Reggie be—"

"Let's not talk about *him* until tomorrow, okay, sister?" There was a long pause. "I'm sorry, Aletha, if I snapped at you. Just come on up. You know I'm *here* for you."

"Look . . . Desiree . . . i-is it o-okay if I bring my dog Sparky with me? Is your dog friendly?"

"Of course, Aletha. Don't worry, Hemingway loves company."

"All right, I'll see you in a while. I love you, big sister." Aletha's crisp and practiced control asserted itself again. She put down the receiver and started to pack.

Desiree stood stunned in the silence of her kitchen.

I hope she doesn't love me as much as she loves Reginald, she mused, and then started to giggle.

She felt guilty about giggling, but she knew that everyone was driven to think about shooting someone, at some time in their life. But to actually shoot them and have them *survive*—and not run you down to the police? Now *that* was a wild fantasy! God, she had no idea that Aletha was in such a state as to sneak into some guy's apartment and shoot him. Though she and her sister hadn't been very close over the years, since they had been leading such different lifestyles, and even though Desiree had seen a lot of clients who had done a lot of irrational things, even this was nearly too much to believe.

Desiree constantly shook her head, acknowledging the irony of Aletha telling her that her choice of a career in psychology was absurd—always saying that black folks didn't *need* shrinks. What did Aletha want, less therapist's offices and more firing ranges? And why on earth was her fabulously successful baby sister shooting little boy writers?

Though she knew she should have known better, Desiree would never have imagined one of the Brown sisters involved in something like this!

Desiree reached into the cupboard for a bottle of merlot. She poured herself a glass. Then, leaning against the island counter in her kitchen, she shook her dreadlocked head in disbelief.

Desiree knew that no matter what Reggie would try to arrange, this mess would be all over the papers by tomorrow morning.

She and her sister had a lot to talk about. Maybe if they had stayed closer, this would not have happened—but then, maybe it would have anyway.

Desiree had learned long ago that most women—whether they were friends or patients—really didn't want advice concerning their relationships with men. For the most part, women came to her looking for quick-fix answers and a magic wand—fairy dust and happily ever after.

Those willing to invest a little time in improving their relationships were nearly as bad. They figured that since Desiree had been happily married for over twenty years, she had to have some kind of secret recipe. All they needed was the list of ingredients and the steps, and they, too, would have a happy life. What they didn't realize was the key ingredients—the two people—were the most unpredictable and unique ones of all.

Sometimes those women simply had designs on David.

Yet, Aletha was neither a patient nor a girlfriend. Desiree had to admit that a sister was an entirely different case altogether. She knew that proceeding with caution was crucial, especially since she loved her baby sister and didn't want to push her farther away. Despite their differences in age and the circumstances of their lives, Aletha had come to her in a moment of great crisis, and that pleased Desiree. It felt good to know that Aletha trusted her.

But this situation required a whole lot of trust. "Where on earth did Aletha get a gun anyway?" she asked herself, frowning at the thought.

Well, she wasn't going to deal with her sister's predicament right then. When Aletha arrived, she'd serve her a cup of tea, tuck her into bed, and deal with this scandal the next morning.

With the blizzard continuing the way it was, Aletha might not make it on these Connecticut roads until way after midnight.

Oh, God! She prayed silently to herself that her sister would make it to the house all right and that there could be something she could do to help her. *Really* help her.

Isn't that why Desiree became a psychologist anyway—to *help*? If she couldn't help her own sister, what good was she?

CHAPTER FOUR

*T*he next morning Aletha appraised, with more than just a twinge of envy, the riot of shiny foliage and herbs displayed throughout her sister's magnificently bright, airy, and tastefully decorated kitchen.

The icily bucolic landscape outside was framed by the panes of the bay windows that curved gracefully from three sides of the room. The warm feelings that permeated the room emanated not only from the bright oak counters, closets, and window casings, but also from the peaceful aura that surrounded her sister and her husband, David.

Aletha had awakened before they did and had taken the liberty of exploring their lovely rustic home—eighteenth century, wasn't it? She thought she remembered her sister telling her this some years ago. She had never been to her sister's house before, even though for the past few years, since Aletha moved to New York, they'd been living less than two hours away from each other. She'd just never had the time to visit, although she knew, not all that subconsciously, that she had never *made* the time because she just couldn't handle all this happily-married-couple shit.

She'd only once invited Desiree to her place. Desiree had come to her office a couple of times to take her out for her birthday. They had generally just kept their conversations superficial, as she never wanted to get into the details of her life . . . and she *certainly* didn't want to hear the details of her sister's.

Now that Aletha had heard from their mother that Desiree and David were planning to move to some fancy place outside the country, she realized that she'd probably never really get to know her sister as an adult.

Damn!

It seemed as if Desiree always got *everything* that Aletha wanted. With her own practice, she was self-employed, answering to no one. No sponsors, no demanding and vengeful public. And now that her *writer* husband once again had published another blockbuster book, she'd be closing her practice so that they could tap-dance around the world together. He had written some kind of psychological thriller called *Bombay*. Supposed to be hot. Desiree had sent her a copy of it, of course, although she hadn't yet bothered to read it.

His *fourth* bestselling book, and now they were set for life, it seemed. It took David only a year to write this last one, or any of his others, so she had heard. Reggie'd been working on *his* damned novel ever since she met him.

Oh, shit . . . *Reggie*! Her hand trembled as she remembered why she was at her sister's house, spilling her cup of tea all over her sister's quilted place mat.

"Damn! I'm sorry, sis."

She started to get up, but David was already removing the wet mat as her sister poured her another cup.

"It's okay, Aletha. What I want to know is why you were carrying a gun."

"I've been carrying a gun ever since I was burglarized in Miami, and also because I had a stalker fan for a while, right in New York City! Things like that make one paranoid, you know?" She paused for a moment, throwing a jealous glance toward her sister. "Of course, I guess *you* wouldn't, with your very protected self." She tried to laugh, in order to deflect her unintentionally bitchy comment, but choked on her tea instead.

Desiree stared at her sister in horror and thought, again, about how little she knew of her sister's life and how little Aletha knew about hers. Aletha seemed to feel that because Desiree was married and living outside of the city, she had been living a sheltered life. Desiree had had her own share of stalker fans and enemies over the years. After all, she *was* a psychotherapist! One disgruntled patient had left messages on her office answering machine threatening to "cap her" for some imagined offense. Only David, Desiree, and the authorities knew about another patient who used to manage to show up almost everywhere Desiree happened to be in the city. One morning they had awoken to the smell of freshly brewed coffee. Following the aroma, they ended up in their kitchen, where that same patient sat calmly at the kitchen counter, reading their morning paper. The patient looked up at them, smiled, and said, "Help yourself," pointing over to the pot in front of her.

Then, of course, there were David's fans who either overidentified with him as a writer—one of them claiming that she and David were soul mates from a past life and were being reunited through his books—or the ones who felt that

David and his books were a menace to society and should be eradicated along with their author.

Yeah, right. Protected life, *indeed*! Desiree thought to herself, trying to contain her annoyance toward her sister's presumptions about her life, in order to get back to the problem at hand: Aletha's shooting of poor Reginald Pinkney.

"But, Aletha, Reggie said that you shouted, 'I *own* you, nigger,' then you shot him! 'I *own* you, nigger?!' Aletha, when did you start *owning* people?"

"Did I hurt him bad? Did he go to the hospital?"

"You shot him in the arm. I had him go to your personal physician; no one is going to report it to the police. Now, answer me, when did you start *owning* people, Aletha?"

"You know, Desiree, that bitch that was with him—she was his literary agent! I *knew* that I recognized that 'ho from somewhere . . ."

David got up to leave the room and said, "Look, ladies, I'm going to leave you two alone to talk about this.

"Come on, guys," he said to the two dogs, lying on the floor in the middle of the kitchen—Aletha's Sparky and their mild-mannered golden retriever, Hemingway. They perked up and scampered ahead of him out of the kitchen.

As he left the room, Aletha silently observed that the brothers didn't have a monopoly on juicy buns. Her sister's "nice Jewish boy" certainly filled *his* blue jeans nicely.

While Aletha had spent her college years quietly studying and waiting for the perfect brother to come along—or just ask her out on a date even—sister Desiree had flitted around campus and around the world with her United Colors of Benetton boyfriends, seemingly oblivious to the critical stares and comments of her African American peers.

Her sister had told her once that she thought it strange how so many of the sisters were willing to exercise flexibility in the dangerous consumption of recreational drugs, yet refused to indulge in the healthier pastime of sampling different flavors of men.

She had asked Aletha, how could one possibly know what kind of wine one preferred, without having tried the rosé, the burgundy, the white . . . the French . . . the Italian . . . the Australian. . . .

Aletha remembered shuddering at her sister's weird analogy. It all sounded more like something a man might espouse than what a five-foot-tall, one-hundred-pound woman should have been saying.

Besides, Aletha had a fundamental craving for wide, juicy, full lips on her body and thick electrified hair in her hands. Nothing less would do.

Nevertheless, Desiree got married during her first year in graduate school. Back then, in the early seventies, everybody thought she was crazy to get married at the tender age of twenty-two. She and David hadn't even lived together first. Totally unheard of at that time—or *these* even. Desiree hadn't even been established in a career yet!

Aletha had dated only two men while she was in college. In fact, Reggie was only her second lover. The first one was that pimp, that dick, she had shacked up with for almost two years while she was living in Miami.

He had called himself a lawyer, but he turned out to be a slimy dealer of illegal immigrants, gouging them out of their hard-earned money for falsified green cards and other documents. He was a master of creating false hopes and illusions.

The day the investigators from the INS, the IRS, and the FBI all showed up at her door, Aletha excused herself from that alphabet soup of suspicion and never went back. He was still renting her house, though, with all her lovely things.

So much for living together first, Aletha had finally concluded as she gulped down the last of her tea. Aletha then looked at the disturbed, questioning, and beautifully smooth mahogany face of her big sister. Desiree had those huge, haunting, almond-shaped, jet-black eyes. Those very eyes were probably what seduced everyone into giving her sister every little thing that her heart so desired. Sometimes Aletha had to admit to herself that she just *hated* the girl! Why couldn't Aletha have been the oldest and the one to get all of the attention? Nobody ever took her seriously because she was the baby. Even with millions of dollars in the bank, they *all* still looked at her as if she were "the baby." Now her sister probably thought that she was a complete jerk. Their brother, Marshall, if he ever found out, would probably start chastising her about what he always called her "ridiculous, controlling nature." Well, she'd never tell him about this "Pinkney incident," and she knew that Desiree could be trusted not to tell him.

"Desiree, girl. You know, I *love* your house. What are you going to do with it when you move? Are you going to sell it? This place would be a perfect weekend retreat for me. I'll pay you a handsome price for it."

First, she thinks she owns Reggie and now she wants to *buy* our house from us, Desiree thought, cringing.

"Aletha, you think not only that you can buy *people*, but their lifestyles, as well. That's sad, really sad," Desiree said, managing to hide some of her annoyance—an annoyance that flowered now but had long and tangled roots.

So often when they were growing up, Desiree had felt that Aletha was stalking her. Desiree loved her sister with all her heart, but she was some-times frightened by her, thinking that if Aletha *could*, she would find some way for Desiree to disappear so that she could just walk in and live out Desiree's life. When they were small, even though Aletha was the youngest, she would covet or steal Desiree's toys. When their mother would decide to buy duplicates of something, Aletha would still want Desiree's, as well. Aletha was and would always be a consumer hog. The stalking began to dis-sipate a bit when Aletha found that she and Desiree had very different tal-ents. Desiree was the more outgoing and socially confident of the two of them, but Aletha started winning her prizes in debating and journalism. It took some time and adjustment, but Aletha eventually found her own milieu of achievement. The fact that she found Desiree's attraction for non–African American men rather daunting, kept Aletha from trying to seduce her sister's men, and sent her to find her own world at a predominantly black university. Once Aletha went away to college, the two sisters were living distinctly dif-ferent lives.

But Desiree admired Aletha's discipline and ambition. She was one of the most focused women she had ever met. That's probably why she had become a self-made millionaire before she was even thirty years old. But, Desiree wondered, at what cost had that fame and fortune come? In addition to all of the other pressures that black women have to endure in this country, in Aletha's professional world she knew that she also had the burden of being considered by some in the media "Oprah's little sister"—as if one successful black woman was the standard by which to measure all the others.

"If I am *Oprah*'s little sister, who does that make you, Desiree?" Aletha had asked her one day, annoyed at the nickname that haunted her everywhere she went. Desiree had always been sensitive enough to never refer to the nickname in Aletha's presence. She was also aware that the pressures of Aletha's notoriety made her a target. That the target had fired back at a more or less innocent victim made her sad. On the other hand, what really made Desiree angry was the way that Aletha had somehow gotten Desiree tangled up in this by suggesting that buying her and David's house would somehow solve Aletha's personal problems.

"What is it that you really want *now*, Aletha? First, you try to pay me some outrageous salary to be a resident shrink on your insidious talk show, knowing full well how I feel about all those awful exploitative exhibitions of human frailties. Now you want to buy this house! What on earth would you need with a house in the Connecticut suburbs anyway? You're not exactly what anyone would call call a country kind of girl, you know."

"Sparky could use some room to run outside. I'm telling you girl, I'll *pay* you for it."

"I'm sure you *would*, but we're not selling," she lied. "Besides, Sparky is a city dog and has lived in an apartment all his life. I think your problem is that you think you can buy people, Aletha. Reggie told me that he was in his *own* apartment when you 'caught' him with that girl," she stated simply, as she got up from her chair to go to the refrigerator. "Want some breakfast?"

"No, I can't eat a thing."

"What about some fruit, or some juice? I have some croissants. I *know* you like crois—"

"I *said* I can't eat. I'll just have some more of this tea. Actually, this herbal mess is boring the hell out of me. Don't you have something with a little caffeine or something?" She reached over to pour the tea, lustfully admiring the craftsmanship of the silver pot. "Look, girl, I caught him cheating on me. He's been *my* man for all these years. How *could* he—"

"Aletha, had you noticed anything changing in your relationship? Anything? Even something subtle? Why did you sneak into his apartment?"

"I don't know, girl. I've got pressures, you know? He's no baby—not *really*, anyway—I can't read his fucking mind."

Desiree was trying to understand, but her sister had become an enigma to her. It was so much easier keeping a certain level of objectivity with the patients, who were strangers.

"Aletha, as Eddie Murphy would say—"

"Why would I give a *damn* about what that misogynistic pip-squeak Eddie Murphy would have to say about anything?" How could her sister give credence to that nut anyway? Aletha wondered briefly.

"As Eddie Murphy would say," Desiree continued, 'I don't see no ring on your finger.' He's not your *husband*, girl."

"*Husband?* What's that got to do with it? He cheated on me with that white, redheaded bitch! You wouldn't understand. I don't even know why I'm even talking to you."

"Sorry, but you know, I'm all you've *got*. I certainly can't see you talking to Mom about this—or Marshall." She put a croissant on one of her Lalique dessert plates, returned to her chair across from Aletha, and began tapping a bejeweled and manicured left hand on the oak table.

Aletha grabbed her sister's hand and looked hungrily at the sparkling pear-shaped diamond on the engagement ring and at the diamond-and-sapphire wedding band that smugly and mockingly encircled Desiree's long, dark finger.

"I may not have any 'rings on my fingers,' but I *do* feel that I deserve respect as his woman." She grimaced, reluctantly letting go of Desiree's hand.

"It's not as if he had that woman at *your* place," Desiree stated gently.

"How do I know that she's never been in my place with him?"

Desiree shuddered. "Why would you give a man you're not married to the keys to *your* apartment?"

Desiree reflected back to the night that David proposed to her over twenty years ago.

They had been at her apartment taking a shower. David loved showering with her. Desiree had been the only black woman he had ever dated, and he found her wet hair, which she wore in what was called an Afro in those days, intriguing. He hadn't known that black peoples' hair when wet, shrank. She loved how his eyes widened and a smile spread across his face whenever she washed her hair. He always found this phenomenon wildly fascinating to watch.

"David, hand me the towel, please," she said, smiling at the mesmerized expression on his face.

"No, Dez, just let it dry naturally. The drops of water make it look as if there are diamonds in your hair," he said, playing with a coiled lock.

She reached over and grabbed the towel herself. They had been dating for almost two years by then, and those romantic utterings had begun to feel trite to her. She'd wanted a commitment!

As she turned off the shower and began to towel dry her hair, he took her hand and suggested, "Dez, why don't we move in together?"

She slapped him with the towel and jumped from the shower, butt naked, soaking wet, and mad as hell!

"What's *wrong*?" Startled, he jumped from the shower stall to follow her into the bedroom. "Did I say something—"

"Fuck off, David! You men are all alike!" In her frenzy, she was pacing around the bedroom, searching for her robe and shaking her fist at him. "Don't come near me, David!"

He stood there—shocked—with his mouth agape.

"You macho jerks don't hesitate to go out and get hunting licenses. Gun licenses. Driver's licenses. But then you stand around like dunces, acting like you never even heard of *marriage licenses*. Get out, David! Go home!" She picked up a shoe and threw it at him.

Ducking, David said, "But, Dez—"

"I don't want to be your damned concubine! What would I say to my parents? A white boy's *concubine*! How antiquated! Who do you think I am, Sally—damned—Hemmings or something?" She rolled his clothes into a ball and threw them at him for emphasis.

"But—," he started.

"But *what*, David?" She glared at him with her hands on her hips, her small round breasts quivering with outrage. Her eyes dropped to below his waist, noting that his fat, arrogant cock had begun to swell. She moved her eyes swiftly back to his face. He was grinning, but he looked kind of nervous. She seized her robe from the bed and put it on, closing it firmly and protectively around her body. She then pointed to the door and said, "It's over between us, David. Good-bye."

David laughed and grabbed her by the arms and sat her down on the bed.

"Look, Desiree. Although I have a *driver's license*, I don't hunt, nor do I own a gun. So, now let me rephrase my proposal." He dropped to the floor on bended knee. "Desiree? Why don't we get married!"

A rush of embarrassment seized her, but she'd never let him know it. She jumped up from the bed, ran over to the window, her back facing him, and said, "Okay, then. Go and get a ring or something, David."

David laughed and said, "Desiree, it's one o'clock in the damned morning!"

He went out and bought the ring the very next morning, and they got married a few months later. Since then they had passionately lived the emotional roller-coaster ride that is characteristic of a truly committed relationship.

She knew that she would have been living a personal delusion if she had agreed to live with David in what the French called a concubinage. Desiree Brown Simon had always wanted the boundaries in her personal relationships as crystal clear as possible.

Aletha was staring at her sister, annoyed by Desiree's private, faraway look. Desiree's archaic ideas about relationships had convinced Aletha that she could never tell Desiree about the freaked-out affair she had with that Miami slime lawyer. Desiree was just too out of touch with the realities of Aletha's world.

"Also," Desiree added, pressing crumbs from her flaky croissant, which had fallen on the table, with the tips of her fingers and flicking them onto the plate. "Why on earth would you have keys to some man's apartment, when he never *gave* them to you? Aletha, you have to get a grip. You should have been dating other people, too."

"*Dating* other people?" Aletha looked at her sister in disbelief. "You are insane, right? What on earth are you talking about?" She guessed that having been wed at birth had rendered her sister profoundly naive.

"Forget it, Desiree. You'd never understand. I've just got to call Reggie and apologize. We'll get our relationship back on the right course. What would he want with that silly little bitch anyway? I could buy and sell her!

"You know, Desiree, if Reggie has a craving for red hair, I could *buy* it! If he wants some light skin, I could just pick up the phone and dial Michael Jackson's plastic surgeon."

"Don't be ridiculous, Aletha." Desiree rose with impatience from her chair and went to the refrigerator. She took out a bowl of fruit with one hand and a wedge of Gouda with the other and pushed the door closed with her left hip. She removed a cheese board from the hook over the counter, placed the cheese on it, and returned to the table with the goods, placing them directly in front of her sister.

"If the man wanted a damned dancing girl, I'd put stones in my navel and dance for him. Shit, Desiree, I could even get my stones from Harry Winston's, if Reggie had wanted!"

Desiree reached over to the counter next to her to grab a basket of rolls and then placed them also in front of Aletha.

Aletha flashed a look of nausea at the food, picked up the butter knife in front of her, violently stabbed the offending Gouda, and yelled, "What in the hell do these men *want?*" Aletha then spluttered into one of the most chilling sobs Desiree had ever witnessed inside or outside her office, a sob wet with abject confusion and despair.

Yep, her sister, her dear, rich, and powerful baby sister, Desiree thought, had plummeted into the abyss over her young and apparently uncommitted lover.

"You just wouldn't understand. I—I bought us a house . . . in the Bahamas. I w-was going to ask him to marry me."

Desiree sat down next to Aletha and stared at her.

God! So *that's* why her sister was in Nassau. Reggie didn't tell her this. Knowing Aletha, he probably didn't even know. She put her arm around Aletha's shoulder to comfort her and giggled to herself, surprised and amused by the revelation.

"Aletha, why would you buy Reggie a house? Didn't you think that he would want to buy one of his own?"

"He's not established yet. He can't afford one. Why shouldn't I take care of him while he's struggling?"

"Because he's a *man*, Aletha."

Aletha frowned in pain and shrugged out of her sister's grip. "You supported David while he was struggling—"

Desiree burst out laughing. "I certainly did *not!* We both worked at jobs until he published his first book. That was our deal. David spent years teaching obstreperous high school teenagers English all day and toiled away at his writing at night. If you're going to emulate someone's life, girl, perhaps you should ask questions before you go shooting off your mouth or—" She couldn't resist. "—just *shooting!*"

Before Aletha could respond, Desiree continued. "You're acting like a power-freak white man, Aletha." Desiree snapped her fingers and reached over and selected an orange from the fruit-filled bowl.

"You're *married* to a white man, Desiree."

"No, I'm not. I'm married to a Jewish man." Her thumbnail angrily pierced the orange's thick skin as she eyed Aletha suspiciously, suddenly leery about the curious turn of the conversation.

"Jews are *white*, aren't they, Desiree?" asked Aletha snidely, snickering into her cup.

"Not to *real* white people, they're not. And not to *me* either. I know the difference, too, because I've been with *both*," Desiree snapped again, peeling away the skin and separating the juicy sections.

"Well, if you didn't support David, how did you get this *house* all those years ago then? Don't try to bullshit your own sister," she said, sweeping her hand around the kitchen.

Ignorance breeds stupid gossip and presumptions, Desiree thought to herself, anger welling up inside her. Aletha was a fucking piece of work!

Popping an orange section into her mouth, she calmly and slowly said, "Aletha, since you *asked*, David's parents loaned us the money for this house, and we have paid them back with *interest*."

Aletha got up from her chair, glancing around at the expensive kitchen, and mumbled under her breath, "Usurers."

"*What* did you say, Aletha?" Desiree's voice rose slightly. She heard perfectly well what Aletha had said, plus she had become well aware of the depth of her sister's jealousy. She wanted to slap her. "You know, Aletha. This beats *all*." She clenched and unclenched her jaw, trying desperately to contain the outrage seething in her toward her impertinent baby sister. "You bring your arrogant—" She wanted to say *black ass*. "—*self* up here to *my* house, running like a thief in the night from the police, the news people, or perhaps even the president of the United States himself for all I know, with blood on your hands . . . your eyes all wild and crazy . . . shaking like a leaf in here . . . and . . ."

Aletha was pacing around the kitchen, banging on all the counters. "Okay . . . okay . . . I'm sorry, sister, for what I said about the Jews."

The bitch was incorrigible, Desiree thought as David returned to the kitchen.

"What *about* the Jews?" David asked, having entered the room, the dogs at his heels, panting from their vigorous run around the snow-covered neighborhood. He looked nervously at his sister-in-law, who looked as if she were about to go over the deep end again.

"Nothing your people haven't heard for thousands of years, David," Desiree responded, watching her sister begin to pace again and at the same time continuing to enjoy her piece of fruit.

"Aletha, why don't you sit down and have something to eat," David suggested, picking up a glass from the counter and going over to the refrigerator.

Aletha spun around and screamed, "Why do you people keep offering me your fucking food? What's *wrong* with you two? One would think that you grew up *hungry* or something!"

The dogs started howling.

David dropped the glass he was holding.

Everyone stood in eerie silence.

Job burnout, with a capital B, Desiree thought knowingly; she was wrestling with her *own*, as well.

"Aletha, you've *got* to find a way to take some extended time off," David nervously suggested, glancing at his wife, who was slowly easing herself back in her chair. "Maybe you can get away again. Go lie on the beach in the Caribbean for a while."

"The *Caribbean*!" she yelled at the top of her lungs. "The *Caribbean*? What am I supposed to *do* down in the Caribbean, may I *ask*? You expect me to go d-down . . . there and g-get hustled by green-card s-seekers or . . . or . . . ," she yelled, saliva spraying everywhere. "Or *pig farmers*?"

"*Pig* farmers?" Desiree and David repeated incredulously, their eyes almost crossed with confusion.

"Don't ask me to *explain* myself to you," Aletha said.

"Don't worry, we don't want you to, Aletha," Desiree said quietly and cautiously.

Aletha burst out laughing, suddenly snapping back into focus. Tears streamed down her cheeks.

Aletha's eyes wandered over David's face and locked onto his full, wide, Mick Jagger lips. Desiree caught Aletha's eye. She knew what Aletha was thinking . . . and Aletha knew she knew. They both started giggling uncontrollably, because they had discussed this "thing" before, years ago. Both sisters shared some of the same predilections, after all, Aletha concluded.

David looked at the two women, who were now staring at him in the same peculiar way. He moved apprehensively toward their table, grabbed an apple and a banana, and backed nervously toward the door.

Aletha then noticed David's thick curly hair and thought, her mind wandering in an entirely different direction—about how whenever he and Desiree would come back from one of their vacations, how much David, with his suntan and all, resembled a brother to *her*.

"Tell me something, David. Why do white people *do* that?"

"Why do white people do *what*, sister-in-law?" David's chuckle hid his apprehensive curiosity.

"Why do they burn themselves into dark brown crisps under the sun, then go out and discriminate against black people because of their naturally rich brown color? Why do the white people lie on their backs on sunny beaches and in tanning salons in self-destructive attempts to look like something they're not? To look as though they were wearing someone else's skin? I've wanted to ask somebody this for *years*."

"I dunno. I guess it's one of the hard questions of the day. But as for *me*, I'm a Semite, so I enjoy paying a visit to my long-lost Mediterranean pigmentation from time to time." David laughed, wondering about the purpose of this strange bait that Aletha had decided to toss at him.

"Ahh . . . pish, David." Aletha sighed, fanning her hands in order to dismiss him.

Images of the evil, taunting, project-dwelling skeezer children flashed back into Aletha's head again. And the animal-rights people.

Jealousy, she figured, was the *real* answer, conceding that few white people would be willing to admit it.

Of course, it *never* feels like jealousy when you found yourself a victim of colorism—or any of the other kinds of "isms" for that matter, she thought to herself.

Desiree went over to her sister and held her in her arms, relieved that she seemed to be calming down.

David silently repeated "pig farmers" and fled from the kitchen, forgetting what he had come in there for, the dogs following at his heels.

"Aletha, please listen to me. You know I've only met Reggie a couple of times. But every time I did, I always told David how happy I was that you'd found a man who cared for you so much. A man who cared for you just for being you. And I know you care about him, too. But sometimes when we care about someone too much, we do the strangest things. Sometimes caring for somebody gets all mixed up and confused with other things."

"Other things?"

"Like confusing a personal relationship with a business relationship or vice versa. You have a different set of expectations and appropriate behaviors for each. I mean, Reggie's not like an employee, someone whose loyalty you expect because you pay him. And there are boundaries, too, Aletha. You don't just burst into someone's private home."

Desiree could see that her words weren't having the desired effect, so she tried a different tack. "Sometimes, Aletha, it's difficult to assume that even a man you have a legal commitment with would be completely faithful to you. It's a man thing, you know?"

"No. I don't know." Aletha wiped her eyes with a linen napkin. "Has David ever cheated on you, sister?"

Desiree laughed a deep, throaty chuckle. "I haven't a clue. But you see, I'd have a legal right to punch his lights out if I ever found out that he *had*, and then I'd clean him out so thoroughly that he'd have to live with his parents for the rest of his short and pitiful life."

That's what Desiree *said*. But what she was *thinking* was that she had refused, from the very beginning, to waste a lot of time worrying about the issue of infidelity. No one had *that* much control over someone else's life. What she figured was that the best she could do concerning the subject was to keep her man busy and absorbed on the home front and leave him with as little expendable cash as possible. What *else* could a woman do without driving herself completely mad?

Despite her emotional state, Aletha let out a wicked laugh, which momentarily cheered her up.

Damn . . . that Desiree. She's *something*. Maybe she understood women, after all, Aletha thought, watching her sister go over to make some normal tea.

Desiree looked over her shoulder at Aletha, and for a brief moment they shared a warm, conspiratorial grin.

Aletha sat at the table again. Looking earnestly at her sister, she asked, "Desiree, *really,* what would you do if you found out that David was cheating on you?"

Desiree sat down across from her.

"What do you mean, 'found out'? You mean if I caught him, here, in our bed with another woman?"

"Umm-hmm . . . yeah, that's what I mean," Aletha said, although she realized that she wasn't exactly sure *what* she meant.

"Well, I'd shout and scream and threaten to kill him, although I wouldn't, because no man is worth spending a lifetime in jail over. After all the screaming, I'd probably have him committed into an insane asylum. But I don't spend much time thinking about all this, Aletha, because while the image of another woman in our bed is horrific and David may be a man, he is not a suicidal maniac. If I did somehow find him cheating with another woman, I would suggest that we seek outside help—therapy."

Aletha rolled her eyes.

"That's right, *therapy,* Aletha. But probably, I'd have him committed. I could *do* it, too. Besides, what kind of arrogantly reckless man would get *caught* cheating on his wife, then sit down to eat the food she prepares for him? Ridiculous!"

Aletha shuddered at the thought of something she had never considered and then remembered the voodoo-lady episode of their childhood. Desiree could be one scary broad, Aletha thought.

"Would you throw him out?"

"If it happened only once? No. Why would I just hand over my man to some other woman, because he happened to be 'phallicly challenged' for a moment? As I said, I'd suggest therapy. I'd want to get to the bottom of the real problem in our relationship. Besides, Aletha, David and I have 'decriminalized' adultery in our marriage."

Aletha's eyes widened as large as saucers. "What on earth are you talking about, sister. Decriminalize—"

"I believe if you decriminalize it, it is no longer possible to use it as a weapon, a vindictive tactic, a smoke screen in order to avoid confronting the real problems."

"You're *crazy*, girl." Aletha pushed herself away from the table and stood at the island counter.

"Not really. But Aletha, David and I are *married*. I don't see how a person could commit adultery or be unfaithful to a person they are not legally married to. If David and I weren't married, and we were living in separate places, I'd go out with whomever I wanted and I suspect he would, too."

"I bet David would kick your ass right out of this place if he caught *you* with another *man*."

"Again, we're married, Aletha. He probably *would*, though. But I would have to be a deranged fool to get caught cheating on my rich and famous husband. Especially after all the work I've put into this relationship, molding him into the husband of my own specifications. And I'd hope that you and David would have *me* hospitalized if you found that I was ever involved with some such nonsense."

"So, if you caught David, you'd go to a shrink. If David caught *you*, you would be kicked to the curb. Sounds like a double standard to me."

"So what? What difference does it make? But, sister, this all has nothing to do with you and Reggie. You don't even live together."

"But Reggie and I have been seeing each other for over five years. He has no right to treat me as if I'm just a date," Aletha said. Her tears resumed their course down her cheeks.

"Aletha, I want you to be honest with me. In all of the five years that you have been going with Reggie, have you never—ever—been with another man?"

Aletha felt herself blush as she thought back to her recent extracurricular activities in the Bahamas. And a couple of other times there, as well.

Desiree looked at her suddenly silent sister, pursed her lips, rolled her eyes, and rising from her chair, said, "Aletha, honey, you need to put some time aside for reflection."

Aletha watched her sister walk away from the table and at that instant simultaneously hated and loved her. She decided that she'd better drop the whole conversation about the Reggie conflict before her sister ended up, in that sneaky way of hers, "all up in her business."

David returned to the kitchen with the dogs, carrying Aletha's big New York City Handbag of Essentials.

"Since it appears that we are harboring a fugitive in our home, Aletha," David stated, placing the bag on the table in front of her and unzipping it, "I feel that Desiree and I should know what's in this thing."

Aletha reached over to grab it from him, but he had already dumped the contents onto the table.

Desiree stared with a blank poker face at the contents of Aletha's handbag, taking inventory.

There was a tube of lipstick, a couple of rat-tail combs, her portable phone, three separate sets of keys joined together on a huge, heavy iron key ring, a set of handcuffs, a can of mace, several multicolored condoms, the pistol, and her gun permit.

Aletha even tries to control the color scheme of Reggie's "thing," Desiree thought to herself, noting the colorful array of prophylactics.

Suddenly Aletha noticed loud chirping sounds in the room. She jumped, grabbed the collar of her blouse, and asked breathlessly, "What on earth is that noise?" The dogs had started barking again, but they had moved to the other side of the room.

"Those are finches," Desiree said. "Hadn't you noticed them?"

Aletha then realized that all morning an unrelenting chirping sound had been obnoxiously filling the air. She had blocked it out. Her eyes followed her sister's to the other side of the kitchen, near the side door, where there was a large ornate cage.

The dogs were sitting next to each other looking up and engaging in some kind of loud confabulation with a bunch of raucous, tiny birds.

Aletha got up and walked over to look at the twenty feathered critters who were bunched together chattering about who knew what.

"What do you call these loud things, Desiree?"

"Society finches."

Aletha figured that Desiree was compensating for all those petless years when they were children.

"Look at them! Look at how they sit there all huddled together looking as if they're passing judgment on everyone," Aletha huffed, returning to the table.

"They're only passing judgment on *you*, Aletha," David said snidely. "But right now, I want you to take this pistol apart, and as soon as you leave this house, I suggest you dispose of it somewhere, Aletha. Somewhere far away from here."

Desiree gasped with amazement as her sister grabbed the pistol and took it apart like a pro.

"Where did you learn how to do *that*, girl?"

"Maybe Aletha saw this maneuver in *The Godfather*," David said, equally amazed.

Aletha let out a nervous chuckle, avoiding their eyes.

David looked quizzically from the rat-tail combs, the mace, the handcuffs, and the rubbers to the pistol parts and asked with amusement, "When you find you have to protect yourself, how do you know what to pull out of the bag? I don't think that you understood what doctors meant when they said use protection."

"Stop messing with me, David!" Aletha snapped, jumping up from the table and sweeping her belongings back into her bag. "Are you satisfied now? Have you both sufficiently amused yourselves at my expense?"

"Aletha, you're right. There's nothing amusing about any of this," Desiree said.

David had several questions about the iron key ring; it seemed so . . . so . . . medieval, but he didn't know how to approach the subject. Forget mentioning the handcuffs!

Aletha noticed David staring at her, and asked, "What's *wrong* with you? What do you want to know? Are you going to make me a character in one of your novels or something?" she asked sarcastically, turning away from him to look toward her sister.

"No publisher would find you plausible, Aletha." He laughed, getting up to leave the room.

"Very funny."

David returned to his study, still wondering why Aletha seemed so familiar with implements of restraint.

The dogs followed David out of the room again, probably figuring that his agenda would continue to be a lot more interesting than the sisters'.

"Look at how well Sparky and Hemingway get along, Desiree," Aletha said, impressed.

"Why are you surprised? They *are* first cousins, you know." She laughed, thankful that Aletha seemed to be relaxing. "You realize, Aletha, that this whole episode could have landed you in the slammer . . . probably for *life*."

Aletha let out a rather demented giggle, fanned her hand condescendingly toward her sister, and said, "That's impossible, Desiree."

"What on earth do you mean, *impossible?* People go to prison for shooting and killing people."

"I could never have killed Reggie. I'm too good a shot. Do you think I'd own a gun if I didn't know how to use it? Please, Desiree, don't be irrational. But you know, you just gave me an idea about a show to do. Thanks, sister."

Desiree wasn't about to respond. It was obvious that Aletha was in no position at that moment to rationally discuss any issue associated with her relationship with Reginald Pinkney. They'd have to get back to that later.

So, she and Aletha spent the rest of the day talking about superficial things. That evening Aletha left to return to her complicated world.

Beep. "Reg, call me, baby." *Click.*

Beep. "Reginald, are you okay? *Please,* call me. I didn't mean to get you in so much trouble with Aletha. I'm so sorry." *Click.*

Beep. "Please call me, Reg. I still love you, you know." *Click.*

Beep. "I'm so *sorry*, Reg. I forgive you about the bitch. Call me." *Click.*

Beep. "I bought us a house, baby. In the Bahamas. Please call me, sweetheart." *Click.*

Beep. "It's me, baby. Pick up the damned phone, Reggie! I *know* you're in there!" Pause. *Click.*

Beep. "Reginald, darling, please call your mother. I just heard the most disturbing thing on a gossip show. Is it true, dear?" *Click.*

Reginald Pinkney sat quietly in the darkness of the corner of his bedroom, nursing his wound, staring at the answering machine, which relentlessly summoned him with messages from Aletha, his agent, and his possessive mother.

Reginald Pinkney picked up the Real Estate section of the *New York Times* and shuddered as he realized that he had almost married Aletha Brown. She had turned out to be a gun-toting, Saturday-night Caldonia, and he'd discovered this not a moment too soon.

He then wondered how many other times Aletha had been snooping around his apartment while he wasn't there, and at what point had she made a key to his apartment?

He knew he'd never find a new apartment fast enough.

SNAP TWO

CHAPTER FIVE

"*I*t's a *boy*!" said the blood-smeared doctor, smiling.

The obstetrician's now-exposed face revealed stubble, which painfully reminded Veronica of both Derrick's recently cultivated beard and his absence from one of the most important events of their lives.

"It's a boy child, girl," shrieked her girlfriend Clarisse, jumping up and down like a banshee. She had been acting as Veronica's Lamaze coach, ever since the baby's father had decided to move to Zurich, Switzerland—in order to forget his roots, Veronica presumed.

A boy!

A big ole healthy, blacker-than-black, nine-pound baby boy had been placed on her belly. The spitting image of his daddy!

Thank God, she could *afford* this baby, Veronica thought, as she passed out into the most relieved and yet unsettling slumber known to womankind.

When she regained consciousness, the first person her eyes locked onto was her mother. There was "Muh Dear," standing in her brown, full-length mouton coat and exotic mouton hat, with her arms crossed disapprovingly in front of her, glaring down at the baby.

"Sweet Jesus," she muttered, loud enough for everyone else in the room to hear. "Truly a blessing it is that this child is *not* a girl."

Muh Dear hadn't realized that Veronica was awake and staring at her with mixed emotions.

"What's wrong with my baby, Mother dear?" asked Veronica, groggily.

"Why, this child is blacker than a moonless night!" She blurted out her distressing observation from thin, stern lips before she realized that it was her *daughter* to whom she had been responding.

"Oh, my *girl*, you know what I mean." She forced a twisted smile toward her beautiful, banana-colored, hazel-eyed, curly-haired daughter. "Him so much like that tired, runaway daddy of his, that it makes me—oh, never mind. How are you *feeling*, daughter?" She placed her gloved hand on her daughter's arm, then leaned over to kiss her.

"What you goin' to *name* our boy child, Veronica?" Clarisse asked, peering into the blankets to see the child more clearly. "You should name him something *African*, girlfriend." She looked around at the others in the room and proudly announced, "You see, *I'm* going to be the godmother. I *am* the godmother."

"Oh, who *cares*, girl." Veronica's mother waved away Clarisse's wild histrionics with an arrogant flick of her right hand. "You have always been such a dizzy child!"

"My baby's name is Derrick—after his father. His name is Derrick Thomas, Jr.," Veronica stated definitively.

"But *everyone's* naming their children Afrocentric names, Vee," Clarisse stated with some kind of mysterious authority.

"I'll be damned if *I'll* tolerate a grandson with a name like Abbubu Malick or any of that nonsense." Veronica's mother took off her coat and placed it on the back of her chair. "Even though I don't like the baby's father, at least this child will have a West Indian–sounding name like the rest of the family!"

"What's a West Indian–sounding name, ma'am?" Clarisse asked, mystified by her best friend's mother's open hostility toward such a precious little baby.

Annoyed, the grandmother cut her eyes at Clarisse and sat down with a sigh into her chair.

"I think little Derrick is a fine-looking baby, Veronica, honey," her father reassured her with a tender smile, as he looked at the sleeping baby and wrestled his strong index finger from the baby's already tight little grip. The grandfather was amused by the irony of the baby inheriting both his and the baby's father's rich ebony complexion, distinctly African features. He was equally pleased the baby had none of his color-struck, white-looking blue-eyed wife's or his high-yella daughter's Eurocentric physical characteristics. To his wife's horror, it seemed, their daughter shared her taste in very black-looking men.

He could never understand how women like his wife would go after dark-skinned men then get upset if they had a baby that turned out the same. He was sure this was the reason that Veronica was their *only* child, although he never bothered to discuss it with his wife. He couldn't have possibly expected a rational response from her on the subject anyway.

"I think Derrick Junior is beautiful, too, Daddy." Veronica was deeply distressed at her mother's reaction to her innocent newborn baby. She knew her mother hated Derrick because of his dark complexion. Veronica felt that Derrick was a brother with sterling qualities in almost every way—a graduate of Harvard Business School, a successful banker, and from a good professional, middle-class upbringing. Yet, not only did her mother disapprove of his color, she also couldn't abide her daughter going out with a child of "one of those Southern Negroes." He could have been almost *anything* else—Haitian, Jamaican, a Bajan even—but not one of those "tired American Negroes who are forever complaining about how the white man keeps stepping on their backs." It didn't make a damned bit of difference to her mother that Derrick's father was a successful attorney and his mother was the principal of an elementary school in Westchester. To her, they were just dark-skinned Southern Negroes from Georgia.

"Migrants," she always called them, forgetting that her own and her husband's family had come up from Trinidad to work in white people's homes in order to get a fresh start in America. She conveniently forgot that Derrick's family had been hacking forward in this country for hundreds of years.

At times Veronica would confront her mother on her hypocritical preoccupation with color especially why she had chosen a black-black man. Muh Dear would place her hand on her skinny, white-girl hips and say, "In my time things were different. And I have to tell you, daughter, the dark ones treat you better than the light ones, because when you're a light-skinned woman, they think they've got a prize. But you, child, are not light enough—as pretty as you are—to risk being with someone who looks like your father."

Yes, Muh Dear was one twisted sister.

"So, now where *is* that tired daddy of his anyway, Veronica?"

Veronica sighed and resigned herself to the fact that this was hardly going to qualify as one of the most glorious days in her life. "You *know* he took that position in Switzerland. I told you a million times already, Mother."

"And he can't even appear for the birth of his first child? It *is* his first child, isn't it?" her mother asked snidely.

"Don't do this—"

"Have you even *heard* from the boy, daughter?"

Clarisse decided to jump in and help her girlfriend in her own peculiar Clarisse way. "He's been writing Vee ever since he left. She just won't answer him back, won't take his calls, either. It's just a mess . . . such a mess." Clarisse nearly swooned in exasperation. "I just don't understand you, Vee!"

"I had *asked* him not to take that job. How can I just *leave* my career, which I have worked so hard to build?"

"Girlfriend." Clarisse looked at her in disbelief, as she had for months now regarding this subject. "What kind of job is that anyway for a mother? Those long hours working around all those silly folks who come on a talk show. Folks who run around the country scouting for vulnerable hayseeds who spill out their tired guts on the most unbelievably intimate matters." Clarisse shook her head emphatically. "Your baby, Derrick, needs his mother and father. If I were you, I would *leave* that darn *Aletha Brown Show* and go with my *man* to Switzerland!"

"Well, Clarisse, you're not me. Why don't you all just leave me alone!" she replied angrily, turning away from them and plumping up her pillow to take a nap.

"You can't dismiss your own mother, child," Muh Dear huffed. "I have only wanted what was best for you . . . and now you do *this* to me and your father!"

"Look, let my daughter get some rest," Veronica's father said sympathetically, leaning over to kiss his daughter on the cheek.

"Bruddah . . . hey, bruddah . . . you go Bwookleen? I go Bwookleen!"

"I'm not going to Brooklyn, man! And I am *not* your brother!" Derrick Thomas snapped at the man in the turban.

Where were all the damned New York Yellow Cabs, he wondered, maneuvering himself through the mobs in front of the Swissair terminal at JFK. He had never seen so many dreadlocks and turbans in his natural-born life. And he'd been all *over* the world.

"Hey, mon . . . where you gwine? Man-hat-tan? For you, only hundred fitty dollah!" another wanna-be cabby called out.

"What?" he gasped incredulously, his eyes bulging out of their sockets at the outrageous price of the fare. He waved the thief away.

He had only been away from the States for a few months, but by the looks of things at the airport it had seemed that the whole of the Third World had moved in to replace him since he'd been gone.

"Where you go, meestah?" asked the guy looking up at him from the driver's seat of—finally—a Yellow Cab.

"Manhattan. Fifty-seventh and Madison Avenue," he answered briskly, jumping into the vehicle and slamming the door.

"No bag, meestah?"

"No. Just this shoulder bag."

"I put in trunk!"

"No! That's okay, I'll keep it right here next to me. Now let's *go!*"

"Okeydokey." The man winked at him through the rearview mirror as he took off, turning up the stereo to a supersonic decibel. Some strong nerve-jangling music in some even weirder foreign-sounding language—and Derrick thought he'd heard them all—pounded into the air around him.

"Please, could you turn that down a bit?"

"No problem." The man smiled solicitously and bowed to eagerly turn down the sound.

It had been a long flight and Derrick's nerves were frayed, having pondered for hours over what he was going to say to Veronica. He wasn't even sure why he had decided to come. After all, they hadn't ever talked about having a child together.

He leaned back in his seat.

Why some black women single-handedly decide to make such earthshaking decisions, involving so many people, he'd never understand.

He had always felt that families should be planned. Planned between the two involved parties—preferably a husband and wife.

Life was so challenging that he couldn't understand why *anyone* would choose to bring a child into the world in anything less than an intact family.

He needed to sit down and talk about . . .

"Meestah? Where you from? What country?" The cabby had turned down the music even lower, thank goodness, but had interrupted Derrick's train of thought.

"What?"

"Where you from? Africa? You very black, like African."

"I'm an *American*," Derrick said through gritted teeth.

The cabby burst into laughter. "Of course, you American. We *all* American now, right? But where you *from?*"

"I told you, I'm American. My people have been in this country for more than five generations."

"But where your people *from* . . . in Africa?"

Derrick shook his head in disbelief.

"I am a Black American. We don't know where all of our ancestors came from."

"Oh, no, no, no . . . *everybody know*! You just become too high-hat to *say*, right?" The cabby cackled at his intimate knowledge of the immigration situation and added, "Me, I from Singapore."

Derrick leaned over to look at this ostensibly Chinese man through the rearview mirror, and then glanced at his taxi ID and noted that the name said Raheem Abdullah Shabazz, and there was a photo of a Middle Eastern-looking man next to it.

Derrick shook his head quickly as if trying to wake up and toss out the confusion. He was *not* going to deal with this.

"Look, I just had a long flight. I'd like to take a little nap. You *do* know how to get to Fifty-seventh and Madison, don't you?"

"No problem."

No matter where he was in the world, hearing those words sent chills up his spine. "No problem" had usually been followed by the most outlandish consequences. But he was back in his own country now, so how bad could it get?

He leaned back again and closed his eyes.

Where was he?

Oh, yeah . . . Veronica.

Veronica and Derrick had had an on-again, off-again relationship for a couple of years. It wasn't as if they didn't care for one other, it was just that they had been both so involved in their careers. Derrick had been scheming and planning to land the overseas position for quite a while. A stint in Europe was what he always thought he needed. The slower pace and more cultivated European lifestyle suited him. He also wanted, and needed, a hiatus from the sordid rat race of American corporate life, not to mention escaping the mounting racial tensions that were being stoked these days in the States. Sure, Europe wasn't without its problems, but most of it seemed to be more about immigration than someone's skin color. It would also be a nice breather to live for a while in a country that had a history of neutrality.

Also, he had to admit to himself that he enjoyed what he considered the relaxed and appreciative nature of the Swiss women.

Veronica had known from the start how he felt about all of this—except about the Swiss women, of course.

He enjoyed Veronica's company; she was pretty, smart, and ambitious. He admired ambition in a woman, but he wasn't sure he could learn to take that albatross mother of hers. So, for the foreseeable future, marriage was not even an option to consider. It wasn't that he placed so much importance on a woman's family, but Veronica seemed to be so infuriatingly close to the woman who obviously despised him for reasons too stupid to contemplate.

Derrick just couldn't figure why Veronica had decided at that particular time to get pregnant. Though he didn't like to think about it, he couldn't even be absolutely sure that it was *his* child, since they had been so on-again, off-again. Actually, that's exactly the reason he had decided to make the trip—in order to get a look at the boy.

But what should he do?

"Meestah . . . where Madison? Here One Fifty-seventh Street. You sure *you* live here?"

Derrick's eyes snapped open to see a population of Dominicans mulling around in the streets . . . Latina bodegas *everywhere*!

"Where the hell *are* we?"

"Where Madison?" The cabby was negotiating slowly down a crowded avenue . . . far uptown in Manhattan.

"Don't you understand English, man? I said *Fifty*-seventh Street, you . . . you . . ."

"I sorry. I sorry. I go back. Downtown. No problem!"

"We have a *major* problem here. Turn off that meter! I'm not paying for this."

"No problem, no problem. I go downtown." He turned off the meter and turned the wrong way onto a one-way street, heading directly into oncoming traffic.

"Look, Mr. Shabazz, or whatever your name is, do you think you could get me downtown? Now? *Alive!* I'm not about to get out and try to catch a cab way up here."

The driver maneuvered himself backward out of the traffic and eventually found the road southward.

"Jesus Christ," Derrick muttered, realizing that he was having a hard time being understood in his own country. As a matter of fact, he didn't feel as if he was even *in* his own country. Switzerland made more sense.

They sped down Fifth Avenue after a time, but the traffic got clogged in the Sixties, so he decided to get out and walk. He could use the air and the exercise. Before it got too late in the evening, he wanted to pick up a gift for the baby—he hadn't a clue exactly what it would be—as quickly as possible and get on over to Veronica's place.

"No charge!" the cabby said as Derrick left the car.

"You'd better believe it!" Derrick said, slamming the door.

"Meestah?"

"Yes." Derrick looked back over his shoulder, wondering what this man could possibly want to tell him.

"No be shame of Africa. Good country. Good people! Fine people! Good music. Cloth-es have lots of color. Not like here!"

"Whatever," Derrick muttered as he crossed to the other side of the avenue.

F.A.O. Schwarz was probably the perfect place to find a gift for a baby who, he presumed, already had everything. He mounted the escalator in the incredibly decadent toy store for children, trying to tune out the relentlessly upbeat jingle.

His eyes suddenly shifted to the other side of the room where a familiar figure was lifting and moving huge stuffed fabric beasts into different positions around the room. She stepped back every now and then to assess their looks from their various new angles.

Aletha Brown!

Did she really think that that silly disguise she was wearing would fool anybody? Did she think that a pair of large sunglasses, an oversize raincoat, and a gaudy scarf tied around her head could conceal the identity of one of the most recognizable black women in America?

Derrick turtled his head between his shoulders to avoid being spotted.

That woman was bizarre. News traveled fast in this age of the global media. Derrick had heard and read, all the way in Zurich, that she had broken into her lover's apartment and shot him. He couldn't understand how Veronica could work all these years for this wild and dictatorial woman.

The perks must have been irresistible.

He wondered if she was there to buy a present for his newborn son, as well. Derrick laughed to himself. He wouldn't be surprised if Aletha Brown had made an offer to purchase Veronica's child.

Derrick had met Aletha's lover, Reginald Pinkney, a couple of times in the past and thought he seemed like a nice guy. He tried to imagine what Reggie had done to make her shoot him. As far as Derrick knew, it could have been for something as innocent as being late for a date.

Derrick noticed that Aletha had started looking around the room. He definitely didn't want her to see him and try to engage him in polite conversation. Who knew where it would lead? He backed into a corner and watched her movements. As soon as she turned her back away from him to walk away, he fled to the escalator and escaped in another department.

CHAPTER SIX

*V*eronica ran her fingers through her auburn curls and pulled at them in exasperation. She looked around her otherwise impeccable, antique-filled living room and sighed. This should have been a festive occasion. Her six closest girlfriends in the world had gathered in her home to celebrate little Derrick's arrival. Instead, she surveyed the disorder and gummy filth that had accumulated around her in the less than two hours her friends had been there with their boisterous little monster children and sighed. She figured that as a recent initiate into the club she'd better learn how to deal with this hyperactive madness.

The noise of the shrieking children was deafening. She looked at the half-filled Baccarat fluted champagne glass in front of her, half expecting it to shatter.

Things like *this* would have to go, put away to enjoy at some future date. Probably when little Derrick went off to college.

Her tastefully elegant lifestyle had changed. Maybe she would look for some well-trained nanny to help her out. She didn't have a clue about raising a baby—especially alone—with the kind of demanding career she had. And she'd rather slit her wrists than expose the baby to the kind of poison her mother would inadvertently feed him with her sinister and old-timey prejudices.

She looked over to the other side of the room where the children had gathered and noticed that three of her friends' little girls, of about four or five years old, had encircled the only little boy, of about the same age.

"Let us *see* it! Let us *see* it!" They whispered, screaming, pushing and shoving the boy, who began to cry out for his mother.

The little girls pulled down his pants and squealed with amusement, sounding far more mature than their years.

"Ma-a-a-a!" he yelled.

Veronica got up at the same time that her friend Dee Dee rushed in from the kitchen, carrying a tray of crab cakes. Dee Dee placed the tray on the coffee table next to a large Steuben crystal bowl filled with strawberries and then ran over to grab her little boy. As she yanked up his pants, she shook him and said, "Boy, didn't I tell you to stop showing your thing to little girls?"

She picked him up, returned to the girlfriends, and added, "I've got a baby flasher on my hands. Oversexed, I guess. Just like his daddy—as far as I can remember!"

Everyone laughed except Veronica. In fact, she was speechless. She turned to the little girls, who were sharing some secret, vindictive joke, and said, "Why don't you all go and color in the coloring books we put out for you?"

"No way, José," they all yelled in unison and added a refrain of startlingly familiar baby shrills of laughter.

The little girls quickly dispersed throughout the apartment in search of other attention-getting missions.

"You're so lucky, Veronica," one of her girlfriends said, hugging little Derrick to her chest. "I hope I have a boy the next time. If I ever *get* a chance at a next time."

The women all laughed empathetically, knowing exactly what she meant.

Veronica gently removed her baby from her friend's covetous embrace and returned him to his nursery down the hall.

Clarisse stood in a corner sipping her wine and, it seemed, hyperventilating. Her freckled cheeks were puffed up like apples.

"Clarisse, girl, what's the *matter* with you? You need a doctor or something?" asked Dee Dee, the flasher baby's mother, as she put her child down in front of her, flipped her blond weave over her well-developed shoulders, then reached over to refill an empty champagne glass. She then placed a crab cake on each of six plates and handed them around the table to the women.

"All I know is," Clarisse said, crinkling her nose and fanning away Dee Dee's proffered plate as she pulled back the heavy drapes with her other hand, glancing nervously out of one of the living room windows, "if I had a *fine* brother like Derrick, I'd be in Switzerland and not sitting here with you all, getting plastered on some overpriced bubbly and nibbling on these little bitty strawberries. I'd be in my Swiss chalet, in bed with my man with that gorgeous baby snuggling between us."

"Oh, shut up Clarisse," snapped Dee Dee. "What would you know? You probably haven't been laid in over a decade!"

The women shrieked with laughter, one giving another a high five.

"Yeah, well, when I find the *one*, I'll bet you all that I won't be sitting—"

The shrill sound of the doorman's intercom jolted everyone into temporary silence.

"Are you expecting someone else today, Veronica?" the exotic Polynesian-looking girlfriend purred, uncrossing her long legs.

Clarisse nervously dropped her glass on the Persian rug, and everyone turned to look at her.

"Umm-hmm, what are you *brewing*, Clarisse?" Dee Dee asked suspiciously, glancing around at the others. Clarisse had confided to her that she had called Derrick the day the baby was born.

"Me? Why are you all looking at *me*? Answer the damned doorman, Vee!" She picked up her glass from the floor and ran over to the coffee table around which they had all been sitting, and poured herself more wine.

Veronica picked up the phone. *"Who?"* She turned to her friends, then shot Clarisse a mean stare. "It's Derrick! What on *earth* is he doing in New York?"

A long silence, then everyone focused their stare on Clarisse.

"Go on, have him come up, Veronica," Dee Dee said, a smile of grim satisfaction parting her lips. "We've got your back."

"Send Mr. Thomas up, Juan," Veronica instructed the doorman.

Veronica assessed herself in one of her gilded wall mirrors. Why should she care how she looked, she thought, fluffing up her hair.

She'd never forgotten the day she told Derrick that she was pregnant. He had turned ash-white, as impossible as that may have seemed, and asked Veronica what *she* had planned to do about it. She had assumed that her pregnancy and pending birth, though a shock, would force Derrick to give up the ridiculous idea of working for that Swiss bank. Why on earth would she, or he for that matter, want to raise their black child in the icy whiteness of a European country? There was so much for successful, black American couples like themselves to accomplish right here in their own country.

He had told her that he wasn't ready to start a family.

He didn't even seem ready to get *married*! She'd been hinting for the longest time. She figured that a baby would clinch the deal.

"What do you plan to *do* about it?" he had asked instead.

The muthafucker!

When she said that she planned to have the baby, Derrick's frustration got the best of him, and he asked why she hadn't been using birth control. He repeated that he had told her time and time again that he wouldn't be ready to start a family for at least another two or three years.

Veronica asked him if he thought that she had all the time in the world to wait for *him* to be ready? They had been going together for two years!

He had said that since *she* had made the decision to get pregnant, only *she* could make a decision regarding the child's future.

Arrogant bastard.

Derrick walked out on her and accepted that job in Switzerland.

Muh Dear had claimed that dark-skinned men would treat you as if you were a prize, yet this one had walked out on Veronica and fled all the way to Switzerland in order to get away from her and his responsibilities!

Oh, sure, he had written and left messages on her answering machine, his guilt causing him to offer her financial support and to want occasional access to the child. Why on earth would she need financial support when she had a six-figure salary that more than equaled his own? Aletha Brown *paid* her staff. She was a real "down" sister. With sisters like that in the world, and in your corner, who needed some blue-black scared-of-responsibility Negro in their life?

When the doorbell rang, Veronica glanced back at her girlfriends, who were now situated strategically around the room, leaning against the walls with their arms crossed in front of their chests like poised-to-pounce Black Panthers. All of the children had quietly disappeared into another part of the apartment. Veronica hoped to God that they had decided to go to sleep, or to do something equally as benign.

She opened the door.

The images of Michael Jordan, Denzel Washington, Sidney Poitier, Wesley Snipes, and Hannibal all blended before her into the six-foot-three-inch-tall, powerfully built, successful, and sensual figure of Derrick Thomas, Sr. She looked into his warm and brilliant eyes, which possessed the glistening color of the ripest black olives, and found herself propelled into his sinewy embrace. She kissed him. It was as if she had been loving him for an eternity of lifetimes. She was lost, she had completely lost herself in his regally beguiling and enigmatically masculine universe.

"So, Derrick, my expatriate brother. What brings you back to the land of Uncle Sam?" Dee Dee asked curtly, flipping her hair out of her eyes.

Dee Dee's greeting pulled Veronica back to those more urgent and practical matters.

Veronica wistfully removed the sumptuous cashmere overcoat from his shoulders—wistfully because the fragrance of his Lagerfeld cologne had produced a sharp stab of memory reminding Veronica of how much she had longed to feel his embraces again.

It had been too long.

Derrick strode into the living room and greeted the hostile visages of Veronica's girlfriends with a warmth that could have melted a village of igloos. Nothing less could have saved his skin in *that* room.

"Hello, ladies!"

Derrick did not like most of Veronica's so-called girlfriends. At least one ... no, two ... *damn* ... no, *three* of these women, in this very living room, had made a pass at him at one time or another over the past two years. The one with the big yapping mouth and the peculiar blond hair had even had the audacity to call *his* house once.

The woman *had* to have known that Veronica was away at that broadcasters convention, but she had called him under the pretense of looking for her. He didn't even know who she *was* at first, having met her only a couple of times. Then when she identified herself, cooing indecently into the receiver, he remembered who she was.

"Oh ... *Derrick* ... I'm Veronica's *friend*, Dee Dee," she had said seductively.

He had cut her off abruptly. "If you are truly Veronica's friend, why are you calling *my* house?" he had asked bluntly. "I'm sure you know that she's out of town!"

The woman then hung up the phone abruptly, but not before she hissed defensively, "Jive-ass turkey," into the receiver.

Derrick thought that strategic maneuvers like that put men in a precarious position. If he had informed Veronica of her girlfriend's behavior—a woman she had known longer than she'd known *him*—she would probably have accused Derrick of having given off signals encouraging Dee Dee. And, of course, if Veronica had confronted her about this, Dee Dee would certainly have denied any dubious intentions and would have taken something he'd done out of context to make him look guilty, thus intentionally driving a wedge between him and Veronica.

So, he never said a thing about it to anyone. Besides, it was nothing new. That kind of thing had happened with most of the women he had dated in his life.

He figured that maybe *one day*—although, he wasn't about to hold his breath on it—women would learn that the only thing scheming, undercover bitches would ever hope to sink their claws into was a pack of scheming, underhanded *bastards*. Who else could possibly feel secure with those kinds of women? Men have too many pressures to waste time dealing with the webs of confusion that women like Dee Dee liked to weave. Derrick leveled his most condescending stare at each one of Veronica McPheerson's misguided "sister friends."

The only one of her manless friends that he cared for at all was her childhood friend Clarisse. Everyone said she was a little dizzy, but she was a straight shooter and, as far as he could tell, seemed to be genuinely in Veronica's corner.

Suddenly, Veronica remembered that Derrick had brought something to the apartment with him. She ran back into the foyer and found a gigantic, eight-foot-tall, F.A.O. Schwarz blue baby elephant.

Must have cost a fortune, she thought, hugging it before she dragged it into the living room.

Clarisse ran over to Derrick and embraced him like a long-lost brother. "Wait till you see your son. He's so-o-o-o gorgeous. He looks just like *you*, Derrick!"

"So, you think a big, expensive elephant is supposed to compensate for your absence all these months, brother?" one of the girlfriends snarled. Derrick swore he saw flames and smoke coming at him from her mean, thin, scarlet, dragon-lady lips.

"Come, let's see the baby," Clarisse said, dragging Derrick and Veronica by the hands and into the opulently cluttered nursery.

"Damn, girl, what is the baby going to do with all of this stuff? Open his own toy store?" Derrick frowned, stumbling over some stuffed animals. Then, looking into the crib, he picked up the baby and a cloud-clearing smile spread across his majestically chiseled face. Yes . . . this was *definitely* his son. No doubt about it.

"Hey, Junior. I'm your *daddy*."

Clarisse left the family in privacy, tiptoeing out of the room like an animated sleuth.

Veronica's eyes hardened as she remembered the aching loneliness she had felt when she was carrying the baby that he was now so proudly handling as if it were one of his fancy tennis trophies.

"So, why are you here, Derrick? Are you coming back to us, or is this some kind of ego trip of yours?"

"Why don't you want to communicate with me? You know, we never talked about having a baby. But you come up with this zinger just when I'm getting my career in order, and figure . . . actually, I don't know *what* you figured."

"I figured you'd marry me and help me raise our child."

"Tell me something. Did you ever give me a chance to ask you to marry me?"

"Two years was long enough."

"*Had* I asked you to marry me?"

"No."

"Then you planned this baby as a trap, right, Veronica?"

Unlike a lot of men placed in a similar situation, at least he was willing to acknowledge the child as his own and arrange to help support his son, Derrick reflected. He had thought that she had to know how much he had wanted that assignment in Zurich and that he had to do some fancy footwork around the white boys in order to get it. But she had acted as if he were some kind of race traitor, saying that black couples like themselves had so much to accomplish right here in their own country. Yet *she* worked for a television show that, despite the presence of a black host, seemed to portray black folks—*all* folks actually—in an unsavory light.

"Look, I think we should talk," he said, sweeping some toys from a chair and sitting.

She stood stubbornly in front of him with her hands on her hips, her middle-class veneer dissolving, unconsciously snapping her head from right to left in that familiar way some black women have when they're about to get all worked up about something, like a metronome swinging between pissed off and fed up. Derrick hated when she did that.

"Don't try that Sapphire—or should I say—Jezebel number on me, standing there looking like Miss Anne with your white-looking self. Sit your behind down, woman!"

Veronica sat, but not without rolling her eyes at him in retaliation.

"First, let me tell you that I came back here to see if this baby was mine . . . if he looked at all like me—"

Outraged she shouted, "Of course, he's *yours*! But how in the hell can you tell if a newborn baby looks like—"

"As I said," Derrick calmly interrupted, 'I came to *see*, and I accept that he's my son."

"*Accept?* What do you *mean* 'accept,' nigger?"

"Nigger? You know, Veronica, I haven't heard that word since I've been in Switzerland."

"That's because they don't know what you really *are* yet," she said viciously.

Shocked at the venom oozing from between her thin, rigid lips, Derrick picked up a rattle and shook it. He smiled at its sound. "What have I *done* to make you hate me so, Veronica? I told you that I had plans. That I wanted to get my career on track. Personally, I don't understand why you feel that you have the time yourself, at the moment, to raise a child. *I* certainly don't!"

"A woman doesn't have all the time in the world. You know how old I am. Plus, you and I have been together for—"

"Sporadically for *two years*. We hadn't even had a chance to work out our differences."

Veronica thew her hands up in exasperation. "Well, you moved out after only six months."

"First of all, you kept pushing me to move in with you and I *did*."

"And you kept your damned apartment the whole time." She pointed accusingly at him.

"Of course, I kept it. We hardly knew each other. Then for six months we were both flying here and there, working late and leaving notes on the door. Nobody was ever home."

"To make you dinner, huh?"

"Veronica, you know I don't care about any damned dinner! Don't play these games. It doesn't become you."

"I don't want to talk to you, Derrick." Veronica got up from her chair and walked toward the door. "Besides, my friends are in the living room waiting for me."

"No . . . no, they're not. They're in there drinking up all your booze, most of them having the time of their lives bad-mouthing me. So let's get back to what we're going to do about the baby."

"*Do* about the baby? I *had* him, I'll take care of him. I'm not some charity case!" Veronica folded her arms and leaned against the door.

"I may not have planned him, but he is mine, too."

"And what's wrong with your parents, Derrick? They just finally got around to seeing the baby, after I left the hospital. Treated the event like an afterthought!"

"Are you *really* surprised that they didn't come to the hospital, with *your* folks there and all? They know how your parents feel about us . . . *them*. I'm surprised that your folks hadn't suggested that you give this 'inappropriate-looking' baby up for adoption or something." He looked directly into her angry, hazel-colored eyes.

She looked quickly away, remembering that her mother had demanded she get an abortion rather than risk having a dark-skinned bastard child. Muh Dear couldn't help it, she was an Island Creole and was brought up to think that way. Veronica knew that her mother only wanted what she thought was the best for her family, as misguided as she often seemed about the subject of colored people's color.

She nibbled nervously on the nail of her left index finger and said sadly, "Instead of moving out, Derrick, we should have tried harder to make things work between us."

"I realized that I just wasn't ready and I told you that. But you ended up getting pregnant in order to force the issue. You decided to bring an innocent newborn baby into the world in an attempt to manipulate me into a lifetime of something I was and am not ready for. Such selfish, manipulative behavior convinces me, unequivocally—"

"Unequivocally," she mocked, pulling a condescending face in an attempt to mimic his arrogance.

"That's right . . . that you are *definitely* not the woman for me," he said, standing up and glancing over at the baby who had just begun wailing in his crib.

"You're fucked up, Derrick!" Veronica and Derrick both walked over to the crib and stood on opposite sides staring at one another.

"*Me?* Was it me who decided to change the destiny of the world through irresponsible sex?"

"What? It takes *two*, you know!"

"Why didn't you tell me what you were planning to do, Veronica? Or do you take your lessons from that certifiable boss of yours, Aletha Brown? I read in the papers that—"

"What in the hell do you know about it? What makes you think that what you read in some foreign paper is accurate . . . especially about the sisters?"

Despite both their efforts to soothe him, the baby was still crying.

"Clarisse, please come in here and get this baby!" Veronica yelled toward the living room.

Instead, it was Dee Dee who ran into the room to fetch the wailing infant.

Derrick took one look at the insolent, sneaky Dee Dee and picked up his child himself.

Dee Dee sneered at Derrick, sucked her teeth with annoyance, and asked, "Are you okay, Veronica, honey?"

The baby had stopped crying. Derrick hugged him for a moment longer then placed him back in the crib.

"I'm okay. I'll be out there in a minute," she answered, waving her away.

When the woman left and closed the door—almost—behind her, Derrick turned to Veronica and said, "I've decided, I'll contribute a monthly stipend for the child in the amount of—"

"*You* decided? Who the *hell* do you think—"

"I see that we're not going to work anything out here face to face," he interrupted, "now or probably ever. In a civilized manner anyway. So I'll take it all up with my attorney. If you have any problems with my arrangements, talk to my lawyer. You leave me no other choice but to handle it this way."

He thinks he's *so* smooth, with his leather and cashmere, and million-dollar haircut, and Yuppie-tailored beard, she thought.

Fuck him!

"I don't need you, Derrick. I am perfectly able to raise this child myself. Go away. Leave us alone. You've seen the child now, so just get out of our lives!"

"Are you saying that you don't want me in any way involved in the life of my son?"

"Get out, Derrick!" she wailed, going over and slapping him.

"What was that all about, Veronica?" Derrick thought that he'd suddenly stepped into some melodramatic soap opera.

The buzzer from the doorman sounded again.

"Dammit. Clarisse, somebody please answer that for me," Veronica yelled toward the living room, trying not to lose any more control than she already had.

"Will you be okay, Veronica?" Derrick held her face tenderly between his hands.

She desperately wanted to kiss him. To make love to him, desperately. But she knew he just didn't love her enough. She was not his "prize."

"Aletha Brown is here, Vee," Clarisse yelled from the living room.

"Go . . . go back to Switzerland, Derrick. I don't need you. I have my friends; I have my job."

Derrick sat slump shouldered in his seat, suddenly looking very tired and feeling even older. He pushed himself out of the chair, like a beaten fighter about to throw in the towel.

But as he trooped through the living room and searched for his coat, he looked at Veronica's evil-looking, high-yella girlfriends and felt a surge of indignation. This was *it*. No more black women for him. As fine as they were, they all thought they should run a brother's life. He had never promised any of them anything he hadn't delivered. They didn't even want to accept the things he *could* offer.

He had flown all the way from Switzerland to see a baby he had never even thought about having and gotten slapped in the face. The woman didn't even want him to support his own son.

Those arrogant wenches could take a walk as far as he was concerned. Who did they think they were anyway? He had always known that her mother hated his black skin. She'd hate him even if he had the money of Donald damned Trump.

Fuck it!

Derrick Thomas was going back to Switzerland, to his plum job, and as for women, he would look for the *real* thing: blond, accommodating, blue-eyed, and white, white, white, white, white!

Oh, shit! He had heard that Aletha Brown was there. He had managed to escape her a few hours ago, and he had no intention of meeting up with her at that moment—especially with all those other witches in Veronica's place.

He walked out the door and slammed it behind him, leaving all those evil glares behind him forever!

Just as he reached the elevator, the door opened, and the first thing he saw was a giant, eight-foot, F.A.O. Schwarz blue baby elephant tumbling from the elevator door.

That little, fig-colored big shot, Aletha Brown, was pushing it ahead of her. Veronica was right. She didn't need him. Her own employer could bring, for a simple baby present, the same two-thousand-dollar toy that he had brought for his own son.

"Derrick, is that *you*?" puffed Aletha. "Help me with this, will you?"

"No," he said simply and got on the elevator.

Everyone fell out in riotous laughter of approval over Aletha's present.

Except Veronica. She sat thinking about how things just weren't working out the way she had planned. She was a successful, attractive woman. She might have been a busy woman, but she knew how to create a beautiful home, nevertheless. She knew that she was a competent lover because they had always come back for more, that was, until she demanded something more substantial and permanent. Over the last decade there had been four men—all of whom had fled like geese in the winter as soon as she broached the subject of marriage.

What *was* it that men wanted, she wondered, looking over at Aletha.

Veronica smiled to herself, thinking that she understood why Aletha had felt compelled to shoot Reginald Pinkney after he betrayed her. Anyway, the tabloids claimed that she had, although Aletha had firmly denied it. Nevertheless, Derrick had been lucky that she didn't keep a gun in *her* apartment!

Aletha reached into her enormous New York City Handbag of Essentials . . . and pulled out a stack of eight-by-ten glossy autographed publicity photos of herself. Presumptuously shoving one in each of the women's hands, she said, "Hello, ladies. Now, *where's* the baby? I want to lay my hands on that sweet thing."

Aletha adjusted her rings and bracelets, noting that all of Veronica McPheerson's friends were white-looking black women—the kind she had always been envious of. That is, until she had made her first million.

Aletha's eyes devoured Veronica's tastefully appointed apartment.

Aletha Brown decided on the spot that she no longer liked her producer one bit. Sure, she had been a good and imaginative employee, but *look* at the setup! A fabulous apartment on Central Park West, all those incredible antiques, those fancy high-yella friends. And where'd she get the money for all of this? And how did she show her appreciation to her oh-so-generous boss? By getting herself knocked up. Veronica did not deserve that unbelievably delectable-looking, blue-black, sexy hunk who would, no doubt, never give a dark-skinned woman like Aletha the time of day, and now, a baby boy named after that terrific-looking man. A heifer like Veronica deserved a bum, pimp, gigolo, like that Reggie she had wasted too many years of her life on. She'd almost destroyed her life over that sorry Negro.

Aletha threw a covetous glance around the nursery . . . the paintings, that expensive wallpaper, the unbelievable crib, and that *baby*!

What a sweet little baby, she thought. Kidnapping crossed Aletha's mind as she picked up and caressed little Derrick, noticing how easily he could pass for her very own son. They *were* the same complexion. The baby didn't need to be with all those banana-colored blacks; he would be much happier growing up with a mother who looked a lot more like him.

Aletha didn't even try to hide her envy as she looked over at her producer. Veronica tried to take her baby from Aletha, but Aletha quickly walked to the other side of the nursery, kissing and snuggling the little boy in her arms.

"I have the name of a good nanny," lied Aletha. She'd find one if she *had* to.

Aletha's indomitable will pushed back the jealous tears that had begun welling up in her eyes. She'd never want her employee to suspect that Aletha Brown had any unfulfilled desires.

She so desperately wanted some babies of her own. Her biological clock had begun ticking as loudly and tenaciously as Big Ben. Maybe *she* should have just gotten pregnant, herself. Maybe then, Reggie would still be with her. But what if Reggie had left her anyway? God, she knew that she couldn't walk around single *and* pregnant on her prime-time talk show. With all those right-wing sponsors of hers crowing about family values, they'd cancel her black ass in a New York minute!

"Aletha, I'd like to find a nanny on my own. That's why I'd like to ask you for a few more weeks off, although, I had thought I'd come back to work sooner. This is all so new to me, as you can imagine, Aletha. I want to spend time with my baby and find a suitable person to take care of him while I am at work. Plus, it *is* the Christmas season, and I have so many personal things—"

"What about one of these *friends* of yours? Aren't they qualified?" Aletha said.

"They all have their own careers, Aletha."

I bet they *do*, thought Aletha, holding the baby closer to her. The bitches probably had great careers and fabulous nooky, too.

"I can't give you extra time, Miss Veronica. We have that special show to put together, and . . . I . . . *need you!*"

"Not even a couple of *weeks*?" At first, Veronica was panicked, then she relaxed. What on earth could Aletha *do*? She was her executive producer—*had* been for *years*, too. Aletha couldn't fire her. Besides, maternity leave entitled her to a few more months.

"No. I can't afford not to have you around the studio for even another day. You are my most valuable employee."

Aletha decided, on the spot, that she would have to fire Miss Perfect. What would her producer do, *sue* her? The last thing in the world Aletha needed was a reminder of what she couldn't have with Reggie. She imagined Veronica wandering around the offices, an I-gotta-man-and-a-baby smile plastered across her face. Worse yet, the incessant stream of baby pictures, her office converted into a gallery of bliss. No, Aletha definitely did not need any of that.

That "banana" Veronica McPheerson would definitely have to go—no matter if she got bruised. Aletha quickly squelched whatever guilt she felt for thinking of firing her by reminding herself that Veronica's too-too-too fine man would provide her in ways financial and physical. He was a man who could produce and reproduce. None of that struggling writer bullshit like she'd put up with with Reggie.

Aletha walked over to Veronica and handed the baby back to Veronica. She quickly clutched the child to her chest.

Aletha considered for a moment how the media might react to her firing a new mother. She knew that it wouldn't look good, and at certain times it didn't feel good to think that she was capable of such cruelty. But when she looked around that apartment, saw that gorgeous baby in that hussy's arms, her heart hardened into a tight fist of remorseless envy.

Aletha smiled.

Veronica retreated to a safe position behind the crib. She held Derrick ham-mocked in her arms, just about to set him back down but reconsidered. She stood in that awkward position, feeling the strain in her arms and back. Turning her head toward Aletha, she saw that smile again. But this smile was different.

Aletha dimmed her smile a few watts, just to keep Veronica guessing. She loved to give people little tests. Nothing they could study for ahead of time, no grading on a curve. Pass/fail. Sink or swim. Aletha was feeling a bit parched, and she didn't feel like going home alone to her apartment. If Veronica offered her a drink, she could keep her job. If not, she was gone.

Aletha sighed and said, "Well, Miss Veronica, I have to go. Congratula-tions on your new little arrival."

She stared at Veronica. Waiting.

Veronica noticed something . . . something weird going on in Aletha's eyes. "Wh-why, of course, A-Aletha. Thank you for coming by."

Aletha's eyes daggered into hers. "Aren't you going to offer me a drink or something? Some of those delightful little snacks your *friends* are munching on?" She pointed with her well-manicured index finger toward the living room, then curled it back toward her palm as though summoning the hounds of hell.

"Of course, Aletha. Where are my manners?" Veronica paused for a moment, every instinct in her telling her to keep silent, but the words came out anyway. "What can I get for you?"

Aletha was miffed that she had to ask. Well, bye-bye, girlfriend, Aletha thought to herself smugly. "Nada." Aletha engaged her best perky smile. "Must go. But thanks for the offer. Busy, busy, busy, you know. Aletha draped her coat over her shoulders and swept dramatically from the room.

Only when Veronica heard her front door slam was she able to rouse herself from her stupor. She checked the baby's hands and feet, wanting to be sure that nothing was missing. She felt as though she'd lost something in the last few moments, but she couldn't be certain what it was.

CHAPTER SEVEN

A week later, while decorating her Christmas tree, Veronica collapsed onto her baby-soiled sofa in a pool of overwhelming sadness.

The baby was screaming for one of his endless feedings.

She had lost her job working for that vindictive, crazy Aletha Brown. The weird, unstable chick had made it look as though Veronica had pocketed money from the show. She had implied that Veronica had two choices: She could take a generous severance pay, minus the missing sum, or Aletha would report her to the proper authorities.

Veronica had been too tired with the baby and her new life to do anything about Aletha's madness, and her friends were no help with advice, since more than one of them had asked her how they could apply for her old job.

She had figured that she'd never hear from her baby's father again, but as her friend Dee Dee had said months ago, she'd be better off without him and his arrogant ways anyway.

"Clarisse, you can't keep spending all your money on presents for this baby." Veronica sighed, taking the shopping bag, kissing her girlfriend on the cheek, and motioning for her to come into the apartment.

"Derrick Junior is my godson, and I bought him some books. He must be properly educated."

Veronica laughed at her dizzy girlfriend and said, "Honey, he's only two weeks old. He can't read yet!" She placed the festively colorful bag under the Christmas tree.

"How do you know? You were reading stories to him the whole time you were pregnant. I have read in journals that—"

"Clarisse, do you want something to eat?"

"Of course. I have also come over to make you Sunday brunch. Let me go into the kitchen and I'll whip something up in a jiffy. Besides, I can see from your sorry-assed, disheveled looks that you haven't had any breakfast yet." Clarisse smiled broadly, melting the frost from her harsh words.

"Look, Clarisse—"

"Go fix yourself up. You look like an overworked, poor Irish maid," Clarisse said. She hastily brushed past Veronica and took off her heavy wool red cape coat, sweater, and red Persian lamb beret and tossed them onto a chair. Veronica's eyes followed Clarisse's jaunty, tight-butt, splay-foot ballerina walk—a permanent remnant, it seemed, of their childhood dance lessons—as Clarisse walked toward the kitchen. She was clad in her usual uniform of black stretch pants, black suede, low-heeled, thigh-high boots, and black wool turtle-neck sweater accessorized with a huge silver and turquoise squash-blossom necklace. Clarisse still wore her sandy-colored brown hair the same way she did way back in high school—parted in the middle with her thick, wavy tresses forming a triangle around her olive-complexioned heart-shaped face. She looked more like a Left Bank Parisian sculptress of the early seventies than the elementary school teacher that she had been for nearly a decade.

"Girl, I am *so-o-o* tired." Veronica sighed with fatigue. "The baby . . ."

"I don't want to hear it, Vee! If it was up to me, you would be in Switzerland with Derrick Senior." Clarisse scanned the refrigerator's shelves, trying to find eggs amid all the clutter. "I bet he'd even have hired you a maid and one of those au pair girls to help you out."

"First of all, Clarisse, Derrick never invited me to go to Switzerland with him—"

"Whatever—"

"Besides, what would I want with an au pair? I have never understood, myself, why women would hire young, nubile nymphets to live in their homes around their men anyway."

"Doesn't matter, Vee. You don't *have* a man anymore. You're just a poor old, unemployed, scraggly-looking colored woman with a fatherless child. Now go fix yourself up!" Clarisse yelled above rattling pans in the kitchen.

Smiling and grateful for her girlfriend's temporary rescue from the doldrums of domesticity, Veronica picked up Clarisse's coat, sweater, and hat from the armchair in the living room to hang them up in the bedroom out of sight. Disorder had always unnerved her, she thought to herself as she remembered that with a child she would have loads of adjustments to adapt to the high-strung and demanding life of single motherhood. She had watched her friends, Dee Dee and the others, and although it looked rather intimidating, she was sure she was cut out of equally sturdy cloth.

"Hey, Vee, I bet you when our folks laid out all that money for our cotillion—our coming-out party—they didn't figure that we'd end up middle-aged women with no men and one of us supporting a child in a state of unwed motherhood, huh?" Clarisse laughed, yelling from the kitchen.

"I suppose not," Veronica muttered to herself, silently cursing Derrick Senior for her predicament.

Veronica remembered the cotillion she and Clarisse had way back around their sixteenth birthdays. At the Waldorf-Astoria, no less. She recalled how it had been one of the most humiliating days of her life. Why some middle-class black families chose to have their daughters and sons participate in such an abhorrent custom—which mimicked the misguided ritual that upper-class whites had of displaying their teenage daughters to so-called society—neither she nor Clarisse could ever understand. All it was, actually, was meaningless and pretentious upper-middle-class Negro mothers' materialistic and social climbing exhibitionism.

Clarisse had told her that she asked her mother, back then, what exactly they thought young colored girls were *coming out* to?

It had been a useless question because this was what families like theirs did: they belonged to the right organizations like the Urban League and social clubs like the Links and gave their daughters piano, ballet, and ballroom dancing lessons and coming-out parties. That was that. And then off to college to get a degree and marry a properly focused well-credentialed brother!

As far as Veronica was concerned, it turned out that their cotillion merely trumpeted their arrival as future affirmative-action tokens and sociopolitical threats to the status quo. As for being introduced to "proper young men," half of the brothers in those days ended up getting shipped off to Vietnam, and the other half? Well, for an answer to that she just needed to look at where she was *now*!

Veronica looked over into the crib, which—for the sake of convenience—she had moved from the nursery into her bedroom, and became mesmerized by her plump, beautiful, and quietly sleeping baby. This was a nocturnal child—crying, laughing, and gurgling all night then sleeping peacefully nearly all day. Their clocks definitely were not compatible. Veronica was a morning person who loved watching the sunrise and the rare luxury, because of her demanding job, of hitting the pillows by ten-thirty at night. Derrick

Junior was obviously destined to be the first man to dominate and transform her life.

"Tell me something, Vee," Clarisse yelled from the kitchen.

"Wait, I'll be out there in a second. Give me a chance to pull it together and we'll talk."

Veronica pulled a brush through her hair, staring in the mirror over the dresser at the bags under her eyes, and slowly shook her head in disbelief. She was over forty, but everyone had thought she was twenty-two. Not anymore. She looked to herself as if she was seventy years old.

She applied concealer under her eyes, a little mascara, then twisted her curly red and gray-streaked hair—she hadn't had a chance to touch it up—into a bun. She walked into her closet and stared at all the beautiful working woman's clothes she had no idea when she'd ever wear again and pulled out a colorful floral print silk robe, threw off her wrinkled nightgown, and put it on.

She leaned over into the crib and kissed her sweet, serenely sleeping baby on the forehead and went to the kitchen to see what Clarisse was up to.

Clarisse had already set the table with two plates of poached eggs, hot, spicy sausage patties, slices of whole wheat toast slathered with butter, a pitcher of mango juice, and a large bowl of peeled citrus fruit in the center.

"You look like you need a cup of coffee, girl. Is it okay to have coffee when you're breast-feeding?"

"I'm sure one cup won't render the baby a junkie."

"Tell me something, Vee."

"What?" Veronica sat down and pierced a poached egg with her fork. Clarisse always made the most perfectly formed poached eggs. It was almost a shame to break the yolk, but it was half the fun of eating them. She took a toast triangle and dipped it into the delicious, golden yellow pocket of condensed cholesterol and asked, "What is it that you want me to tell you?"

Clarisse placed the coffeepot on the table then sat down across from her.

"What are you going to do now about a job? When you go back to work, what are you going to do with Derrick Junior? When do you plan to go back to work? When—"

"Stop, girl! I have no idea *what* I'm going to do. Not yet anyway. I figure I can comfortably stay home for about a year—"

"*This*, I cannot imagine. Not with *you*, my friend. You are a workaholic. I know you. I'd hate to see you end up taking it out on the baby."

"What do you mean?" She dropped her fork, horrified at her girlfriend's statement.

"Well . . . you know . . . life is funny, isn't it?"

Silence. Then, "Hardie, har, har . . ."

"Vee, I always imagined you as the high-powered media mogul, maybe married, but sitting in a big-time office wielding big-time power at some big-time television station. I figured I'd be the one who'd be a housewife with a baby, changing diapers, making formula, and shopping for politically correct books, toys, and games for my children."

"Me, too. So what's your point, Clarisse? You think I'm going to be an unfit mother to little Derrick because it looks as though I won't be vice president of CBS by sundown?"

"No, I just want to know what you're going to do about this situation. Aletha Brown did you a dirty turn. Just say the word and I'll go over and kick the bitch's ass!"

Veronica laughed. "And she'll blow you to the Pearly Gates with the pistol with which she shot Reginald Pinkney!"

"Do you believe she really shot him?"

"Considering what has been laid out before me, what do *you* think?" she asked, taking a quick sip of the delicious mango nectar then throwing her girlfriend an impatient frown.

"That is one crazy heifer! I think you can sue her tyrannical black behind for sex discrimination, Vee. You better go talk to your lawyer about this. Do you think she fired you because she is jealous?"

Veronica sliced off a piece of sausage and asked, "What could *she* possibly be jealous of? She's rich, famous, powerful, had an absolutely *fi-i-i-ne* brother who jumped at her bidding—from what I could tell—not some creep like Derrick who was afraid to make a commitment and—" Veronica waved a piece of sausage around in a tight circle, "—let me tell you, she has the most fabulous penthouse apartment a sister could ever dream of having in this city of money-gouging landlords and pompous co-op boards."

"Well, you never know what other people's problems are. Besides, if Aletha's man was so perfect, why did she find it necessary to shoot him?"

Ignoring the question, Veronica said, "Personally, I think that she was pissed off with me because she lost the talk show award again. Probably blames it on me. Maybe she's right. If I had put together a show on hermaphrodite marriages or something, maybe we could have won it."

Clarisse couldn't believe what she was hearing. She gulped down some coffee and said, "Are you for real?"

"Sometimes I wish I had become a schoolteacher like you are, Clarisse. Children are much more real than adults."

"Yeah, well, I *love* teaching because I love the kids, but teachers have problems, too. Honey, I'm working under a principal who kicks my ass every day of the week." She laughed, sopping up the last of her yolk with her toast. "And I suspect it's only because I'm skinnier than she is and probably half her age—"

"Half your *age*? How old *are* you these days, Clarisse? Please keep me posted." Veronica laughed, slapping her hand on the table.

Clarisse laughed, also, and continued, "'Cause I *know* I am a damned good teacher. And *you*, girl, were a damned good producer! Too good for that sick, lame shit you spent your time worrying your increasingly gray head of hair about. I think you should change your profession, Vee."

"You know, my *profession* is not the problem. My problem is that Derrick let me down."

Clarisse stood up from her chair and hissed, "Oooh no, girlfriend. He did not. You let *him* down. I've known you forever. I have been with you through all of the episodes with your half-baked boyfriends and could see that there was some real potential with Derrick. You just let your biological clock drive you insane, and so you put the cart before the horse. Derrick is an ambitious brother—upwardly *mo-bile*! You dragged him down with this ghettolike, premature baby-making tactic."

"What?"

"You heard me." Clarisse sat back down and stabbed a slice of grapefruit from the bowl with her fork.

"The asshole took off to Switzerland, girl!"

"You have *got* to admit that one of the many reasons that you admire and respect Derrick is that he is an Ivy League brother. An image to which you have always been attracted. I *know*!"

"So what?"

Clarisse leaned forward and rested her forearms on the table, her palms up. "You can't possibly tell me that you never realized that the brothers of the Ivy League were trained and programmed, in school, to service the needs and agendas of rich and powerful white men for a living."

"What *are* you babbling about, Clarisse?"

"Derrick is simply making a living at what he was trained to do. If you really loved him, you would support him in his career and enjoy the perks, as well. You can't have it both ways, Vee. A down-home brother who at the same time has credentials from *Harvard*? Not possible! You're not being realistic!"

"What do *you* know? You don't even have a man. Haven't had one in, what . . . *how* many years?"

"Doesn't matter. But if I were to find someone of substance I would take my time and try to understand the brother's needs before going off hog-wild—"

"Hog-wild? What kind of expression is that?"

"One of those hillbilly expressions that keep cropping up on that Aletha Brown show, or don't you recall?"

Veronica broke into uproarious laughter at her girlfriend.

A dark, melancholy expression settled in Clarisse's eyes.

"You know I *mean* what I say. It is so rare and special to find a person who loves you for yourself just as you are. It takes time. Since Michael passed, there hasn't been a soul who could measure up to all of his qualities."

Clarisse always said that Michael had "passed," but the reality of the situation was that her wonderful and devoted Michael had been blown to pieces over in Nam trying to rescue some destitute Indo-Chinese family from their flaming village.

His name was one of thousands carved on that memorial down in Washington, D.C.

After a long, dark, meditative moment, desperately searching for a lighter subject—about almost anything—Veronica asked, "Clarisse, remember how when your family moved across the street from us and we found out we were the same age . . . seven . . ."

"Yeah. And your mom got all upset about us playing together, since my folks were what she called 'migrants.' " She started giggling at the ridiculous recollection.

"I guess she eventually got over it because you were, despite your unfortunate family origins, the right color—light, bright, and damned near white."

"Oh, girl, you don't remember it right. Your mom got all friendly after my mother invited your folks over for cocktails and she realized that our house was almost entirely furnished in that French Provincial junk that they had purchased from your parents' furniture store."

They both broke out into warm, profuse waves of laughter.

"It also helped that your father decked out my mother's sugarcane-ravaged immigrant mouth with some fancy, heavily discounted bridgework and caps so that she could do the TV ad for their store with my father."

" 'Live like European aristocrats . . . Shop at the Furniture King!' " they both chimed, standing up from their chairs to mimic her parents' stiff posturing while reciting their company's slogan.

"Lord . . . *parents* . . . they can wear you out!" Veronica said, gasping from almost breathless laughter.

"Especially *yours*, girl!" Clarisse said, grinning. She pushed back her chair and moved from the table to begin putting the dishes in the dishwasher. "This baby certainly has ole Muh Dear knotted up beside her snooty, elitist self, doesn't he?"

"Umm-hmm. Clarisse, sit down. I can do those dishes later. Let's just go in the living room. Want to play some Scrabble?" she asked, leaving the kitchen and the dirty dishes. She glanced back at her lifelong girlfriend, and a winter chill shot through her as she pictured the two of them years from now—old women, living together in the same house like a pair of twenty-first-century Delaney sisters. What if it were to turn out that Clarisse was her true soul mate in that rather inconvenient female packaging?

Lord, have mercy!

"Vee, I need to know, exactly what you were thinking when you decided to just get pregnant without ever discussing this with Derrick? Did you feel that he would just drop everything, get married, and stay with you in New York so that you could continue working for that crazy Aletha Brown?"

"I felt that he would act responsibly."

"And what does that mean?" Clarisse asked, setting up the Scrabble board.

"By marrying me."

"Why? Because you got knocked up? This isn't the nineteen thirties you know. People have choices these days—both the men and the women, in case you haven't noticed."

"I know what year it is, Clarisse. Derrick is just a jerk." Veronica sat staring at one of the letter tiles. It was a B. "Anyway, I think you're right. I'm going to sue Aletha. I think she's terribly prejudiced."

"What are you saying? Aletha is prejudiced against babies . . . women with babies . . . or what?"

"No, you know Aletha has always been kind of a bitch to work with. I've always felt that because of my color that I've always been under the pressure of proving to her that I was a real 'down' sister. You know how some of these dark-skinned sisters are. They try to make you feel inferior. Make you feel as if you aren't really black."

"If that were the case, why did she hire you in the first place and why did she decide to fire you now after all these years? No . . . I don't think—"

"She's always treated me rather high-handed, the same way she treats the white female employees. I'm always trying to prove—"

Clarisse jumped up from her chair and laughed. "Vee, *that* explains everything! Girl, I've been wondering about you."

"About what?" Veronica wrinkled her brow in consternation.

"I've known you since childhood, yet ever since you started working for that pompous flake, you've taken on the personality of what seems to be your idea of what a real black woman is like. I just couldn't put my finger on it before. That's why you seemed to have become some kind of pale-faced clone of Miss Aletha Brown. You McPheersons have this color thing all mixed up in your heads. Always have. That explains why all the men you've ever dated had complexions as black as tar. You weren't *dating* men. You were proving how black you were."

"Oh, Clarisse, *stop. You* know, I'm sure, how those dark women—"

"Vee, I have never allowed anyone to drag me down those paths," Clarisse said, sitting down again, laughing and noting the doubtful look on her girl-friend's face.

"Well, I don't care what you say," Veronica said, ignoring her friend's laughter. "I'm going to sue the bitch. I'm not going to have her dismiss me as if I were some kind of incompetent fluff of a white woman."

"You should cut that out, Vee. I know for a fact that white women are as competent as anyone else, and so do you. You were fired by a jealous woman, who in my opinion now, has done you a favor."

"A *favor*?"

"Umm-hmm. You can sue her, get your compensation, set up your own business, and get your personality back. Get out of the shadows, you know? Probably if you stayed any longer with that woman, you'd have ended up shooting some poor black guy and I'd have to visit you up in Rikers Island or something." Clarisse laughed.

"What kind of business do you think I should start, my dear Miss Know-It-All?"

"Maybe set up your own production company. Make documentaries or something, on subjects like female jealousy or black people's color complexes. Do something constructive with your neuroses, girl."

Veronica hadn't been ready to admit it to her face, but she knew that Clarisse was right. Most of her friends considered Clarisse dizzy, but she had always known that she could trust the woman to be honest—brutally honest at times—and very grounded.

"Documentaries, huh?"

"Yep." They were obviously not going to be playing Scrabble, so Clarisse put the board away. "You know, Vee, I love Derrick Junior almost as much as you do," she said cautiously, "but how are you going to raise him without the proper male figure? You don't even have any brothers."

"Well, he *does* have a grandfather, and although my family is steeped in young'uns of the female persuasion, I *do* have a cousin, Eric, who's just moved east to Philadelphia, I've heard. Maybe I'll give him a call. I haven't seen him since we were kids."

"He's the one with the white mother, right?"

"His *father* is black, though. He was raised by a black man, Clarisse."

"Ohhh, nooo . . . I wasn't trying to imply anything contrary about his parents. I was just trying to place him in my mind. I think I remember him. I remember his family visiting your folks a couple of times with their brood of a gazillion offspring." Clarisse laughed.

"It was only *five*, girl."

"*Only* five, huh? Sounds like a mob of crumb snatchers to *me*."

"And *you're* a schoolteacher! *Shame* on you, Clarisse."

At that instant the intercom from the doorman's desk rang.

Veronica got up from the table to answer it.

"Yes, Juan? Who is it? My father? Of course. Send him up."

Clarisse followed her to the door. "Who is it, Vee? You want me to leave?"

"No, it's just my dad." She leaned against the door, waiting for the bell to ring.

"Why do you think he's here?"

"Don't know. Probably to see the baby."

"Well, I'll go clean up in the kitchen," Clarisse said, leaving her friend to await the arrival of her father.

When Veronica opened the door, her father stood for a minute scrutinizing her with an unsettled look as if he were seeing her for the first time.

"Hi, Dad. What are you doing here? Why aren't you with Muh Dear? Did she throw you out of the house of something?" she asked, warmly embracing her smiling father.

"No, Veronica. Despite what you seem to believe, we are not attached at the hip. I've come to see how my daughter and my grandson are doing," he said, patting her on the shoulder and walking toward the nursery.

"No, Dad. He's in *my* room." She placed her hands on his shoulders, redirecting his route.

"Hi, Mr. McPheerson!" shouted Clarisse from the kitchen.

"Is that Clarisse in there?" he asked, looking around.

"Yes, Daddy. She came over to make me brunch."

Clarisse ran into Veronica's bedroom and hugged Veronica's father as if he were her own.

"Been to any Holy Roller churches lately, Clarisse?" he asked, grinning at his daughter's friend, remembering how the two women, when they were kids, used to cut Sunday School classes at what they had thought was their parents' highbrow Lutheran church in order to listen to the loud, garish—in his opinion—music of the Pentecostal church nearby.

Veronica had told him that they liked the tambourines.

"As a matter of fact, Mr. McPheerson, I attended a service just this morning!"

He shook his head and said, "Clarisse, you will never change."

"Why should I?"

"I'm not suggesting that you do. It is just an observation," he said, leaning over the baby, looking as if he was going to pick him up.

"Please, Daddy, don't," Veronica whispered. "Let him sleep. He had me up all night. I need some rest. Why don't you take off your coat?"

"Okay, honey," he agreed, removing his overcoat and handing it to his daughter. "I came over because I wanted to have a talk with you."

"You want me to leave?" Clarisse asked again, defensively.

"No. As a matter of fact, since you're here, maybe you can baby-sit Derrick Junior for a few hours, if it's okay with the two of you, because I'd like to take Veronica to lunch."

"I told you, I just *ate*, Daddy."

"Well then, you can just watch me eat, or have a dessert or something. How's that?"

"I'd love to watch the baby. You two go on!" Clarisse said, plopping herself down on the chair next to the crib and picking up a magazine from the floor next to it.

"Well then, the two of you get out of here and let me dress. I'll be ready in a second."

CHAPTER EIGHT

*V*eronica pulled her long beige wool coat tightly around her against the numbing, icy winds and shook her head in disapproval as her father threw open the door from the inside of his brand-new black Lincoln Town Car.

She slid into the seat beside him and slammed the door.

"Daddy, why do you keep buying this make of car? I'm sure everyone out there thinks you're a chauffeur driving around in this thing."

"I suppose you think I should buy a Jeep or maybe some kind of sports car, huh?"

"No. Maybe something classy and appropriate for you like a Lexus or a BMW or—"

"A BMW? You know I don't like those foreign cars. I'm an American and I *buy* American, Veronica. You know that."

"It's not possible to know anymore whether a product is actually American or not, but—"

"Look, child, if they think I'm a chauffeur, at least none of these white cops will find it necessary to pull me over under suspicion of robbing a bank or selling dope or something. Besides, you know I never cared much about what other people think about who I am. People think all kinds of stupid things about other folks. Especially about black folks. Even other black folks."

"Well, I think you're stuck. Break out, Daddy! Do something different and daring for a change."

"You seem to be doing enough breaking out for all of us, child. Don't worry about me," he said, adroitly maneuvering around the chaos that predictably occurred at Fifty-ninth Street and Columbus Circle at any hour of the day. "You are the one we're all worried about. Gonna raise a baby all by yourself. And now on top of everything, that Aletha Scrooge Brown fires you, just in time for Christmas and all."

"I hope you didn't come over here from Queens to lecture me. I get enough of that from Muh Dear."

"I *do* want to talk to you, but why don't you take a nap while I drive down to Brooklyn for some callaloo."

"Yuck! You and that down-homey food. Why don't you both just move on back to Trinidad. Where are we going anyway?"

"To Dexter's Caribbean Hideaway—"

"Yeah, *some* hideaway. That place is always a mob scene, especially on Sundays."

"Doesn't matter to *me*. They've got the best callaloo, curried goat, and calypso rice in New York City. But what I want to know is, what you are going to do about a job, child?" he asked gently, with his eyes steadfast on the avenue.

"Look, I'm going to take that nap that you suggested," she snapped, leaning back and closing her eyes.

Despite what Clarisse had said about starting her own business, she didn't feel that she was ready to make that move yet. She would soon be needing another nine-to-five. How was she ever going to find another job of the caliber of the one she had? And as a new mother, no less. The job with *The Aletha Brown Show* had come to her in the most preposterous way that fate could have conjured up. She figured that weird twists of fate were the primary ways in which people found their most interesting employment.

She had been working as a production assistant for years on an insignificant children's program at the station. She had taken the entry-level job after a sizable number of peculiarly lonely years selling advertising time for a radio station in LA where she had gone to college. Her expensive masters degree in broadcast journalism was going entirely to waste, in her opinion. She had taken the modest assistant's job in television because it had gotten her back to New York City and into the visual media, which was what she had really wanted.

That job had been no bargain either.

She had been considering quitting to find something else the day she stood on line arguing with the cashier about her change for lunch at the station's commissary, when the most outlandish thing happened.

A bigwig smelling of alcohol and mischief stumbled over toward her as she took her tray and began searching for an isolated table at which to sit.

"So *you're* the girl, huh?"

"What?"

"You're the girl that opened the couch."

"What on earth are you talking about, sir? *What* couch?" She began to panic. Drunken men were always something to panic about, especially when their eyes focused like lasers on your breasts and they spoke of couches.

"You've certainly grown into quite an attractive young woman," the man breathed lasciviously, touching her hand and gallantly, or so he probably thought, taking her tray and motioning his balding pinhead toward a table.

"I think you have me mistaken for someone else," she said briskly, trying to retrieve her tray of food.

"You work with Ed, over there in production, don't you?" he asked, glancing over at the man who dressed up and starred as Squeaky the Squirrel on the program where she worked.

"Yes, I do, but—"

"Yeah, that's what he said. He says that your father is king of the furniture. You're the Castro Convertible girl, right?" he said, smiling knowingly, placing her tray on the table he had chosen for them.

Veronica thought that she was about to go insane.

"Mister, first of all, my father is owner of a furniture store called the Furniture King. We having nothing *at all* to do with the Castro company," she snapped, flustered and offended simultaneously. "And secondly I am not old enough to have been that Castro Convertible girl, as you call her."

The bigwig stood with his mouth spreading into a big gaping hole in his face. "Oh . . . I . . . uh . . . uh . . ."

"Also," she drawled slyly, smiling at the man with delicious anticipation, "I am a *black* woman, so I couldn't possibly be that person, could I, sir?"

The little color that he had, drained from his face, as his eyes formed into beady little marbles trying to discern something about her that he had clearly overlooked.

She loved the infinite variety of baffled expressions that swept over the faces of white people when they suddenly discovered she was not exactly who they thought she was. She had always enjoyed catching them in the midst of moronic ethnic jokes or snide racial remarks behind some other black person's back. Weird situations like those also compensated for the peculiar curse she was forced to bear of having a deceptive skin color that allowed her access to the kinds of information to which she had really never wanted to be privy.

That was one of the reasons she had always made it a point of getting involved only with dark-skinned black men. She wanted to give her children enough color—enough so that certain kinds of white folks could see them coming, forcing them into brief periods of racial civility—even if it was superficial or forced.

"I-I'm so sorry. I didn't notice that . . ." the pinhead stuttered.

What could he have possibly *noticed* anyway? Veronica thought, laughing coyly in his face. To most Caucasians she looked like a member of any number of the swarthy tribes of Europeans, just as her own mother had wished for her.

"It's okay. It happens all the time." She winked at him, then sat at the table where he had placed her tray and began to eat her lunch.

"Well, you're still pretty anyway," the pinhead added awkwardly.

"Anyway? What do you mean—"

He fled before she could finish her sentence.

Somehow guilt about the mistaken identity had lingered in the man's conscience, because when there was an opening for a producer of the new *Aletha Brown Show* a month later, he had seen to it that she was offered the job.

She had taken it without even a second thought.

"Veronica, honey, wake up. We're here." Her father nudged her.

"I'm awake," she said, pulling up the collar of her coat, readying herself against the cold. Relieved, she noticed that her father had miraculously found parking directly in front of the restaurant.

"A table for two, sir?" the waiter asked with that admiring and respectful look men give to older men who appear to be dating a much younger woman.

"Yes, please," her father responded, as he removed his daughter's coat with a possessive gesture. Mr. McPheerson was at the age where he enjoyed encouraging the charade. Actually, Veronica had to admit that she enjoyed it, too, especially since her father was such a handsome man, with his head full of stylishly coiffed gray hair and his prosperously distinguished manner.

Dexter's was packed to its maximum, teeming with every West Indian who lived within a hundred-mile radius of Brooklyn. The restaurant and its decor had what Veronica considered a chic pre–Castro Havana–like ambience. The walls were covered in bright colored murals of tropical scenes, and the few spaces not crowded with tables were filled with wicker and potted palms.

The convivial cacophony of animated West Indian conversation mixed with calypso music playing softly in the background created, for Veronica, a satisfying diversion from the repetitious demands of motherhood.

The aromatic fusion of pumpkin, plantain, onion, thyme, garlic, pepper, cumin, and curry wafted throughout the dining room, calling forth memories of Sunday afternoons in her mother's kitchen.

"I'm having the callaloo and a ginger beer. What are you having, dear?" her father asked, tapping her hand with his finger, forcing her thoughts back to the present.

"Just an Earl Grey tea and key lime pie."

When the waiter left with their orders, Veronica looked at her father, feeling a flicker of foreboding, and asked, "What do you want to talk about, Daddy?"

"Derrick."

"The baby?"

"No, the father."

"Why on earth would I want to talk about him? He's a selfish and irresponsible jerk! It's over between us." She tapped her fingers with agitation on the pink tablecloth.

"Your mother said that Clarisse called and told her that Derrick had flown all the way from Switzerland to see the baby. That does not sound irresponsible to *me*," he said gently, a bewildered tone coloring his voice.

"He had arrogantly said that he wanted to see if the baby was really *his*." In an effort to keep her frustration in check, Veronica's voice came out in a choked whisper.

Her father moved uncomfortably in his chair and cleared his throat with a short cough.

Veronica saw the dubious look on her father's face and continued, "Well . . . that's what he said!"

"Can you blame him? Now, you are my daughter and I love you more than life, but you played one of the oldest tricks in the world, dear. What did you expect he'd do?" He shook his head. "I thought you modern women had moved beyond all those old-fashioned games."

Veronica looked over at the next table at the young couple engaged in intimate conversation.

"Derrick is a good man. A smart man," her father continued. "He was probably upset that you thought that you could trap him like that. He was just trying to save face by telling you that he wasn't sure he was the father. But he's convinced now, isn't he?"

"Umm-hmm. So what? He doesn't want to marry me, so I told him to take a hike." She snickered, taking a sip from her water goblet.

"Take a hike? If you had to tell him to take a hike, as you say, then he must have shown interest in the child. Does he plan to support the boy?"

"I don't want anything from him. He can keep his black—" She stopped short when she noticed her father's eyebrows shoot up toward his scalp, disapprovingly. "He can stay in Switzerland as far as I'm concerned. That seems to be where he prefers to be."

Her father leaned back into his chair and stared at his lovely daughter, wondering how to broach what he wanted to say.

"He doesn't want to marry me, Daddy. In your day, you probably would have shot him, right?"

"In *my* day?" He laughed. "In my day, women did not intentionally put the cart before the horse."

"Sounds like you've been talking to Clarisse."

"Clarisse sounds like an intelligent woman, then," her father said, leaning in toward her. "If Derrick wants to support the child, you should allow him to do that. It is his responsibility and obligation. He should have a part in raising his son. No father should be denied that opportunity. Besides, how do you know that he does not want to marry you?"

"If you remember, we lived together and he never asked," she said defiantly, unable to mask her hurt.

There was silence for a while as her father searched in his mind for a common ground to approach his headstrong daughter.

"Veronica, honey . . . in . . . my . . . *day* . . . women didn't waste their value in uncommitted relationships."

"Value? What do you mean, 'their value'?" she asked, attempting to mock his generation's old-timey perspective on contemporary life.

Bingo! her father thought. He was beginning to make headway.

"Have you young women lost all sense of your own value? If a man cannot make a commitment to you, then he is not worth living with. Why would you squander your charms and other feminine endowments in a relationship that has no future?"

"If a man lives with a woman, he is implying that there is a future, is he not?"

"Why would you build your future on an *implication*, Veronica?"

She looked at her father, confused. She was beginning to get a headache. How could she explain the way things are today to this sixty-something-year-old man?

"Well, answer me, Veronica," he needled.

"Do you believe that a man who lives with a woman, even though they are not married, feels that he is not in a committed relationship, Daddy?"

"Daughter, in case you have forgotten, I am a man, and what I can't understand is why a woman would permit such a situation to exist. If you want a marriage and a family life, you must demand it. Accept nothing less. It is the woman who sets the standards in a relationship—that is, if she wants to be taken seriously," he stated definitively, pressing his index finger onto the table to emphasize his position.

"Why would a man live with a woman he doesn't want to marry?"

"Because the woman allows him to. But I ask you again, how do you know that Derrick didn't want to marry you?"

"He never asked."

"Did you discuss it?"

"I kept hinting, but—"

"Hinting? That is where you made your mistake. Making assumptions and weaving fantasies is immature for a woman of your age. Do you make assumptions when it comes to your career? Do you *hint* at what you want to achieve in your work?"

"Derrick wanted to move to Switzerland," she stated curtly, becoming more and more frustrated by the second. She did not want to discuss the arrogant and selfish creep any further.

"People raise families in Switzerland."

"Yeah, Swiss people do!"

"This is our fault. Your mother and I have spoiled you in such a way as an only child that you believe that everything revolves around you and you alone."

"Maybe you're right, Daddy." Veronica slumped untidily in her seat. "So here I am—unemployed and raising a fatherless child. Okay, it's your fault, then," she almost shouted, but her father put his hand up in a gesture that told her to calm herself.

"The baby *has* a father, and I, as the grandfather of Derrick Junior, ask that you make an effort to reconcile with the baby's father, whether you ever marry or not. It is best. Derrick is a good man, that I know."

"Muh Dear hates his guts."

"She doesn't hate him. She has her peculiar ways, but she knows he is a good man. Besides, the only feelings that are truly important at the moment are those that you and Derrick have for the baby. If you let him become involved with Derrick Junior, you may find yourself pleasantly surprised at the outcome."

The waiter placed their orders in front of them and left.

The smell of the salt meat and crab in her father's plate beckoned her. The deep green slices of okra looked scrumptious. She realized that the troubling conversation had caused her to work up an appetite.

She picked up her fork, reached over her key lime pie, and aimed it at her father's dish. He grabbed her wrist in his hand to stop her and said, "Promise me that you'll call Derrick, honey."

"Yeah, sure, Daddy," she muttered as he released her hand. She dug in and ravenously shoveled a fork full of delicious, spicy, down-homey callaloo into her mouth.

That'll be the day, she resolved willfully. She would call that pompous Oreo cookie Negro when hell freezes over. She would raise her baby by herself.

She would teach Derrick Junior to be responsible. She would also teach him to be proud of his African roots, which would no doubt become diluted by a father who lusted after Europe.

Clarisse and her father would eventually have to learn to accept her decision.

Veronica McPheerson had not sacrificed so much and worked so hard to now have to put up with some man's bullshit.

SNAP THREE

CHAPTER NINE

Beep . . . beep . . . beep . . .

Jeffrey Scott quickly rose on his right elbow, grabbed his watch from the night table beside him, and shut off its alarm. He cautiously turned toward Debra to see if he had awakened her.

He watched the gentle rise of the tangled sheets. She was facing away from him, sleeping on her left side. He kissed her lightly on the back of her neck.

"Sweet," he said, nudging her softly. Jeffrey certainly didn't feel like getting out of her warm bed, but he had to get home to shower, dress, and hopefully make it in time for his eleven o'clock flight to Detroit.

He smiled as he lightly touched her smooth back and reflected on the fact that they never *did* get to dinner last night. He'd arrived at her door and they had immediately begun to tear at each other like two lions in heat.

He was *not* complaining.

Debra would probably say that it was perfectly natural for two Leos like themselves to greet this way.

He chuckled and nudged her again. She let out a long groan and flung her strong, thin, little body onto her back, her right hand pushing him with such unexpected force that he fell from the bed onto the floor with a thud.

Boy, she is a deep sleeper, he thought, getting up and searching for his clothes. They were scattered about her lacy, aggressively feminine bedroom as if they had been superfluous impediments.

Once dressed, he gazed down at her still-sleeping and naked body lying spread-eagle before him. A fierce, primal desire mounted and pulsated in his groin.

This is the kind of woman, he mused, with whom you could run around buck naked in Tahiti.

Maybe he would arrange it. But they'd at least have to go out to dinner first.

He was definitely going to call this one as soon as he got back from his business trip.

He leaned over and tried to rouse her again.

Damn, this girl could sleep. He stared incredulously at her sleeping like a baby . . . *still*! He pulled the covers over her and looked around for her alarm clock. It was on the night table on the other side of the bed. He walked over and pushed it closer to her ear, to make sure she wouldn't be late for work, all because of *him*. It looked like she had another hour of grace, anyway, according to the clock.

He reached into his shirt pocket to make sure the numbers she had given him were still there. He compared her home phone number to the number printed on her telephone and placed it back in his pocket.

He pulled out one of his business cards from his wallet and placed it on the pillow next to her cheek.

Right before he left the room, stumbling over one of her spike-heeled shoes, he *remembered* . . .

Jeffrey turned around, picked up the card, and added his home phone number. They didn't exactly know each other well, and he didn't want her to think that he was married.

As he walked toward the door, her little Yorkshire terrier started yapping at him like an idiot. Why did women like these silly ratlike dogs, he wondered, figuring that this pooch probably had certainly awakened her now.

He reached over to pet the dog, who instantly bared her teeth and snapped at his hand. Jumping back, he called out toward the bedroom, "Debra . . . I'll call you next week, okay?"

Silence.

The next day, Debra Parker paused for a moment, sighed, leaned back against the cushions of the office couch, and crossed her long, thin legs. Annoyed, she surveyed the damage on her brand-new Ferragamo boots, which had been assaulted by the salt and snow-covered New York City streets. Then she sighed with irritation and continued with the session.

"Dr. Simon, you *know* how I dread flying home to Chicago for Christmas."

"Yes, I do," Desiree stated, nodding lightly. She placed her yellow legal-size writing pad on the end table next to her armchair, which sat directly facing her patient.

"This year the whole tribe will be at the house: my mother, my grandmother, my two aunts, their husbands, their four daughters, my cousins, with *their* husbands and their six precious little hatchlings, my nieces and nephews! The women will end up all up in my face asking why I'm still not—"

"Married," Desiree completed the sentence for her.

"Right! I'm just sick of it! I just don't want to go. All I'll be doing is spending my hard-earned money on an airplane ticket and a billion dollars in Christmas presents for the pleasure of enduring the condescending scrutiny of my personal life by Mother and her gang."

"Why are you going, if it's not something you really want to do?"

"It's my *mother*, Dr. Simon. Don't *you* have a mother?"

"So, it's out of loyalty to your mother?"

"No! Well ... I mean ... of course, I want to *see* her. It's just the Christmas thing, you know? Also, it's because I'd never hear the end of it if I didn't show. Her only daughter—her *baby*—refusing to visit her poor little mother for the holidays. She'd only end up flying out here, figuring that either I was too broke to come or sick or something. *That* I definitely don't need."

"Have you ever discussed your feelings about the situation with her?"

"I can't."

"Why not?"

Debra began playing nervously with one of the braids of her exotic coiffure that sat piled on her head like an intricately woven basket and answered, "Because I know her. She just wouldn't understand. Frankly, she scares the shit out of me. Always has. Especially ever since my father left and they got their divorce. If I told her I wasn't coming for Christmas, she'd probably just start on a long litany of complaints about the loneliness of—" She stopped suddenly in midsentence, leaned forward, elbows resting on her knees, and asked, "Dr. Simon, tell me something."

"Umm?"

"How is it possible that a woman who I have never heard say a single positive thing about the male of the species can be so anxious for her daughter to marry one of them? You know, whenever members of my family get together for these large family dinners, the men all end up in one room together drinking and looking at some ball game on the television while the women gather in another room drinking and competing over which of them has the best story about their own experiences with male insensitivity, cruelty, or betrayal. Why would I want to become a member of that club, I ask?"

"Would you want to be married someday, Ms. Parker?"

"Look," Debra became agitated, rapidly tapping her left foot on the floor. "I have been going out with men since I was sixteen years old, and now I'm almost forty. I've even lived with a couple of them but haven't yet found anyone who I could trust with my life. Besides, the brothers just get on my last nerve! I get along just fine with my pet Yorkie, though."

"Would you like being married one day?" Desiree repeated, reaching over to retrieve her writing pad.

"I take care of myself very well. I make a good living. I have some great girlfriends. But you know, Doctor . . ."

"Umm?"

"Whenever the shit hits the fan at work, I think of how nice it would be if I had someone who could help me take a break for a while. I get so tired of being alone . . . *sometimes*." She sighed softly, and a dark haze seemed to settle in front of her eyes.

"Do you want to talk about—?" Dr. Simon asked.

"Actually . . . ," Debra interrupted suddenly, like flipping a light switch from her somber mood to a bright, giddy one—her eyes smiling devilishly at Desiree. "Actually, Dr. Simon, I met this absolutely fi-i-i-ne brother the other day. We went out."

Debra shuffled anxiously in her seat, glanced sideways, and coyly tilted her head. "Well . . . we never actually *left* my apartment," she snickered slyly.

Checking first to be sure her client wasn't watching, Desiree glanced at her watch and waited for her to continue.

"I guess I met him a little too late to have him accompany me to my mom's house for Christmas." She laughed. "But maybe we can get something on for New Year's Eve. Actually the only time I hate being single is on New Year's Eve."

"Why is that, Ms. Parker?"

"Because it reminds me that yet another year has passed without my having found my soul mate."

"This is the *only* time, Ms. Parker?" Desiree asked, trying to suppress a tone of doubt.

"Okay . . . not really," Debra conceded, flashing a cold scowl toward the doctor.

"I guess I also feel it every time the landlord raises the rent on my apart-ment!" she replied sarcastically.

Beep . . . beep . . . beep . . . Dr. Simon's clock indicated that Debra Parker's time was up.

Debra glared at the calendar on her office desk, fuming. Two weeks have passed now, and the nigger *still* hasn't called! She was so frustrated and humiliated that she wanted to cry. Perhaps she shouldn't have let her passions run so wild as to have sex with a veritable stranger on their first date, she thought with resignation.

"Why should a man buy the cow if he can get the milk for free?" Her mother's warning smacked her squarely on her guilt lobe. She should have listened to the advice.

Debra Parker thought that she and Jeffrey had had a fabulous evening together. What on *earth* could have turned him off?

She had decided to go out to lunch with two women at the firm—the only other black women who worked at Noonan, Craft, Johnson, and Wells Adver-tising Agency, where she was creative director.

Life for this ambitious, single, New York City, African American woman had become overwhelmingly empty, she conceded, pulling on her coat to meet the girls in the lobby.

"Going to lunch, Debra?" one of her colleagues asked good-naturedly, peeking her blond head through the office door.

"Umm-hmm," she responded to no one—since the woman had walked away before she could even open her mouth to answer the question.

Debra Parker wanted to meet some wonderful man to marry who could "sit her down," as her mother would say.

She didn't need this shit anymore. She had been promoted to vice president, creative director, and the company had decided to target her account Sunny Day Shampoo to the African American market, using all those famous black female singers as spokespersons. Sales had gone up *4000* percent! It was amazing that white people made any *real* money at all, stubbornly ignoring huge target groups of consumers like they did.

She had ascertained over the years that without outside pressures—or the more recent popularity of big-bucks black sports figures and rock stars—

advertisers wouldn't care one way or the other about the nonwhite American consumers' needs.

But on the other hand maybe she just had been overestimating the marketing savvy of big business enterprises. Perhaps they were simply ignorant of the fact that *all* kinds of folks washed their hair.

Despite all her hard work and her promotion, Debra could feel the big boys closing in like vultures on a carcass, ready to make her the victim of a Pac-Man-type merger and corporate downsizing. She was not only making too much money now, but at thirty years old—at least, that's what she had *told* them—she was now too damned old. They wanted fresh, young, cheap—and *white*—meat.

What could she expect? It was downright pathetic that shit like this turned out to be the kind of coveted big-time "opportunities" that blacks had fought to get.

It just wasn't worth it in the final analysis. Even the white boys descended into alcoholism, drug abuse, and dropped dead from heart attacks as a result of this mess, with their marriages exploding and shattering all over the place.

She wished that she had followed her dream of pursuing a career as an artist, instead of having gotten herself contained in all these rigid corporate boxes. Besides, she thought, glancing down at her rather conservative—for *her*—tan, lamb suede Ralph Lauren shirtdress, she would much prefer spending her days in a paint-spotted smock with her hair wrapped in a babushka, inhaling the exhilarating perfumes of Grumbacher's luscious pigments, her turpentine and linseed oils.

Coincidentally, when she got on the elevator her two friends, a media director and a woman from account services, were already there. Her white coworkers present looked at them with nervous expressions, as the three women warmly greeted one another. Surely they couldn't possibly think that these black women were planning a corporate takeover.

She ignored them.

Sitting cozily in a booth at the crowded and trendy Gleason's restaurant, the women paused their small talk as the waitress delivered their first courses.

When the woman was out of earshot, the media director asked, "Okay, Debra, what's this big, hard question you want to pose?"

Debra took a sip of her water and began. "Well, I met this terrific brother— or so I thought—a couple of weeks ago."

The account services friend, who happened to be married, sighed. "Oh, no, not *another* one of those stories."

"Easy for *you* to say," snapped Media Director in Debra's defense. "Go on, girl, what *happened*?"

"Of course, go ahead, Debra." Account Services smiled, leaning in toward her, helping herself to a glistening and succulent asparagus from her plate of vinaigrette.

Debra continued. "We had a *terrific* time—" Slightly embarrassed. "—if you get my drift." She looked up quickly from her lobster bisque.

"Umm-hmm. We get your *drift*, girl." Account Services grinned, crinkling her nose with amused empathy.

"He seemed to enjoy himself, too, you know?"

"They *always* enjoy themselves, girl! What you're saying is that the nigger hasn't called you back, right?" Media Director's words stabbed the air in front of Debra with the same force that she used to rip the tail from one of the big, fat, coral-colored shrimps in her salad. "So, what do you want to know from *us*? You just jumped into the sack with another loser? No big deal. New York City is polluted with them. Just pick up your panties and go on with your life."

Debra felt tears trying to break through.

Account Services' heart went out to her. She liked Debra. To *her*, Debra seemed, despite her sometimes aggressive and practiced self-sufficient ways, like the kind of woman who should be married and at home raising some children and painting landscapes or something. "Debra," she said, "I assume that you gave the man your number, and he gave you *his*, right?"

"So?" The lobster bisque was delicious, as always, Debra thought, savoring another spoonful.

"He is *fine*, right?"

"*Too* fine, girl. " A giggle leaked out from between her near tears.

"Mrs. Account Services reached over, touched Debra's hand, and continued. "He's terrific in the sack, right?"

"Of course, he *is*," snapped Ms. Media Director. "Why do you think she's sitting there about to cry all over our *food*?"

Debra knew that at some point she'd have to tell someone that she'd been living a lie. Sex with a man had never been fulfilling. She'd consoled herself by saying that maybe she overestimated the importance of sex, that having someone she could share all parts of her life with was more important. What was the big deal with sex anyway?

What she wasn't sure she could tell anyone about was how confused her feelings were for the media director at her firm. Debra was sure that on some level she loved the woman, but she wasn't prepared for a bring-the-girlfriend-home-to-meet-mother kind of moment.

"Shut up, girl, let me talk." Account Services glanced impatiently at the bitter and still single female and asked Debra gently, "Does he have a *job*?"

"He's an architect for Richmond, Gardiner, Pitt, and Newhouse."

Relieved, Account Services said, "*You* call *him*, girl . . . and right away!"

Ms. Media Director gasped, almost falling off her seat. "What are you saying? Are you *crazy*, girl? A man—a *real* man—*always* calls a lady after he makes love to her. Don't make a fool of yourself, Debra."

"Debra, what have you got to lose?" Account Services fanned her hand at Media Director with exasperation. "Maybe he lost your number. It *is* unlisted, remember?"

"Sure," grunted Media Director with bitter skepticism. "The man is just a dog. Forget him!"

Debra looked from one to the other of her girlfriends, took another sip of water, and reflected for a long moment. Media Director was right. She would take *her* advice. After all, this woman was higher up on the corporate ladder than Account Services was, so she *must* know what she was talking about. Plus Account Services was married and had been out of the single scene for some ten- or eleven-odd years. She didn't have a clue about the world *they* lived in.

She finally looked over at Media Director and said, "I agree with *you*, girl. I'm not so desperate that I have to chase an ungrateful *man*! Fuck him!"

Debra would also consult her shrink about this, too, before making a final decision.

"Good girl." Media Director sighed, relieved that her friend had decided not to make a total ass of herself.

Account Services was struck dumb.

She looked from one to the other of these women, then called out to the waitress, interjecting a voice of frustration into what she thought was the misguided air around them. "Miss? I need a *drink*."

CHAPTER TEN

*R*achel Moskowitz shook her head of thick black curls in bewilderment.

"You know, Dr. Simon, you probably won't understand this the way I do, but it's television shows like that nanny show that make my situation as a single Jewish woman all the more difficult. You have a sister in the business. How does she explain all the perfidiously insulting stereotypes and dangerous messages that are being pounded relentlessly into the heads of viewers? It's not even subtle."

"What do you object to about the program?" Desiree asked cautiously. She had a pretty good idea of what could be bothering her patient about that sitcom. Desiree found it patently offensive. But since she was not a white Jewish woman, she wanted to confirm her perceptions. Since there had been no protest from the Jewish community nor the Anti-Defamation League that she was aware of, perhaps she had gotten it all wrong. Perhaps her sense of humor was lacking.

"I find it to be the most racist, most anti-Semitic show on television. Maybe in the entire *history* of television," said Rachel, banging her hand on the coffee table. "I mean no presumption or disrespect, Dr. Simon, but I am convinced that if the Jewish characters in the nanny show were African American, the NAACP would have organized a boycott. How many Jewish women have you heard of making a living raising Anglo-Saxon children, I ask you? Jewish women don't do that kind of work. As far as I know, nannies are primarily immigrants eager to have an American experience."

"In what specific ways do you find that program anti-Semitic, Ms. Moskowitz?"

"How is the show anti-Semitic? Have you ever *seen* it?"

"A couple of times."

"It's bad *food*, Doctor! It shows a young Jewish woman as loud and crass, begging for the opportunity to fall into the bed of her rich, Gentile employer. Week after week, three generations of Jewish women—the nanny, her mother, and her grandmother—are portrayed as obnoxious, money grubbing, overeating intruders into a supposedly genteel, WASP world. And there is not a single Jewish man in sight who might defend their honor or integrity. In fact, Jewish men, even in their absence, are denigrated."

Ms. Moskowitz's voice had begun to quiver and rise in pitch.

"The star is a gorgeous woman who is always outfitted in expensive clothes, and it is implied that this wardrobe is a reflection of Jewish women's grasping and shopaholic materialism. Whenever this woman opens her mouth, which is constantly—I guess she *is* the star—a stream of loud, obnoxious honking sounds blasts from her lips. I'm appalled to think that this is someone's idea of how a New York Jewish woman speaks. I was born and raised in New York, and absolutely no one I know speaks like this. Do *you*, Dr. Simon?"

Desiree reflected on her in-laws, various friends, past teachers, professors, and her Jewish colleagues and neighbors, "Actually, no, I do not. But it is supposed to be a comedy—an exaggeration."

Rachel rolled her eyes with exasperation and responded, "A bit extreme, in my opinion. It's so blatant, Doctor, that I sense a strange condescension from my colleagues whenever I arrive at work the morning after the show was aired. Of course, I could be becoming paranoid!"

"Take it easy, Ms. Moskowitz."

"I'm sorry, but it just offends me to no end. I haven't watched it in a while, but I hear it's an extremely popular show. You know, one episode—the last one I watched—was about how a woman of a rich black family was looking for her long-lost daughter and had traced her search to this nanny character. Because the black woman was *rich*, the nanny's own mother was willing to give away her *own* daughter to that black woman. I mean no offense, Dr. Simon . . ."

"None taken."

"That's the obvious stereotype that a Jew would sell his own flesh and blood for a dollar. Do you understand, Doctor, why I'm pissed off with this? It even goes as far as portraying these characters as having an insatiable and hypocritical lust for crustaceans—always searching for lobster dinners and crab cakes. I realize that most Jewish people these days aren't exactly living by the laws of kashruth, but it's the context, Doctor!"

"How do you feel that this television program personally affects *you* and your life?"

"One of the main reasons that anti-Semitism exists is because people have been told for centuries in so many different ways that Jews are lowlife money-grubbers and—"

"How exactly do you feel that this affects *your* life?"

"If black women were consistently portrayed in this manner, don't you think that it could affect your relationships with black men? Perhaps it's programs like that one that create a climate where I am personally finding it difficult to meet eligible Jewish men who take me seriously as a romantic possibility. I don't even remember the last time I *had* an intimate relationship with a Jewish man, or," she added with a disarming smile, "*any* man for that matter! Jewish men all seem to prefer Catholic shiksas and everyone else."

Desiree tried to stifle a nervous cough but couldn't.

"But then who can blame them, considering the kind of press Jewish women get. It's really an outrage. The other day, I rented a movie starring a tremendously famous Jewish actress. The plot involved her entering into a sexless marriage with a dysfunctional Anglo guy," she said, looking directly into Desiree's eyes, then lifted an eyebrow and rolled her eyes in exasperation.

"And you know, Dr. Simon, during the course of this bizarre plot, after a number of months in this unconsummated marriage, the woman demands sex from her husband, who ultimately refuses to oblige her by saying, 'I have taken specific precautions in choosing a wife who I would not be attracted to' or something to that effect. Can you *imagine?*"

"I do not know this movie, but it does sound like an implausible scenario, Ms. Moskowitz."

"If that weren't enough, the woman asks her mother if she had ever been pretty. And, by the way, the actress is quite attractive. And the mother says, 'Yes, you *were* pretty,' and then hands her a baby picture of herself when she had been a *blonde!*" Rachel Moskowitz sighed and leaned back in her chair, spent from anger.

"Do you feel the mother's sentiment in this movie to be implausible, Ms. Moskowitz?"

There was a long silence. Rachel frowned pensively, looking at Desiree, and said, "Unfortunately, no. My own mother has been frustrated for years because I refuse to straighten my hair and dye it blond."

"And why do you think she wants you to do this?"

"I guess she feels I would be more successful or happier if I looked more like Christie Brinkley, or somebody. I guess she wants me to look less 'Jewish,' " she finally admitted, a deep well of melancholy vibrating in her voice.

This woman's distress, Desiree silently noted, was a mirror image of what many African Americans experience in their communities when they don't possess the Caucasian features of "good hair" or light skin color—especially the women.

Ms. Moskowitz continued with her observations. "Have you noticed that the expression *Jewish princess* is usually uttered with ridicule and disdain, while the expression *blond shiksa goddess* is always sighed breathlessly by someone bedazzled and in awe? Haven't you noticed that, Dr. Simon?"

"Ms. Moskowitz, in regard to that television program that offends you, I'm sure that you, in particular, realize that you have the right to write a letter of protest to the network, the show, or its sponsors. As a matter of fact, it's quite possible that if you were to use your legal letterhead with your communications that the offending thrust of the program might change seemingly overnight."

"You're right. I've thought about it, but I have a problem with it."

"What is the problem?" Desiree ran her fingers through her dreadlocks, trying to suppress a look of anxious curiosity.

"You see, I believe that protests might cause them to cancel the show altogether. I don't want anyone to lose their jobs. These days, it seems that *any* excuse is enough for the big boys to toss people out onto the streets, jobless and in debt. I simply feel they should change the direction of the scripts."

Rachel Moskowitz hesitated for a moment, leaned back in her seat, and continued, "I remember a black program, starring a famous black actress, way back in the sixties or seventies, where she played a widowed black mother of a little boy. She was a nurse, if I remember. The black community felt that her lifestyle was not realistically represented, and they were also upset about the fact that the story did not include a strong black male character."

"Yes, I remember the show. The star was a famous black singer," Desiree recalled, nodding her head.

"That's right. Yet, I can swear to you, Dr. Simon, that of all the times I have watched the nanny show they have never portrayed a positive Jewish *male* character, either. But as far as I know, not a single Jew has expressed any concern or offense."

Ms. Moskowitz frowned for a minute, looked down at her hands, and continued. "Dr. Simon, in my opinion, that black actress's show wasn't even a fraction as offensive—if at all—to the black community as the nanny show is to the Jews! But I heard that the woman's show was *canceled* because of the complaints."

"As I understand it, Ms. Moskowitz, the writers of that nanny show are Jewish themselves," Desiree stated, wondering what Ms. Moskowitz's response would be.

She looked at Desiree accusingly and raised her voice. "And there were Jewish collaborators during the war, too! So what?" At that instant Rachel Moskowitz looked at Desiree, smiled, and said, "Thank you, Dr. Simon."

"There is no need to thank me, Ms. Moskowitz. You are here to air the things that disturb you."

"I've just decided to write a letter suggesting that they fix the script. I can no longer quietly sit by, watching or trying to ignore the flagrantly insulting mockery of my own people. Maybe I could suggest that they drop the negative ethnic stereotype thing, and give it more of a Lucy and Desi Arnaz dynamic. Funny, but without racial condescension, you know?" she said dreamily.

"Umm-hmm." Desiree nodded slightly, smiling to herself. Exactly what we all needed these days, less complaining and bitching and more creative problem solving, she thought.

"Besides—" She started to laugh. "—I want to find a nice Jewish boy to marry!"

Jewish women shared a common dilemma with African American women, Desiree noted. It seemed that both groups were finding it increasingly difficult to find suitable men from their particular ethnic tribes with whom they could form relationships and build families.

Desiree had observed in her practice over the past fifteen years or so, that there was no other group of American women with this problem. Not a single Hispanic, Asian, or Anglo American female patient of hers had ever expressed concern over the theft of "their" men by the shiksa, the Clairol girl . . . or anyone else. In fact, African American and Jewish American women were the only ones who appeared to believe that they could actually lay exclusive claim on a specific population of men.

"By the way, Dr. Simon, what does your sister think of all the insanity dominating the television talk show circuit these days?"

"My sister may appear to be powerful, but it's stressful and complicated no matter how beloved she may be. She is merely an employee of a large communications conglomerate," Desiree said with a tone that she hoped sounded empathetic.

Rachel Moskowitz winked, then tossed her hair over her shoulders. "I'll call you, Dr. Simon."

She smiled, shaking Desiree's hand before sweeping confidently out the door.

As Desiree watched Ms. Moskowitz depart she laughed to herself, knowing that this young lady would just *plotz* if she knew that her very own shrink had used her own nappy locks, high, round, black-lady derriere, and exotic, cherry-wood complexion to "steal" a prized Jewish boy to be her very own.

Having stared at Ms. Moskowitz's mass of dark kinky hair, her mind quickly switched to a subject that she had been pondering for years—particularly whenever she was confronted with a white Jewish person's African-looking tresses.

She had often wondered what undisclosed aspect of European history would explain the prevalence of this kind of African hair texture among so many Jews from Eastern Europe. It had obviously been actively suppressed since she had never heard any explanation for this phenomenon. African Americans spoke openly about the historical dynamics that had contributed to the hair of diluted African characteristics that many of them possessed. What's the big secret with the European Jews? Was it because they were suppressing a period of history in which bands of Africans raped and pillaged European Jewish communities—she doubted this—or was it something much more positive that had been pushed back in historical memory by the negative impact of European colonialism and its distorted concepts of racial supremacy?

She wondered.

Nevertheless, getting back to Ms. Moskowitz's search for a nice Jewish man, Desiree had realized at an early age that finding a proper lover or mate had a lot less to do with which racial or religious group one was born into, than it did with a mutual physical attraction and—more importantly—shared values.

She was in complete agreement, though, with Ms. Moskowitz in the opinion that media images played a large part in how people related to or approached one another and that these days it's being played from the dark side.

Thinking about all of her black female patients and their quest to find a suitable black mate, Desiree grinned to herself as she realized that she was no longer sure what being "black" actually meant these days. Aletha's Reggie could physically pass for an Italian or any other Mediterranean-type "white" man. Her sister's producer, Veronica McPheerson, looked more white than Ms. Moskowitz, and as far as she could surmise, McPheerson's features hadn't even been cosmetically tampered with in any way. She had also known numerous unmistakably black-skinned, kinky-haired African Americans whose value systems chillingly reflected ideas and attitudes normally attributed to right-wing, conservative Anglo-Saxon whites.

The crux of this attractive, unmarried, thirty-five-year-old Rachel Moskowitz's deep distress had to do with the kinds of unrelenting negative racial messages being disseminated. They touched members of every so-called ethnic minority on one level or another in this country.

In her case, it was compounded by the fact that her parents, much like her patient Debra Parker's mother, were no help. Moskowitz had said that they had been pressuring her for over a decade to find a husband as quickly as possible and give them, Desiree noted with more than a bit of amused irony, blond-haired, blue-eyed Jewish grandchildren.

Aryan Hebrews, Desiree supposed.

Rachel Moskowitz didn't get a single bit of credit from them for her ability to rise to the fierce challenges of being a young Jewish woman and becoming a partner at one of the city's largest law firms, by the age of thirty-two. She was simply an unmarried woman with a good job, in their eyes, Ms. Moskowitz had said.

It was no wonder, thought Desiree, that perfectly intelligent people all over this nation were losing their friggin' minds.

Desiree almost laughed out loud as she leaned back in her chair to indulge in the recollection of the day she had first met her husband's parents.

When David had introduced her to his parents in their suburban Scarsdale,

New York, home, his father had been graciously open and welcoming, while his mother had kept staring at her as if she were a scornful, taunting black ghost, while intermittently praising all the lovely colored maids she had known throughout her life.

After a while Desiree noticed that David's mother had chosen to assert the family's Jewishness in the menu she had decided to serve everyone that evening.

Desiree had had nothing against the appetizers of gefilte fish, creamed herring, and matzo; in fact, she loved it. But when they sat down in the dining room and found that, in addition, dinner was to be cabbage borscht, brisket, potato kugel with vegetables, Mount Hermon Israeli wine, and cheesecake for dessert, she began to feel an uncomfortable twinge of alienation—which had quite obviously been David's mother's intent.

Relief swept over her when David looked at the table, laughed, and said, "Mom, what's with you? You cook Italian!"

He looked over at Desiree and his father with a flicker of astonishment and added, "The only time we ever ate Jewish food, Desiree, was when our grandparents were visiting. In fact—" David stared suspiciously at his mother, who had started to nervously blush. "—we've always celebrated Christmas *and* Hanukkah and had baked ham with pineapple for Easter."

"And breakfast would have never been complete without bacon or pork sausage, probably just like at your family's home, Desiree." David's father boomed with laughter, then winked at his wife.

Desiree decided to join in the preposterous scenario by cunningly interjecting. "*We* usually ate lox, cream cheese, onions, and capers with bagels for breakfast, Doctor."

Mrs. Simon appeared to come undone, but pulled herself together quickly and began to talk about the days when she and her husband rode the Freedom Buses and participated in the March on Washington and witnessed Dr. King's speech.

It was a truly bizarre evening, as it apparently usually is—from all accounts—the first time anyone meets their future in-laws.

Later David told her that when he was alone with his mother, she had asked him why he couldn't find a nice Jewish girl to marry, although she was sure that this Desiree would make a splendid wife for some "nice colored boy."

David told her that he had looked his mother squarely in the eyes and demanded to know why she hadn't bothered to ask him if Desiree was, in fact, a Jewish girl. After all, anyone with half a brain, he had said to her, knew that being Jewish was less a race than it was a philosophical way of living.

David's mother was struck dumb. She turned red in the face and walked away abruptly, muttering something to the affect of "You know what I mean," although Mrs. Simon realized she was no longer certain that she understood *anything* anymore.

David's father was of no help to his wife; he had been seduced by Desiree's charm, intelligence, and sensually exotic good looks, or so David had told her. Dr. Simon was a *man*, after all. A Jewish man, at that. His ostensibly easy acceptance of Desiree had been no surprise to her since it seemed— considering the large percentage of intermarriage among Jewish men—that they have always expressed a profound appreciation for the female aesthetic and personality in all its diversity.

Of course, over the years of meeting her various boyfriends' parents Desiree had mastered the skillful balancing act that involved charming the fathers without threatening the mothers in such a way that would make them feel as if Desiree could steal both the husbands *and* the sons.

According to David, his father had said that if he was lucky enough to attract and get this lovely "Zipporah woman," as he had called her, to marry him, more power to him. Maybe she'd even be willing to convert to Judaism. There were certainly a lot more *serious* problems in the world than *this*!

Desiree had, while exploring the possibility of conversion, met a number of what she had come to call Nazi rabbis, usually among the Reform denomination. They were people who had been born in Jewish families, but were actually closet Gentiles in their thinking and cultural allegiances, lustfully wishing on most levels to be accepted by the white Christian majority.

She had also learned that David's father had nearly exhausted himself over the years, trying to convince his son to become a doctor, as he himself was, but had now come to the conclusion that this son, like David's brother who was also an artist, had opted for a more interesting life. Dr. Simon had found that David pretty much did exactly whatever he chose to do and that most of his choices had worked out fine.

"Mazel tov, son!" Dr. Simon had given his son his blessings, assuring David that his mother would soon come around.

A year later, after they were married in their simple civil ceremony, David and Desiree held the most delightful Seder at their home that the Simon family could remember, or at least, that's what they said.

Of course, to Desiree blacks and Jews celebrating the liberation from slavery and oppression together seemed perfectly reasonable and appropriate.

Of all the marriages in the two families, it was David and Desiree's that had endured . . . and blossomed.

As for Aletha, she had been with the same Reginald for years, looking for emotional fulfillment in, evidently, the completely wrong place or wrong *way*. Their brother, Marshall, on the other hand, preferred to lead his life in private, making an occasional appearance with a woman named Janeen who appeared at family gatherings with him every now and then.

David's younger brother, Elliot, a filmmaker in Los Angeles, for years had had nothing but a long line of serially monogamous live-in relationships with seemingly passive and jittery Anglo-Saxon, Christian-like blondes. It seemed that each and every one, to her knowledge, ended up starring in one of his movies. In these films they consistently portrayed shallow, morally deficient, neurotically unpredictable companions to some poor, complex, passionate Jewish man with noble ethical qualities. Or else they played the poor-white-trash wives of some run-of-the-mill white man who lived in a trailer park or dirty shack on the wrong side of town.

Elliot Simon had very few fans among black folks—if any. As one of her clients, a struggling black actress, had complained to her, Elliot never used black actors in major roles in his films. Blacks were always merely sidekicks or extras. Desiree knew that she would have been highly insulted if he *had* decided to include black people in prominent roles in his films. But she couldn't say that to her client, nor could she tell the young woman that Elliot Simon was her brother-in-law. She had personally reassured Elliot years ago that blacks could hardly play, effectively or plausibly in her mind, any signifi-cant role in the peculiar neurotic scenarios of Elliot Simon's cinematic white people.

Desiree got up from her comfortable armchair, walked over to sit behind her desk. She shook her head wearily and laughed to herself, thinking about how pathetically obsessed Elliot was with white Gentiles. She feared that one day if he didn't resolve this problem, he might bring devastating pain upon one of his unsuspecting Gentile paramours. Knowing Elliot's penchant for melodrama, it would probably be something odious like vindictively throwing some nonwhite woman in his white Gentile woman's face.

She was glad that her husband's brother lived on the other side of the country. While others might find him quirky or eccentric, she thought he was strange.

She rummaged through her desk drawers in search of a cigarette. It had been six days since her last one, and the craving still hadn't gone away. A girlfriend of hers had given her the name of a Chinese herbalist who she claimed could concoct a tea that would take away the withdrawal symptoms. Time to schedule an appointment with him, she remembered.

She unearthed a crumpled pack of stale cigarettes pushed under some papers way back in the drawer. There were matches folded between the cellophane and the paper of the cigarette pack. She pulled out the bent, torn, and yellowing tube of tantalizing tobacco, and rolled it between her thumb and forefinger to give it back its rounded shape. As she hypnotically lifted it to her lips a guilty knot formed in her abdomen.

She quickly dropped the cigarette and tore each and every remaining one into a flaky pile of toxic debris, determined to make it "clean" into the seventh day.

Desiree swept this garbage off her desk into the trash pail. How appropriate, she thought. Now that she was getting close to leaving her practice, she thought that she should rid the files in her head of a life's worth of accumulated nonsense.

Desiree thought back to the day she had announced to *her* folks her intention to marry David. They had reacted as if her choice of a husband was some act of betrayal. She was not at all surprised by her father's initial silent disapproval upon meeting David, nor was she surprised that his reaction gradually changed to respect and then a warm acceptance. It had made sense to her that her father might have felt slighted by his daughter's choice of a man who seemed, at least on the surface, completely different from himself. It would naturally appear as a form of personal rejection in favor of the "enemy."

Her mother's reaction, on the other hand, was confusing, to say the least.

In all of Desiree's years of growing up in the Brown home, she had never heard her mother express anything but contempt toward black men, even though she had been married to one—the same one—for almost half a century. It was always, "Can't trust a black man to do this," or, "You can't trust a black man to do that." It was evident that her mother was living in a marriage where she was unfulfilled in some way, and she had always applied this sweeping generalization to *all* black men, for as far back as Desiree could remember.

Mothers! They can wear you out, she thought, trying to control her annoyance toward what she had considered her mother's hypocritical stance on the issue of her marriage to David. Her mother had never, as far as she could remember, expressed any reservations about interracial relationships. In fact, the message that Desiree had received in her formative years was one that made her feel that if she wanted to find happiness and gratification, that she'd just better avoid the whole find-a-good-black-man crusade that the majority of the sisters were embroiled in.

Desiree's dating patterns hadn't really posed any particular problem in her social life. She had dated the men whom she had fancied and who had fancied her.

There were a couple of blond, blue-eyed WASPs. These affairs were rather brief because she, quite frankly, felt she could never completely trust their intentions.

In her experience, they never brought much to the table in a relationship. They were too opportunistic, always out to maximize their profits, even in the area of romance. Of course, perhaps there was really nothing there at all—for *her*, at least. Desiree had no way of knowing, and she certainly didn't have the patience to find out. Life was too short to mess around with a bunch of guys who initially appeared to enjoy her gregarious ethnicity, then after a while attempted to transform her into a vapid, grinningly submissive Stepford wife.

Besides, a frightening number of her white friends' mothers and several patients were married to WASP men who had become, over the years, tight-lipped, lockjawed alcoholics. Desiree had had no intention of setting herself up to live in a world in which she had to shroud herself in a blanket of chemical dependency in order to manage some kind of pseudocompatibility with her husband.

She had eventually grown weary and annoyed by the need that some of them had to use their relationship and her race as fodder for social rebellion. A couple of times she had thought that her presence in those boyfriends' parents' homes was accompanied by some silent appeal for visibility on the men's part. It often felt as if they were saying to their folks, "Look what I brought home, Mummy! Do you *see* me now? Do you *really* see me?"

In addition to the Anglo-Saxon boys, she dated Philip Akai, a terrific and gorgeous Japanese American law student. They had sort of drifted apart after he graduated from law school.

After months of unsuccessfully looking for work on the East Coast, where he had preferred to live, he finally had to accept a position in San Francisco. The West Coast, he had told her, was more tolerant toward Asian Americans. When she last heard from him, not long ago, he happily informed her that he had opened up his own practice—Akai, Chin, and Sanchez—with a Chinese American and a Filipino lawyer in Honolulu.

Desiree found that she preferred Jewish men, anyway. In her experience, they never came into a relationship either emotionally or intellectually empty-handed. None were ever threatened by her intelligence, and consequently, each one brought out some latent talent or asset.

She had also found that Jewish men made wonderfully attentive and imaginative lovers. But then, Desiree smiled wryly to herself, perhaps she was not giving herself enough credit that she just knew what to do with them.

While she was in college, a sister would sometimes dare to confront her about her dating habits. They always started with the issue of the rape of black women by white men. She had often felt that they should have rejoiced in the fact that she was one less black woman in competition for a member of this "endangered group" of men.

Surprisingly, the brothers never bothered her at all. She figured it was because one black woman dating nonblack men had done nothing to diminish their own deep pool of available women of every color in the rainbow.

Before her marriage to David, her mother had asked the inevitable—as did David's: "What about the children?"

The "one-drop theory" of American racial definitions assured that the children would quite simply be black. This question would have been less galling if she, Desiree, had been a white woman. After all, she felt that white women would undoubtedly find it challenging to raise black children, having never been black themselves, but what African American woman could possibly have problems raising a child of her own race? Black women have historically raised all shades and types of black children, and those children of white American families, as well.

David's response to his mother had simply been that their children would obviously be black, but look like Israelis.

Desiree had told her in-laws that if she and David found that they were committed to Jewish values, she'd simply convert and raise the children as Jews. Like many American children they would probably eventually choose their own religion.

Nevertheless, Desiree and David had decided that they had absolutely no intention of having any children at all. She wouldn't want children even if she were married to a man of her *own* race . . . and neither would he. She felt that the world was just too sick at the moment. They'd leave that child-rearing stuff to braver souls.

Her plan had been to just do her part by practicing psychology as long as she was able, and David would write entertaining novels.

Over the years Desiree had found that her patient list had become exclusively female. This was not at all by design. It had just turned out that way.

Recently, however, Desiree Simon had grown exhausted. Fed up with it all. She needed a long and overdue sabbatical.

Desiree got up from her desk to make a cup of tea. As she sipped the warm drink she looked out her office window onto the cold, icy New York City streets and thought about how she and her husband were so anxious to close the deal on the sale of their house and move on to explore warmer, sunnier climes.

First, they planned to spend six months in Maui. From there, they would travel through the South Sea Islands, then on to Europe, where they would begin to look for a house to buy someplace in their favorite area—the Amalfi Coast of Italy. They had been dreaming of this ever since they had spent their honeymoon there. They had returned every chance they could get over the past twenty years. Now that David was firmly established as a writer, they could live anywhere in the world. Desiree would now be able to recuperate from this burnout from working with troubled patients and start to paint again. Maybe she'd finally study sculpture. She'd always wanted to, having never had the time before.

She and David would begin a whole new life.

The problems that oppress New York City single women couldn't possibly be at the center of the world's most pressing concerns. Desiree and David Simon planned to live out the next chapter of their lives searching for the meaning of life, on a broader and more global scale.

A nagging personal revelation came into sharp focus in Desiree's mind. She didn't want to sell her house at all. She realized that she needed a permanent release from this type of helping profession, but she didn't want to just give up her house. They had put so much work into it over the years, and she loved the memories that they'd created there. It had been David's idea that they shed, as he called it, all the excess baggage in order to begin a new life. She had been so wrapped up in her burnout and escape fantasies that she had never told him how uncomfortable she was with the idea. What if they settled into some foreign country and then things changed in such a way that, as foreigners, they found themselves unwelcomed? The thought made her shudder as if she were outside right then in that blizzard coatless.

She was going to have to break it to him. The sooner the better. He'd probably think she was being capricious, but since they hadn't found any buyers yet, as far as she knew, this revised plan shouldn't pose any major problems.

Desiree returned to her desk and sat down, unbuttoning the jacket of her gray pinstriped Bill Blass wool pantsuit. She reached over for the newspaper in the magazine rack and sighed sadly as she thumbed through the paper.

Wars. Famine. Downsizing. Domestic violence. Racial strife. Gang violence. Ethnic cleansing. Evil *everywhere* . . . or so it appeared. Despite it all, she and David had decided not to allow all this frightening news to deter them from traveling and enjoying the world. They'd just have to be cautious and stay informed. And not sell their house, she laughed to herself, realizing that she could use the headlines to bolster her reservations.

She shuffled absentmindedly through the day's mail. A bright red envelope popped from the pile and landed on the floor next to her. Probably a Christmas card, she thought, picking it up and turning it over to check the return address. She smiled and quickly tore it open with her brass letter opener. The card was from her life-long friend, Joy. She and Joy had become friends way back in high school.

It wasn't a Christmas card, but a note saying that the family would be in New York with their two children for the Christmas holiday and would like to get together for dinner.

Whenever Joy came in from Monterrey, California, where they had lived for the last five years, Desiree and David usually had them up for dinner at their home in Connecticut on Christmas Eve.

Joy was one of the few women that Desiree knew that did not have a chip on her shoulder toward men. Joy and her husband were one of the two couples that Desiree knew who had been married as long as she and David.

She reached in her desk to get her pocketbook. Before dropping the card in the handbag, she noticed that on the back there was a tale printed in a beautiful calligraphy script by a writer named Helen Chu. It read:

Legend of the Sleeping Princess

It is said that an empress began the practice of footbinding. In ancient times, everyone admired large feet. The feet of the Empress Tu Chin were considered particularly large and beautiful. But the empress had one bad habit. She walked in her sleep. Every night while everyone else was asleep, the empress crept out of bed. Dreaming of cool night air, bright moonlight, birds, and wild beasts, she would wander into the forest. The emperor, fearing for her safety, consulted the court physician. He said, "perhaps it's her feet. They are large and need to walk much. They do not get enough during the day and so they wander off at night." Then he magically reduced her feet to a third of their size. The empress cried for shame at her tiny feet. To remedy the problem, the emperor ordered everyone to copy the empress.

From that time on, tiny feet were quite fashionable.

Desiree giggled at the tale and its contrast to the usual theme of her patient sessions, dropped the card in her purse, and snapped it shut.

The receptionist buzzed the intercom and announced to Desiree that Mr. Simon had arrived to take her out to lunch.

Desiree prayed that David didn't plan to take her to any restaurant farther than a block away. She reached under her desk for her boots and put them on. Lord knew that she was sick and tired of trekking around in all this cold, snowy weather.

She grabbed her pocketbook, opened it again, dug around, and took out her small compact. She quickly dusted the shine off the tip of her nose, snapped the compact shut, dropped it back into the bag, and got up to meet her husband.

Desiree arrived in the reception area just as her secretary struck up a conversation with David.

He was standing next to the woman's desk, covered in snow, with a black, knit sock hat pulled down past his eyebrows, talking with that warm, big-lipped, crooked smile of his that graced the photographs on the back covers of all his novels.

He was tall, dark, curly-haired, and handsome, she thought to herself, in that Semitic way found in Jewish boys with heavy doses of Russian blood. And "Miss Thing" was fluttering her eyelashes all over her silly face, grinning at him like a ninny.

The woman was talking to Desiree's husband in that high-pitched, little-girl voice that certain types of black women put on when talking to white men who were married to or involved with black women. She tried to contain her annoyance at this asinine behavior, thinking that her secretary was exactly the kind of black woman who was the most likely candidate to make a pass at her husband. This was the kind of cowardly woman who came on to white guys who they *knew* were involved with sisters, because they were too timid to risk rejection from those who they weren't sure were attracted to black women.

David noticed the peculiar look on his wife's face and quickly explained, "Uh . . . Desiree . . . Ms. Johnson here was just asking me if I thought that Michael Jackson's marriages were publicity stunts." David had no idea what triggered those cold, blank looks on Desiree's face in certain situations, and he didn't bother to delve into it. He knew that if it was important, she would most definitely explain it to him sooner or later. Besides, he knew he hadn't been guilty of anything. He smiled at his wife, who then rolled her eyes with boredom at the subject at hand. "I told her that I didn't see why Michael Jackson would need to get married for publicity. Why would Jackson need to generate any more publicity than he already—"

"Umm-hmm," Desiree mumbled, still fighting a laugh. She turned away from the two of them while reaching into her closet to take out her heavy Mongolian lambskin coat.

Even though she was convinced that David was innocently unaware of it, she knew that this silly bitch was using a discussion of Michael Jackson to make a sly dig at the Simons' interracial marriage, implying that there had to be motives other than love—most likely material ones—for mixed-race alliances.

Ms. Johnson watched David put his arm around his wife's furry waist as they walked out the door. She then leaned back, put her feet up on the desk, and picked up the phone to make a call.

CHAPTER ELEVEN

*D*espite the horrible weather, Chez Josette restaurant was crowded as usual. At least David had chosen a place that was just around the corner from Desiree's office. The waiter whisked them to their usual booth and took their coats away.

At that same moment a big, blond, hard-looking young woman approached their booth and shoved a book in her husband's face.

"Oooh, Mr. Simon," the woman said. "Please autograph this for me. I've read *all* your novels. I'm your number one fan!"

How did these people manage to know when some writer is going to show up in a restaurant? Did they carry books around with them every day hoping to run into the author?

It was downright weird!

David noticed that strange look on his wife's face again. It always made him nervous because sometimes it was followed by an increasingly emotional lecture. After over twenty years of marriage he had become extremely sensitive to her moods and tried to accommodate her, but she had an artist's temperament, despite the fact that she was a shrink. It must be a Brown family thing.

"I would be happy to sign your book, miss."

"To Ethel Cox, please." She placed the book in front of him, oblivious to the hostile stare from Desiree.

David was not.

"Ms. Cox, I'd like you to meet my wife, Dr. Desiree Simon." He glanced over at his wife and began to sign the title page of his latest book, *Bombay*.

Ethel Cox glanced quickly and indifferently at Desiree.

Desiree rose abruptly from her seat.

"Darling," she said, possessively, placing her hand on his forearm. She glanced at her husband, then at the smitten woman, who had a decidedly predatory look on her face. "I'm going to the ladies' room. I'll be right back." She gave his arm a viselike squeeze and released it.

As she quickly walked away, David watched her quizzically. He handed the book back to the woman and signaled the waiter.

In the other corner of the dining room, Debra Parker sat, her mouth agape.

Even though she was sitting in a corner area, snugly protected by a potted corn plant, she could see the entire room. When Ms. Parker had decided to have a quick lunch at Chez Josette she never expected she'd run into something like *this*.

She slammed closed the book that she had been reading. It was the latest in the series of thriller books that one of her favorite authors, David Simon, recently had published. Debra looked at the back-cover picture of the author's face, then glared back over at the man that was accompanying her psychologist, Dr. Desiree Simon.

It was the same man.

"Oh, my God . . . oh my God . . . ," Debra gasped to herself. "Bombay, my ass. More like ofay. Girlfriend is married to . . . a *white* man! She never would have ever connected the name Simon to both the writer and her psychologist.

It was an outrage!

Debra Parker didn't believe in interracial relationships. In her opinion, people involved in mixed matches were all self-hating sellouts, people whose lifestyles confused the important issues of ethnic allegiances in this racist society.

She sniffed with indignation, stabbed into one of the shrimp on her plate of *curry de crevettes*, violently trying to pierce one of the embryonic-looking crustaceans, and sent it flying into the plate of the diner at the table next to her.

"I'm so sorry, sir," she apologized to the man who had jolted with a start at the sudden intrusion into his soup.

"That's okay, dear," the man responded cordially, then returned to his dish.

How could Dr. Simon help the people when she was actually a collaborator with men who oppress people of color? Debra thought.

Besides, what could that Dr. Simon bitch know about the problems she faced with the brothers, when she wasn't even involved with one?

At that moment, as she watched Desiree disappear into the ladies' room, Debra Parker felt profoundly betrayed and abused.

In the bathroom, Desiree stood leaning against the washbasin and stared into the mirror at her immaculately made-up face.

She realized—and had been pondering over it for some time now—that when she closed her practice she would graduate to the status of a homeless— although David would probably call it carefree—"lady of leisure nobody" married to a famous novelist. The mere thought of being regarded that way frightened her.

Wherever they went, people would be flocking all over her husband and canceling her out with looks of dismissal or indifference—just like that Ethel Cox.

As she washed her hands with the deliciously scented soap that Chez Josette supplied, she remembered with not a small bit of relief that in the places they planned to go, people weren't as intrusive and starstruck as they were in the United States. Whenever she and David had traveled out of the country, she recalled, they were always able to enjoy a certain degree of anonymity. Even in places where her husband *was* recognized, the most that would happen would be that some restaurant manager or waiter would send them a bottle of wine, on the house. She knew that she was blessed by the fact that David always showed sensitivity toward her feelings about their lives among his adoring public. They had learned together over the years exactly how to watch each other's backs in that milieu. The public, as fawning as they may appear, could be erratic in their loyalties and oftentimes potentially dangerous.

When she arrived back at their table, the fan, Ethel Cox, had already departed and David had ordered some bizarre-looking cocktails. The two glasses were filled with a piña colada–looking substance, but sticking out of the liquid were two bananas in each glass—one naked and one covered in chocolate.

"What the hell is *this*, David?"

"I call it 'gringos on the beach,' in honor of our new lives in the sun." He laughed mischievously.

"Very funny," she said dryly. Unfortunately she wasn't in the mood to enjoy his eccentric sense of humor at the moment. Job burnout was getting to her.

"David, I've got to go back to work. I can't drink anything alcoholic. I won't be fit for—"

"So . . . . we'll just toast to our new lives," he interrupted, trying to inject some much-needed humor. "I ordered you the special—the *cuisses de poulet a la tomate et au basilic*. I hope you don't mind. I remember that you enjoyed it the last time we were here. I'm having the fish—the *dos de cabillaud au beurre blanc*."

"You've got to cut back on butter, David. Remember your cholesterol," Desiree snapped. She *had* minded that he had presumptuously ordered for her before she even had a chance to think about what she wanted to eat. Nevertheless, it was cold outside and that warm dish was what she probably needed.

"David, have you ever seen that sitcom about the Jewish nanny?" she asked before taking a sip from her water glass.

"Yes, of course. Why?"

"Do you find it offensive to Jewish people?"

David laughed and said, "To tell you the truth, Dez, I find it an extremely misogynistic program. *All* of the women on that show are treated like buffoons. Why do you ask?"

"I was just wondering if you found it anti-Semitic."

David reflected for a while and said, "I guess it could be interpreted that way. But the way I see it is that right now we seem to be in some kind of media cycle where *everyone* is being attacked or ridiculed. This kind of dynamic surfaces, as you know, whenever there is confusion in the economy. During times like these, they create an environment where no one has any credibility and everyone becomes suspicious of everybody."

"Who is *they*?" asked Desiree.

"I dunno."

"Are you afraid or concerned about this, David?"

"Yep."

"What do you think our responsibility is in the matter?"

"I dunno. Just to do what we're planning to do, I guess—be a moving target." He laughed, reaching over to take his wife's hand.

"I guess. But you know what really gets to me, David?"

"What's that, hon?"

"So many of my patients come to therapy for help, when in reality they are quite reasonably disturbed by irrational situations that seem to be imposed on them by neurotics, psychotics, and plain misguided, narrow-minded, mean-spirited people—the kind of people who would never go for therapy themselves."

Desiree knew that a necessary reality of life in the nineties was having a stress-relieving mechanism in place. Without it, everyone was at risk of suffering a premillennium meltdown. In many ways, that was her role as a therapist. But she and David also knew that they had to perform that function for one another, as well.

As the holidays drew near, Desiree's clients grew more agitated, felt more out of sorts, and a few became outright despondent. The responsibility she felt toward them weighed heavily on her shoulders. Aletha's misadventures compounded the pressure on Desiree. As a result, Desiree and David had increased the frequency of these getaway lunches.

She'd even developed a kind of shorthand to let David know what to expect. This was venting day, a relatively harmless but extremely important expulsion of frustrations; other times she would tell him to anticipate lava flow—a few tears, free-flowing anger. Both of those were necessary to prevent the extremely rare full-scale eruption, complete with yelling and a tossed object or two.

Depending on the type of alert Desiree sent out, David would calm or challenge, commiserate or cower. As a writer, he was by nature an observer, and he appreciated the variety of Desiree's displays. David and Desiree both knew that it was the people who walked around like placid peaks who posed the most threat, who were most likely to erupt without warning. They were the kind of people about whom—following some catastrophic episode—neighbors would say, "He was always such a quiet person."

"Well, Dez, they come to you in order to have a safe, nonjudgmental place to air their frustrations and concerns. That's important. I would call it good preventative medicine," he said, hoping to reassure her.

"But I've been feeling for years now that my efforts have been wasted exercises in futility."

"I can understand how you can feel that way sometimes, Desiree, but you know that you've helped a lot of people. Imagine what this place would be like if no one went to therapy."

"I don't think I want to." Desiree smiled.

"Oh, that reminds me. Aletha left a message on the machine this morning."

Desiree shot David a concerned look, "What did she have to say?"

"She said that you should call her. She claimed that she had written a ten-page letter to Reggie, asking for forgiveness, I suppose; but it was returned to her stamped 'moved; no forwarding address.' "

"Oh, shock and amazement," laughed Desiree sarcastically. "So, what am *I* supposed to do? Shit, David, I'm sick and tired of talking about other people's problems. I have a few of my own, you know. I can't play both big sister and therapist to Aletha. She needs to go see her own private shrink or something."

"That's what she's trying to do, in her own Aletha way. Call her, Dez. You know you're the only one she ever listens to. I think you should sit down and talk to her again. She seems to still be teetering over the deep end. Her voice sounded peculiar. You've got to make her understand that if you shoot somebody—"

"David, why don't *you* sit down and talk to your brother, Elliot, about his sordid relationship with *his* women?" she asked with a slight grin curling at her upper lip.

"I can't," David said simply. "He doesn't listen to me."

"Exactly," said Desiree definitively.

"But, Desiree, Elliot hasn't broken into anyone's house in an attempt to blow them to smithereens—"

"Not *yet*," Desiree teased, thinking about Elliot and the fact that gun play wasn't an entirely impossible scenario. In her opinion, Elliot was just as much of a control freak as her sister. Maybe that's why he'd chosen moviemaking as a career, she thought.

"Really, Desiree, I think you should call her. Have dinner with her. She's your sister and she needs you, you know."

She smiled at David. She loved him for the fact, among numerous other reasons, that he did not regard her sister as a raving lunatic. She loved him because she knew that he liked Aletha and respected her drive and ambition.

The whole damned Brown and Simon clans shared the same characteristics in that area.

"David, I love Aletha, but I have my own problems, you know?"

Of course, he knew.

He held up his glass to make a toast and pointed to hers for her to do the same. They clinked glasses as he said, "We've sold the house, kid. So now, we're on our way."

Desiree's expression wasn't what he expected. In fact, she looked like she was passing a kidney stone.

He was perfectly aware that she was frightened about the prospect of losing her identity in their new life, but he also knew that she was bone tired. Fifteen years of dealing with other people's emotional problems was beginning to get to her. He had never mentioned to Desiree that he noticed the thin new lines of tension under her eyes or the recently accentuated gravelly sound in her voice. Five years ago, when they had become financially independent because of his book sales, he had tried to convince her to close her practice and rest. Begin painting again, or do anything else she might want to do. David wanted his wife to relax and luxuriate in his success. She wouldn't quit, though, because she said that she couldn't abandon her patients.

"I can't believe you're not rejoicing over the fact that we are actually about to realize our goal."

"I'm just too tired to take it all in, that's all."

Maybe I should tell him about the house now, she thought, reaching over to take a tiny sip of her gringos on the beach. But she let the moment pass into thoughts of Aletha.

Over the years, as he had watched her patient list grow longer, David had begun to worry that she might develop high blood pressure from the stress. He had read that black people were more prone to this condition than others, and it seemed to run in her family. He refused to let her work herself into a stroke or a heart attack.

He had suggested that she retire and maybe try to write some self-help books since she was so worried about her patients. She would just smile and tell him it was a great idea, yet she had done nothing to make it happen. This had pissed him off. Desiree's stubbornness and occasional self-righteousness

had frustrated him over the years. She had no idea that he had secretly nick-
named her Saint Dez.

Yet, he understood her, which was why he wanted to get his wife out of
America for a while, to places where people's worth wasn't defined or mea-
sured by a title or the number of hours one spent on a job site.

David could empathize; after all, he was a writer. When he quit his teaching
job to write full time, he'd had a hard time adjusting to people treating him as
if he was unemployed. Neighbors would watch his wife leave their home to
drive to the city every day, and shake their heads with misguided condescension when he went out on their front lawn with his cup of morning coffee to
pick up the mail. They probably figured that black Desiree was this white
man's slave. He was glad that Louis Farrakhan, with his Jewish slave-owner
theories, didn't live next door. He would have been in big trouble, he laughed
to himself.

"David, I just can't deal with Aletha's drama. We haven't been all that
close in years. Why should I begin to cultivate a friendship now when we'll
soon be moving away from here? You *know* that the only time she *initiates*
any kind of contact is when she needs something."

"Yeah, but she's your sister. I don't believe that you can hold your
relatives—especially close ones—to the same behavior standards that you do
friends."

"Oh, David ... *pul-eese*! You treat your relationship with your brother,
Elliot, the same way I treat mine with Aletha."

"But can't you just have dinner with her? She can be pretty entertaining;
it's not like she's one of your patients. She's going to do what she wants
anyway. She probably just needs a sounding board."

"That's what I do for a living, David," she said as the waiter returned with
their dishes.

"Those ladies over there would like to buy you a drink, Mr. Simon," the
waiter said, pointing over to three giggling women who were sitting at the bar
waving.

"Thanks, but no thanks," he said quickly, noticing Desiree's growing
agitation.

"As you wish." The waiter smiled, looking at Desiree. He walked away.

"Don't be annoyed, honey. Think about it, Dez. At least I'm not a rock star," he said, responding to his wife's look of annoyance, then glanced quickly over again at the women at the bar.

He had to admit that he enjoyed the recognition, though. Most of his days were spent locked up in his lonely study, pounding away at the computer, tussling with pushy, demanding fictional characters.

"Whatever." She sighed, slicing into her chicken.

"You realize, Dez, that your sister, being hugely famous and all, probably doesn't have a single friend she can confide in. This fish is delicious! Would you like to try some?"

"No thanks."

"Do you like the chicken?" he asked apprehensively, acknowledging to himself that he had been rather cavalier in assuming that it was what she would have chosen.

"Yes. It's delicious. Good choice, David," she said, smiling to herself, having noticed his guilty expression.

"Anyway Aletha—being who she is—probably gets most of her feedback from the masses who watch her show. As a matter of fact, yesterday her show was about domestic violence perpetrated by women," he said, picking at a slice of steamed eggplant on his plate. "A couple of the women had even been interviewed from prison."

The irony of it caused them both to break out into hysterical laughter.

"She could have ended up a guest on her own program!" Desiree gasped for breath, tears of laughter streaming down her face.

"It's really not funny. It's—it's tragic." David was trying to place it all back in its proper perspective, but he was trapped in an uncontrollable laughing jag.

"Drink some water, honey," Desiree said, looking away from him so she wouldn't lose control again, as well. "By the way, David?"

"Yes, hon?"

"I don't want to sell the house."

David stared at her in disbelief. It had been Desiree who had rushed around frantically marking most of their belongings for storage, until they could find their new house. He was convinced that both of them had become tired of

living in a place where they had to shovel themselves out of snow and drive—
or rather, skid around—in ice for almost half of every year. He wondered
what had happened to make her change her mind so suddenly.

"Why don't you want to sell the house?" he repeated calmly. "Why have
you changed your mind just when we have finally found buyers?"

"I never really wanted to sell, David. It was all your idea."

"It *was?* Well, why didn't you say something earlier? Since when have I
tried to force decisions on you?"

"I guess I never got a chance to really think this sale thing out because I've
been so bogged down with other people's issues. That's why. Also I didn't
want to rain on your parade."

"My parade? I thought we were in this parade together, Dez. Why don't
you want to sell the house?"

"Because . . . I'd feel rootless. Like a homeless person. A vagabond."

David wanted to laugh because it had certainly not been his intention to
make his wife feel like a homeless person. God, he thought, one never knew.
He sat silently, waiting for Desiree to continue.

"What if we decide after all of our travels that we want to come back to
Connecticut? We'd have to look for a place all over again. I love our house
and all the things we've done with it, David. It's part of my personality and
our life together."

A bright light of possible resolution lit up in his eyes. He took a sip of water
and began to try to unravel the conflict. "Desiree?"

"Yes, David." She looked at his expression and was relieved. She could see
that he was taking her seriously and not judging her.

"Sometimes it's funny how things work out, isn't it?"

"What do you mean?"

"Before Aletha shot back into our lives—pun intended—this could never
have occurred to me as a possibility, but—"

"Aletha? What does Aletha have to do with—"

"Hear me out. Remember when you told me that Aletha had offered to buy
our house 'for a handsome price'? You told me that she had said that she
could use a weekend retreat for herself and Sparky."

"You want to sell—"

"No. Not sell it to her, but *lease* it to her. She could take care of the taxes and other expenses until we either decide to sell or return to Connecticut. How does that sound?"

She sat stunned. Creative problem solving, *twice* in one day, she thought, first with Ms. Moskowitz and now with David.

"I'm sure Aletha would close the deal in a nanosecond," he said, smiling and proud of himself.

Desiree was sure that Aletha would, too.

"If Aletha agrees to our offer, you won't even have to put our things away in storage. We'd be able to return to our home exactly the way we left it, if you like. How's that?"

"Fine," she conceded, embarrassed that she had never broached this issue earlier, having instead agonized and fretted, worrying her blood pressure up.

"So, as I said, go have dinner with Aletha. It'll probably work out for everybody. Now," he said, reaching over for her hand. "Are there any other secrets you want to tell your poor old husband?"

"I . . . I guess not. Oh, by the way, I just got a card from the Shapiros. They will be in New York for the holidays this week, so we've got to plan a menu."

"Are you sure you feel like cooking this year? Why don't we all just go out to dinner?"

"Nahhh, that's okay. It's more comfortable at the house. We'll just make it simple. Besides, Joy loves to help."

"Well, how are they anyway? Did she say what Ira's working on these days?" he asked, sopping up the last of the butter from his fish with a chunk of crispy baguette.

"Umm-hmm," Desiree said, starting to giggle.

"What's he up to?" David asked, and drained his glass of gringos on the beach.

"He's working on a score for a new Broadway musical."

"Yeah? What's it called?"

"The Nuremberg Trials—The Musical!"

David almost choked on his drink as he sat back abruptly in his chair, the frown on his face frozen into an expression of horrified disbelief.

"You're kidding!"

"Nope."

"*She's* kidding then?"

"Nope."

As the waiter approached their table to ask if they wanted anything else, another fan, this time a prissy-looking black guy in a three-piece pinstriped suit, pushed in front of the waiter, brandishing a book.

"Hey, David Simon. Here . . . autograph this book; I'm your number one fan," he squealed, winking at her husband suggestively.

David looked nervously at his wife.

Desiree crossed her eyes then winked, picked up her napkin from her lap, and dabbed her lips with it.

Signing the book with the flourish of a contented celebrity, David handed it back to the man and returned his attention to his wife.

"The *what*?"

"That's right . . . the musical!"

CHAPTER TWELVE

Debra Parker had had a long arduous day. The deadlines in her department at the agency were wiping her out, and like most people who worked in corporations, she had almost no support staff. She was so tired at that moment that her whole body ached. The weather sucked and she still hadn't heard from that lying brother Jeffrey Scott. She figured that she might as well just lay his shit to rest. Then, on top of it all, while trying to treat herself to a pleasant lunch, there was her therapist, sitting with her damned white husband! All those months of confiding in this woman had proven to be a horrible mistake. How could that woman help her when she was obviously screwed up herself?

She turned, standing in one of the aisles of the produce market, and felt overwhelmed by the tumultuous profusion of garishly colorful fruits and vegetables stacked to the ceiling in their stalls, screaming for her to make her choice. She continued lethargically pushing her shopping cart ahead of her, knowing that she really wasn't up to cooking tonight. She also didn't feel like eating alone, but couldn't think of a soul that she knew—all working stiffs like herself—who wouldn't be working late. "Oh, well," she sighed as she began picking through the stack of fresh spinach leaves.

"Excuse me, miss?" Someone tapped her shoulder from behind.

She jumped, instinctively ready to defend herself. When she turned, her eyes met with those of a tall, dark-eyed, mocha-complexioned brother with the longest eyelashes of any man she'd ever seen in her life. The brother was f-i-i-i-ne!

Another one trying to run a game, she figured, turning away from the joker in order to continue to concentrate on her spinach leaves.

The young man decided to persist, since he figured that it was probably perfectly normal for a woman in New York City to be wary of strangers. "Excuse me, miss. I only wanted to ask you what you call the name of this . . . in English."

She turned back around to see that he was holding up an exotic fruit for her to identify.

"It's a papaya!" she answered shortly, giving him a hard, uninviting look, which was meant to convey her message to back off.

"A pa-pay-ah," he repeated with a warm smile. "And how do you eat this? Do you cook it, or what?"

The brother *was* fine, but what was with the friggin' accent? His vowels were as round as tomatoes, and he clipped his consonants in an exaggerated enunciation. Debra immediately thought of double-deck buses and Union Jacks, James Bond, and evil villains.

"Beats the hell out of me! Puerto Ricans and West Indians eat that stuff, and *I* am neither!" she snapped, abandoning her spinach and quickly pushing her cart away from the intruder.

Deciding to follow her, he maneuvered himself in front of her cart and blocked her path.

She glared at him, pursed her lips in annoyance, and said, "Look, mister, I told you that—"

"I heard what you told me." He smiled mischievously. "And to tell you the truth, I know exactly what to do with a papaya. It's just that you're a very beautiful lady, and I had been watching you shop—" He pointed with amusement into her empty cart. "—wearing that lovely coat with the stripes like a tiger, and decided that I'd have to summon my courage and talk to you."

"About *what*, I don't even know you." Her eyes furtively checked out the brother's broad frame in the Burberry trench coat, the perfectly styled curly hair, and the straightest, whitest teeth than she had seen in a long time.

So what? Big deal.

Good-looking brothers were a dime a dozen in New York. This one might be worth fifty cents, with the fake accent and all, but he was probably just another urban predator, she thought.

"My name is Kamil—"

"Do you think I should *care*, brother?" Debra noticed his finger pointing into her empty cart, so she quickly threw a bag of carrots into it. She tried to move forward, pushing into him with the cart, but he stood steadfast, blocking her attempt to escape.

"What the hell kind of name is Ka-meel, anyway?"

"I'm from Iran."

"Oh. A foreigner, huh? An Arab wetback, are you?" She snickered in an attempt to discourage any further conversation.

"I said that I was *from* Iran. I am an American. I have been for a couple of years now. And I am not an Arab, I am Persian."

"Whatever," she drawled, rolling her eyes.

"And what country are *you* from, miss?"

"These United States of America. What did you think?" She gave up trying to escape. Maybe he'd just go away.

Maybe not.

"You didn't tell me your name." He knew he had made some headway with this difficult but attractive New York City woman.

"Debra. Debra Parker."

"As I said, my name is Kamil. Kamil Mouamed."

"Well, glad to have made your acquaintance. Now will you let me shop, mister—"

"Kamil." He reached into her cart, removed the bag of carrots, and gently placed them back in the bin where she had gotten them. "It is obvious that you haven't had dinner yet . . . and neither have I. So, why don't we have dinner together? This evening."

"Just like *that*?" She asked, snapping the thumb and middle fingers of her right hand.

"Why not?"

"Because I don't even know who you are. You could be a serial killer."

"I couldn't kill you in a public place, with hundreds of witnesses, now could I?"

A smooth operator, she smirked to herself.

"Look. I just left work. I'm tired and I'd have to change clothes and—"

"So I can meet you at a place of your choice. You pick the time and I'll make the reservation."

"You're offering me a free hot meal, Mr. Mouamed?"

Debra watched his face go from shock to uncertainty before it composed itself into something close to regal, sophisticated, unflappable.

"I'd love to take you to dinner, yes."

She thought back to the fact that Jeffrey had neither taken her to dinner nor called her for a second date. She looked at the good-looking brother—she *supposed* he was a brother—were Persians brothers?—standing in front of her. She weighed her options for the evening, came up with nothing, and thought, What the hell.

She figured she'd pick an expensive restaurant and eat herself to distraction. Make him pay cash for the crimes of all the other smooth-talking, no-account men she'd known.

"Okay, Mr. Mouamed. Winterhaven. At eight o'clock. Be there!" she said curtly, whisking past him without a even backward glance.

She was forty-five minutes late. Intentionally. She lived only a block from the restaurant. But how would *he* have known that she was making him pay for all the others of the past? If he decided to leave, well then, fuck him! If he decided to wait and he was mad, then he could just kiss her black . . .

When she entered the restaurant, she saw that he was sitting at the bar drinking a club soda and glancing at his watch.

His face lit up when he saw her.

He stood up and walked over to help her out of her coat and to take her umbrella.

"Miss Parker—I mean, Debra—are you late or did I get the time wrong?"

The waiter took her belongings and led them to their table.

"I had things to do. You could have left, you know."

"Well, I figured that I'd give you another fifteen minutes. I know how the traffic can be in this city, sometimes." He pulled out the chair for her to sit.

Why was he being so solicitous? she wondered. Probably just plotting to get me into bed! She knew the type, accent or no accent.

"Actually, I live just up the block," she challenged.

"You look very lovely."

"You said that already . . . in the market."

"Well, you still do." Taking the wine menu from the waiter, he asked her, "Would you like something to drink? A cocktail, or perhaps a wine with the meal?"

Your damned tootin', she thought to herself, pointing to the most expensive wine on the menu, her mind flashing back to Jeffrey Scott.

Kamil nodded to the waiter.

"So, Debra, what do you do?"

"I work in advertising," she murmured, and leaned back to take in the lavish decor of the restaurant. She had wanted to come to Winterhaven for years but could never afford it. Even with her recent promotion. She felt that she had lucked out that this oil-rich Arab could afford it.

"And what do *you* do, Camel?"

"Ka-meel."

"Whatever."

"I have an import-export business."

"I hope it's legal." She laughed derisively, taking a sip of water.

"We deal in household accessories. Objets d'art. And what do you advertise?"

She ignored his question, because she had decided earlier on that she would work on her own agenda that evening. Since he was a foreigner, she had decided that he had some serious explaining to do.

"So, Kamil. How many native-born black Americans have you hired in your company to work for you? You must feel you owe *something* to the American people for allowing you to have an opportunity to make money in our country, don't you?"

"I'm not sure I understand the nature of your question," he asked, completely confounded.

"*You* know what I'm saying!"

He took a breath and looked around the restaurant before leaning forward to speak. "I don't know what you're talking about. But I have a feeling that we are not starting off on the right foot. Do you have a problem with me because I am a foreigner? If so, why are we having dinner together?"

"Because you begged."

"Begged?"

The waiter placed the expensive bottle of wine in front of them. He started to pour a bit into Kamil's glass, but Kamil held his hand up to stop him.

"Just the lady," he said, pointing to Debra's glass.

The waiter poured, Debra sipped, nodded, and the waiter left, leaving behind the food menu.

"Aren't you having any, Kamil?"

"I don't drink," he responded calmly, a frown casting a shadow across his face.

"Oh. Too bad for you. Anyway, I'd like you to answer my question."

"No, there are no black Americans, as you say, in my company. It is a family business. But why, I must ask you, are you taking such an antagonistic position?"

"I'd like to know something. If you really *are* a foreigner, why do you speak English so well? 'Antagonistic position.' That's quite a sophisticated expression for an immigrant!"

Kamil set his menu aside and folded his hands.

"Miss Parker, first of all, I'd like you to know that I studied at the university in Tehran, then I went to Oxford in England. Also, I am not an Arab. I am Persian. Different people, different culture, although the same alphabet. I am not an immigrant, I am a political refugee, as are the other members of my family. We run a family business. We were forced to leave our country. So, now that I've told you all of this, why can't we enjoy a pleasant meal simply as a man and a woman? Or is it that you've had a problem with Arab men in your past?"

"I've never been with any foreigner before," she said, refilling her glass. "Look, this menu is divine. I chose this place because they have the best loin of pork in New York. You must try it."

Debra watched his face knot up and then relax.

"Order it, if you like. I don't eat the meat of the . . . how do you say it, in English? Ah yes, the meat of the *swine*. He tugged at the cuffs of his shirt and straightened his tie. "I am a Muslim."

"A Muslim, huh? Am I to believe that, or—"

"Miss Parker, please. I thought you were attractive, and I asked you out to dinner. Do you like men? Or are you a lesbian?"

"Because I am not acting grateful for a meal and gullible to your men's bullshit, you think I'm a lesbian?"

"That is not at all what I meant to suggest. I'm sorry. It's simply that you act as if I killed your mother. If you have a problem, perhaps you would like to talk about it. But if you really don't want to have dinner with me, please let me know, and I shall release you."

Debra scanned his suddenly flushed face.

"Release me? I didn't know that your intention was to trap me."

The waiter returned for their orders.

"Just one moment, please," Kamil waved the waiter away.

"Tell me, Miss Parker, for I should like to know. What is the problem?" Kamil leaned back and rested his chin on his fingertips.

"I don't have one."

"Yes. Yes, I believe you do." He scratched his head before continuing. "You know, Debra . . . Miss Parker."

"What?"

"First, you attack my nationality. You call me a wetback, when in fact my family and many others like us were forced by oppressive regimes to leave our country."

"Have you ever asked yourselves why this happened to you all? Maybe you did something wrong," she said glibly, gulping down some wine.

"You are a very spoiled American lady. You should not be so smug. Especially someone as vulnerable as you are." Kamil picked up his menu and began leafing through it.

"*Me* vulnerable? Ha!"

"You are a member of a minority group in your country. I read the papers. I watch television. I have seen and heard your skinhead groups. I have also studied your history, and it seems to me that your countrymen are not so terribly in love with you. How do you know whether one day you might be thrown out of *your* country?"

"This is the United States of America, you ignorant foreigner, not some backward dictatorship!"

"You attack my family's business. If you were thrown out of this country, where would *you* go? What would you *do* for a living? Your American *advertising*? What would your family's business be?"

Debra could see that he was trying to control his temper, so when he took a sip of water she attempted to cut in, but he continued in a condescending tone. "I bet the only language you speak is American. As for *me* I speak Farsi, Arabic, English, French, Swahili, Wolof, and Japanese."

"Big deal. Who cares!"

"You don't even know the name of your tribe—Negro, black, Afro, African American! You are not an African. The African ladies that I know don't carry around such hostility. They have grace and charm, not this . . . this . . ." His hand fanned the air, trying to find the word.

"We don't have tribes here. This is America. Nevertheless my ancestors are all from Africa, Mr. Mouamed!"

"Everyone on this planet has origins in Africa, Miss Parker." He took a breath and continued. "This attitude of yours. Such anger. Such intolerance. It seems to be a black American lady thing."

"What would *you* know about it?"

He leaned back in his chair, his eyes gazing over the beautiful face of this strange woman. His voice tinged with regret, he said, "Personally, since I have been in America, I have found myself attracted to black American ladies. You are, generally, the most beautiful and sensual women in this country, in my opinion. In the world! Yet, whenever I ask one of you out, I am met with hostility and defensiveness. Arrogance and rigidity. You are all—at least the ones I have met—reminiscent of British colonialists. They come to a dark, generous country and then spit on the natives."

"You are not a native of this country, Mr. Mouamed."

"No, I am not. And from what I understand you are not an American Indian. So why are you hostile toward me? What is it that is going on here in this country that creates this kind of madness among such beautiful women?"

"You men never call back after you have slept with us."

"If you women treat the men you meet the way you have so far treated me this evening, it is no wonder. It would be a miracle that any of you have any love in your lives at all."

"I guess you could not begin to understand. You are not an American. Not *really* anyway."

"Well, I certainly don't understand why you didn't even give me a chance. If your American men are so incompatible with you, why don't you give someone else a chance?"

"Why should I . . . we? It's all the same. You men are all the same."

"I can tell you from experience that women are not all the same, so how could it be possible that men are all the same, my dear woman?"

Silence.

"It appears that *you* are having problems with your sex life. Perhaps you should seek some counseling. But then, you are in all probability the kind of woman who would go to a doctor for help and then throw the cure right back in the doctor's face!" He laughed, motioning the waiter to return to the table.

"Are you finished, Mr. Mouamed?"

"Yes, that is all. I don't know about you, but I am going to order *my* meal now," he said with a tone of dismissal.

"Fuck you!" Debra slammed her empty glass on the table and stood up to leave.

"I wish you well, Miss Parker."

She swept away from the table without even a backward glance.

Debra had been savoring her usual morning coffee and bran muffin, enjoying the quiet-before-the-storm moments in her office, when the messenger approached to deliver a huge bunch of tiger lilies.

Her favorite.

She was shocked to find that they were intended for her. She looked at the card to see who could have possibly sent this unexpected gift.

Jeffrey Scott!

She couldn't believe it.

She tore up the card and dumped the flowers in the wastebasket.

Just at that moment the phone rang.

She answered it, figuring it to be either her mother calling to find out what day she planned to arrive in Chicago for the family's annual Christmas dinner or her good friend the media director, who also liked to come in early to enjoy the quiet.

"Who?"

She was so outraged, so . . . so . . . *mad* that she spilled her coffee all over her impeccably neat desk. All over her fucking storyboards, no less!

A little over two weeks had passed, and *now* he decided to pick up the phone. She couldn't believe his nerve. She and the media director had discussed and agreed on how they both despised the reprehensibly cavalier way men treated women and their feelings.

"Hello, sweet lady, did you get the flowers?" he said brightly, albeit a bit nervously, into her ear. "I'm sorry it took me so long to get back to you, but . . . look, let's have dinner—the dinner we never got around to, okay?"

"So why on *earth* do you bother *now*, Jeffrey, after all this time?" she hissed with all the venom that she could muster. "What is it? You only get hungry every couple of weeks or so?"

Who did he think he was anyway? She was no sniveling wimp!

Jeffrey felt the humiliating crawl of raw egg oozing down his face, over his nose, his lips, and under his chin, but he persisted. "Look, Debra . . . *baby* . . ." He was about to plead, but thought, Shit, I am a *man*, not some sniveling wimp! "Debra, I meant to call, but I misplaced your number. And it's—"

"*Sure*, Jeffrey. Don't hand me that crap. I'm a busy woman, and I don't have time for your fucking shenanigans!"

"Look, when I got back from Detroit I sent my shirts to the laundry and—"

"Look, Mr. Scott, you don't have to give me one of those infantile stories you throw at other women. Try it with a nineteen-year-old," she said dryly, squeezing the receiver, her knuckles becoming beige with the accumulated rage of waiting by the phone all those days.

Damn, he thought; he was afraid that something like this might happen, but what was he to do, never call her again—out of *fear?*

"Look, Debra, I thought we had a great time. When you hadn't heard from me after a few days, why didn't *you* call *me*? I left you my number."

Debra, thinking she heard laughing hyenas mocking her, said, "I don't call men. Men are supposed to call ladies!"

"Well, I'm sorry. But as I said, I lost your number."

"Go to hell, Jeffrey. I'm not so desperate that I have to—"

"What on earth is wrong with you, sister? We had one little date. I misplaced your number, and now it's the end of the world! What's the big deal? Oh . . . I get it, you have that PMS thing, right? That's okay. Let's have dinner and we'll talk about it, okay?"

"Oh . . . so now you're being condescending, right? What the hell is wrong with you men, anyway?"

"I am not 'you men.' What is wrong with *you*, Debra? This is a pretty extreme reaction, don't you think? You've got to check yourself, sister. You've got problems that I realize now I could never even begin to handle."

"Handle? Who the hell are *you* to handle—"

"Oh, I get it. You're one of those lesbians or—"

She gasped. That word again. Debra Parker panicked and slammed down the phone.

A lesbian? Bullshit, she thought. Men always started throwing that word around whenever a woman stood her ground or offended their egos in some way.

Jeffrey Scott shook his head and mumbled, *"Black women*!" They won't even cut a brother some slack! He didn't have time to worry about this shit; he had to get to work.

Besides, obviously he had made a big mistake about this woman. He nearly drove himself crazy fantasizing about her and tearing his house apart looking for her number. He couldn't help it if he couldn't remember what building she lived in. She lived in New York City and all those Chelsea neighborhood brownstones looked alike. What was *he* supposed to do, hang around her neighborhood like a stalker looking for her?

He shook his head again and put down the phone.

Maybe the bitch forgot to take her medication or something, he thought as he geared down and eased his Ferrari onto the exit off the Merrick Parkway.

CHAPTER THIRTEEN

"Send Ms. Parker in," Desiree replied calmly into the intercom.

She rolled her cup of green tea in her hands, warming them, then took a sip as she looked toward the door.

Debra Parker's disturbingly thin, fabulously dramatic, red, fake-fur-clad figure bounded through the door breathlessly.

"I'm so sorry I'm late, Dr. Simon, but you know, just as I was walking out the door of my office that architect I told you about called. And you *know* I had to talk to him—to tell him off!"

"Take off your coat and sit down, Ms. Parker," said Desiree evenly, successfully controlling her annoyance toward this patient. She was so tired of people who not only squandered *her* time, but in doing so, squandered their *own* money, since she didn't give her patients any discounts for tardiness.

The red coat was a nice touch, though.

Without a doubt, she thought, God gave women like herself and Ms. Parker brown skin in order to bring utter joy to the world by having them parade around in such wildly dramatic hues as red, yellow, green, and orange.

This was an attractive woman, but her bulimic sveltness unnerved Desiree. As she focused more closely on the patient's presence she locked on the girl's eyes.

Dilated pupils . . . *damn!* Girlfriend was as high as Mount McKinley—had lost all track of time and was now blaming it all on some phone call.

"So, how are you feeling today, Ms. Parker? Is there anything you want to talk about—that phone call maybe?"

"You remember I told you about that guy Jeffrey that I met? The one that fucked me and never called back?"

A calm silence from Desiree, who was now anxiously tapping her left foot under her desk.

She was always nervous when she found herself alone in a room with a patient who came to her high on something.

"Well, the nigger *called*. Just this *morning*."

Desiree's heart skipped a beat as she realized that Ms. Parker had just told her only moments ago that he had called her as she was on her way to this very *afternoon's* appointment.

She'd never dare correct her. Ms. Parker would probably only freak out, accusing the good doctor of not paying attention.

"He acted as if nothing had happened. When I asked him why he hadn't called me in all this time . . ."

A lousy *two* weeks, Desiree recalled with exasperation, from the last session.

". . . he said that he had lost my phone number. You know, I wasn't born yesterday. I *know* the nigger was *lying!*"

Nigger . . . there was that word again, Desiree sighed to herself with disgust.

"Do you think that perhaps he may have been telling the *truth*?"

"Of course not. The only indication I had that he had even been in my house was the business card he left on my pillow. He has not called since. Not even a peep from him."

"Why didn't *you* call *him*?" Desiree asked.

"Why would I *call* him? A gentleman should always call a lady after he's made love to her."

A *lady*? Desiree thought, perplexed.

What was the definition of a lady these days? she wondered. An adult woman goes to bed with a stranger the first night they are together, and then decides to get virginal? What kind of game was this?

"Sometimes men require just as much of a display of interest as women, Ms. Parker."

Debra went ballistic.

"I would *never* call a man! That's *his* job to make sure that I'm okay."

"Weren't you even curious to know whether this man was okay or not? What if he were in a coma in a hospital or something? Or perhaps he did lose your phone number. It *is* an unlisted one, isn't it?"

Desiree knew from her own experience that if she had been attracted to a man to the point of sleeping with him on the very day she met him—and had enjoyed it—she would have made sure she contacted him for the repeat performance that she would definitely be craving.

All the brother could say was no! Or yes!

Debra Parker's hairs stood up on her neck as she looked at this arrogant Oreo cookie doctor. What on earth could this bitch possibly know about black men and their tired-ass lines?

"Of course, I *know* that the nigger was lying. He said my number was in his jacket pocket that he had sent to the cleaners. What bull!"

"So, are you going to see him again?"

"*Hell*, no!" she screamed, looking at Desiree as though she had lost her mind. "I'm not going to allow any man to treat *me* that way."

Desiree looked at Debra Parker's face—a closed and hostile mask—waiting for her to continue. Maybe she was completely out of touch with the dating games of the day.

"You know, Doctor, I don't feel comfortable talking to you anymore. You don't know a thing about black men. It's not your world."

So, Miss Thing had discovered that her husband was white, Desiree deduced. Probably thought now that she was some kind of race traitor. Desiree had decided long ago that if not sitting around verbally crucifying black men made her a traitor to the sisterhood then so be it.

"Just because you wear those dreadlocks, sister, doesn't make you black, you know."

"Why are you being hostile toward me?" Desiree asked calmly, taking a sip of tea. She looked over at her calendar and ticked off the months before she would leave this exhausting endeavor. "The session is about you, Debra, not me. But for your information, I have a black family that includes not only my sister, but my mother and my *father*, my *brother*, my *uncles*, and my *male* cousins."

"You don't know a thing about *dating* brothers. If you did, you'd know that this one is running a game on me. The niggers all think they are something special; treat the sisters as if we're bonbons in some damned candy store."

Desiree was definitely tired of all this "nigger this" and "nigger that." If Debra Parker really felt this way about black men, as she certainly appeared to, why didn't she just try something else? Desiree wondered impatiently.

Desiree had decided during the black-male-bashing eighties that perhaps African American women should look at themselves and their mothers more closely; they had to come to terms with their participation in the gender war.

Who did they *think* had been primarily responsible for the care, feeding, and social development of these men anyway? Black women needed to examine their contributions to black men's so-called objectionable characteristics.

"It seems that you don't like black men, Ms. Parker. You are always recounting stories of how they never meet your expectations."

"I *love* black men, Doctor." She smiled, blushing.

"What is it then that you like about black men? *Tell* me."

Ms. Parker's pupils disappeared northward as she searched, far too long it seemed to Desiree, for an answer.

"The brothers are *so fi-i-i-n-e*! They are hot and they . . ."

Ms. Parker drifted off into an intoxicated confusion, dark brown irises surrounded by dull, bloodshot eyeballs shooting rapidly from left to right and back again.

Loyalty to dysfunctional brothers, especially for these types of women, seemed to be simply a manifestation of low self-esteem. They did not feel confident enough in their femininity to explore relationships with men who treated them well and other options. Debra Parker had not come up with a single reason for why she kept putting up with the so-called abuse of black men.

Desiree thought that if she were a black man herself, she would have been hard-pressed to go out with a sister like Debra Parker. Who would want a woman who was only attracted to you because you were *fine*?

Maybe black women needed to employ a new strategy of reverse psychology and give these guys a run for their money. Let sisters start avidly exploring the assets of other groups of men, and the brothers might suddenly find them more valuable commodities, Desiree mused.

"You realize, Ms. Parker, that *this* man did call you back. Maybe he's interested in you. Don't you think it might be worthwhile, giving him a chance?"

"No!"

"Why not?" Desiree asked, wondering again how Debra had found out that her husband was white.

"As my mother would say—"

Bingo! thought Desiree. The *mother*! As she reflected over the past sessions, she realized that this young woman had absorbed the poison of her own mother's disillusionment with black men.

"Your mother? As I understand it, your mother had a challenging marriage with your father and a very difficult divorce. Am I correct?"

"Damn straight, she did. I was there through it all!"

"And your mother has never remarried?"

"No. She loved my father."

"Has she had any significant relationships with any other men since?"

"No. She loved my father. He's the only man she's ever loved, and he hurt her deeply . . . with his womanizing and all. My mother was a virgin when she married him."

"And you have allowed your mother, who has loved only one man in her entire life, to give you advice on how to handle *men*?"

"She's my mother. She doesn't want me to end up in her position. Lonely, alone, and hurt. What's wrong with that?"

Desiree sat silent, waiting to see if the message would sink in that that was *exactly* the kind of life that Debra was actually living.

"From my experience with black men, Doctor, it appears that my mother is absolutely right. They don't treat us right. They are thoughtless and—"

"If black men disturb you so much, Ms. Parker, and you are looking for love in your life, why don't you explore other options?"

"What do you mean, other options, Doctor?"

"Nonblack men."

"Nonblack men, as you call them, have never been an option for me. I can't sleep with the enemy!"

"Who do you feel is the enemy, Ms. Parker?"

"White men, of course! *You,* in particular, Doctor, could never possibly understand my position."

"Why not?" Desiree asked.

"You are married to a white man!"

"Yes, that is true. Nevertheless, the human species is not limited to just black and white men, you know."

Debra felt her dander rise. "You know, Dr. Simon, you just don't understand. You're just like all the other lying, cheating black men who make excuses for themselves and never take a sister's feelings into account!" she yelled, emotionally overwrought.

Desiree couldn't believe her ears. She had just been called a black man!

The true nature of Ms. Parker's problem just took a turn in a direction that she had suspected for quite some time now.

"You said that *I* was just like 'all the other black *men*' who—"

"You know what I meant!"

"Do you think it's possible that you are simply just not attracted to *men* at all, Ms. Parker? I want you to think carefully about what I've just said," Desiree soothed.

Debra didn't appear to be interested in or attracted to men. Society had been forcing penises on her for all her life. It was no wonder she was such an angry woman, Desiree concluded.

"You don't understand. The brothers just don't know how to make love to a sister, nor do they know how to talk to a sister! But, of course, this isn't your world, is it?"

Debra Parker recalled her secret and knew that she had never in her life ever *really* enjoyed her sexual relations with men. The last thing she would do at that moment would be to explore the issue with a white-flesh-loving black woman! There was no point to it anyway. The problem was not Debra Parker, it was Desiree Simon. She was going to look for another more politically and emotionally correct doctor. This Dr. Simon was a fake. A charlatan!

"Look, Doc, I'll spell it out for you. The sucker I was talking to you about—Jeffrey Scott—slept with me in *my* bed, didn't even take me out to dinner, and then he didn't bother to call me back until today! What does *that* tell you, Doctor?"

Beep ... beep ... beep ... Doctor Simon's clock signaled that Ms. Parker's time was up.

SNAP FOUR

CHAPTER FOURTEEN

Dr. Brian Morgan was convinced and had been for some time now that he was the last of a lonely, dying breed. He adjusted the rearview mirror and turned on the ignition.

As he eased out of his garage onto the palm-lined street of the cul-de-sac on which he, his wife, and daughter had now lived for over ten years, he thought about the three-and-a-half hour flight he was about to take from Miami to New York. He hadn't been to New York in years. The weather report said that it was a frigid twenty degrees today up there.

He turned up the air conditioner in his gunmetal gray Mercedes 600 and smiled at the palm-studded Miami vista that flew by as he pressed down on the accelerator. He hadn't planned to visit New York at all this year, but it seemed like a perfect opportunity to pop in to visit his folks in Brooklyn, killing two birds with one stone. Instead of them flying down to Miami this year for Christmas, he'd decided that he, his wife, and daughter would celebrate the holidays in Puerto Rico with his wife, Marta's, family. That would be terrific for their three-year-old daughter, who was now perfectly bilingual.

He lowered his Armani sunglasses from his smooth, shiny, dark-brown pate onto the high bridge of his narrow, prominent nose.

Yeah, even though he enjoyed his work and provided his family with a comfortably luxurious life in the sun, he often felt he should have specialized in cardiology, radiology, internal medicine—anything other than the family medicine he practiced. He had never felt properly appreciated or respected—that is, until those people from *The Aletha Brown Show* in New York called to invite him to speak on the subject of family medicine with a panel of his colleagues. They claimed that they had read his recent article in *The Medical Review* on the subject and were impressed.

Dr. Morgan had never actually *seen The Aletha Brown Show*, but he remembered the big hullabaloo over her successful talk show when she was living down in Miami. He was proud of the fact that she had become another of the growing number of powerful black women of the day and was looking forward to meeting her.

He knew that his wife watched the program often and loved it, so he supposed it was quite appropriate that he go. Since Marta had already left for Río Piedras with their daughter, he hadn't gotten a chance to tell her that he was going to be on the show. But, he had decided, he would just surprise her when his broadcast aired. She'd get a kick out of it, he was sure.

It was a nice touch that these shows supplied the guests with a first-class round-trip ticket and a stay at a first-class hotel.

Dr. Morgan didn't recall every having stayed at a hotel in New York. He usually just stayed in Park Slope, in Brooklyn, with his parents whenever he found it necessary to be in New York.

Actually, even though he grew up there, he had never liked the place. Too uptight, crowded, and the winters could kick your behind!

He had literally clicked his heels when he had gotten his residency in Houston, Texas—way back when. Brian Morgan was a warm-weather, mellow-paced brother.

CHAPTER FIFTEEN

*L*ouise Washington had just *loved* her book tour!

Those jaunts had given her the opportunity to visit cities in the United States that she would never otherwise have ever seen. Actually, she couldn't call them *jaunts*—just pit stops.

Nevertheless, the experience so far had been a hoot!

Then, there were all those pleasant surprises, as well, like the fact that in business class and first class the airlines—at least, this one in particular—served regional food reflecting the destination to which the passengers were headed.

The attendant had just placed Louisiana gumbo in front of her, a tantalizing appetizer to preview the flavors that were awaiting Louise at her next destination—New Orleans.

Hot diggidy dog! Creole food at thirty thousand feet! Life didn't get any better than *this*, she giggled to herself. It was astonishing that mere airline food reached those new heights . . . ha, ha, ha! The dish had all the ingredients she loved: ham, crab meat, shrimp, chili, and cayenne pepper. It was absolutely orgasmic.

Careful not to spill anything on her burgundy cashmere turtleneck sweater, she sprinkled on a few drops of hot sauce, then devoured a forkful of crab meat, okra, rice, ham, and shrimp, perfumed with thyme and who knew what all else. She could *live* in a city that specialized in food like this, she thought.

Slowly savoring the taste of her dish, she leaned back in her seat and took a sip of champagne.

"Catherine, is that *you*?"

That familiar voice from a faraway time, another world, descended upon her like a speeding Mack truck. She sat paralyzed as her glass of champagne slipped from her hand to the floor.

She didn't want to look at the place from where the voice had come.

Louise turned her head and looked up at the tall, captivating man standing next to her. His deep-hued eyes—the color of beer, she thought wryly to herself—spilled with an all too familiar longing into her astonished, black ones.

If she had a parachute, she would have jumped.

Except for a few strands of white hair artfully threaded through the thick undulating waves of his full head of jet-black, he didn't look a day older than the last time she saw him, a lifetime ago.

She slowly recovered and almost said inaudibly, "My name is Louise, Louise Washington now . . . Father McCarthy."

She noticed that he wasn't wearing a collar, but a smart-looking, gray wool sports jacket, a burgundy turtleneck sweater, and a pair of jeans.

"Please, Ca—I mean, Louise, may I sit down?" he asked, his eyes pleading with her.

"Yes . . . yes . . . of course." She motioned for him to sit, then looked away into the clouds outside.

If she had watched him, she would have seen his eyes flash with relief and gratitude as he sat down next to her.

"I didn't think I'd ever see you again, Louise."

She turned back to look at him. The pain that had begun to throb in her temples had become almost unbearable.

"I never thought I'd ever see *you* again either, Father Mc—"

"I'd like *you* to know," he interrupted gently, "I am no longer Father McCarthy. I am just Jack. Professor Jack McCarthy. Have been for years. I teach theology in New Orleans."

"So . . . you left the priesthood," she said flatly.

"I told you I would, Louise."

"No! No, that's not exactly what you told me, *Jack*!" she challenged, pushing her meal away. She had completely lost her appetite. Why had fate decided to bring Jack McCarthy back into her life on this particular day after all these years? Perhaps it was her penance—God's jest in order to ruin her taste for gumbo!

He leaned over to pick up her empty glass from the floor.

"Would you like me to ask them to bring you another glass?" He reached over and touched her hand.

She couldn't find the breath or energy to respond.

"Louise?"

"Yes. Yes. Of course. Please do," she said, staring at him in disbelief, feeling as though she had fallen out of her body and into a pile of old manure.

They had fallen in love when she was a young novice in the convent in Baltimore, way back when. It had been the most confusing, soul-wrenching, and painful time of her life. She thought that she had put that all behind her forever. But there he was, sitting next to her.

The love of her life. The life-altering and *unconsummated* love of her life!

She had almost forgotten how the disquieting passion she felt for him had created a turbulent wake in the calm waters of the life she'd chosen. The improper feelings—by themselves a kind of infidelity—that had inexplicably blossomed between a priest and a novice had convinced her, beyond a shadow of a doubt, that she could not take her final vows.

At first she tortured herself, thinking that she was unfit or, worse, unworthy of the religious life. The guilt gradually subsided over the years, and she concluded that no mere twenty-year-old girl with no experience in the world should have been expected to make such an irrevocable vow. But *he* had been a twenty-nine-year-old man who had already *taken* a vow.

A vow to *God*!

He should not have taken advantage of her naive vulnerability. After all, she had planned to become a nun. Father McCarthy had twisted and ruined her life!

Over the years, in light of what he had allowed to happen between them, she had come to question his devotion. She had become deeply skeptical about the ability of any man to commit to anything larger than himself.

Jack handed her a fresh glass of champagne, and she placed it on the tray in front of her, unable to drink.

"I looked for you, Louise."

"*Did* you, now?" Her words dripped with more than a hint of sarcasm. She layered it on in an attempt to mask the hot flashes of acrimony she shot toward him. Unfortunately, they boomeranged right back, piercing her rapidly beating heart.

"I told you that I wanted to take time at the retreat in order to reflect on our situation. To ask for guidance."

"A retreat? Going to China is more than a retreat, Professor." She picked up the champagne and downed it in one long gulp.

"I told you that I would let you know my decision."

"I wanted to marry you, Jack! I left the convent for you. And you—" She stabbed her recently manicured index finger into his thigh. "—you went to China, leaving vague promises behind. How long did you expect me to wait for you?"

She was close to spiraling into a sea of tears, but not wanting to ruin her makeup, she pulled out of the dive just in time. She wanted to look good for the publicity people meeting her at the airport in New Orleans—and for *him*.

"I was only away for six months. When I came to look for you, you were gone. I couldn't find a trace of you!" His eyes flickered with controlled anger at the memory.

"I decided to start a new life."

"Evidently. A new life without *me*. You didn't leave a trace."

"Not a difficult thing for an orphan to do," she said smugly. She wanted to hurt him for all the years of turmoil he had caused her.

"What did you do? Where did you go, Louise?" he asked, taking her hand and squeezing it.

"I went where I went, Professor," she said enigmatically.

"Please, tell me about your life, sweetheart."

"My name is *Louise*! It is *not* 'sweetheart,' Jack!"

The flight attendant approached them and asked him if he wanted to be served his lunch.

"No, thank you. I'm not hungry," he said, dismissing the attendant and returning his attention to Louise Washington. "I apologize for the impropriety, Louise."

"So, what else is new," she mumbled under her breath to herself.

She had regained her appetite. Or perhaps her body had begun to demand the fuel she had felt that she needed in order to let him have it! In the chin! In the chest! In the fucking balls!

"Tell me what happened." He brought her hand to his lips, and her anger just melted away like snow in a spring thaw.

"I changed my life. My identity. It was easy. It was easier than being in the witness protection program, Jack." Her eyes pierced his. "Having been raised, as you know, in a convent orphanage, I had no family to worry about. No one would come looking for me."

"I went looking for you, Louise."

Ignoring his statement, she continued. "So, I decided to begin a new life with a clean slate. To start a family of my own. Of course, how could *you* ever understand how I felt? You come from a huge loving family. With support and traditions and everything that you could obviously go back to."

"It was not so loving, as you well know, Ca—I mean, Louise."

"So you *said*," she said nastily, looking abruptly away from him, back outside into the clouds.

"I understood you better than you were willing to acknowledge, you know. You felt that I was abandoning you—like your birth parents had done. Unlike them, I had gotten to know you and then fell in love with you. I could never have left you."

"But you *did*. You left me and went to a retreat all the way in China," she said, turning back to look at him again, batting her eyelashes with sarcasm.

"You had said that you understood and respected my decision."

"I was only a kid, Jack! A Little Orphan Annie child. You allowed me to leave the only family I had ever known, to flounder about in the world all alone."

"It was never my intent—"

"That's what they all say!"

"Who, Louise?"

She felt that he could not possibly expect her to dignify that question with a response. After all these years, it was certainly no business of his, so she sat in silence, wondering if she should ask him to remove himself from her presence.

"Where did you go?"

"New York. To Harlem. A person can easily get lost in a place like New York. Anonymity there is a prelude to reinvention."

"Why did you want to reinvent yourself—as you say—alone? Why couldn't we have done that together?"

"I did not see it as an option. But then, you should understand that. You had decided to reinvent, undo—or whatever you might have chosen to call it—yourself in China, right?"

"Not at all. Anyway, what did you decide to do for a living? Did you teach?"

"No. I decided to go to business school. I've done okay for myself."

"Where do you live now, Louise?"

"In Harlem."

Jack McCarthy did a double take and said, "You've spent all of your adult life in Harlem?"

"That's right. So what *of* it?" she asked defensively.

"Are you married?"

"I'm a widow." She felt a pang of guilt at the lie, but shit, he wasn't a priest anymore, so she could say what she pleased.

"I'm sorry. So very sorry, Louise."

You *should* be, sucker, she thought to herself, but instead she said, in an attempt to further prey on his guilt, "My husband was killed in Vietnam. I have a son who is going to medical school this year. His father was a doctor, too. He is my pride and joy. My greatest success."

"I am happy for you." He sincerely *was*. "What was your husband like, Louise? What kind of a doctor was he? What was to have been his specialty?"

Louise cleared her throat, moved uncomfortably in her seat, and said curtly, "I have no desire to discuss my dead husband. Especially with *you*!"

He looked at Louise, at her body language, and saw the lie. Despite the years that had passed between them, he knew her well. In fact, he pretty much watched her grow into womanhood. He knew beyond the shadow of a doubt that she had no dead husband. Had never been married. He was convinced that the son was real, though.

"You know, Jack, I figured that you had chickened out over the prospect of marrying a black woman."

"How could you think such a thing? Your race was insignificant in the face of vows I had made, Louise. Besides, it's not exactly as if I didn't know what color you were the first day I laid eyes on you." He had laughed incredulously, lightly stroking the sable-colored flesh of her hand. He continued, "I loved you. I thought you *knew* that. Actually, I still do, but I have made a new life for myself, too."

"Umm-hmm," she mumbled skeptically.

"Louise, when I couldn't find you, I thought I was going to lose my mind." He kissed her hand again.

She pulled her hand away and helped herself to more of her gumbo.

"Well, then, tell me. How on earth *did* you feel that your big old Irish family would have reacted to your leaving the priesthood in order to go off and marry a black woman? They probably would have thought that I had put a voodoo spell on you, right, Jack?" she asked, looking directly into his Guinness stout eyes with a sardonic grin.

"Evidently, it is *you* who had reservations about an interracial marriage. I am certain that you can recall nothing in our relationship that would have made you feel that I had any concerns at all about your color."

"Well, despite the fact that I had been cloistered all my life, I was not too naive to realize that we would definitely face some serious issues out in the world because of—"

"Those issues weren't important to me, nothing I felt that we couldn't have handled together. Besides, while I was a priest and in the years since, I have met many mixed-race couples who had very successful marriages. It appears to me that the only important thing is that a couple share the same faith—you know—religious and spiritual values."

"Yeah, whatever."

"Look, Louise, you know as well as I did that they—my family—felt that I was the chosen one. The fact that I left the priesthood was enough for them to be convinced that I had failed them. Nothing else I would have chosen to do with my life could have mattered to them at all."

"What did they say when you left, Jack?"

"Nothing."

"What do you mean?"

"I haven't spoken to them since. After I left, we no longer had anything to say to one another. When I couldn't find you, I, too, was left floundering about in the world alone, as you say. In their minds it looked as if I had left the priesthood in order to go off and marry a woman who didn't exist . . ." His voice trailed off into the dry air of the cabin around them.

"Are you married, Jack?"

"Yes. I have two sons. Would you like to see their pictures?"

She really didn't, but instead she said, "Why, of course."

He pulled out his wallet and opened it to a picture of his family.

A chill shot down her spine as she looked at the image of his wife. Although the woman appeared to be olive-skinned Caucasian and Louise was a brown-skinned Negro, she could have been Louise's light-skinned twin!

"Is your wife a colored woman?" she asked, holding the picture closer to her eyes.

"No. My wife is Italian. She is a wonderful wife and mother. Do you have a picture of your son?"

"Yes. Look over there in my handbag. In the red wallet," she responded, fanning her hand in the direction of her bag while steadfastly staring at the picture of his wife.

He found the photo.

"Your son is a handsome man. He could have been ours, you know, if you hadn't been so impatient and capricious." Jack closed the wallet and placed it back in her bag.

"Call it what you want to call it, Jack," she replied crisply, tossing his wallet of photos onto his lap.

"So, you are on a business trip in New Orleans, Louise? You know . . . I *do* like your chosen name."

"Yes. Actually, I'm on a book tour. I wrote a book."

"How interesting," he said, intrigued. "You wrote a book about business?"

"No! Well . . . yes."

A wave of embarrassment swept over her as she realized that there was no way that she was going to tell him to his face what her book was about. After all, he *had* been a priest, and he might think she was preposterous.

"What is it about?"

He noted, again, her uncomfortable expression, a fleeting look of guilt. After all, he *had* been a priest. He could spot the need for confession a mile away.

"Why don't you just go to a bookstore and buy it? I could always use another sale." She smiled nervously, looking away from him.

He wanted to laugh out loud. Her last statement was the last piece of the puzzle. Louise Washington was an opportunistic woman. She'd probably even written a book about a subject she knew nothing about. He'd suspected that the young woman he knew from the convent was much more than the naive innocent she presented to the world. No one lived in a series of foster homes and orphanages without becoming at least a bit streetwise. Her cunning simply took some time to show itself more publicly. Perhaps she had even used him as a means to avoid making a commitment to the sisterhood—the religious kind.

He also knew that he would just love to have dinner with her and hear the story of her life.

"Is it possible that we might have dinner together while you are in New Orleans? I would be honored . . . you know?"

She was momentarily startled as she felt him place his hand on her lap.

Their eyes met.

Louise tilted her head, narrowed her eyes, and then glared down accusingly at his hand, which lay brazenly on her thigh. She believed that his face held that familiar look of counterfeit innocence that men displayed around women when they were trying to get away with something stupid and inappropriate.

He removed his hand.

"New Orleans has wonderful restaurants, Louise. We could go someplace nice and intimate like—"

"I wouldn't *dare*, Jack McCarthy! You have already left the priesthood for me. I wouldn't want to—"

"Aren't you even *curious* about—"

Louise widened her eyes and lifted her eyebrows as if scandalized and gasped, "Curious about *what*, Jack?"

She was tickled and wanted to burst out laughing. Instead, she held her fraudulently shocked expression in check, her eyes challenging him to explain his proposition.

He stuttered defensively, "I—I—what I m-mean is—"

"Yes, Jack?"

"I mean—a-aren't you even curious about wh-what it would be like if we were to dine out for the first time together like—like normal, everyday friends?"

"Like everyday *what*?"

"My wife wouldn't mind," he interjected quickly.

"But I *would*!" She exploded in a tension-relieving laughter, and added, "Why don't we just enjoy the rest of the flight together and then leave things as they were before today?"

Louise Washington leaned over and kissed Jack McCarthy on the cheek, pressing her full breasts into his arm, pleased at how his face flushed.

"Black women." He sighed with a hint of exasperation at her mixed signals.

"What? What would *you* know about black women, Professor? I thought you said that you are a professor of theology—not women's studies! Besides, how many black women have *you* been involved with?"

"Enough to have formed an opinion, Louise," he responded, chuckling as he noticed her shocked expression.

"Oh? And what are these opinions of yours?" She was sorry that she had asked, because she realized that she was about to get some kind of long dissertation. He *was* a professor, after all.

"Of course, I mean *American* black women. I have no experience with the other nationalities."

"Go ahead, Jack. I'm listening."

"You all have a kind of power that other women are lacking. The kind of power that would drive someone like a Shirley Chisolm to run for president of the United States, for example, whereas women of other races would probably find it a sign of female progress that a woman is asked to be a mere running mate with some male candidate. Black women in this country have a power for greatness, yet a vast majority of you squander this power and drive, by manipulating for *small* things. We have so many problems in this country, and you all have what it takes to help put this country on the right track. But, instead—"

Louise, profoundly confused by the direction of the conversation, asked, "Jack McCarthy, what on earth does this all have to do with *me*?"

"Okay, let's take *you*, for instance—"

"*Now*, you're talking!" She chuckled, like the true Aries that she was.

"When you left the convent, and a possible future with me, you had the whole country—the whole world, in fact—in front of you to choose as a place to begin a new life. Instead, you chose a small neighborhood in New York City to live out your *entire* life. I suppose you chose Harlem in order to explore your 'roots.' Is that it?"

"It's possible. I *did* grow up among all those white—"

"Exactly. Your black community left you on the steps of a Catholic church. You were raised, nurtured, and educated by white Christians." He ran his fingers over her hand.

She pulled it away and snapped, "Oh, are you saying that I should never have tried to explore my black culture, Professor? Are you crazy or something?"

"I'm not saying that at all. Personally, I feel that if you wanted to explore your roots, you should have begun by searching for your birth parents—your *blood*!"

"Why should I? They didn't come looking for me, so why on earth should I go looking for them? I'd only have been opening a can of worms."

"Perhaps not. Maybe you would have learned of the kind of conditions that existed for your parents, in their time, that had caused them to make such a painful decision."

"Easy for *you* to say, Jack!" she said, looking down at her dish, moving the remains of her meal around with her fork.

"Maybe the information would have enabled you to understand and help others who have had to endure similar conditions. Pain is not for us to bear alone. It is to be understood, and the insights are supposed to be shared with others. That's how I see it."

No one had ever spoken to Louise Washington like this before. *Never!* And she definitely resented this presumptuous man preaching to her. She began to search for words that would end this conversation—forever!

"Also, this book that you wrote—"

"What about it? That's right, I wrote a book. I was tired of working like a *slave*, helping to make other people rich on my sweat. But, of course, you wouldn't know anything about that, would you, Jack?"

"The opportunity to write and publish a book should come with a huge sense of social responsibility. Published words are engraved in stone."

"So? What are you trying to say? What are you accusing me of, Professor?"

He smiled at her indignant look and said, "What I am saying is, the fact that you refuse to tell me what your book is about leads me to believe that you used—or abused, I should say—your talents and skills in order to capitalize on something that you know absolutely nothing about. Am I correct?"

"Maybe. Maybe not. It's for me to know and you to find out," she said with finality.

"Umm-hmm. So, Louise, why don't we talk some more . . . over dinner this evening, if this is possible for you."

"I think *not*, Jack! I am in no mood nor need for another lecture. I have business to attend to and the last thing I need is to put up with more of your Catholic guilt trips! This isn't the time of the Inquisition, haven't you noticed?" she huffed and pressed herself against her seat.

"Let me tell you another thing!" she continued. "You have no right to come over to my seat, after decades of absence, to criticize my life. You don't know me anymore! As a black person or as a woman. You have no idea of where I have been or what I have been through. I'd like you to go back to your seat and your life, but before you do, let me leave you with this last thought."

"Yes?"

The unmitigated *nerve*! she thought to herself as she felt tears welling up in her eyes, "I am a survivor. *Not* an idealist, Mr. Man. Now go!"

She dismissed him with a flick of her wrist.

"Pity." He sighed, returning to his seat with regret.

CHAPTER SIXTEEN

*T*hat evening, up in New York, Aletha was giving her sister, Desiree, a tour of the apartment, showing off the new alterations that her decorator had made in her penthouse. They were standing in the doorway of what would have been Reggie's study.

"Absolute perfection." Aletha sighed dreamily. "Don't you think, Desiree? And here I stand like an idiot, after spending all this money . . . and no Reggie! I could kill a horse!"

"Please, don't go shooting any horses, Aletha," Desiree said, staring at the papier-mâché moose head over the fireplace in disbelief. Nodding in its direction, she asked, "Aletha, did you shoot the moose, *too*?"

Aletha cut her eyes with annoyance at Desiree's sarcastic remark and said, "Don't be a wiseass."

They were both silent for a moment as Desiree's eyes explored the safari fantasy surrounding them.

"This is a very interesting room. I'm sure Reggie would have liked it, Aletha." Desiree tried to sound convincing . . . but then who *knew*?

Perhaps Reggie *would* have enjoyed it. She had met him only a couple of times, so she had no idea what kind of taste he had in decor. Since he had been attracted to her flamboyant sister, perhaps he would have thrived in this ostentatiously kitschy den.

"Ahh pish, Desiree!" Aletha sniffed, fanning away her fleeting fantasy image of Reggie lying naked except for his briefs on one of the faux zebra-skin rugs. With a flick of her wrist, she added definitively, "The nigger can burn in hell for all I care!"

"You *know* how I feel about that word, Aletha. I wish you'd stop using it. You should wash *it* and any other racial vituperations from your mind forever, girl!"

"Oh, Desiree, lighten up. I'm just angry at the sucker. If you were angry with David, wouldn't you call him a—"

"Never . . . *ever*!" she interrupted, appalled at the thought.

"And David wouldn't ever slip up and call you a—"

"Aletha, don't be insane! I've told you, neither of us has a death wish."

"It's only words, Des—"

"You work in the media. What do you mean, *only* words? No wonder television has reached such an all-time low, if its stars and other big shots feel so cavalier about—"

"Okay! *Okay!* Desiree! Don't start preaching to me. You know, big sister, you should have become an ordained minister or something, the way you like to moralize to all of us wayward, pathetic, and unprincipled souls." Aletha laughed, touching Desiree affectionately on the shoulder.

"I guess I should feel secure in the knowledge that very few people in my social life are black, huh, Aletha?"

"Why is *that*?"

"Because it's becoming frighteningly clear to me, chances are the only time I'd ever be called a 'nigger' by a so-called ally would be by some black person these days. It's perverted!"

Aletha rolled her eyes impatiently at her sister and said, "That word coming from the mouth of a black person isn't the same as—"

"Why *isn't* it, Aletha?"

"Oh, who *cares*." Aletha sucked her teeth. "Just stop preaching, okay?"

At that instant, a divergent thought formed in Aletha's head. "Desiree, since Reggie is gone, do you think that David would like a moose head for *his* study for Christmas? Men like this sort of thing, you know. I could wrap it up and give it to you guys for—"

"No! I don't think so, Aletha!" Desiree gasped, mortified at the image of such a thing hanging on a wall in her house.

"Oh, okay. Well, anyway, I think my girl has our dinner ready in the dining room, so let's go and eat!"

They walked down the hallway toward the dining room, which Aletha had lined with floor-to-ceiling bookcases weighed down heavily with expensive, well-worn volumes. Passing a small gateleg table, Desiree noticed a book with a bright cover lying open on top of a stack of others. The author's photo on the back cover beckoned her. She picked it up and read the title.

"Aletha, are you kidding? Are you reading this?"

"What?"

"*Black Men: How to Find One, How to Get One, How to Keep One. The Twelve-*

Step Program? Really!" In turning the book in her hands and flipping through the pages, Desiree felt something bogus about the energy emanating from it.

"Oh, *that*. The publisher sent me that copy. The author is booked to appear on my show in a few weeks. I figured I'd better read it."

"Learn anything?"

"Go to hell, Desiree!" Aletha laughed, turning away from her sister and continuing to head for the dining room.

Desiree sat enjoying the panoramic view from one of the glass-enclosed terraces of Aletha's penthouse. Aletha had cleverly created an outdoor dining room in this area, where they now sat savoring their dinner wine with the twinkling lights of the other Manhattan high-rise buildings as a backdrop embracing them. Aletha sat across from her at the elegantly set table. The light from the flickering flames of her gold-trimmed Lalique crystal candlesticks bounced off the silverware, wineglasses, and water glasses and onto Aletha's dark eyes, revealing that an alarming plot was hatching in her brain.

"Aletha, what are you thinking? You're scaring me, little sister."

Aletha's maid placed their dishes in front of them and discreetly retreated from the room.

Desiree noticed that Aletha's maid was a young Caucasian woman. She remembered that Aletha's previous maid had been a black woman from one of the Islands. She wondered when and where she had found this one and whether her presence as a domestic had anything to do with her having found Reggie in bed with another woman who happened to have been white. Desiree remembered Aletha's statement about being able to "buy and sell" her.

"Aletha?" Desiree looked suspiciously at her sister, having decided to skim the issue.

"Yes, Desiree?"

"Didn't you have a *Haitian* housekeeper working for you? When did you hire this young woman?"

"Oh, you mean my new girl? My old one had to leave . . . had to go back to Port-au-Prince to take care of some sick relatives."

Desiree doubted this.

"I hired this one just the other day. She is a good girl. Would you like to borrow her sometime?" Aletha asked good-naturedly, completely unaware of what she had just revealed.

"No, thank you," Desiree said firmly, having satisfactorily confirmed what she had theorized.

Desiree looked over at Aletha's plate of lobster Newburg, then apprehensively looked into her own dish.

Aletha smiled knowingly and said, "Don't worry, Desiree, I know you don't eat this sort of thing. I ordered you the chicken paprika."

Desiree's skeptical eyes deciphered her dish, and she sighed with relief.

"Girl, I think you have been Jewish all your life! You never ate pork." Aletha chuckled, having noted her sister's highbrow look of consternation.

"I'm allergic, Aletha."

"Umm-hmm! And you would break out in hives whenever Mom cooked any *kind* of crustacean."

"I'm *allergic* to those things, Aletha."

"Whatever." Aletha chuckled. "But all I know is that it seems that you were *born* Jewish. A bona fide, American, black Jew!" She cackled. "I can tell you right now, girl, that you have missed out on some good shit over the years."

Desiree imagined herself rolling her eyes at Aletha and said, "I don't eat shit—as you call it—Aletha. Anyway, I asked you a question. What were you thinking about? You had one of those strange looks on your face."

"I told you that Reggie moved, right?"

"Aletha, you've got to accept the fact that you chased Reggie—at gunpoint—out of your life. The end."

"You got a cigarette, Desiree?" asked Aletha, all fidgety now.

"I quit. And I thought you did, too."

"Girl, I've got pressures. Anyway, you've got to help me, Desiree. I want you to help me get my man back!"

Desiree sat stupefied at the request. "Aletha, I can't get involved in this. What on earth would you want *me* to do? No, Aletha, I can't get involved in your obsessive plots and schemes."

"If you don't help me, sister, I'll just call Geraldo. He'll help me out, I'm sure."

"Who?"

Desiree felt the dreadlocks on her head stand on end. She watched Aletha shoot up from the table and begin to pace around the room.

It was amazing. Aletha and her personality seemed larger than life, but watching her pace around her pretty dining room with her ivory-colored silk robe swirling about her long shapely legs—Desiree had always wished she had legs like Aletha's—she silently noted that her sister was just a mere slip of a woman. Hardly five feet tall and couldn't possibly be any more than a hundred five, maybe ten, pounds soaking wet. A tiny woman who wielded a huge gun.

Aletha came back to the table, forked up some lobster, and gulped her wine, looking as if she had discovered a new mission in life.

This was getting scary.

"Yeah, that's it. I'll get Geraldo to help me."

At that instant Sparky entered the room from the kitchen, barking with alarm.

"Oh, shut up, Sparky! What's wrong with you? Here, have some lobster," she offered, dangling a piece with her fingers.

Sparky sniffed, let out an outraged yelp, and then quickly sought sanctuary under the table.

Desiree noted with amusement that Sparky seemed to be discerning about his diet, as well. "Sparky must be keeping kosher, too."

"What?"

"Never mind. Aletha, who is this Geraldo?"

"Yeah . . . I could ask him to do a show on 'Men Who Cheat on Their Women.' Then he could call Reggie's agent, saying that he wants to do an interview with him on one of his articles—"

This was madness. "Geraldo?" Then Desiree suddenly understood. She gasped, "You mean that talk show host on channel—"

Sparky growled from under the table.

"Yeah, him. I know *he*'d help me. He—"

"Get a grip, Aletha!" Desiree yelled, struggling to calm herself. "If you do this, I will have you committed—put away! And you *know* I could do it, too. How can you stoop so low as to conjure up such an idea anyway?"

Thankfully, Aletha started laughing.

"I bet you'd freak out, big sister, if David left you for a white woman, wouldn't you?"

Adroitly avoiding an entirely lopsided question, Desiree sighed. "First of all, Reggie didn't leave you for any woman. You broke into his apartment and shot him! You could have killed him."

"But he was with that redheaded, white—"

"This is not *about* white women, Aletha. It never is," Desiree said, slicing off a piece of chicken from her plate and offering it under the table to Sparky.

Sparky snapped it up with canine gratitude.

"What do you mean?" Aletha asked, looking incredulously at her sister.

Desiree thought to herself that, at this very moment with Aletha's thick hair falling wildly around her face, her sister looked like a black Medusa.

"Just what I said," Desiree said simply, slicing a piece of chicken for herself. "This is delicious, Aletha."

"I'm glad you like it. These dishes were prepared especially for me at Gleason's," she said, then added smugly, as if it should make a difference, "It's *expensive*, Desiree!"

That was *pure* Aletha, Desiree thought, smiling at her sister.

"Anyway, as I was going to say, the brothers are always chasing after white women, Desiree. Haven't you noticed?" Then Aletha added mischievously, "I guess it's not *your* world, huh?"

"Look, little sister, I'm willing to talk to you about this, but I want you to remember that I am *not* Reginald Pinkney and I do not intend to sit around dodging your bullets all evening!" she shot back.

"Sorry," Aletha said, picking up her napkin, placing it on her lips, and smirking behind it.

"I have noticed, Aletha, that some black men like white women and that some white women like black men. Actually, it seems to me that it's the white women who are leaving white *men* in *droves*."

"What do you mean?" Aletha asked with what had turned instantly into an intense interest.

"Have you ever wondered why a group of women who have access to the most powerful men in the world would throw this all away to be with a relatively powerless man? Why they would risk public ostracism, humiliation, and a certain degree of social status to be with these men? Why they would choose to bring biracial children into the world who would most probably be shunned by their very own parents?"

"They want the big, black *bamboo*, girl." Aletha laughed hysterically.

"Be serious, Aletha."

"I have no idea. Tell me, Doctor."

"Maybe they are fleeing from controlling, power-freak white men."

Sparky, bored with the conversation, came from under the table and left the room to search for more intriguing subjects.

Aletha was silent for a moment, then said. "That reminds me of something you said up at your house. I wanted to talk to you about it. You said that *I* was acting like a power-freak white male!"

"I see that you are beginning to follow me. Get my drift, Aletha?" Desiree smiled and took a sip of her wine.

"How can *I*, a bona fide black woman, ever be like a white man? I don't have all those privileges in this society. I'm a double minority! Don't be ridiculous, Desiree."

"*You* in particular, Aletha, earn more in a year than most white men in America—or anywhere, for that matter—will ever see in their lives. You do whatever it is you want. You always have and you *know* it! *You* are not what anyone could call an oppressed minority."

"I've got *problems.* I'm a black—"

"All of God's children got problems, Aletha." Desiree laughed, taking another sip of her wine.

"Well, how else, besides my money, am I like a white man?"

"You're kidding, right?"

"I am *not*! Tell me. I'm listening."

"You try to control everyone's life. You think you can buy and sell people. You were down in the Islands buying Reggie some house he knew nothing about. He said you were buying him little expensive gifts all the time, knowing that he doesn't have the kind of money—"

"I'm *rich*, Desiree!" Aletha said, banging her hand on the table in a typical Aletha Brown outburst. "Why shouldn't I share my wealth with the people I love!"

"Aletha, you were trying to turn Reggie into an obedient, dependent, white, Anglo-Saxon housewife—if you ask me—and the brother ran for his life just to save his balls."

Aletha sat dumbfounded.

"You broke into his home like some kind of freaked-out colonialist with a gun. Honey, you shot him and got away with it just like some racist white man."

Silence from Aletha.

"And remember, you shouted at him, 'I *own* you, nigger.' Sounds familiar in more ways than one, doesn't it?"

Aletha was no dummy. She realized that she had a lot to think about.

"You know, Aletha, I feel that black women who are interested in finding fulfillment with a brother had better start to understand their needs and agendas, because if not, there are millions of other women out there waiting in the wings prepared to take them off your hands."

"Humpf!" Aletha grunted with impatience, fanning her hands at Desiree.

"By the way, Aletha."

"Yes, big sister?"

"How's your producer, Veronica McPheerson?" Desiree had read that her sister had hired a new woman to replace her. She was curious about what the woman could have possibly done to cause Aletha to replace her.

"I fired the bitch. She was stealing from me."

"Why don't I believe you, little sister?" Desiree said pointedly.

Aletha stifled the smile that threatened to form on her face and stared at Desiree, who she realized knew her better than anyone else on the planet.

Aletha sat watching her sister enjoying her meal and decided to ask her a question she'd never asked before.

"Sister?"

"Yes, Aletha?" Desiree asked, picking up her glass of wine and smiling into it, knowing instinctively the direction that Aletha was about to take their conversation.

"Have you ever even *dated* a brother, girl?"

"*Dated?* Of course. But that's not what you're asking, I'm sure. You want to know if I've ever had a black lover."

"Yes."

"It always seemed like the kind of black men that I was attracted to were never attracted to black women like me."

"It's probably because of your haughty-taughty, big, flapping preachy mouth. You probably frighten the brothers, girl!" Aletha laughed.

"At least I don't pack a gun," Desiree said simply, enjoying another helping of her chicken.

"What do you have against black men, Desiree?"

"Absolutely nothing. Did I *say* I had anything against black men? In fact, I find black men to be exceedingly attractive. It's just that the type of black men that I found myself really attracted to all look like Marshall. It's too weird."

"Marshall is handsome, Desiree. What's wrong with *that*?"

"Too incestuous for me. Besides, it seems that once a black woman starts dating nonblack men, *particularly* white ones, the brothers stay away. Black women like me who date others have a saying: 'Once you date white, the brothers no longer bite.' It's like the other guys leave a stamp on you that says, 'One of ours.' Anyway, in my opinion, Aletha, the fact that we call black men *brothers* and they call us *sisters* seems to imply that we black folks have inadvertently put up a wall of taboo between us. It's weird karma. Maybe that's why the so-called brothers and sisters are having such a hard time hooking up with one another these days. Who would want to sleep with one's relatives?"

"Damn, Desiree! You get on my nerves. Why can't you leave your psychology shit in the office where it belongs? Why can't you talk like everybody else—at least for a minute and a half anyway," Aletha complained, holding up her wineglass and twirling the liquid in it around in the candlelight.

Desiree stuck her tongue out at Aletha, and then continued to eat.

"If you weren't so damned superior, distancing yourself from us mere mortals, you'd realize that you're not as psychologically sound as you think you are. Damn girl, are you *blind*? If you were to dump David into a vat of chocolate, he'd look just like Marshall himself. Haven't you ever noticed that?"

"I'm not going for it, Aletha. David is my husband and my lover—*not* my brother."

"Ahh pish, Desiree," Aletha said, fanning her hands again, this time at her sister's evasiveness. Shrinks! Aletha thought with exasperation. They're nothing but another group of pompous, high-handed doctors, she thought to herself, downing another sip of her wine.

"You asked me a question and I answered it. What more do you want from me?"

"Okay," Aletha conceded. Her eyes lit up at the thought of taking another scrumptious bite out of her sister's private life.

"Okay, *what*?" Desiree snapped.

"I want to know—since you have diverse experiences with men—do you believe it's true what they say about black men? You *know* . . ."

"What do they say, Aletha?"

"Go to hell, Desiree! You know what I'm asking."

"No. Spell it out."

"That black men have bigger sausages than—"

"Sausages? How would I know, Aletha? Even if I *had* slept with any, I certainly couldn't have slept with enough to have come to any sound conclusions. Besides, the big-penis theory was started by white men in order to frighten white women away from dating and sleeping with black men."

"It certainly hasn't worked, has it?" Aletha asked, frowning as she thought back to Reggie in bed with that redhead.

"No it hasn't." Desiree laughed, then added, "Nevertheless, my lovers have all been sufficiently endowed for me. I've never made any racial comparisons."

"Well, then, who has been your *best* lover?"

"David, of course. Perhaps that's part of the reason that he is my husband."

"You've had an Asian lover, right?"

"Umm-hmm."

"Are they as—"

"Aletha, think about this. As black women, we have a reputation of being highly sexual. They say that our male counterparts have huge members. Do you think that a man of any race would approach us if he felt that he was insufficient in that area?"

"What are you saying?"

"I suspect that *any* man with a small penis—from any tribe—would be hesitant to approach a black woman, given the kind of press—"

"So what you are saying is—"

"What I'm saying is that all the men I have ever been with are pretty much the same in that department. Of course, the lovemaking skills are different."

"Skills?"

"My husband is the best lover I have ever had. But, of course, this has a lot to do with the fact that he is not only competent in bed with *me*, but he also satisfies my mind."

"Give me a break, Desiree."

"Why don't you go to a nude beach or something, if you are interested in penile diversity. Or comparisons."

"A nude beach?"

"Umm-hmm. Pick a place somewhere on the Mediterranean where you'll find a cross section of tribal diversity, and check out the dicks. When you *do*, let me in on your findings." Desiree laughed at Aletha's expression, which seemed to indicate that she was seriously considering the idea.

"*You've* spent a lot of time in Europe. Have you ever done this?"

Desiree winked at Aletha and sliced into her salad.

Changing the subject, Aletha asked, "By the way, have you spoken to Marshall lately?"

"Umm-hmm," she said, picking at a piece of chicken. "He read about you and Reggie in the tabloids and was pressuring me for details."

Aletha panicked. "You didn't tell him anything, did you?"

"Of course not, Aletha! What kind of question is that anyway? You *know* me," Desiree snapped, looking at her sister with disbelief.

Desiree had always been the keeper of the secrets. She had enough dirt on the whole Brown family—Aletha, Marshall, their father, and their mother—to bury them all. It was the price of being the oldest. At a very premature age, their mother, having been unable to communicate with their father, had taken her as a confidante—a heavy burden to place on a child. Of course, in the beginning Desiree had felt honored, but had soon realized that she was becoming privy to the kinds of adult problems she couldn't possibly understand, and didn't want to. Their father used Desiree as an intermediary, passing messages on to his wife on subjects he didn't want to confront her with—usually things dealing with issues of money and disciplinary suggestions concerning Marshall and Aletha. Not that Aletha ever got any major reprimands; she was the baby, after all.

Plus, everyone in the family, except Desiree, appeared to be afraid of Aletha, even as a baby. She was always throwing temper tantrums in order to get her way and pushing in everywhere in order to be the center of attention.

"Well, you know, Desiree." Aletha sniffed with indignation. "Those tabloids are full of lies!"

"What do you mean?"

"I really didn't shoot Reggie. The bullet never hit him. It—it—" She got up from her seat and flicked her right hand in the air. "—it just grazed his shoulder. I just wanted to scare him, girl!"

"Sure, Aletha." Desiree laughed, looking away from her sister toward the New York skyline. She had spoken with Reggie herself, of which Aletha was perfectly aware, if she'd just think back to the night of the shooting.

"I'm telling the truth, Desiree! Anyway, forget it. It's not important anymore." Finishing up her lobster, she continued. "Marshall *is* coming up for Christmas, right?"

"Of course, Aletha."

"What do you mean, of course? When was the last time he went up to see the folks? He's probably only coming up because this is *your* last Christmas around here for a while. He wouldn't make any special trips up there for *me*," she said huffily.

"How can you be so ridiculous! When you moved back to New York, he came all the way up to the folks' place to see you . . . and you *know* how he feels about going up there. He, Mom, and Dad always end up getting into loud altercations. Who needs it?"

"Well, Desiree, can you blame them? He moved out . . . just *moved* out, remember? Took his stuff out of the house without telling anyone where he went. Not a warning!"

"He left a note, Aletha, and that was almost two decades ago. Everybody needs to just let it go, don't you agree?"

"No, he just left me. My big brother just left without saying good-bye or anything!"

Desiree broke out laughing at her preposterous baby sister and said, "You were fifteen years old and couldn't wait to get out of that house yourself. You were just jealous it wasn't *you*. You couldn't wait to get out there to be the star in your own movie . . . and you know it!"

"Desiree, Marshall just wanted to go out there and run around like a wild man with all those wild, artsy-fartsy hoochies who used to flock around him. He always liked those light-skinned, big-haired chicks . . . just like the rest of the brothers."

Desiree's eyes widened at her sister's assessment of their brother's lifestyle, then she squeezed them shut, forcing back another Brown family secret.

"Is he bringing that Janeen girl with him?"

"He usually does, Aletha."

"He's been going with her for *how* long? Seems like forever."

"She's just his friend, Aletha."

"Do you know her well? What's she like?"

"No, I don't know her that well, but she seems nice."

"Why doesn't Marshall just marry her? Have some children. It looks like I'll never have any, and since you and David don't want any, he's my only hope!"

"Only *hope*? What does *that* mean?"

"My only hope of becoming an aunt!"

"Oh, I see." Desiree laughed.

"Look, if you and David wanted children you could just do it now—" She leaned toward her sister grinning and snapped her fingers, the candlelight flickering in her eyes. "—and I'd spoil them rotten, too. And if Marshall married Janeen, *they* could have some kids, but *me*—poor little me, what can *I* do? I'm almost forty. It's over for me. Reggie has ruined everything!"

"You know, Aletha, I read in some paper that there's a woman in Russia who had a baby at the age of sixty-seven." Desiree tried to look serious but lost control of her laughter and spewed wine from her mouth all over the table and her—thank goodness—rust-colored slacks.

Aletha just stared at her sister and handed her a napkin. "You know, Desiree, I've learned over the years that you can't believe everything you read in the papers."

Sparky returned to the dining room with one of his squeaky toys. He placed it on Aletha's foot and sat on his hind legs wagging his tail with anticipation.

"Looks like Sparky wants to play," Desiree said, finishing up her dinner.

"Later, Sparky," Aletha responded, rubbing his head. He lay down next to her feet.

"Aletha, this meal was absolutely delicious," Desiree said, pushing herself away from the table. She got up and began looking around at the various sculptures that were dramatically displayed under spotlights in the room.

"You have quite an impressive art collection, baby sister."

"Thank you. Reggie picked out most of it. I don't know much about art. I just know what I like."

It seemed that Reggie had terrific taste in art, Desiree thought to herself.

"That's all you need to know in order to buy art. I never understood why people think they need a Ph.D. in art history in order to buy something beautiful for themselves."

"Some of the shows in the downtown galleries are a complete mystery to me, Desiree. You're an artist, so it's easy for you," Aletha said, pouring herself another glass of wine.

"A lot of those pieces are an overpriced mockery of public taste, Aletha—art dealers just playing on people's insecurities, that's all." She laughed, continuing to admire Aletha's gallery of wonderful imaginative works. "You know, about twenty years ago I attended a gallery talk at the Museum of Modern Art. The lecturer spent almost two long hours explaining *minimalism*!" Desiree chuckled derisively at the memory. "Just buy what you like. That's what life is really all about, when you have money to indulge your taste, right?"

"I suppose so," Aletha said, remembering with a certain amount of discomfort the numerous things she had bought in her life that she didn't understand at all, just because some expert had pronounced the acquisition as a good investment.

"Desiree, come back over here and have some more wine," Aletha demanded, leaning over to refill her sister's glass.

"Thanks," said Desiree, returning to the table, wondering what Aletha wanted to talk about next. She had a feeling, from the looks of things, that the topic wasn't exactly going to be as tame as a discussion of art.

"Desiree, how is that friend of yours? You know, the one you went to high school with."

"You mean Joy? She's okay. She and her husband are coming out for Christmas."

"No, not *that* friend. The other one. The one who always used to wear the big earrings with the coins hanging from them."

Desiree frowned, trying to think of who Aletha was talking about.

"You know, Desiree, you always have had such exotic friends. I guess you married folks just have a much more interesting social life than us singles," Aletha stated, sipping some wine.

"The friends we socialize with are mostly people we met back in school. Actually, it's difficult for couples to have any real friends."

"Why is that?"

"Oh, it usually seems that either one member of a couple doesn't get along with one of the other couple, or that the men involved feel threatened by the relationship between the women."

"Yeah, I have seen that—a lot—on my show."

"Then, of course, single women friends often express jealousy toward married women. It's screwed up!"

Aletha, perplexed, just shrugged. She didn't know anything about all that. Her only real friend for years had been Reggie.

"Well, at least you and David have each other. You're lucky."

"I know. But, Aletha, *who* are you talking about—the girl who used to wear the big—"

"*You* know. The Latina girl—Diaz, I think her name is. You went to high school with her, and then the two of you went to the same shrink school. She's a psychologist, too, right? You know who I mean."

"Oh . . . Annunciata! She's married. She's Annunciata DaSilva, now." Desiree laughed as she suddenly realized why Aletha was asking about that particular friend. "She's fine, Aletha. I had lunch with her just last week. Why do you ask?"

"Does she still do those tarot card readings on the side?"

"She's a professional psychic, Aletha."

"I thought she was a shrink, like you."

Annunciata Diaz had always possessed incredible psychic abilities, even when they were young girls, Desiree reflected. Although she had gone to school for her degree and was licensed as a psychotherapist, she had decided to combine her talents to practice a unique nontraditional type of therapy, which had proven to be quite successful.

"Annunciata is a therapist, and she's also a very talented psychic, as well. Do you want to make an appointment with her?"

"Do you think she would see me?" Aletha asked tentatively, a bit embarrassed.

"Aletha, you amaze me," she said, giggling into her glass. "You don't believe in shrinks, but you want to consult a psychic? How do you explain that?"

"I can't explain it. But I'd like to make an appointment with her. How much does she charge?"

"The same as I do for a session, dear," Desiree said sarcastically.

"She won't charge me *more* 'cause I'm a celebrity, will she?"

"Of course not."

"I think I could definitely use a reading. Weird things have been happening to me lately—things I can't even tell *you* about! I am at a totally confusing point in my life, and I need to know what's going to happen next."

"I see."

"Do you think she'd make a house call, or do psychic therapists *do* that?"

"I'm sure she would, for *you*. I'll give you her number before I leave," Desiree said, agreeing that Aletha probably *could* actually benefit from a session with Annunciata.

There was a moment of silence, so Desiree decided to broach the subject of her house.

"Aletha, I want to ask you a favor."

"Me? Why, of—of *course*, Desiree! I would do *anything* . . ." Aletha was flattered and flabbergasted at once. Desiree had never asked *her* for a favor. Desiree always seemed to be *above* asking anyone for favors, Aletha thought.

"You know I told you that David and I were selling our house, right?"

"Uh-huh . . ."

"Well, I really don't want to sell it."

Aletha laughed and said, "I had wondered about that, Desiree. I just couldn't imagine you selling your beautiful home to wander around the earth with your husband and a big dog. It just didn't sound like you . . . but I was afraid to ask."

"Afraid? Are you afraid of me, Aletha?"

"Not of *you*, but I always feel if I don't understand something the way you do, that it's because I'm not as smart as you in some way. And I hate to have you mad at me or to think that you'll be disappointed in me."

"I'm sorry that I made you feel that way. I didn't know."

"It's no big deal, girl. Let's get back to the house. Do you want me to buy it from you?"

"No. What I'd like to know is if you were serious that you would like to have it as a weekend retreat."

"That *would* be nice. So, what are you proposing?"

"While David and I are away, deciding whether we really want to sell it or not, we'd like to know if you'd take care of it. Use it as often as you wish."

"What's in it for *you*, sis?"

"You'd pay the taxes and expenses. Take care of it for us."

"That's *all*?"

"That's all."

"Girl, you certainly don't ask for much. I'd be happy to do it. It's the least I can do considering what I've put you guys through lately. Your place is so lovely. It would be a pleasure."

"Then it's a done deal, huh?" Desiree asked, a huge weight disappearing from her shoulders.

"Done, big sister! No problem." Aletha looked toward the maid who had entered the dining room. "Ahh . . . here comes the dessert! You're going to *love* this, Desiree," Aletha chimed, her eyes sparkling as the maid placed their tea and two plates of the mocha-layered chocolate opera cake in front of them.

"The tea is that herbal crap that you like, Desiree—oolong kabong, or whatever it is they call it," Aletha teased, reaching over and pouring tea into her sister's cup.

The next morning, Aletha Brown was in makeup getting the roots of her hair touched up before the taping of her special Christmas show.

She had had an awful urge to take a drag on a cigarette ever since that unfortunate Reginald Pinkney incident, but so far she had successfully resisted.

All the tabloid rags had reported outrageously distorted tales of the shooting. One had even called it a stabbing. She denied everything and told her staff to do the same, if asked. Why on earth would Aletha Brown shoot or try to hurt anyone?

She was known to be a fine woman—generous to a fault, it had been said. She paid her staff outrageous salaries, and they all have the best perks in the business: all-expense-paid vacations in the Caribbean in the winter and wherever they wanted to go in Europe in the summer months, plus a very generous clothing allowance. She firmly believed that people—especially people associated with *her* show—should have exposure to other cultures. She didn't want to work around a bunch of poorly dressed ignoramuses.

Yet try as she might to hold things together around her, Aletha realized that her life had entered a terrifying cycle. Everything in her life seemed to be crumbling around her. Even things from the past had come back to haunt her.

First, she caught Reggie in bed with another woman, then she found out that the jackass in Miami, who she had left living in her beachfront home, had burned it down! He had fallen asleep with a cigarette in his hand and had let her house go up in flames. Her lovely furniture—gone! Her beautiful Steinway piano—gone! All those beautiful clothes and books she had left behind that now she would never see again—*gone*!

She had lived with the nut because she had thought that having a man around her house would be good protection from that stalker fan she had acquired while doing her show in Miami. Look what it had got her!

Nevertheless, everyone was jealous of Miss Aletha Brown—of her "success" they called it. Shit! Life was a bitch and then you died.

What could possibly happen next?

Perhaps, she thought, picking up a pen as if it were a cigarette, this was the worst that could happen.

The new producer seemed to be working out pretty well, although she was no Veronica McPheerson. At least she was dedicated to the job, since she didn't have any other distractions, like an old man or a baby.

Mary Beth Dean had graduated cum laude from the University of North Carolina at Chapel Hill. Aletha Brown always bought the best of *everything*, she thought, reflecting on her new producer.

Although her salary was quite ample, this strawberry blond Irish Southern belle, Mary Beth Dean, lived in a modest apartment in the east Fifties in Manhattan.

Yep, this country-time, starry-eyed white girl, Miss Dean, would have to do for the time being. She certainly had done a good job putting together this Christmas show for Aletha. She was calling it her "Family Reunion show." She'd be bringing together family members who had either lost touch with each other or who had never met.

It would be a real tearjerker. Just the kind of show for this sappy, sentimental season to bring in some good ratings. They had been steadily dropping over the past year. Even though she was ready to retire, she really preferred to retire on top of the world, not like some kind of tired ole dog, walking away with its tail between its mangy legs.

Aletha decided to do this reunion show when she received a touching letter from a young brother from Harlem, Brian Washington, who had asked her if she could use her resources to help him find his father whom he'd never met. He said that he was finishing college this year and was hoping he could meet his father and have him attend his graduation—especially since he was graduating at the very top of his class. This young brother was about to attend Stanford Medical School in the fall.

Aletha's diligent staff had tracked down the father—who was, coincidentally, a doctor—at his practice in Miami. They invited the good doctor to the show under the pretense of doing a program on his work in family medicine.

Aletha had read that about 65 percent of African American children were being raised in single-parent households with the mothers being the head of the family unit.

Where were the fathers?

Aletha, Desiree, and their brother, Marshall, were obviously part of a privileged class. Their father had always been present, committed to them and their mother, and remained gainfully employed.

Well, the least this well-to-do Dr. Morgan could do was help his son with medical school!

She could never understand how these men got off so easily from their responsibilities.

"Mary Beth," Aletha commanded, "as soon as Dr. Morgan arrives, take him to Bruce in makeup. Don't let him take his coffee in the green room with the others. Serve it to him while he's with Bruce."

"Yes, ma'am."

"I told you to stop calling me ma'am. This is not the South. And make sure that you have a tape of an old show playing on the monitor in the makeup room; he's not to suspect a thing, okay, girl?"

"Yes, Miss Brown. Anything else?"

Aletha shook her head crisply, and the producer scurried from the room, like an appropriately intimidated child.

Aletha smiled. Keeping her employees well paid and in awe of her power kept them from cranking up the rumor mill.

CHAPTER SEVENTEEN

*A*s he was whisked through the green room and into makeup, Dr. Morgan noted with a pang of discomfort that the other guests didn't seem like doctors waiting to discuss their work.

Aletha Brown's knees almost buckled under her when she saw this fi-i-i-ne bald-headed Adonis of a doctor leaning back in his chair. It was obvious from the way Bruce puffed himself up and flitted around the man that he shared the same opinion of Dr. Brian Morgan.

"Good afternoon, Dr. Morgan." She couldn't resist putting her hand on his broad shoulder. "I—I—am Aletha B-Brown." The electricity emanating from his body caused Aletha to snatch her hand away, jamming it into the pocket of her suit jacket. She didn't want this man to take notice of her sweaty palms. *He* was just *too* handsome for *her* own good.

"It's a pleasure to meet you, Miss Brown." He started to shake her hand, but pulled back as he noticed something strange going on in her eyes. What a beautiful woman, but Brian sensed something unbalanced about her that he couldn't pinpoint.

The next thing he knew, he was sitting on a metal folding chair on stage, cameras rolling, with a panel of some rather peculiar-looking characters surrounding him—certainly not colleagues of his.

After a long while, Aletha made her announcement with a gracious calm.

"Dr. Morgan, we told you that we were doing a show about family medicine. Well, the truth is—" She smiled at him with a look of demented glee. "—this is our Christmas family reunion show. We have someone here who has been dying to meet you for years. We'd like to introduce you to Brian Washington—your *son*!"

Aletha looked up at the monitor. Under the face of Dr. Morgan, she found that some assistant had entered copy that read "Deadbeat Father"!

Oh, *Lord*! she thought, fighting a silent note of panic.

Utter and complete confusion created a wave of nausea that started in Dr. Morgan's feet and crawled upward to his naked scalp.

A tall, dapper young man, a mirror image of Dr. Brian Morgan even down to the shaved head, walked onto the stage and stood in front of him.

Since when did he have a son? This must be some kind of a sick joke. Perhaps someone wanted to extort money from him or something.

He tried to retrieve a mental list of his enemies. He could think of no one who would pull a ridiculously plebeian prank like *this*. Yet this young man definitely looked as if he could be his very own son.

"Jesus," he murmured under his breath as he shook the boy's hand.

Strong grip.

Brian Washington. Washington? He just couldn't recall what woman he had gone out with whose name was Washington.

He drew a complete blank.

The show went on around him, as he tried to fight his way out of this tide of confusion.

Washington . . .

He looked across the table at the young man who claimed to be his son. He had agreed to have lunch with him at Tavern on the Green—courtesy of *The Aletha Brown Show*—in order to decipher this mystery.

They both ordered the steak—medium rare—and agreed to share a bottle of Mouton Cadet.

"What did you say your mother's name is again?"

"Louise . . . Louise Washington," young Brian repeated impatiently.

He watched the young man cut into his steak with eerily familiar movements; he was a southpaw, too, just like Dr. Morgan.

"I don't remember dating a Louise—"

"At first, she told me that my father was killed in Vietnam," young Brian interrupted.

He was convinced that the doctor was lying about not remembering his mother. How could anyone forget his cute, sassy, outgoing mother?

"Then when I was about fifteen years old, she told me that you weren't dead, as far as she knew, but had left her after she told you that she was pregnant with me. She said you just went off to medical school in Texas. She raised me alone. She never married."

"I did my *residency* in Houston—" Dr. Morgan stated as he suddenly recalled who this Miss Washington was.

He had dated her exactly *twice*. It was a blind date. One of his friends had fixed him up with a cute secretary, encouraging him to take a respite from his backbreaking studies.

The first date he doubled with his friend, and they all went out to dinner.

He could see her in his mind clearly now.

They had all met in front of the restaurant in Chinatown.

When she got out of the taxi with her girlfriend, his friend's date, he had seen her face . . . *pow*! She was gorgeous! His eyes had dropped down to those big, full breasts . . . *blam*!! Then to those wide swinging hips . . . *kapowee*!!! And then to those wickedly shapely legs . . . *boom*!!!! She was a physical gold mine!

When they sat down at the table, she criticized the men's choice of restaurant, saying, "I never eat Chinese food. All this mess is, is scraps—leftovers. China is a poor country, you know." She leaned forward and whispered conspiratorially, "They say it's chicken, but I hear it's more like Rover or Boots."

Dr. Morgan shook his head. "Rubber boots?"

Louise rolled her eyes and said, a little too loudly, "Dogs and cats. They eat dogs and cats."

Dr. Morgan shrank in his chair. He had noticed that despite her assessment of the food she ate everything she ordered plus half of everyone else's dish.

He found it quite hilarious, at first. He thought she had been joking about the Chinese until, later on during the dinner, she decided to get "political" on them.

She had said, *sagely* she thought, "You know, it has been my policy to never eat down here in Chinatown. You see all these black folks eating in these here Chinese restaurants, but never . . . I have *never* seen any Chinese people up in Harlem eating *soul food*! Have any of you?"

Okay, so she had been a little weird, but those hips and legs were beckoning him for a second date.

The second date, a week later, she invited him over to her place where she made a rather tasty catfish dinner. His mother had cooked this quite a lot when he was growing up, but he had decided that when he left home and became a doctor he'd never look at another piece of catfish again in his natural-born life!

Talk about your poor people's food!

After dinner they had sex. She had that great body and all, but he felt that he was in bed with a traffic cop.

He'd spoken to her a couple of times after that, but they both seemed to agree that they had very little in common.

He focused back on his son. Why on earth would a woman go to bed with a man she hardly knew, without using some kind of contraception? That was the pre-AIDS era, when men didn't feel pressured to wear condoms.

She'd never even told him that she was pregnant. She must have known . . . long before he went off to Houston.

What on earth could he tell this boy about his almost nonexistent relationship with his mother?

"Look, Brian, I only dated your mother two times—"

"Oh, I see," the young man commented skeptically.

What was this man trying to suggest? Was he trying to imply that Louise Washington was some kind of two-bit tramp, who'd sleep with a man after only one date? Dr. Morgan *had* to be nuts. What did he take his son for— some kind of bastard fool?

"Well, exactly what did your mother tell you? What kind of things did she say about me?"

Young Brian realized with an unsettling certainty that his mother never really described this man at all. She had simply told him that they had dated and he had left her with child.

Perhaps the doctor was telling the truth.

Perhaps his mother couldn't say much about him, because she really didn't *know* much about the man.

"You know, Doc, my mother almost had a coronary when I told her I intended to become a doctor. I guess it's because you're one, huh, Doc?" A half smile twitched across his lips as he took a drink from his wineglass.

"What did she want you to be?"

"I don't know. Probably anything else but that. But you see, I was a straight-A student all the way through school, and there was no way I was going to be anything but a doctor."

"Of course," he responded, looking at the young man with a puzzled expression. Why would a mother with a brilliant son want to discourage him, for any reason, from being a doctor, he wondered.

Perhaps that's why he had dated her only twice. Obviously her vision was dangerously limited.

He laughed to himself as he thought about his wife, Marta, and what she would make of this whole situation. Thank God, he thought, stabbing a chunk of baked potato, that his son had been born quite a few years before they were married. The shit would have definitely hit the fan.

So, what was he supposed to do now with this full-grown, out-of-wedlock son? What did the young man want?

"So, what do you want from me, Brian?"

"Nothing, Doc. Don't worry, I'm not hitting you up for money or anything. I just wanted to know who my father is. I've been feeling all my life that a whole half of my being was just a big, empty question mark."

Dr. Morgan looked down at his plate, his face moving through phases of relief, anger, and then regret.

"How would you feel if your mother told you for years that your father was dead, only to find out years later that he was a living, breathing entity somewhere?"

"I don't honestly know," admitted Dr. Morgan, thinking that this young man seemed to have been raised well, despite the circumstances. "So your mother told you that I abandoned her, did she?"

Young Brian laughed and said, "As a matter of fact, that's *exactly* the word she used."

That weird talk show host, Aletha Brown, may have tricked him into flying to New York under devious intentions, but she had certainly made this Christmas unforgettable.

"Look, Brian, I'm in New York for a couple of days visiting my relatives. Why don't you and I call your mother and straighten out this abandonment issue?"

"You're *jiving*, man!" Young Brian smiled with excitement.

"I most certainly am not 'jiving', as you say." Brian Morgan decided that he was going to make sure that his good reputation remained intact. He was going to confront the boy's mother with her fabricated story.

"All *right!*" Young Brian lifted his glass in a toast, his handsome face glowing with a pleasure he had never known before. "To family reunions, huh, Doc?"

"Yes, son." He tapped glasses with the young man. "To family reunions . . . and to erroneous tales of *abandonment!*"

They shared a hearty laugh and a pleasurably novel kind of male bonding on that particularly cold, yet bright sunny late afternoon in Manhattan.

Dr. Morgan had arranged to meet Louise Washington at what she said was her favorite restaurant, Alphonse's Louisiana Garden, up in Harlem.

When she got out of the cab, he felt déjà vu propelling him back in time.

Bam! Blam!! Boom!!! Kapowee!!!!

Her big floppy fox fur hat and long fox fur coat only enhanced what he already knew was underneath it all. She was still, over two decades later, an absolute knockout. She had gained a little weight, but he liked that kind of woman. In fact, he was glad that after the birth of his daughter, his wife, Marta, had put on a bit of weight. He was encouraging her to keep it on, too, because he preferred "healthy" ladies.

In the restaurant, over her *catfish* dinner, Louise talked on and on about her life and some book tour she had been on. Apparently, she had written some kind of self-help book; he couldn't catch its theme or what it was all about.

She never asked him a single thing about himself.

After over an hour she hadn't even broached the subject of why they were having dinner together.

This was one self-absorbed woman, he thought.

"Louise, I told Brian that I would speak with you because I am quite disturbed by the fact that you told him that I abandoned you, when you were pregnant."

"You weren't *there*, were you?" She laughed in a disarmingly pretty way.

"You never told me—"

"We had exactly *two* dates, Doctor. Why would I tell you something like that? What would you have *done*?" she asked now, having finished her food and taking a stab at some carrots on *his* plate.

"Well, don't you think I should have been informed?"

"I asked you, Brian, what would you have *done*?"

He felt as if someone had just shot off his testicles, as he realized that he really couldn't lay claim to any choices in this matter. He certainly wouldn't have *married* her. He didn't even know her very well. Plus they both knew that they had absolutely nothing in common.

"Why would you smear my reputation by telling our son that I abandoned you, when I didn't even know that he existed?" he asked, watching her stab at a piece of *his* baked potato.

"*Reputation? Your* reputation? Should I have told my son that I was a dumb little hick who opened her unprotected thighs to a man she hardly knew, Brian?"

She was heaving those breasts toward him now.

He wrestled his thoughts back to his wife, who was *way* down in Puerto Rico. Then he cleared his throat and said, "Look, Louise, I think you should have told me. You never even gave me the chance to do the right thing."

"And *what* would that have *been*?" she sneered, then cracked up laughing. "Look, Doctor, I was pregnant. I didn't want to have an abortion or anything like that, and I certainly didn't want you to think that I wanted to *marry* you—trap you, you know?"

"First you told him I was a dead man, then you implied that I was an irresponsible jerk—"

"Dr. Morgan, I had a son to raise. I had an image to maintain as his mother, you know?" Leaning in toward him, those huge bosoms challenging him again, she added wickedly, "I had my *reputation* to consider. Why should I have wasted one minute worrying about you and your reputation when I didn't even know who you were, really? *I did what I had to do!* As I said to someone recently, I am a survivor, *not* an idealist!"

"Louise, you and I both know that I did not *abandon* you," he said with finality.

"Who gives a shit, Dr. Morgan?" Louise Washington said defensively, cackling loudly, sounding an awful lot like the Wicked Witch of the West.

SNAP FIVE

CHAPTER EIGHTEEN

*J*aneen Davis was famished!

Pangs of hunger pierced her in the gut.

She was leaning against the wall, beginning to feel light-headed, in the corner of the huge dining room of this Mainline Pennsylvania mansion that her company, Davis Creations, had decorated in its entirety. One of the servants approached, presenting before her a tray of little, teeny, tiny appetizers like precious jewels on velvet. Foodlets, she called this insubstantial mess. The rich it seemed, at least the white Protestant ones, subsisted on this faux food and massive doses of alcohol.

The long, anorexically glamorous hostess came toward her, arms open, with a drink in each hand. "Janeen, daaaarling," she drawled with lockjawed sophistication and enthusiasm. "How are you, darling? Here's your drink. You left it on the bar in the living room." She handed Janeen her lipstick-smeared martini, and added, "Come, I have someone I want you to meet. She's just bought this unbelievable place over in Bala-Cynwd, and she might want to speak with you about it."

Janeen Davis had become the hot young decorator among this set. She was the flavor of the month. A social darling. The money was astronomical, but she was beginning to suspect that she was developing an alcohol problem—one of the occupational hazards of this kind of business, she supposed.

Weak with hunger she grabbed her hostess by the arm to follow her back into the living room, quickly and discreetly dumping the martini into the ficus plant in the hallway.

It was the fourth, fifth, sixth, or *tenth*—as far as she could remember now—party in the usual series of pre-Christmas festivities she had to attend at her clients' rambling estates.

How could she complain? She'd made more money in the past year, despite the recession, than she had ever made in her life. She had been able to redecorate her own place exactly as she had always wanted to but never had before because she lacked the time or the money. She'd even managed to squeeze in a nice long two-week vacation on the beach on a splendid Greek island, as well, last summer. Nevertheless, she had grown tired of traveling alone to romantic places. She was also tired of going home alone to her gorgeous apartment. Janeen wanted someone to share it all with.

Greece.

Just as she started reminiscing about her vacation her eyes fell on her tall, effeminate assistant, who was flitting around having the time of his life. He winked at her.

Janeen Davis was sick and tired of his petty gossip and wild melodrama, but what could she do? She was an interior decorator and her business was just flooded with such occupational blessings. Nevertheless, her assistant was a bright young talent just like the others she had hired. She was just fed up with not having a real date and having to show up at all these functions with these male facsimiles.

While she was being introduced to a Mrs. . . . *Somebody* . . . managing to go through the motions of holiday small talk, her mind was elsewhere. She had left a couple of messages on Marshall Brown's answering machine, and she hadn't heard a peep from him. She was expecting to go with him up to his folks' house for their Christmas party—Aletha Brown was going to be there—and he hadn't called her back with the logistics. He had been acting awfully strange since he had returned from his trip to France this summer. He wouldn't even talk to her about it, and they used to talk about everything! She hoped that nothing was wrong.

She'd have to sneak away from this group at some point to call her place and see if she had any messages. The Brown party was only a couple of days away, and since she was already so close to Philadelphia, where Marshall lived, she figured that they could drive up to his folks' house in Connecticut together.

As another tray of foodlets zipped past her, she started fantasizing about what would probably be served at the Brown family dinner party: a big, fat bronzed turkey with chestnut stuffing, a juicy clove-scented ham covered in honey, macaroni smothered and dripping with cheese, collard greens cooked with ham, baked sweet potato soufflés covered with marshmallows, cranberry sauce, hot buttered corn bread, pecan pies, mincemeat pies . . . and who *knows* what all else. Her mouth watered.

Janeen Davis was famished.

"Dinner is served," the hostess announced, as she slowly led everyone into the dining room—too slowly in Janeen's opinion.

Janeen daintily sipped some of her wine, sitting prettily with her red lips slicing a silly social grin on her perfectly made-up tan face when suddenly the hostess's surly black maid rudely slammed the main course down in front of her. She jolted back, and her eyes met with the woman's, who challenged under her breath. "You need to put some meat on those bones, chile!" and then haughtily turned away to continue serving.

Quickly recovering from the shock of this entirely undeserved insult, she looked at her plate.

Lord, have mercy! More foodlets! There, staring up at her, was a thin piece of some kind of fish covered in a white sauce, exactly three thin slices of carrot, a radish flower, and four of the skinniest, tiniest asparagus spears she had ever seen in her life. The soup had been a broth with a few lonely scallions floating around in it, and the salad was romaine lettuce with exactly five—count 'em—five slices of a black olive and a couple of croutons as garnish.

She wanted to get up and scream, *"White people! You must be stopped!"*

Instead she just sat there, feeling faint.

"Janeen, daaarling, are you all right?" the hostess asked with alarm, having noticed her pale, tired, and perplexed expression.

"I'm feeling a bit under the weather. I'm sorry, but I think I need to lie down."

"I will take you to the guest room, sweetheart," the hostess cooed, getting up quickly to escort her upstairs.

She heard a rustle of activity as she walked from the room, not missing the sarcastic "humph" from the maid, who stood chuckling by the door.

"I'll have your drink sent up to you, sweetheart," the hostess said reassuringly.

In the guest room, she lay on the bed and searched through her handbag for her portable phone to call Marshall. Frustrated with all the mess that had piled up in the pocketbook, she sighed and dumped all of its contents in front of her. Just as she was about to dial Marshall's number, the maid knocked firmly on the door and entered the room with a tray that held a large goblet of ice water and a covered dish.

She placed it on the side table next to the bed, cracked a small sympathetic smile toward Janeen, and quickly left the room.

Janeen lifted the cover and found a copious plate of baked chicken, mashed potatoes with gravy, some sauteed spinach with a slice of buttered corn bread on the side. It must have been from the maid's private stash, she thought as she picked up the knife and fork and gratefully began to dig in.

Janeen Davis was famished.

The next morning Janeen quickly brushed a thick layer of snow from her charcoal gray Ralph Lauren wrap coat and stamped her leather boots clean of it, as well, on the welcome mat so as not to leave puddles on the floor of the doctor's office. Janeen then nervously pressed the buzzer to the ground-floor office suite in the discreetly elegant town house building on upper Fifth Avenue. She had never done anything like this before, and her embarrassment about it colored her cheeks and ears, but who would ever find out?

The sound of a buzzer from the inside responded, permitting her to enter the office.

Her eyes met with a festive riot of color and an exotic collection of sculpture, paintings, silk screens, and masks that appeared to have had their origins in Asia, Africa, and the Caribbean. She walked into the arched foyer and approached the pleasantly open-faced young receptionist, who had been sitting reading at her desk, which seemed to have been constructed using highly polished planks of driftwood.

Interesting, she thought to herself, removing her elbow-length navy blue wool gloves. She ran her fingers lightly over the slick surface, pursing her lips and nodding her head slightly with approval.

"May I help you?" the receptionist asked, flashing perfectly straight white teeth—teeth as highly polished as the surface of the desk at which she sat. She had a slight accent, which Janeen couldn't place, just as she couldn't discern the woman's race. She looked as if she were an exotic mélange of Europe, Asia, and a touch of the tar brush—but she knew it had to be something Caribbean.

"I have a nine o'clock appointment with Dr. DaSilva," she said as she watched the receptionist put down her book in order to check the appointment calendar.

Janeen felt a bit ill at ease when she noticed the title of the book. It was called *Romancing the Shadow: Illuminating the Dark Side of the Soul.* She didn't know whether it was one of those traditional types of psychology books or one of the para-whatever-they-called-it kind, but what she did know was that at that very moment the whole scenario made her want to bolt.

"Ah yes, Ms. Davis. Please, have a seat. The doctor will be right out," the receptionist said, motioning for her to take a seat in one of the tropically colorful upholstered sofas.

She sat nervously on the couch and picked up a magazine from the coffee table in front of her. It was the latest issue of *Elle* magazine—French edition. Using the paltry remnants of her college-level French, she waded slowly through the thick publication, inevitably stopping at the numerology page.

She made the calculations based on her month and date of birth and found that she was in an eight year—whatever that meant.

Just as she had begun to pick through the predictions for the month, an incredibly chic Hispanic woman—her right hand sweeping jet-black, waist-long ringlets over her shoulders—strode gracefully into the waiting room from what Janeen supposed was her office off to the left side.

The lady held out a willowy mestizo-colored hand with immaculately manicured nails clothed in a neutral polish, and introduced herself.

Janeen took in the black pinstriped wool Oscar de la Renta pantsuit and the fabulous burgundy, spike-heeled, faux python Donna Karan boots. She realized that although she really hadn't been sure what to expect, she had been imagining a heavy-set Latina outfitted like a modern-day gypsy in some gaudy, dangling earrings and a rainbow muumuu.

"Miss Davis, welcome. I am Dr. Annunciata DaSilva. Please come in. The weather outside is just awful, isn't it?" she asked, graciously leading Janeen into her office, which, in shocking contrast to the waiting room, was starkly modern and sophisticated urban North American.

A rough, pumped-up-looking man dressed incongruously in a dark three-piece suit peeked from around a corner at them. He was munching on a chunk of apple that he had evidently sliced off with what at first appeared, in her nervous state, to be a glittering switchblade, but turned out to be a utilitarian Swiss Army knife.

"Don't let Miguel make you nervous, *querida.* I work alone here—just me and my receptionist, Odile, so I need extra security. Many people get upset about the things that I tell them, you know? He will not threaten you as long as you don't threaten me." She smiled cryptically.

Janeen was feeling overwhelmed by this new experience and a bit scared, but what the hell she thought, this was no big deal, really. This was Fifth Avenue. She'd survived Bedford-Stuyvesant!

The doctor motioned with her hand for Janeen to sit on the black leather couch, which sat across from her own cream-colored leather armchair.

As Janeen gazed about the room she became unnerved by the dramatic contrasts she'd been experiencing. Suddenly she had no idea where she was or what she was doing in such a place.

"You appear to be uncomfortable, *querida*. Would you like a cup of tea?" the doctor asked, hesitating before seating herself.

"N-no. No thank you, Dr. DaSilva," she responded softly, nervous about what would happen next.

"I know that I asked you over the phone when you made your appointment, but refresh my memory. Who referred you to my office?" she asked, sitting down and snuggling comfortably into her chair.

"Oh! No one. I—I mean—I read about you in a magazine. I don't remember which one. Perhaps *People*, or *Elle*, or *Town and Country*. I just don't remember. I read so many magazines, you know. It's part of my business."

"Yes, you are an interior decorator," the doctor responded, trying to ease her tension.

"Oh? You know my work?"

"I don't believe I do, but I can read it on your face."

Janeen was definitely growing even more uncomfortable.

"Look . . . Doctor," she started gently, not wanting to sound like an idiot, since it had been entirely her own idea to make an appointment for a consultation with the woman. "I've never been to either a psychic or a psychologist before, and since you are *both*, I am rather anxious. I don't know what to say or what to expect."

She knew, though, glancing down at the doctor's feet, that she would have loved to know where the woman had bought those outrageously gorgeous boots she was wearing.

Dr. DaSilva smiled into Janeen's eyes, and said, "I bought these boots at Bendel's."

Janeen Davis was momentarily speechless!

"How did you know . . . ," she started to respond as she emerged from the shock.

"It's my job. Besides, I'm in your aura now. So, tell me, what kinds of things would you like to discuss?"

"I—I don't know. I have heard from people that they have been helped by psychics. I've never been to one. So I decided to see you, because as I said, I read about your work and I need to sort out some things in my personal life."

"Let me tell you first, *querida*, that you must begin to look more carefully at the people in your personal life. I realize that this is a particular challenge for you, considering the environment in which you grew up."

"What do you mean?" Janeen asked, gasping with discomfort.

"You were an only child and there was substance abuse in your family when you were growing up. Your father, in particular, I believe."

"Yes! But . . . how . . . what?"

"You didn't become aware of the nature of your father's problem until years after you left home. This means that you survived to adulthood so far by too often having to adapt to someone else's distorted sense of reality. There was a lot of denial. Your mother denied the inconsistencies in the world of your immediate family. She wanted to create a rosy picture, despite the turbulence. You were forced to doubt your own perceptions of the things that you saw. You began to escape into the world of art. You chose a career of creating perfect and harmonious environments for other people. Am I correct?"

Janeen was stupefied. She had never told anyone that she had discovered that her father had been an alcoholic.

"It is not uncommon for people growing up in this kind of environment to have been socialized by their parents or other relatives to interpret things in ways completely different from the reality surrounding them. Do you understand what I am saying?"

"Yes, I do," she responded, acknowledging something that she had just recently begun to decipher about her upbringing. She had realized that despite the fact that her family had spent their lives trying to convince her that she had been living a charmed, rich, and blessed childhood, in reality she had managed to survive an alcohol-drenched, codependent snake pit of hell.

"Then, you do realize that you have been programmed to see things as you want to see them as opposed to the way they are?" Dr. DaSilva asked with doubt catching in her throat.

"I said yes, Doctor."

"You must begin to trust your own eyes."

"I do!"

Dr. DaSilva cleared her throat and continued. "Okay, then, would you like to talk, or would you like some predictions, Ms. Davis?"

"Predictions, I—I guess."

"Most people do. Most people come to me because they want to know what is going to happen in their lives. But let me tell you something about predictions."

Dr. DaSilva sat back comfortably in her chair, looking like a statue of a guardian angel in some Latin American cathedral.

"I am not a guardian angel, *querida*. I am an ordinary person who has a talent to pick up a person's concerns and guide them. You understand?"

Silence.

"The prophecies I make are based simply on the actions you are presently taking in your life. I offer what the logical sequence of events will be as of this moment. You have the power to change the predictions I make, based on your own ability to understand and alter your present circumstances based on your own actions. Do you understand?"

"I'm not sure," Janeen finally uttered.

"I'll give you a simple example. Let's say that you have to take a test for a license of some kind. Let's say you have come to me to find out if you would pass this test."

"Okay," Janeen said, leaning forward toward the doctor.

"If you were sufficiently prepared, the answer would most likely be yes. But if you had been distracted and not doing your work, the answer could be no. But you see, you could change the "no" outcome by focusing and studying for the result that you want. Does that make sense to you?"

"I suppose."

"Okay. Let me tell you again that you *must* look more closely at the people in your life. You want something from someone close to you, who cannot, never could, and never will be able to fulfill your needs. You could have known this years ago, but I don't feel it even mattered much to you before, so you really weren't looking very carefully."

Janeen began reflecting on all of her employees, wondering which one of them was deceiving her or perhaps even stealing from her.

"Is it a man or a woman?"

"A man."

"Someone I work with?"

"No. Someone in your personal life."

"That's weird. All I do is work." Janeen shrugged her shoulders, dismissing it all.

"Also, you are very successful in your business and will become even more so. You will be going to a place—ironically an isolated place—where there are a large group of rich people who will be interested in buying your designing talents."

"I just came back from a trip in Greece. I met a number of interesting people there."

"That is the past! I'm talking about the future. You haven't met the people I am speaking of yet."

"Well, I was at a client dinner party recently with a number of rich people who want me to decorate—"

"No, this is something else. It'll be marvelous for you. But it begins in an isolated place. A retreat of some kind."

The woman is talking gibberish, Janeen thought. She never went to isolated places. All of her business came from parties.

"I want to know, Doctor, if I will find a husband soon."

"No, I don't see a husband in the near future."

The woman was a charlatan, Janeen decided at that moment. How much could she possibly know about her life anyway?

"There is someone who wants to humiliate you. A man who feels threatened by you. If you would just relax and reflect, I believe that you could find where the problem is and avert an embarrassing confrontation."

Janeen figured that if what the woman was saying was true, it was probably her ambitious assistant that she had taken with her to the party in Philadelphia.

Maybe it was curtains time. Knowing his taste, something gauzy sheer for him. Or maybe leather since he *did* seem to be becoming more aggressive lately.

"Ms. Davis, you have the possibility to fulfill all of your dreams, but you must first learn to look at things differently than you have until now."

"This has been very interesting, Dr. DaSilva, but I'm not sure if I believe in this sort of thing that you're doing."

"That's okay, Ms. Davis," the doctor said, watching her get up to leave the session. "But let me add one last thing—"

"What's that?" Janeen replied, anxious to get out of this office and finish her Christmas shopping for the Brown family's Christmas party tomorrow.

"There is a dark man who lives with antiques who has something extremely important to reveal to you. In a very short time, you will know what it is and you won't even have to ask him."

"All right," Janeen said, dismissing this crazy kind of therapist, suddenly realizing what the perfect Christmas present for Marshall would be.

"Good-bye, Dr. DaSilva. I will not waste any more of your time," she stated with finality, reaching in her handbag for her checkbook. "You do accept checks, don't you, Doctor?"

Annunciata DaSilva knew, instinctively, that Janeen Davis's check would clear.

"Of course."

Janeen wrote out and signed her check then handed it to the doctor.

"Thank you and good-bye, Ms. Davis. Have a Merry Christmas," the doctor said politely as she stood to shake Janeen's hand.

She left the room with a dramatic flourish, rudely dismissing Dr. DaSilva's proffered handshake.

I'll never do this again, Janeen thought, glancing at her watch, relieved to find that she had wasted only fifteen minutes with that weird broad.

She fled the office, terrified by it all. She was happy that she had left New York City years ago, after design school. Janeen was convinced at that moment that the city had deteriorated into an insane asylum overpopulated with eccentrics and hucksters.

* * *

"I'm so happy that you could make it on such short notice, Annunciata. I can call you Annunciata, right?" Aletha asked, taking the doctor's coat.

"Of course. Your sister and I are old friends, as you know, so I guess that would make us friends-in-law, *verdad*?" Annunciata laughed. "Taking in the tasteful decor of the living room, she added, "Your home is lovely, Aletha."

Aletha's eyes bulged out at the lush sable coat in her arms.

"Thank you. And this, my dear, is gorgeous! Aren't you afraid of wearing this expensive thing around the city?"

"What do you mean, Aletha?" Annunciata frowned in puzzlement, forcing her gaze away from Aletha's interesting collection of art and objets d'art back to her now worried-looking countenance.

"Don't rampaging lesbians with paint rollers attack you for wearing fur?"

"What?" Then, understanding, she collapsed into peals of laughter. "No, no, dear, you don't mean lesbians, you mean animal-rights activists. No, I haven't met up with any of them lately. I mostly drive anyway. They can't get to me."

"I'm chauffeured around everywhere I go," Aletha huffed, motioning for the doctor to sit on the couch. "But they got me at the airport a couple of weeks ago."

"Well, I'd better watch it tomorrow, I guess. I'll be at the airport," Annunciata said as Aletha went to hang up the coat in the foyer closet.

"You're going to be at the airport on Christmas day?" Aletha asked incredulously, returning to sit across from Annunciata.

"Yes. My husband and I are leaving for Rio tomorrow to visit his family for the holidays."

Aletha looked down at Annunciata's ring finger and said, "Let's hope that those animal-rights dingbats will be at home eating turkey tomorrow and won't bother you. But be careful when you get back. Maybe you shouldn't wear it coming back into the city."

Annunciata smiled and reached over for the pot of tea that Aletha had on the coffee table and helped herself.

"I am a Caribbean person, *querida*. I wear what's warm. I don't care what they—"

"So you're married, huh?" Aletha asked. "How long have you been married?"

"Almost twenty years."

"Like Desiree, huh?" Aletha sighed, and sipped some of her tea. "I should have gone to school with you all. Maybe I'd be married by now, too."

Annunciata smiled, remembering back to the days when little Aletha used to trail behind her and Desiree, trying to get into all of their business. Aletha used to wear a big Afro poof ponytail hairstyle that complemented her shining, big, black, always startled-looking eyes. Now, there she was sitting regally in this lovely penthouse apartment in her beautiful rose-colored silk caftan—one of the country's most famous television personalities. Life was a fun journey, she thought to herself, sipping some more warm tea.

"Aletha, remember when you begged us to take you with us to see *The Graduate*, with Dustin Hoffman? We couldn't believe that you were interested in something like that. You were just a little bitty thing!"

Aletha instantly became defensive, believing that Annunciata might be trying to make some sly reference to her relationship with Reggie, so she replied, "No, I do not! You must be thinking of some other little girl."

"No, you don't *remember*?" Then picking up Aletha's vibe of discomfort, she added quickly, "You were always such a precocious child."

"It's not as if you're that much older than me, Annunciata."

"Oh, thank you, *querida*! Anyway—" She decided to drop the subject. "—you know, Aletha, I always knew that you'd be in television."

"You did? You knew that psychically?"

"No, I just couldn't imagine you in any other business but something very high profile."

"Oh. Me neither." Then, forcing the direction of the conversation back to what really interested her, she asked, "So, your husband is Brazilian, huh?"

"Yes. He was born and raised there."

"Oh? Where did you meet?"

"We were all at Columbia together."

"Like I said, I should have gone to school with you guys."

Annunciata laughed and said, "It's all in the luck of the draw, Aletha."

"I've never been to Brazil, nor have I ever met any Brazilians," Aletha said, adding Rio to her mental list of places to visit on future vacations.

"You should definitely make a trip sometime. The people are wonderful, and you will find all the flavors there, you know?" She smiled mischievously.

Silently coveting the woman's Versace suede and leather form-hugging getup, Aletha thought her sister's friend to be quite elegant despite, in her opinion, the odd career path she had chosen.

"What does your husband do?" Aletha asked, curious to know what kind of a man a psychic would attract, although she was certain that *any* man would have been attracted to this knockout.

"My husband is an opthamologist."

Aletha looked at her in disbelief; their eyes locked and both burst into laughter.

"You're kidding, right?"

"I am serious, Aletha."

"That's some funny shit! Would you like something to eat?" Aletha asked, starting to get up.

"No. Sit down, Aletha. I'm fine."

"So your husband is an opthamologist and you are a psychic. He helps people see, and so do you. What a hoot! You know, that reminds me of my stockbroker. You know what he used to do for a living? He used to be a—"

"A weatherman, right?"

"You know my stockbroker?" Aletha asked, dropping her spoon onto the floor.

"No, I don't. I just knew what you were going to say."

Aletha picked up her spoon, laid it on the table, and stared at her sister's friend.

"Amazing," she murmured.

Annunciata smiled and said, "Weatherman, stockbroker, it's pretty much the same thing, isn't it? Not all that much different from being a psychic, is it?"

"I don't know. You are going to be the first I have ever consulted. Desiree has always believed in this sort of thing. Me, I've always been a skeptic. But, you know, these days I need all the help I can get. I've got problems, girl."

"Yes, I guess you do. We *all* do." Annunciata smiled.

What kind of problem could a woman like this possibly have? wondered

Aletha. Desiree had told her that the woman's husband was some kind of hot number and that they lived in some fancy duplex on Central Park South. Those DaSilvas had a perfect son in a perfect school on the East Side, and they had a summer retreat on the Cape. Aletha thought to herself with a touch of envy, I should have such problems!

"I guess you've read things in the papers about me, Annunciata."

"Of course, but that won't interfere with my ability to help you sort things out."

"Okay, what can you do with this?" Aletha asked, reaching into the pocket of her caftan and pulling out a comb. She tossed it on the coffee table in front of Annunciata.

"What is that?" Annunciata looked concerned.

"It's a comb. My ex-boyfriend's comb. He left it here, and it has some of his hairs. Can you do something with it so that I can get him back?"

Annunciata jumped up in a panic from her seat. She calmed herself as she realized that Aletha didn't have a clue as to what she was asking her to do.

"You are thinking of voodoo spells, Aletha. I don't do that sort of thing, and I suggest you stay away from anyone who claims that they can. You see, you can't force things. You should have learned this life lesson by now, Aletha. When you try to force things, on any level, you never get the results that you wish. No one does. Try to remember that." She sat back down.

"Oh," Aletha said simply. "Well, tell me what you think I should know. Do I have to ask any questions?"

"Only if you want to. Or you can let me tell you what I see, and you can ask me questions after."

"Don't you need some tarot cards or tea leaves or something, girl? A crystal ball, maybe? Don't you need *tools*?"

"No. Not really. My eyes are all the tools I need. But if you like, I could read the tarot for you."

"If it's not necessary, then just go ahead—*talk*, Doctor."

"First of all, the chapter with your ex-boyfriend is over. The sooner you let it go the sooner that your new and much more rewarding life can begin."

Aletha sighed, disappointed.

"You focus too much on what you don't have and act out on others who you feel have things that you want. It's unhealthy and it's blocking your spiritual advancement."

"Advancement? Where do I go from *here*? My life is a shambles. The ratings for my show are going into the toilet!"

"Oh, they're going to shoot up again, but not for reasons that will please you. This particular career is about to be a closed chapter, as well, but not until you realize that you cannot change things back to the way they were before. There is a new regime, so to speak, controlling your professional world, and if you continue to push, you will meet nothing but disaster. Not to you personally, but to people around you in your professional world. The karma is just bad. You must find a way to remove yourself, Aletha."

Aletha figured that this proved that she had made just the right move by firing that hussy Veronica and hiring the new girl, Mary Beth.

"It doesn't matter who you hire or who you fire," Annunciata said after picking Aletha's brain.

"But things have begun to take a more positive turn lately. Overall, I believe."

"No. Not really. It may appear that way at the moment, but you will soon experience a major outburst around you. Consequently, there will appear to be a calm after the storm. But, *querida*, don't let this fool you. The same—I should say Machiavellian—dynamics that you have seen in the past will still be very present. They will have just moved underground and as a result have a stronger and more powerful influence in the media. You will see. Again, my advice to you is to get out."

"Holy cow!"

"Also, your personal life is going to move forward now."

That was impossible, Aletha thought, since she had no personal life at all, now that Reggie was gone.

"Your sister will have a part in your new life."

"Desiree? Ridiculous! We hardly ever see each other, and she's about to leave the country with her husband."

"So will you. You will probably live somewhere around Asia. You will live there for a while and then return home to become involved in a huge political event. Your world, Aletha, is going to become bigger and bigger. It's really wonderful for you."

Aletha laughed and said, "What? I'm going to run for office?"

"No. Something more important. I can't see what it is, exactly, because it's just beginning to formulate. I can't explain it. Aletha, you have to learn to relax. Take yoga or something."

"Yoga?"

"Yes. It will be marvelous for you. There will be a lot of love coming to you in your life, on so many levels. You don't have to push."

"I've had to push for everything I've ever had, girl."

"Well, that is about to change."

"I doubt that," Aletha said, leaning back and thinking about the things that had transpired over the years.

"Your brother is in love with someone who is going to become a close friend. This person is related to someone who used to work with you."

Thinking of that Janeen person he had been dating for years, she doubted this prediction. Aletha Brown had never been too successful in having girlfriends. Actually, the idea of a girlfriend was downright preposterous.

"By the way, *querida*."

"Yes?"

"Someone, at this very moment, is writing, in secret, a book about you. Well, what I mean is, a character like you is central to this work. This person is someone close to you. It's going to be very successful, and the author will clean up. There will be a movie made based on this novel."

"About *me*? An unauthorized biography? I think *not*!" Aletha banged her hand on the table. It must be Veronica McPheerson whom she had fired not long ago who was writing a book about her. She'd never let it happen.

"It's not a biography. It's a novel."

What if Reggie was writing a book about her? She'd have the nigger stopped. She'd sue his ass off! How *dare* he, she fumed to herself, but smiled at Annunciata, thinking how she'd use this information to protect her privacy. As soon as her appointment was over she'd call her lawyer and figure out some way to keep Reggie's book from getting published. There was no way she'd allow her business to be splashed all over the pages of some tawdry book written by a never-has-been hack. It had definitely been a good idea to set up this appointment with Desiree's friend.

"Is there anything else you would like to know, Aletha?"

"Nope! You've told me everything I need to know. Now, would you like a piece of cake? I have some fruitcake, Annunciata."

"Yes, I think I will, Aletha. Also, I'd love you to give me a tour of your apartment. It seems you've done a fabulous job."

"Why, of course," Aletha said, jumping up enthusiastically, her smile carving happy dimples in her cheeks. She loved to show off her place. She'd never had many visitors, and this one had certainly turned out to be a charming and welcome one.

CHAPTER NINETEEN

*A*lmost suffocating from the heat of his bristling anger, Marshall catapulted himself from his plush, red velvet Queen Anne wing chair and flung the day's newspaper into the fireplace next to him. He almost fell over the intricately carved walnut footstool as he ran over to extinguish the tiny red-hot embers that had flown out in response, landing on his brand-new Moroccan rug.

He picked up the remote and turned on the television.

Damn!

He couldn't even read or look at the news anymore without being assaulted by another story about some white cop being acquitted after beating or killing some black man.

He turned off the television.

He jammed his sweaty hands into the pockets of his silk kimono as he gazed over the mantel at the gilt-framed portrait that his sister Desiree had lovingly painted for him last Christmas. It was mesmerizing how she had used those burnt umbers and siennas, cadmium reds and Prussian blues of hers to create a likeness that revealed the Cherokee in his cheekbones, the Irish in his dark freckles, and the African in his broad nose, thick jet-black locks, and espresso-colored skin.

It was the African in him that instinctively knew that the nineties were about the lynching of black American men. It started off with suspicious stuff like Magic Johnson and the death of Arthur Ashe. Where were the big-name, high-powered *white* heterosexual males with AIDS? Was the media trying to imply that black men were so outrageously whorish that even the filthy rich heterosexual ones contract the disease, while wealthy white heterosexual males lead their lives with much more discretion, always practicing safe sex and entirely drug-free? Obviously this whole approach was an update, feeding into the age-old rumor portraying black men as sexually out-of-control, decadent drug freaks.

Well, Marshall Brown knew from personal experience that some so-called straight white men could be some of the biggest sluts the world has ever known. He'd had a number of them himself.

Creepy mothafuckers—a lot of them.

He'd had experience with more than one of those so-called heterosexual assholes—no pun intended—chasing him all over the world begging to dive into his pants.

He often felt sorry for women. So many of them spent their every waking hour worried that their men were out chasing some other woman when, in fact, their men might actually be sleeping with their very own brothers.

What was it with all the cops who had lately been arresting high-profile black men driving expensive cars? The average citizen could recognize a movie star from the other side of the earth, but let a brother be out in his own posh neighborhood, driving to his health club or whatever in his well-earned Ferrari, and suddenly this same movie star becomes a suspected criminal!

The decade of the thirties must have been exactly *this* way in Europe for the Jews. History *did* repeat itself, Marshall had learned years ago.

Marshall felt that there was a conspiracy going on to discredit and destroy the lives of American black men.

His brother-in-law, David, had agreed with him, saying that it would be no surprise to him, especially from the point of view of a Jewish man whose family had been chased out of Europe, that black men—especially prosperous black men—might be the victims of conspiracies and frame-ups. He had said that if it hadn't been for the systematic murder, anti-Semitic oppression, frame-ups, and conspiracies, his own family and the families of most white European Jews in America would still be enjoying their hard-earned prosperity in Europe.

Marshall pulled his pipe out of his pocket and looked around for his humidor of tobacco.

Marshall suddenly jumped as he felt a hand tweak his hard, muscular rear end.

"Oh no, you don't. Don't you *dare* light up that smelly thing! Come on, Marshall. Loverman, why do you look so down in the mouth anyway? It's Christmas Eve; let's unwrap our presents." Eric breathed suggestively into Marshall's ear, seductively easing his elegantly tapered, copper-colored fingers under Marshall's robe and stroking the naked flesh underneath.

Goose bumps erupted all over Marshall Brown's hairy chest, legs, and arms. He kissed his lover on the lips, which tasted to him, as always, like those juicy, black August plums. He ran his tongue softly along the inside of Eric's plump bottom lip to his wide, angular jawbone and to the lobe of his left ear, which until that moment had been hidden under long, thick curly locks. His luscious mane grew like sandy-colored corkscrews, which cascaded over those same broad, smooth golden shoulders that had captivated Marshall from the moment they met on the beach in France this past August.

He had never before laid eyes on such a sensuously beautiful black man. It must have been Eric's mother's French blood that added the exotic arch to his eyebrows, which hung over a thick fringe of light brown lashes that framed smoldering sometimes gray, sometimes green, hazel eyes.

Eric McPheerson had been taking a break between his modeling assignments in Paris, when they met at one of Saint-Tropez's private beaches called La Voile Blanche. Marshall had been exploring the cities and villages of Provence in search of some antiques his clients had requested and had decided to take a break by driving over to Saint-Tropez, the one place on the French Riviera he had never had a chance to visit before.

When he first noticed Eric's long, sinewy thighs and graceful cinnamon-toast-colored dancer's body, he had at first assumed he was one of those Moroccan or Algerian boys. It turned out that he was a homeboy from San Francisco. He should have known, at the sight of those deliciously round buns, that he couldn't have been anything else *but* an African American male, although Eric had later informed Marshall that his mother was a French woman, whose family was from Provence, married to a black American whose family came from Trinidad. Thirty-nine-year-old Marshall fell in love with this twenty-nine-year-old charming and sexy angel the first night they spent together. They fit together like soul mates and appeared to share everything in common.

Marshall extended his stay in the south of France to three weeks. There they passionately cemented their relationship during the Technicolor, lilac, lemon, and garlic-scented Mediterranean afternoons, exploring the grottoes and elegantly Gallic hamlets of the French Riviera. Often they passed their days basting each other with suntan oil and sailing or jet skiing in the soothing sun at one of the rocky private beaches and being served foie gras, carpaccio, champagne, and *tarte aux poires* by young, cute, and scantily clad garçons. Their evenings had been spent making love at their sumptuous little hide-

away at Château d'Eza, which lay cozily perched over the sparkling Mediterranean Sea.

He brought Eric back to live with him in his town house in Philadelphia.
Eric loved the house and the neighborhood, Society Hill, because it reminded
him of Paris.

Marshall felt it was more to his advantage to have Eric live in the house
rather than to pass through from time to time from the West Coast. Most of
Eric's modeling assignments were in Europe, after all, so this setup would be
even more convenient for his work.

"Can you guess what I got you for Christmas, Eric?"

Eric rolled his eyes coyly, tossing back his curls, and giggled, "I know what
you got for me, sweet cakes, but what I *don't* know is what you bought for me."

Marshall smiled and winked at him. As they both sat down beside the gift-
laden, twelve-foot-tall blue spruce tree, the phone interrupted.

"Let it ring, Marshall. The answering machine is on."

Eric pulled Marshall, who had started to go to the phone, down next to him
on the floor and put his head on Marshall's lap. He picked up a small gaily
wrapped package and began to slowly untie the ribbon, looking up flirta-
tiously into Marshall's warm, black eyes. "Now what have we here?"

Eric thought to himself how much his lover looked like that famous sister
of his, Aletha Brown.

"Shush, Eric. I want to hear who it is on the phone." He ran his index finger
across Eric's smooth, high forehead.

"Hi, Marshall, this is Janeen. I'm going to be in New York for Christmas.
Since I haven't heard from you about your plans, I took it upon myself to call
your mom to tell her that I'll be there to have dinner with you all. I heard that
Aletha is coming. If I don't hear from you tonight, I'll just see you tomorrow
at dinner. Bye-bye."

As Janeen spoke out her message, Marshall's two neutered male Siamese
cats—Napoleon and Josephine—began wailing like fire engines, in protest.

"I agree, you guys." Eric snickered, stroking the cats as they passed by
briefly before returning to the corner where they had been playing tug-of-war
with a ball of yarn.

Shit! That bitch kept calling Marshall. Suspicion rose, again, in Eric's gut
as to what *really* went on around there while he was away on his assignments.

"Umm . . . sweet cheeks . . . don't tell me that you still haven't told *Miss Thing* about us?" Eric was sick of this broad hovering around *his* man. "We've been together for four months, already."

Eric's voice quivered as he looked directly into his lover's eyes and noticed that Marshall quickly averted them.

The single bone of contention that he had with Marshall was the stupid manner in which he handled his homosexuality. The man was almost forty years old, but kept this broad around so that his family wouldn't suspect he was gay. He said it might have negative ramifications on his big-time sister's career.

As far as Eric was concerned, it would probably just boost her ratings, which he had read were about to plunge into the toilet bowl.

Finally, he was going to meet Marshall's family. He didn't exactly like the idea of meeting his family for the first time with that horrid Janeen Davis there.

He'd never met the woman, although he had asked Marshall to introduce her to him several times. Marshall just kept saying, "Soon, when the time is right."

Well, his presence tomorrow should rock the little moppet's world.

"Marshall . . . baby," he asked nervously. "When was the last time you saw this Janeen?"

"Just a few weeks ago, when you were over in Italy. I told you. I always tell you who I'm with when I'm not with you."

"I'll never understand why, if she's really your good, *platonic* girlfriend, you can't tell her about me. She surely tells *you*, I bet, about the men in *her* life."

Eric had no intention of sharing Marshall with any woman on any level except for his mother and sisters, Desiree and Aletha.

This Janeen Davis would definitely have to go!

Eric had grown up poor, being one of five children with a chronically unemployed musician father. He had struggled through college and then acting school and was beginning to make a name for himself as a model in Europe, making plenty of money. He had had more than his share of fiscally predatory, sorry-assed, self-absorbed gay lovers, and now that he'd finally met himself a real man, he would be damned if he'd let some woman disrupt his life or make him feel guilty about his lifestyle.

Marshall was the best thing that ever happened to him. He was a wonderful friend and lover, financially secure, classy, and had those outrageously fabulous sisters, who he had every intention of charming to death tomorrow.

Aletha Brown was as rich as *mousse au chocolat* and probably could help him with his acting career, and that shrink sister of his, with the bestselling mystery-writing husband, was about to live all over the world, giving Eric and Marshall the possibility of spending their vacations with them in some of the most fabulous places on earth.

He was not going to give that Janeen, or any other woman, a chance to move in on his man, his lifestyle, or his beautiful new home. He'd piss out his territory by broadcasting his relationship on *The Aletha Brown Show*, if he had to, and Marshall knew it, too. No doubt this was why he had decided to finally break the news formally to his family.

"Janeen will meet you tomorrow, Eric. It's no big deal. Like you've been saying, it's time she knew." Marshall sighed, watching Eric remove the solid gold band from the satin-lined jewelry box.

Grinning with wicked satisfaction, Eric looked up at him sideways as he twirled the ring around on his index finger, "I see, Marshall, it's too big for my finger and too small for my wrist . . . almost." Marshall leaned over and kissed him.

Eric sat up eagerly, and they began to tear open the rest of the presents.

Marshall had been picking up some really weird vibes from Janeen lately. They'd known each other since design school, and even though he had never mentioned his sexual preferences to her, he had never given her any indication that there could be anything more than just a platonic friendship between them.

He had always preferred men.

He had never felt that he had to explain himself to any woman, considering that he had never made any passes at any of them, and none of them, like Janeen, had ever seen him with or heard him talk about any intimate relationships with a woman.

His relationship with Janeen had always been platonic. They might have dinner or go to a show together, or spend an evening talking about art, current events, or gossiping about her girlfriends or her latest boyfriend. And whenever she found herself between affairs, Marshall would escort her to whatever function she needed to attend with a male presence.

On the other hand, whenever he had on rare occasions gone up to see his folks, in order to prevent them from digging too deeply into his personal life, he'd brought Janeen.

Lately, Marshall had begun to feel hunted in some peculiar way.

Granted, Janeen lived out of town, in D.C., so there wasn't exactly constant exposure, but her interior design business had curiously taken her more often to Philly lately, and the messages that she'd been leaving on his phone contained a new and odd undercurrent.

Tomorrow's dinner should be quite interesting. Besides this Janeen problem, he'd been dying to ask Aletha if there was any truth to the tabloid claims that she had shot her boyfriend, Reggie.

It would be the first time in he didn't remember how long that the entire clan would be gathered together.

He looked around to see that he and Eric were almost buried in a melee of suedes and leathers, silks, gold, silver, and hats, and scarves and gloves, and books and liqueurs and . . . God, did they *ever* spend money on each other—like some kind of demented, nouveau-riche Hollywood brats.

It was really special for Marshall to finally have found a companion who was not only young and profoundly desirable, but who also had his own resources.

Exhausted from the long day and the madness of the Christmas season, which was finally beginning to dissipate, Marshall stood up and stretched his long arms toward the ceiling then rubbed his sleepy eyes with the back of his hand.

"Lover, I'm tired. Let's go to bed."

"Marshall, honey, how tired *are* you?"

"Not *that* tired." He smiled, touching Eric's chin with the tip of his index finger, tilting his head back in order to kiss him.

As Eric moved his lips toward Marshall's, his lover straightened up abruptly, winked at him mischievously, turned away, and sauntered toward the spiral staircase leading to their bedroom, letting his kimono fall from his body onto the floor.

"Oh, by the way, Eric—" Marshall turned to glance at him over his right shoulder. "—wear that Adolfo getup tomorrow that you brought back from

Rome. It brings out the green in your eyes. And bring that gift in the jewelry box upstairs with you when you come to bed. I'll help you slip it on."

The light from the fireplace licked and caressed the colors and shapes of Marshall Brown's magnificently naked body, which now beckoned to Eric as he ascended the staircase.

The sight took his breath away.

CHAPTER TWENTY

*H*emingway, the Simons' golden retriever, was wagging his tail with delight. The holidays always brought a lively series of guests who patted his head, stroked his belly, and bore gifts of round bouncing things and brand-new squeaky toys. Their presence was always accompanied by aromas and tastes from the kitchen that kept him feeling as if he were in canine heaven. And the bones—ah yes—the bones! He could smell that there was going to be chicken that night. He was wishing that his new friend Sparky could have been there, so that they could goof on birds together and enjoy the festivities.

"So, have you read any good books lately, Hemingway?" Ira Shapiro asked, handing the dog a package and his coat to David at the same time.

Stamping his boots free of powdery snow on the steps outside, Ira Shapiro said emphatically, "This mess is a reminder of why we moved to the West Coast. You can *keep* your damned white Christmases!"

"Oh, shut up, you nouveau West Coast suntan and come on in the house!" David said, giving his friend a bear hug.

"Desiree! You have dreadlocks! When did you do *that*? They're fabulous! What did you do, become a Rasta woman since last year? Actually you look adorable, kind of look like Whoopi Goldberg." Joy Chiang Shapiro pushed past the men to grab her old friend by the shoulders.

They gave each other kisses squarely on the cheeks.

The four of them almost tripped over Hemingway, who had decided to lie in front of the doorway, using his front paws and teeth to open his present.

"Take that to your place, Hemingway," Desiree said as their dog backed out of the way.

Joy and Desiree walked toward the living room as the guys retreated to another part of the house to hang up the wet coats and hats.

"Let me look at you, Dez! What made you do dreadlocks? They're irreversible, you know." Joy flopped down in an armchair and pulled off her boots. "Don't get me wrong; I think they really become you." She got up and placed her boots in front of the fireplace on the mat that Desiree had put out.

"You want a drink?"

"What do you think?"

Desiree smiled and went over to the bar where she had already set out their glasses.

"You know, Joy, I figured that since we're going to be traveling around, to some places where I doubt they'd have a beauty salon that could service nappy-headed black women, I'd—"

"You know, that's a terrific idea. You've always been a person to think of *everything*, Desiree. Dreadlocks! Do you think that perhaps that was exactly how they came to be? Black people traveling among straight-haired people? Could make an interesting article. You know—" She continued without taking a breath, which was pure Joy Chiang, a friend Desiree had known and loved for ages. "—I've been thinking of doing something with this raggedy mop of mine, but I haven't even had the time to think about such personal things with those boisterous kids of ours and all. Please, tell me, Desiree, why did Ira and I decide to have children this late in our lives? Sometimes I think I'm too old for it."

"Girlfriend, your biological clock just snuck up and got the best of you." Desiree grinned as she brought Joy her glass of Beaujolais. Desiree sat back and waited for another breathless onslaught of words from her longtime friend.

"You mean my biological clock got the best of *Ira*. You know it was mostly his idea. And *me* . . . I do most of the work, while he spends most of his days going 'bing, bang, ching, ching' on the piano composing ditties for freaked-out actors and producers."

"How are the kids?"

Joy looked up at Desiree and crossed her eyes in exaggerated exasperation. She reached for her wine. "What do *you think*?"

Desiree held back the glass and laughed. "And how are *you*, Joy?"

"You won't believe this. We just arrived at La Guardia today—this very afternoon! Our flight had been overbooked." She grabbed her glass from Desiree and took a sip.

David and Ira entered the living room.

"That's what you get. Jews shouldn't be traveling for Christmas. As Desiree would say, it's bad karma, right, honey?" David interrupted, and then went into the kitchen to get a couple of beers.

"Tell *that* to my Chinese Baptist mother and father. They'd have coronary arrests if we didn't show up with the little snips."

"At least we managed to get them to drop the Santa Claus bit," Ira said, sitting down on the couch and running his fingers through his bushy red hair.

"Yeah, well, whatever. At least I am finally free again and able to enjoy some adult conversation for a while. We've left the little rug rats with my folks in Queens for the evening."

"Rug rats? You have a six-year-old and a ten-year-old. How can you still call them rug rats?" Desiree asked.

"The way I've been feeling these days, anyone younger than sixteen is a rug rat to *me*." Joy sighed, stretching her toes toward the warmth of the fireplace.

David returned with beer and two mugs. Ira took his mug and beer and placed them on the coffee table in front of him.

"By the way, how are Annunciata and Paolo? We haven't seen them in ages," Joy asked.

"She's fine. I had dinner with her last week. You know they're off to Rio for the holidays."

"As usual, huh? I wish we could have caught up with them this year. Especially Annunciata. I could really use a reading."

"What about that woman you go to back at home? Isn't she good enough?" Ira chuckled, taking a swig of beer from the bottle.

"You have a glass right in front of you, Ira. Don't act like a fraternity jock on holiday," Joy said, narrowing her almond-sliver eyes at her husband. "Everyone needs a second opinion, now and then, right, Desiree?"

Desiree grinned and said, "I suppose so. You'll never believe this, but I sent Aletha to Annunciata. I think she saw her yesterday or today."

Ira cracked up laughing and said, "Now *that's* a woman who could truly use some help from a psychic friend, from what I've been hearing. Is it true?"

Desiree looked over at David, who shrugged and held his hand out, palm up, signaling that she had the floor. Desiree gave them a brief summary of the Reggie incident, stressing that Aletha's version and reality were separated by a wide gulf.

"Good God!" Joy put her hand to her mouth in shock.

"What on earth was she thinking of? Doesn't she realize that she could have ended up in Attica, or Devil's Island, or something?" Ira asked, trying to hold back his laughter at the insanity of it all.

"Let's drop the subject of Aletha. Reggie's not dead and Aletha's not in jail. There's a lot more going on in the world than Aletha's misadventures." Desiree's tone was more peevish than she intended. She looked at Ira and Joy and smiled. "I'm sorry. I know you're just curious. If she weren't my sister, I suppose I'd find something amusing about it all, too. But I suppose there's some lesson to be learned from all this."

"Yeah . . . like women should stop sulking around looking for dirt." Joy laughed.

"You know, so many of my patients are having problems in finding mates," Desiree said, steering the conversation away from the subject of Aletha.

"It's not just women, it's men, too. Both need to try a different approach in finding their soul mates."

"What do you mean, David?" Ira asked, leaning back in his chair.

"Well, I think most women are still looking for this idealized man, someone who has everything their mothers have told them they should have."

"That's true," Joy said, taking another sip of her wine. "Times have changed. Our mothers' needs were much simpler. Their priorities were basically to find someone from their own tribe who could support them financially—and who wouldn't beat them."

"And men simply looked for women who could keep house and raise children," David continued, crossing his legs.

"And what happened is that now women want to find someone who can be a friend and a partner," Desiree said. "Your reality and someone else's expectations have to collide. You have this one set of ideas drilled into you. It's hard to get them out."

"That's for sure," Joy agreed. "What my parents wanted for me was to find a nice Chinese boy with a good profession. Frankly, I needed a man with a sense of humor, and in my own personal experience Chinese guys just didn't fit the bill."

David laughed and said, "Well, I certainly had no desire to marry someone like my mother. I didn't want to deal with all of that Jewish guilt and female manipulation."

"As for me," Ira said, "and don't ever let this leave the room, I just didn't want to eat any more damned matzo brei!"

They all exchanged knowing looks.

"*Jewish* guilt and manipulation? Don't you find black women manipulative, too, David? You don't have to look that far—just look at Aletha." Joy glanced over at David with a puzzled look.

"I don't have all that much experience with black women, but Desiree isn't manipulative. But then again, you've always been kind of on the fringes of your tribe, haven't you, hon?" David chuckled into his mug and glanced up at his wife.

"That's true," Joy responded, agreeing with David and laughing sardonically. "Back in college you never sat at the 'black table,' right, Desiree?"

"Actually, I was sort of excommunicated. Didn't follow lockstep with the rules of the seventies blackness agenda. Wasn't 'black' enough, you know?"

"You look black to *me*, Desiree. Always have. Actually, you were one of the few black women I was able to approach without trepidation. If I had been a man, I would have been frightened to approach one of them. Too much anger, bitterness, and obsessive demands for conformity." Joy laughed.

"Well, I think a lot of the problem for women finding mates today is that they are looking for a certified member of a particular *group*, rather than simply trying to discover another human being with certain admirable and compatible qualities. For instance, I have a patient who I suspect is gay, yet she is looking for a brother to marry. I don't think a single brother deserves to end up in *that* movie. She's as frustrated as hell, yet she won't even work with me any longer because she discovered that my husband is white."

"Screwed up, isn't it? Like, what does *that* have to do with anything? You know, women say that men look at them too often as a piece of meat. You know what I found?" Ira asked, pointing his index finger into his chest. "I found that a lot of women look at men as though we were pocketbooks or sperm banks. Or proper images to include in a family photo. When I met Joy, I knew that she liked me and then fell in love with me because of who I am as an individual. And I, her."

"Maybe you and I, Ira, should write a book from a male's point of view about the difficulty for men to find a proper mate, huh?"

"*You're* the writer, David. Not me. But I certainly think we need a male voice in the matter. I don't think we men are such ogres. We have needs and feelings, too."

"You don't have to convince the women in *this* room, Ira." Desiree smiled at his look of vulnerability.

"It seems to me in all these women's novels you have women making a lot of foolish choices or assumptions about men, and then you get these graphic descriptions of how these men have let them down. Yet you never get the man's point of view. It's downright *colonialist!*" Ira said.

"I agree with you, Ira, but you know, it's just not *our* problem is it?" David stated conclusively, noticing Desiree's look of boredom with the topic.

"Okay, y'all. Let's talk about something else. Please!" Desiree said with finality, placing her feet up on her leather ottoman for emphasis.

Responding to Desiree's annoyance, David said, "Let's talk about our move overseas."

"So, when are you moving? Have you decided?" Joy asked.

"Within the next few months. Probably in the spring," Desiree said.

"That's pretty exciting. Where are you guys going first?" Joy asked, enthusiasm coloring her tone.

"We rented a house in Maui. With a swimming pool. You know, Dez and I have never been to Hawaii."

"You're going to love it. Of course, if you don't, you have the whole world of places to try out next, right?" Joy said.

"You better stop by our place before you leave the mainland, and see the kids again before they get too old to be cute anymore." Ira laughed.

"Where else are you planning to visit before you get to Italy?" Joy asked.

"Anywhere our American passports allow. You see, Desiree and I are going to try to track down that despot out there who is trying to ruin the quality of everyone's lives. There's *got* to be some jerk out there who is misusing his power in such a way that the world looks like it does at the moment. Maybe the sucker just needs a hug. He's obviously got some serious problems." David smiled, diluting whatever bitterness had crept into his tone.

"You mean like some Arab potentate or something?" Joy asked.

"Who the hell knows? It could be *anybody*. That's what we're going to try and find out, right, Dez? Think about it—if Aletha could shoot Reggie, imagine what an angry, frustrated despot could do."

Desiree rolled her eyes at his silliness. "Leave Aletha out of this."

"A hug, huh? You better watch it, David. Those are usually the types with a bottomless pit of need. He—or she for that matter—would probably end up asking you to kiss him on the lips, as well." Ira laughed.

"I hadn't thought about that, Ira."

"You'd *better*! Are you taking Hemingway with you?"

"Of course, we're taking Hemingway. What kind of question is that, Ira? He's a member of our—" Desiree was interrupted by Ira's finger pointing in the direction of the kitchen door.

"What's that clumpy shit all over Hemingway's mouth, Desiree?" Ira asked, laughing, sliding his small, round, wire-rimmed glasses down on the bridge of his long narrow nose.

"Oh, no . . . the chèvre!" she shouted, jumping up from her chair.

"Hemingway likes *goat cheese*?" Ira asked.

"Hemingway likes anything edible," David said, standing up to go clean the dog, who already had been deeply into his own private party.

Hemingway fled to another part of the house. David went after him, and Ira decided to join in the chase.

"I think that's Hemingway's sign that it's time to get dinner ready," Desiree said, walking toward the kitchen.

"You *know* I want to help," said Joy, jumping up from her chair to follow her. "I could use the therapy."

Joy cleaned up what was left of the chèvre smeared all over the floor.

"Yuck!" she said, dumping a cheesy paper towel into the trash compactor. "This is just like being at home with the kids. So . . . you have sold the house, huh? Getting rid of all the baggage of the past, as you said, right?"

"Actually, Joy." Desiree smiled almost gleefully. "We've decided not to sell. I really didn't want to. It turns out that Aletha has agreed to take care of it for us."

"You know, Desiree, Ira and I had been wondering about that. We just couldn't picture you—*you* in particular—selling this gorgeous place and running around the planet without your roots, just you and David and a big dog!" She laughed, touching her girlfriend on the shoulder.

"Aletha said the same thing," Desiree responded, looking at her friend with an expression of pleasant surprise at the insight. "By the way, Joy, I loved that card you sent me, the one with the tale of the sleeping empress. I loved it."

"I figured I'd better send it as a balance, considering what you've been writing me about your patients and their disillusionments with men. We both know that men are *not* always the problem. Sometimes it's just that men and women show love differently, you know?"

"If you let most of my patients tell it, men are the complete and total problem." She sighed pulling up a chair and sitting at the counter.

"You're tired of it all, aren't you, Dez?"

"Damned straight. I want to concentrate on my *own* life. I want to paint again, like you're doing. I hope I haven't lost my touch."

"I'm sure you haven't. I saw the painting that you did of Marshall last year. It is wonderful!"

"Thanks. But I feel so drained. *Pressé comme un citron*—pressed like a lemon—as the French say."

The last statement caused Joy's eyes to lock onto a platter on the counter with a beautifully prepared appetizer.

"What is that, Desiree?"

"Those are leeks stuffed with white cheese and pistachio. It's called *barquettes de poireaux au fromage aux pistaches*."

"French, huh? You made it *yourself*?" Joy asked with a sly grin.

"Yep."

"Umm-hmm," she murmured knowingly. Pointing over at a bowl of what looked like a rice and mushroom mixture, Joy asked, "Is that for the stuffing?"

"Yeah. Could you pour me another glass of wine?"

"Sure, I'll pour us both some. And I'll stuff those birds for you," she said, going over to the counter and filling fresh glasses.

Setting Desiree's glass in front of her, Joy touched her on the shoulder and asked, "Desiree, what do you call this dish that you are making with the hens?"

"It's *pintade fermiere farcie, riz avec les herbes et a l'ail*—"

"Stop, Dez! Do you hear yourself?"

"What?" asked Desiree, looking up at her friend. She smiled and noticed that Joy looked so pretty and exotic in her red silk Armani wrap dress. With her long Asian black hair twisted up on her head, she reminded Desiree of a bust of Nefertiti.

"What are you two planning to eventually move to *Italy* for anyway?" Joy asked, finally getting up enough nerve to broach a subject that she had wanted to for a while now.

"We love Italy, Joy. Why do you ask?" Desiree looked at Joy, thinking she must be dense after all the years they'd known each other, her asking such a lame question. "Where do *you* suggest we live—Serbia?"

"Look around you, Dez. You cook French food. Besides, most of the stuff in your house has been imported from France. Look at what's on your dining table—the faience . . . the Baccarat. You speak French almost like a native. You both should be moving to *France*!"

"France is too expensive, Joy. You know that."

"*Expensive?* Earth to Desiree, earth to Desiree! Don't you realize that your husband's books have been on the bestseller lists for the last five years? Your husband is loaded! They've made two movies from his body of work. And, girl, you and Aletha have always managed to do the kinds of creative things with money that Ira and I could only dream of. I'm certain that you have a decent nest egg of your own."

"I'm not sure I can live in France. You know, spend our money there."

"Why not?" Joy had begun to stuff the Cornish hens.

"You know for years when I'd really get run down, I'd take little breaks by going to the south of France. Well, a few years ago David gave me a little diamond Star of David pendant. I went to a restaurant one day, the same one where they had always nearly fallen over themselves waiting on me—you know how the French are about black women—"

"Yep!"

"On that particular day I happened to be wearing that necklace. You're not going to believe me—"

"Try me!"

"But on that day when I asked for a salade Niçoise, which you know is a vegetable salad with tuna fish, those jerks served me a shrimp salad."

"They served you trafe, huh? What did you do?" Joy began to laugh.

"I told them to take it back, and I left. You see, I can't live in France. I can't trade one kind of bigotry for another. I can't even begin to count the number of people I've been personally acquainted with over there, Joy, who've made anti-Semitic comments in conversations with me, not realizing that—"

"And so you think that the Italians aren't anti-Semitic, as well? Girl, you know that it's a *European* sickness, don't you? Trying to avoid anti-Semitism in Europe would be like trying to avoid racism against black people in the New World, Desiree. Get a grip!"

"Get a grip?"

"That's what I said. Besides, you have already spent a fortune in that country anyway. Live where it really suits your aesthetic tastes and defend your position."

"I hear you. I really *do!*"

"It's just your burnout showing, friend. It's so deep, you couldn't even see straight enough to recognize where you ought to be planning to settle."

"What are you trying to talk Desiree into now, Joy?" Ira asked. He and David had come into the kitchen in order to check out the status of dinner.

"I can't talk Desiree into anything. She was just telling me about how people were trying to make her eat shrimp over in France, because she was wearing a Star of David."

"Hmm . . . like publicly forcing Jews to eat pig products in the town square, is that it?" Ira asked, chuckling to himself. "So you're a triple minority, huh, Desiree?"

"A quadruple. I'm left-handed also, remember?"

"Desiree has often said that anti-Semitism—racism in general—is a result of the toxins contained in the diet," David said.

Everyone stared at Desiree.

"Well, how else would you explain it?" she asked, grabbing a bunch of asparagus.

"Interesting point. It's that you-are-what-you-eat theory, isn't it?" Ira asked, sitting at the counter with the women.

"For example, have you ever noticed, Joy, how when a group of women sit around eating crabs, the conversation rapidly deteriorates into pettiness and backbiting? If we all watched more carefully the quality of what we consume, perhaps a shrink's job would be a great deal easier."

"Desiree?" Ira asked, pointing over at the stuffed leeks.

"Yeah, Ira?"

"Is it okay if I just pick?"

"Eat all you want. That's what it's there for."

David and Ira started digging into the appetizers.

Joy rolled her eyes at them and changed the subject. "Desiree, what I want to know is if Marshall is still involved in that traveling sideshow with Miss Janeen Davis?"

"Yep. She's coming with him to my folks' house tomorrow for Christmas dinner."

"Imagine, after all these years! Still living that double life. Who does he think he's fooling? I knew he was gay when I was—when you and I were—in college, Desiree."

"I know. He and Janeen seem to be locked into some kind of aberrant charade that neither of them can get out of."

"It's called codependency, isn't it?" Ira asked, through a mouthful of food.

"I don't know. Never thought about it that way. What would be in it for her, do you think?" Desiree asked, seasoning the Cornish hens.

Joy helped herself to some appetizers. "This is delicious, Desiree."

"Yes, it is," Ira agreed, licking his fingers. "Maybe Janeen's just helping Marshall along for your parents' sake, Desiree."

"Well," Desiree started to try to come up with something when Joy interrupted.

"I think she's in love with Marshall. Remember, Ira, about two years ago, we went up with David and Desiree to the Browns' Christmas dinner? Janeen was there. I swear, she was fawning all over Marshall as if he were her lover."

"I thought it was part of their act," Ira said.

"I didn't! And to tell you the truth, I figured that you two—" Joy pointed at David and Desiree. "—had shared some sadistic reason for not trying to tip the girl off!"

"Why would we be involved in some kind of a plot like that?" David said, mildly offended. "It's not as if we spend a hell of a lot of time with Marshall, or think much about getting involved in his private life."

"Man, Marshall always seemed as gay as Truman Capote to me. I can't imagine any woman believing that Marshall had any interest at all in a female sexually," Ira said, a perplexed look clouding his face.

"Janeen is just the type of woman who falls for gay men. Women in those gay-dominated businesses like fashion and decorating are always surrounded by those well-put-together men with a hip fashion sense who have an interest in ballet and the theater. Those guys seduce women like Janeen without even having to try," Joy said, sitting down next to her husband. "I've even known some women who feel that they can *convert* those men."

"Yeah, I've had some of those as patients. But, you know, I haven't thought much about Janeen. I have just been frustrated all these years about why Marshall wouldn't just come out of the closet with my parents. I *certainly* never imagined that Janeen would think—"

David, still mildly pissed off that their friends would think they were party in any way to encouraging Janeen's misconceptions about Marshall, interjected, "We never felt that Janeen could be dumb enough to—"

"I didn't say she was dumb, David," Joy said.

"Despite what Marshall believes he's pulling over on his folks, anyone breathing would know Marshall's sexual inclination the moment they laid eyes on him. *I* certainly did," David stated impatiently.

Desiree giggled at the look on David's face, knowing that he was about to tell his favorite story.

"It was funny. After Desiree and I had announced that we were getting married, Marshall called and invited me to lunch. Marshall said that he had a family secret to tell me and he figured it would be better that I hear it firsthand from him than through someone else—even Desiree."

"Didn't want you to be scandalized, did he?" Ira asked, laughing. Then he added, "The Brown family just cracks me up."

"I agreed to meet Marshall at a restaurant in Little Italy. I figured he was going to tell me that he had actually been raised by wolves and that the Browns had found him under a bush on a camping trip or something."

"Come now, David!" Desiree laughed.

"That's David's writer's mind talking, you all." Ira chuckled. "Go on."

Laughing, Joy almost fell off her chair.

"Instead, Marshall, wearing his mauve-colored velvet jacket, gray linen pants, and a gold and diamond bracelet that Desiree would have died for, leaned over toward me, picking up his glass of San Pellegrino, and said shyly, "You know, David, I am a homosexual.""

"You're lying!" gasped Joy, grabbing her chest.

"No, he's not," Desiree said, grinning and nodding her head.

"Almost choking on my antipasto, I said, 'You're kidding, Marshall.' Then I realized that he actually believed that I was surprised at his revelation."

"Astonishing," said Ira with disbelief.

"Then Marshall sighed—*gravely* I must add—'No, I am not kidding, David. I am gay, and I am telling you this because although Desiree already knows, my folks, whether you believe it or not, don't have a clue. And it's not any of their business!' "

"Then what did you say?" Joy asked with anticipation.

"I said, 'Sure, Marshall. Whatever you say. I appreciate the fact that you feel that you can be so open with me. We don't have to speak on it any further, Marshall. Your secret is safe with me.' "

Anticipating an awkward moment of silence, Desiree interjected, "The point is that neither David nor I ever thought that Marshall could ever fool *anyone*, especially Janeen, who has known him for years. Now, our parents— that's another story! They quite naturally, like many other parents in situations similar to this, are in complete denial."

"I know my folks would be," Joy said. "You know, Desiree, maybe Janeen doesn't care whether Marshall is gay or not. She *is* an interior decorator. She is trained to create environments that look good. She probably feels that she and Marshall make an attractive couple. You know, look good together. You've got to admit, they really do look terrific as a couple."

"You mean that Marshall would look good next to her on top of that wedding cake, huh?" Desiree chuckled.

"It would be a fine wedding cake, I guess," Ira said snidely. "As long as you don't have to eat it!"

Everyone then collapsed into a kind of hysteria.

"You are all lost in the damned Twilight Zone of analysis." David laughed, getting another stuffed leek.

"You know, Desiree, Marshall will probably come out of the closet when he finds some man he has really fallen for and wants to build a life with," Ira said sympathetically.

"I wonder when he'd break it to Janeen?" Joy asked, draining her wineglass.

"Maybe she'll be the first one he tells," Desiree said hopefully.

"Yeah, right," Joy said doubtfully, getting up from the table to put the hens in the oven.

"So, what time do we eat?" David asked, closing the subject.

At that instant, the Simons' golden retriever, Hemingway, dashed into the kitchen and plopped down beside his mistress.

Everyone laughed.

CHAPTER TWENTY-ONE

*D*espite the fact that there always seemed to be something too perfect about Marshall, Janeen's feminine instincts told her that he was just the kind of man she needed to settle down with.

She realized that she had fallen in love with him right after he'd returned from France this past summer.

He had invited her over to show off the tastefully elegant objets d'art he'd gathered while on his shopping expedition there, prepared for her one of his fabulous gourmet home-cooked meals, and plied her with some expensive champagne he had brought back from the wine country.

It had been such a lovely and intimate dinner.

In fact, it was the first time he had ever prepared dinner for her at his town house in all the years they'd known each other.

It seemed that Marshall was initiating a romantic shift in their relationship. She was definitely ready for something serious, too. She hadn't been involved in anything meaningful in almost three years.

At one point during the evening it seemed as if he had something that he wanted to tell her, but he never got up the nerve. She had always found his shyness rather endearing. She adored those rare kinds of brothers who were unafraid of showing their feminine, sensitive sides.

Janeen put the conditioner, then the shower cap over her thick bush of sandy-colored hair, then reached over for the knob to turn on the shower.

She turned to look at her slim russet-brown figure in the bathroom mirror and wondered if Marshall liked small breasts like hers. She used to have a complex about her tiny titties, but fortunately for her, thin silhouettes started getting better press at the advent of the women's lib movement—right at the time that she had started dating.

Since black women tended to be rather voluptuous in build, she had for quite a while thought that her skinny and somewhat flat behind would put her at a disadvantage in attracting the type of brother she was looking for.

To her surprise, it had become evident that it was the more prosperous brothers who preferred their women on the thin side—just like the rich white guys did.

Janeen figured that after all these years she'd finally found him—a prosperous and secure gentleman—in the handsomely masculine Marshall Brown. Marshall had the type of impeccable taste and refinement that a woman seldom found in brothers with all those baseball caps worn backward and the Reeboks and urban oversize that passed for comfortable clothing these days.

She never had to drag him to art gallery openings or to the ballet. These were the kinds of things that they actually enjoyed doing together.

Maybe he would take her to France for a holiday or a shopping spree. They were even in similar businesses. He was an antiques dealer, and she was an interior decorator. Maybe they could become a terrific husband and wife team and go into business together.

Hmm . . .

The only change she would demand in his life were those two ridiculous cats. They would have to go! Why he would name two male cats Napoleon and Josephine she could never figure out. Maybe that's why they were so neurotic. Throughout the entire dinner at his house those two cats screamed like sirens, making her want to run away into the night. They would definitely have to go, she laughed.

As the foam from her lavender soap trickled soothingly over her body, she thought about how terrifically matched she and Marshall looked as a couple when they went to functions together.

He was also the exceptional kind of brother whose eyes didn't wander all over every female body in the room.

She leaned her head back under the powerfully therapeutic rush of steamy water gushing from the shower nozzle to rinse out the conditioner and started to become aroused as she reflected on her plans.

Yesterday afternoon, Christmas Eve, she had driven into New York to do some last-minute shopping for gifts to take to the Brown family. Janeen didn't know the taste of the various members of the family, so she had settled on some colorful stemware from a small shop on Madison Avenue for Marshall's parents, and she picked up two small smoky Lalique crystal cats—one for Desiree and her husband and one for Aletha. For Marshall, she had bought an exotic gold bracelet of skillful workmanship made in Benin, from an African boutique in SoHo. She had never given Marshall a present that personal before, so the message should make it clear to him that she, too, was ready to take their relationship to the next level.

Her American Express bill was definitely going to be a horror next month, but so be it!

She was on an important mission.

Last night she had checked into the Plaza Hotel where she had passed the night in an insomniatic restlessness, planning her strategy. After driving up to Greenwich for the dinner party and chatting up his relatives, she was going to make a move and tempt him back to Manhattan to her hotel room. How could he resist staying the evening with her in Manhattan, when his only other choices would be to sleep at his folks' weird, oversize house up in WASP-ville, or drive for three hours all the way back to Philadelphia?

Perhaps after rendering him helpless under the spell of her feminine wiles, she would talk him into taking a week off in New York where they could spend New Year's Eve together. Of course, she wouldn't mind it at all if he invited her to spend the holiday at his gorgeous town house, in that regal Victorian, tiger-oak bed of his.

Janeen stepped out of the shower, dried off, tied the towel around her gleaming body, and went over to the night table to look at the clock.

Noon. The trip to Greenwich was about an hour away, so she'd better skedaddle. Of course, it might be more beneficial for her to arrive late, making a grand entrance right before dinner was served at three o'clock.

She had laid out a formfitting cream-colored dress. It was an ankle-length cashmere frock with tiny mother-of-pearl buttons down the back, which met a coquettish split that reached up to about an inch below her derriere. With this dress and nothing but her pantyhose underneath and her tan, ankle-high Italian leather boots, Marshall would have to be numb in the nuts not to accept an invitation to her rented boudoir.

She returned quickly to the bathroom in order to blow-dry her hair into a come-hither, big-haired, run-your-hands-through-it style.

"Oooh, girl, why don't you wear *this* sexy red number," Bruce shrieked with his high-drama attitude, lustfully fondling Aletha's three-piece red wool pinstriped suit. He was in hairdresser heaven as he hypnotically surveyed all the lovely clothes and shoes tossed about in disarray in Her Majesty's walk-in closet.

With her long fingers, she fanned away his latest suggestion, rolling her eyes. "Bruce, I'm not wearing a suit to my *own* folks' house. Forget it!"

"Girlfriend, you are the *star* of this gathering. You've got to keep your image up. And what about the first impression on this date you have coming here in a few minutes?"

Aletha glanced around her clothes-strewn dressing room, which had gotten worse over the last couple of high-pressured weeks, and decided to throw all of the mess into her closet and close the door for a while, until she regained the energy to try to organize her life again.

"So, you're just going to wear a pair of jeans and a sweatshirt to Greenwich, Connecticut?" he asked, crinkling his nose with disapproval at Aletha's uninspiring getup.

"Yep. I bought the place for them, so I don't have to impress anyone up there," Aletha said, smoothly twisting her heavy hair into a chignon.

"Can I borrow your mink, darling?" Bruce asked, swishing around the room in her full-length Blackglama.

"Of course."

She watched Bruce with amusement as he primped in front of the floor-length mirror in her bedroom, flipping his thick head of blond curls over the high collar of her black mink. His cobalt blue eyes smiled back in approval of his reflection.

Aletha Brown's warm regard for Bruce suddenly turned cold. Bruce was the first man she'd had in her bedroom since Reggie.

She looked at this gay boy's tight derriere packed neatly into slim velvet slacks. What a fucking waste!

The doorman rang the intercom. Bruce ran to answer it.

"Girlfriend, the chauffeur has arrived with Mary Beth and your date, Chester Lockwood. What do you want me to tell him?"

"We'll be right down. Bruce, you take down the presents. One for Desiree and David, one marked for my parents, and one for Marshall. The white leather bag on the couch has the doodads for the rest of the folks."

"Yes, ma'am," Bruce said as he flipped his shiny hair over his right shoulder and went to gather up all the booty.

Aletha watched Bruce dutifully and with good humor take care of his chores. She thought to herself that maybe she should try a white boy next, since her relationships with the brothers tended to take rather disastrous turns. The only problem Aletha had in that regard was that all the white ones that she'd ever found attractive were like Bruce, musicians who preferred to play instruments she didn't have. She figured it might be one of the consequences of living in New York City.

Well, she couldn't wait to meet this Chester Lockwood, who she had hired to be her date for the day. She should have ordered a white man instead of a dark-skinned conservative-looking brother, she thought. But then Desiree would probably think that Aletha was jealous of her relationship with David.

No, if Aletha decided to start dating white men, she'd wait until Desiree and David moved to wherever they were going.

There was no way she was going up to her parents' house without a date, though, knowing that everyone there would be coupled off—her sister and her husband, and Marshall there with his girlfriend, Janeen.

She was sure they would all be there waiting to meet Reggie.

Aletha once met a woman on one of her plane trips who had told her how she used escort services to hire a man whenever she needed one for functions where she would have preferred a date. Aletha had never thought about doing such a thing until she realized that she'd probably never hear from Reggie again.

It turned out to be an interesting proposition when she understood that in hiring such a man, she could also—since she was *paying*—demand sexual services if she so desired.

She hadn't had sex in the longest time. Maybe paying for it, on her own terms, would be quite rewarding. That was why she had ended up calling Big Apple Escorts for a date. She'd have 'em shut down faster than a roadrunner if they ever leaked this out to the press.

As Aletha swept past the doorman on their way out, she handed him a card containing five one-hundred-dollar bills.

"Merry Christmas, George."

"Merry Christmas to you, Miss Brown."

Jim, the chauffeur, opened the door for them.

"Hi, Mary Beth. Merry Christmas." Aletha looked past her producer to her date, Chester Lockwood.

Not bad, she smiled to herself.

"Hello, Aletha. Merry Christmas." He had a sexy drawl, which she instantly knew was not exactly authentic, but who cared? At a thousand dollars for the day, he had better put on the performance of his life for her.

Bruce peeked into the car to get a glimpse of Aletha's date. His eyes locked for a moment with Chester's before he got into the front seat next to the chauffeur. He grinned cryptically as Jim slammed the door shut.

Bruce Jacobson wasn't fooled for a second.

Eric reached over Marshall's reclining body to answer the phone.

Quickly, Marshall grabbed his hand, squeezed, and with a stern reproach, snapped, "I told you, I'll get it!"

Eric's look of outrage soon melted away as Marshall placed the palm of Eric's hand to his lips and gently kissed it.

"Eric, after today you can answer the phone anytime you wish."

Eric got up to make their morning coffee. He reached over to the Louis XIV chair, one of the many things he had sent for from his apartment in San Francisco, grabbed his G-string underpants, and put them on.

As he started to leave the room for the kitchen, Marshall sighed something into the receiver that made Eric pause.

"Yes. . . . Hello, Mother. . . . Umm-hmm, I know that dinner is being served at three. . . . Yes, I know that Janeen is coming. . . . No, I *couldn't* drive her up to the house because I was just never able to get in touch with her. I figured she'd call you anyway."

Marshall looked over at his lover, who was now staring at him, his eyebrows crashing into each other in an angry scowl. Eric leaned against the door frame with his arms crossed in front of him.

"Mom, I told you, we'll *be* there by three. . . . Umm-hmm, yes, I said *we*. I'm bringing a special friend with me, someone I feel it's time for you to meet. . . .

"Her name? Uh, the name is Eric, ah, Mom, you'll—"

Eric started yelling angrily as he immediately noted that with a tricky twist of syllables, Marshall had made it sound as if his name was *Erica!*

"Erica! Now my name is *Erica?*" He picked up a box of condoms from the top of the dresser and threw it at Marshall.

Marshall covered the mouth of the receiver with his hand. "Shhh!" He placed his index finger to his lips. "Mom says that you sound loud, Erica."

With that, Eric held up his middle finger.

Marshall winked at Eric again, and with his hand still over the receiver, said, "I will later, baby. Go make us some coffee."

Eric stomped down the stairs, two at a time.

All these games about *nothing!* Marshall should have told his folks about his life years ago. Maybe his parents were so old now, that they'd take one look at him and drop dead from heart attacks.

Eric had told his relatives about himself when he had started acting school and had his first real relationship with a man. Sure, they weren't too happy about it, but he had just moved into his own apartment and begun to live his own life. He knew that if all the people in this world knew anything at all about love, or really, truly had ever experienced passion, they could never, *ever* criticize with whom a person chose to share his life.

Hypnotized by his upset, Eric let the glass coffeepot slip from his grasp, and it shattered on the floor. Eric took a couple of deep breaths and sat down in order to pull himself together.

When he returned to the bedroom, carrying the silver tray with the coffee and a couple of chocolate croissants, he noticed that his lover was lying on his back with his arms folded over his eyes.

"Oh, my poor, big ole tortured soul," he said mockingly as he set the tray down on the highly polished cherry table next to the bed.

Marshall eased himself up with his dark, powerful arms and leaned back against the pillow.

Eric stood looking down at him, his eyes following the lines of Marshall's strong, black, well-sculptured body, and asked, "Marshall, are you ashamed of me?"

Marshall looked at Eric with a pained expression of disbelief and said, "I'm in love with you, Eric. How could I ever be ashamed of you?"

When Eric crawled onto the bed, they slid, with the black satin sheets, to the floor and into each other's arms.

"I love you, too, Marshall," he whispered breathlessly, kissing him tenderly on the neck. "Merry Christmas."

"Merry Christmas, Eric."

Marshall ran his index finger down the spine of Eric's golden back. His fingers entwined with the flimsy fabric of Eric's G-string. Marshall's powerful hand pulled roughly, ripping the silly thing from Eric's round, hard bottom.

David watched his wife stand in front of the bathroom mirror and wind a wildly colorful Kente cloth scarf around her hair.

The effect was dazzling.

Desiree realized, with an already tired sigh, that although she was obligated this year to go to her parents' Christmas dinner since she and David were moving across the world soon, it would be the nationally famous Aletha who would be the star at the party this afternoon.

"David, get the phone, will you please?"

She glanced at him in the mirror's reflection and began to line her large, almond-shaped eyes with navy blue liner.

He called her from the bedroom. "Dez, it's your mom."

She strode reluctantly to the telephone. As she removed the receiver from David's hand, she made comic faces.

He grinned and leaned over to press his lips tenderly to her collarbone. He inhaled to enjoy the fragrance of her perfume, which seemed to him reminiscent of some sweet and spicy fruit.

He leaned back, propping himself up with the pillows on their bed to watch his wife's interaction with her mother.

He was glad that his folks were away in Florida for the holidays. David knew he didn't have the strength this year to deal with the high drama of both the Hebrews and the blacks.

"Hi, Mother. Merry Christmas to you, too." She pulled up the antenna of the cordless phone. "Yes, we'll be there by three. . . . *What?* You say Marshall's bringing his new *fiancée*, Erica, to the dinner? What about Janeen? Didn't you tell me yesterday that Janeen was coming?"

She turned to look at David, who was now sitting straight up in the bed with a newly intense, typical writerlike interest.

His characteristically crooked smile began to spread over his amused and swarthy face.

"Mom, look, I know you've got a houseful of guests you're expecting, so why don't we have this discussion when I get there. We'll see all of you in a few hours. Bye-bye, Mother."

She firmly hung up the phone.

Desiree looked around at her husband again, who was now motioning for her to come to the bed with him.

She placed her knee on the thick, down-filled comforter, which they had bought in Iceland last year, and sat down.

"I'd give anything to be at your parents' house in nice, warm West Palm Beach, Florida, right now, rather than to be at what is probably going to be the biggest circus of the season, with Aletha jumping from ring to ring."

She's got to be kidding, David thought, laughing to himself. He wouldn't miss this party for the world. Who wanted to spend the holiday listening to a bunch of old Jews complain about the humidity in South Florida, when he could watch high drama unfold at the Greenwich, Connecticut, mansion of some wild and colorful African Americans?

He pulled his wife to him and had her lean back to nestle in his arms.

The phone rang again.

Desiree reached over to pick it up.

"Oh, hello, Elliot." It was David's brother calling from Los Angeles. "Yes, Merry Christmas to you, too. . . . Yes, we're fine. David's right here." She abruptly handed her husband the receiver.

She wasn't about to ask Elliot how *he* was doing. The man would only start on his long litany of complaints: how unreliable his actors were, the weather in LA, how his latest woman didn't understand his work.

Fortunately for Desiree, David didn't share any of Elliot's annoying, self-centered characteristics. Elliot Simon was the youngest and truly the baby of the family, like Aletha.

"Hi, Elliot. How's it going? Are you still squandering your millions?" David laughed good-naturedly into the receiver as he pulled his wife to him, cupping her small, round breasts in his hands.

"Man," he brusquely interrupted his brother. "I don't give a damn about your beef with your tax accountant. Fire him, for all I care! Yes, we *did* speak to Mom and Dad. Why don't you call them. They made a point of letting us know that they hadn't heard from you in weeks."

Desiree sighed and got up to go into the kitchen.

"What? What do you want to *know*? You want to know if Aletha really shot Reggie? What do *you* care? Say *what*?" David burst into hysterical laughter. "Your production staff has an office pool going on whether Aletha shot Reggie? You're *sick*, man. Is *that* what you're really calling us about?"

David rubbed his forehead and shook his head in disbelief.

"Elliot? Get a *life!*"

David hung up the phone.

Desiree returned from the kitchen with two glasses of orange juice. She handed David his and sat back down on the bed next to him.

"Dez, guess what? They're wagering bets out there in Los Angeles on whether your sister really shot her boyfriend. Can you believe it?"

"Of course," Desiree answered with a bored shrug of her naked shoulders. "So, did you tell him to get a life?"

"Exactly."

David drained his glass in one long gulp and pulled his wife into his strong, brawny arms.

The contrasting colors of their unclad flesh would invariably excite him, he was sure, for the rest of his life.

David buried his face into his wife's hair as he reflected upon the knowledge that this clinically cool, extraordinarily clever, woman and psychologist was in her very essence and core a passionate painter.

David was extremely pleased that after all these years, with his new success, he could now give his lovely wife the rich and exotic artist's life she deserved.

He would have probably grown up to be a painter himself had he been brought up in a community with all those beautiful colors of people. White people came in shades of pink, beige, and sometimes a suspicious tan. Black folks came in all *those* colors and *more.*

David smiled as he recalled how they had met, over twenty years ago.

One weekend he had decided to go roller-skating at an indoor rink in Greenwich Village. He was in graduate school at the time at New York University in the Village, and she was going to Columbia.

He had been there for about an hour when this absolute fox—a *shwartze* goddess—bedecked in white hot pants and a flimsy white T-shirt and red knee pads skated awkwardly onto the rink. She was accompanied by some big, arrogant, blond, Viking, Ivy League–type schmuck.

The Viking jerk spun around the rink showing off, while Desiree stumbled along, grabbing hold of the railing for support from time to time.

She obviously couldn't skate.

While the blond Nazi spun around like a demented whirling dervish, David decided to make his move. He skated up behind Desiree and tripped her. She literally fell into his arms.

He lied and told her that he was an instructor at the skating rink and offered her lessons—the first one being free of charge.

He then quickly gave her his home phone number and left the place.

She called him to make an appointment for her trial lesson. They agreed to meet at the rink.

She arrived shortly before he did and found out that he didn't work there at all.

When he walked in, she sauntered her pretty little behind over to him and slapped him squarely on the face.

He kissed her. They both laughed, and the rest, as they say, was history.

Score: The Hebrews, 10; the shit-faced Nazis, zip, piss, zero!

"Dez, honey." He moved his hands down to pull her legs up to make it easier for him to stroke her smooth, warm thighs. "Who in hell is Erica? Why has he chosen another woman as his beard? He's almost forty years old. Personally, I can't understand why some women go along with this shit!"

"I have never heard of Erica, and Marshall usually tells me what's going on." She sighed, reaching up to run her fingers through his shiny, black curls. "As you well know. But I will never understand why he continues to insist on living out this ridiculous charade. Maybe Janeen got tired of playing girlfriend. I just hope Marshall hasn't decided to marry this Erica." She sighed and continued, "David, as I've said time and time again, I feel that he should have gotten this out in the open years ago. I'm tired of keeping everyone's secrets!"

"When do you think he should have done this, Dez? When he left home at seventeen with the fifty-year-old guy with the antiques business?" David asked, glancing over at the clock on the end table.

"Maybe after the old guy died. That might have been a good time. When the guy died and left him the business, Marshall could have said that he had some investors and then announced the fact that he was gay. It must be quite a burden to hide yourself from your own parents. What would they *do*, anyway? Disinherit him? Marshall has more money than my parents have ever seen. They probably know anyway. Marshall was always pretty prissy."

"That's for sure." David laughed.

David couldn't wait to meet Marshall's new "friend," Erica, he thought looking over at the clock again.

"We'd better finish getting ready," David teased, as he moved his hands below Desiree's flat, taut belly, resting them in the moist place between her thighs.

She and David were the part of the family, Desiree reminded herself, that lived the closest to her parents.

When Aletha started making her big bucks, she had insisted on buying their parents that outrageously inappropriate minimansion in Greenwich, only twenty minutes from David and Desiree Simon's Weston, Connecticut, home. She could have slapped her sister silly.

Aletha was slick.

By putting their folks closer in proximity to the Simons, she was off the hook, way down in Manhattan, passing familial responsibility primarily on to Desiree.

Well, now things were going to be different. Aletha was going to have to take the heat now that she was going to be the caretaker of David and Desiree's house.

Life was about to change, especially for Desiree, as she had lived for all of her adult life a rather structured life as a therapist. Now she had referred all of her patients to other doctors and would, from now on, be faced with twenty-four-hour days of blissful uncertainty.

She looked over at the clock. It was only one-fifteen.

"You know, darling, we don't *have* to rush. We have plenty of time," she purred, as she straddled his solid, cream-colored, hairy legs between her now hot, dark thighs.

CHAPTER TWENTY-TWO

Mrs. Brown looked around her at the bizarre combination of people gathered in her living room. Most of these folks were here in her Connecticut house because they seemed to be attached in some way to her daughter Aletha. There were even some relatives, normally too intimidated to ever come to Greenwich, roaming about, drinking her booze, and waiting to eat themselves into a stupor just to be able to go back and tell their friends that they had spent Christmas day with the famous Aletha Brown.

Her children, private by inclination anyway, hardly ever visited. She had insisted that this year's Christmas be different. With Desiree and David moving out of the country and her own advancing age coloring all her perceptions, she could not be sure when they would all have a chance to be together again. She couldn't imagine Eugene and herself on a plane to visit whatever far-off place Desiree and David settled.

Actually, Mary Brown secretly wished that it was her other daughter, Aletha, who was moving out of the country.

Ever since that girl had become a high-visibility millionaire, her and her husband's life had become an utter nightmare. The girl had decided to try to run their lives, first by trying unsuccessfully to force them to retire from their administrative jobs with the city of New York, and then by buying them this stupid house in Connecticut—away from all of their friends. Aletha said it was a better investment than the places in Queens that they would have preferred. What did *they* know? They were just working people. Then there were always those newspaper people up in their faces, with pencils or cameras, trying to pry into all the family's business.

So, in order to assert their last vestige of independence, she and her husband met the seven-fifteen commuter train from Greenwich to New York, along with the high-ranking ad agency, television, and banking executives in order to make it on time for their comparatively ordinary city jobs.

Aletha subsequently had hired some of those interior decorators of hers to fix up the place with all this slick, modern stuff.

Sure, Mary and Eugene could probably have resisted Aletha's intrusions on their lifestyle in some way, but they had never had any experience before with this kind of thing. Neither did they have any friends whom they could confide in who wouldn't just think they were bragging. Intimidation and the knowledge that Aletha meant no harm at all had caused them to give in to her.

But it had just become too damned much!

Now, she'd even read in one of those papers that Aletha kept telling them not to read that she had shot her boyfriend—in his very own apartment, no less.

Her other children, Marshall and Desiree, just minded their own business, living their own lives the way one's children *should*.

All she and her husband had ever wanted for their children was for them to get a good education, some good jobs, then get married to some nice people and start their own families. Instead, they found that out of their three children, who all seemed to be bathing in money, not one of them had given them a single grandchild.

Mary walked into her dining room to check how the staff that Aletha had hired was doing as they set up the long glass table, laden with crystal, china, silverware, and those wicked-looking poinsettia plants, for the buffet.

Mary Brown hated poinsettias!

She used to enjoy making holiday dinners herself and entertaining at a sit-down dinner for an intimate group of people. Instead, Aletha had hired caterers from some fancy place called Gleason's where they made overpriced, foreign-tasting food. It was nothing but common food camouflaged in such a way that you never knew exactly what you were eating.

She figured, with remorse, that *this* must be what living the life of Riley was all about.

Just then, she heard a hail of greetings rise from the living room, signaling that Aletha and some of her friends had arrived.

She walked back to the den, where her husband was lying on the couch watching some television show.

"Eugene, Aletha's here. Get away from that TV and come on in the living room and mingle with our guests."

He pointed over at the enormous box he'd opened and the bizarre gift that lay below it on the floor, then asked with a puzzled frown, "Mary, why did Aletha feel compelled to give me a moose head for Christmas? I don't hunt. Never did!"

Mrs. Brown walked over to the papier-mâché masklike object and picked it up. "It's truly ugly, isn't it? I wonder . . ." She then noticed that a small card had fallen on the floor. She picked it up and read it out loud. "Merry Christmas, Pops! I have heard that men like this sort of thing. Love always, Aletha."

"Have I ever expressed an interest in having a moose head, Mary?" he asked, scratching his head in bewilderment. "I have always wondered what went on in the head of that daughter of yours."

"*My* daughter. In case you have forgotten, you were right there with me when she was conceived." She laughed. "But, Eugene, you should do like I do. I don't let Aletha buy me presents anymore. She never gets me anything I can use or even understand. I tell her to just write me a check."

"That doesn't take any thought or imagination at all."

"If it's imagination you want, there you are. You've *got* it—a moose head!"

"Maybe we should save it and give it to Marshall for his birthday."

"I don't think so. Look, Eugene, we've got guests out there!"

"Ah, woman, they aren't *our* guests. Those are Aletha's."

"I *said* to come on, Eugene!"

He ignored her.

Mary lifted up the hem of her diaphanous red caftan and stomped out of the room and down the hallway to greet her daughter.

She stood at the doorway and noticed that the tall, handsome, dark-skinned man beside Aletha wasn't Reggie. Where was Reggie? Maybe she had killed him! She wondered if this man *knew* that her daughter had shot her lover.

Maybe this brother was some kind of a gold digger and didn't even care.

She pushed through the crowd to meet them all.

Aletha grabbed her mother around the waist and kissed her on the cheek. She turned to her friends, who were handing over their coats to a valet, to introduce them.

"Mother, this is Bruce, my hairdresser at the show."

"*Enchanté,* madame," Bruce flirted, holding up Mrs. Brown's hand to kiss it. "Your home is just *lovely!*"

She looked directly into his eyes, and answered, "How would *you* know? You just got here, Bruce."

Taken aback for only a moment, he sniffed, and said, "Touché, Mrs. Brown. Touché! Now where are the drinkie-poohs?"

"Just say what you want, and I assure you, it'll appear in your hand just like magic, right, Aletha?" she said sarcastically, turning away, now looking at the young white woman.

"And this is my producer, Mary Beth Dean, Mother."

"Pleased to meet you, ma'am."

"Sounds like you are from the South, honey. Where from?" Mrs. Brown asked graciously.

Mary Beth had never really known any black people until she started working for Aletha. She'd certainly never been in any black person's home. At first, she was a little anxious, worrying that she might say something ignorant, but looking around this interesting room full of warm-looking people, she instantly relaxed.

"I'm from Wilson, North Carolina, Mrs. Brown."

"I thought you were born in *South* Carolina," interjected Aletha brusquely, suddenly becoming embarrassed that she had revealed that she didn't know everything about a key player in her world.

"No . . ."

"Oh, don't mind Aletha, girl. She's weak on trivial details," Bruce interrupted with bitchy disdain. He wasn't about to let any other employee get close to *his* Aletha Brown.

Aletha laughed nervously as she introduced her date, who was taking in the activity in the room with an amused smirk.

"And, Mother, this is my friend Chester Lockwood. He works in public relations."

Public relations, my *ass*, Aletha's mother thought. She had no idea who this big Negro was, but she was certain that he was *not* in public relations, and she didn't like him one bit.

"Merry Christmas, everyone. Why don't you all mingle," she said, turning away from this Chester character. "And, daughter, I want to talk to you."

Aletha instinctively realized that her mother wanted to talk to her about something she didn't want to deal with at the moment.

"Look, Mom, there's Aunt Agnes—"

"Agatha, girl, your Aunt Agatha."

"Whatever. I'm going to go over and talk to her."

At just that instant, Aletha looked over toward the door and saw her brother, Marshall, hand his coat to one of the help.

"Marshall, big brother, over here." She grabbed the arm of her date and motioned toward her brother, who was now approaching.

Bruce, now with a glass of wine in his hand, gave a passing glance at Marshall, but his jaw dropped when he noticed the splendid mulatto boy toy standing alongside Aletha's brother. He quickly finished his glass of wine. Before he had a chance to think about it, one of the waiters filled his glass again.

Aletha looked at Marshall's friend Eric as if she wanted to devour him on the spot. Her eyes gazed over the tall, sensual, golden man's elegantly clad body, strong jaw, wide mouth with kissably juicy pinkish lips. His sandy blond curls were pulled into a ponytail on the top with the rest of his hair falling over beautiful wide shoulders.

Hanging from his left earlobe was a small, dangling, gold and emerald earring.

She reached up and covetously touched it with her right hand.

"Marshall, don't tell me that you brought this pretty thing for me."

Eric edged back from her.

"Merry Christmas, Aletha," Marshall said, kissing her on the cheek. "I'd like you to meet my friend Eric. Eric McPheerson."

Aletha's eyes popped out as she noticed something familiar in the shape of Eric's head and in the color of his eyes.

"McPheerson . . . McPheerson?" She tried to contain herself. This couldn't possibly be the brother of the producer, with the fabulous little baby, that she had fired recently—Veronica McPheerson. He sure did *look* like her.

Why would he be here with her brother?

"What's wrong, Aletha?" Marshall's tone only hinted at how worried he'd become about his sister. Maybe he'd tell her to seek some professional help. He'd been hearing and reading some very strange things about her.

"Do you have any sisters, Eric?"

"Yes, I have four. They're in California. Why?"

"Do you have one named Veronica?"

"No, I do not." Eric's facial expression flickered back and forth between stunned irritation and wide-eyed perplexity.

"Veronica? What are you talking about, Aletha?" Marshall thought that things were beginning to take a strange turn.

"Oh, yes. . . ." Eric's face suddenly brightened. "I have a *cousin* named Veronica who works in television somewhere on the East Coast, but I'm not that close with my family."

Aletha's face went ashen. In a moment she recovered. "I—I want you to meet my friend Chester Lockwood."

Marshall looked at Eric, who now appeared as though he was seeing a ghost. He looked as if he were about to faint.

He struggled to contain a scream that, no doubt, would have shattered every piece of glass in this demented house.

Chester Lockwood.

That filthy, gold-digging, coke-snorting, faggot slut, who he had thrown out of his apartment a year before he met Marshall! His *ex-lover*—one of the biggest fucking mistakes he'd ever made. What in God's name was he doing here as Marshall's sister's *date*?

Chester stood calmly staring at Eric with a slight and amused smile.

"Pleased to meet you, Marshall—" The corner of the left side of his upper lip rose into a cruel smirk. "—and you, too, Eric McPheerson."

The name McPheerson made Aletha feel as though something ugly was crawling up her back. Suddenly overwhelmed by a feeling that at that moment something was coming to get her, Aletha fled to the kitchen.

What Aletha didn't know was that Eric wanted to join her there. Or anywhere he could escape from Chester Lockwood. Eric had hoped to never lay eyes on the man who spent his whole life siphoning money from other people's bank accounts. Whatever he was doing with Marshall's sister could not end well, he was sure.

Desiree tapped on her brother Marshall's shoulder.

He turned to see his only sensible sister and her normal husband smiling at him. He checked out with approval Desiree's chic khaki-colored leather aviator suit with the tan shearling collar and cuffs. He knew it had to be a Dimitri. She was standing quite comfortably in three-inch-heeled Stuart Weitzman ocelot pumps. Feline patterns were becoming on his big sister. He had always loved her style. Then he glanced at what David was wearing. The usual, he sighed to himself, a brown corduroy sports jacket and a pair of jeans. With all of *his* money, it was an outright scandal! He'd have to give David some fashion tips one of these days.

"Desiree, you look *divine*!" He kissed her on the cheek. "And David. How goes it, brother?" he said, patting him on the shoulder.

"Fine. Fine." David struck a glance at Marshall's friend in covert amazement.

"Merry Christmas, Marshall. Where is this Erica that you want us all to meet?" Desiree asked, looking directly at Eric and trying to suppress a chuckle.

"Desiree, David, I'd like you to meet my friend—" He glanced at Eric, who was still standing paralyzed, glaring, it seemed, at Chester. "—my lover, Eric McPheerson."

Desiree moved to shake Eric's very cold, dry hand.

So, *this* was her brother's "fiancée," she thought, smiling with relief, for her brother had finally come out of the closet.

His man was in some kind of a disturbing trance, though.

David went over to shake Eric's hand. Eric emerged from his distraction, and he looked into the eyes of Marshall's sister and brother-in-law to see if he could catch even a note of disapproval. There was none. None at all. In fact, they were smiling warmly and, he thought, welcomingly at him.

"What do you do for a living, Eric?" David asked. He *knew* he hadn't wanted to miss this party, but he never would have imagined anything like this. He noticed that Janeen was nowhere in sight. He could hardly wait to see what was going to happen next.

"I—I—look . . . I have to *do* something. Marshall, where is the bathroom . . . or someplace private in this house?" Eric glanced desperately about the room.

"There's a room next to the bathroom on the left. Are you okay, Eric?" Marshall asked.

"I'll be fine in a minute!" he snapped.

Marshall stood in shock as he watched Eric drag Chester by the arm out of the room.

"Where's Aletha?" Desiree asked Marshall.

Mrs. Brown returned. She greeted her daughter and son-in-law, then stared at Marshall with a look of apprehension. "Where's Erica?"

At the entrance to the living room, which also led into the dining room, two of the help, who were both male, looked at each other, lifted their eyebrows, giggled, slapped hands, then snapped their fingers in unison. One said to the other, "Now *this* is just the kind of party I truly *live* for—a party given by a *royal* family!"

"Yes, honey," said the other. "An empress and two queens."

"Honey, you mean *three* queens! Did you check out Aletha's *date*?"

"Well, if you scope out the cute blonde with the killer buns she came with—her hairdresser I think I overheard—we've got *four*!"

"Yea, honey, that's the one *I* got my eyes on. He is *too* sweet with his ba-a-ad self!"

Desiree reached over to take a glass of wine from the tray one of the help held before her, and whispered in her husband's ear, "Do you see Janeen anywhere around here?"

More than a few people at the party noticed that things were heating up.

Aunt Agatha approached Desiree and her husband, grabbed Desiree's arm, and demanded, "You *always* knew this about Marshall, didn't you, girl?"

"Mmm-hmm . . ."

"I've been trying to *tell* your mother and father, but they never believed me! That boy has been effeminate all his natural-born life." She lit a cigarette, causing Desiree to back away from her, and added, "That sure is a pretty thing he came in with, though, isn't it? *Decorating!* That choice of a career should have given your parents a clue, don't you think?"

"Marshall is an antiques dealer, Aunt Agatha," Desiree stated flatly, discouraging any further discussion of her brother with this woman who had never been in her own brother's home since they had been placed in Greenwich.

Desiree was nervous. She closed her eyes and made a silent wish that when she opened them again she would find herself sitting next to her husband at the side of the swimming pool at *his* parents' house in Florida.

In the little room behind the bathroom Eric stood with his hand on his hips, hissing at Chester.

"What are you doing here, nigger! What are you doing posing as a date for Aletha Brown? You gold-digging motherfucker!"

"It doesn't seem that you're doing too badly yourself, Eric."

"*Excuse* me? I would say that this is entirely different. Marshall is my man. Aletha happens to be his sister. What's your *game*, I asked you?"

"She hired me," he said simply.

"*Hired* you? You're working for a fucking escort service, now, selling it to rich *women*?"

"Lighten up, Eric. It's no big deal."

"What's no big deal?" Marshall entered the room. He looked around at all of his mother's strange stuff, tossed this way and that, and thought to himself, I never *will* figure out what this room is for.

"Marshall, I used to live with this whore. I threw the nigger out. Now he's here—"

"What?" What was his sister doing dating a faggot?

Marshall calmly looked at Chester, wanting to laugh at the irony of it all, but then his mind flashed to Janeen. Shit! This was going to be a long day.

He regretted not having told Janeen not to come. He should have called her back and told her that he wasn't coming up to his parents' place this year. Actually, he realized that he should have gone on and told her at the dinner he made for them that he was involved with Eric. But he hadn't known how. He wanted to grab Eric and run, but it was too late.

"Mr. Lockwood, what are you doing here with my sister? And why did Eric kick you out?"

"He's a thief and a drug-crazed whore, Marshall!" Eric shrieked, flailing his hands.

Marshall shook his head and, with a tired sigh, put his arm around Eric to escort him from the room. "Come on, let's all go back to the party," he said.

It didn't take much imagination for Marshall to understand what had transpired between Eric and Chester. He had been dragged around the block a number of times himself by selfish faggots, ever since his benefactor had died.

When the three of them confronted Aletha, who was sitting at the bar in the kitchen with her head down on the counter, she simply looked up at Chester, and said, "Look, you can stay here till the end of the party. But let me tell you, if I catch you doing blow, or if I even *think* you are, in my parents' house— which *I* bought, by the way . . ."

Marshall dropped his chin to his chest and shook his head sadly.

Aletha continued. ". . . I'll have you blackballed from every escort service in America!"

She looked at Eric, letting go of her misguided fantasies about him, and said, "I am pleased to meet you. Welcome to the family."

Eric strolled haughtily out of the kitchen with his arm around Marshall's waist.

"I don't want you up in my video anymore, Chester, after today!" Eric yelled.

"Enough, baby," Marshall said to Eric, his large hand squeezing the small of his lover's back.

Now, Marshall knew that he would finally have to confront his parents. He looked around to see if Janeen had arrived yet. He knew that if she had, she'd be up in his mother's face as usual, regaling the woman with some fabricated story about their latest adventures. Janeen was a loyal friend, but he felt guilty that she had fallen in love with him and he had never taken the steps to be an equally loyal friend to her by offering her his honesty and introducing her to Eric.

He had met most of Janeen's boyfriends, as far as he could tell, but he had kept her out of the most intimate parts of his own life. His despicable cowardice had also caused him to treat the love of his life, Eric McPheerson, as if he were an old-time white plantation master's hidden slave mistress.

Marshall Brown was secretly drowning in shame.

Bruce, with a silly drunken cruelty, decided to comment on the Christmas music blaring throughout the house. As he motioned his hand toward Marshall and Eric, who were coming back into the living room, he vengefully winked at the mother and said, "Oh, my dear, *listen.* Isn't that Nat King Cole on the stereo roasting his *chestnuts*?" A self-satisfied and inebriated cackle issued from his mouth.

He'd show her who knew a few things. No matter how long they'd been there. This was his payback for that arrogant "How would *you* know? You just got here, Bruce" statement she had uttered earlier as a greeting.

Bruce Jacobson never, ever, forgot a slight.

Mary Brown stood horrified, looking as though someone's big fist had punched out her eyes.

Mary Brown had always known that her only son was gay, but she never thought she'd ever have to confront it—especially in public, among all their family and friends. At that moment she wanted to snatch her husband from in front of the TV set and run away back to Queens, where they understood the social terrain.

She fled back to the den, where Eugene still lay on the couch, staring at the television.

"You *are* going to eat dinner with the rest of us, aren't you, Eugene?"

"I'll come in as soon as Marshall and that Erica girl of his—"

Mary Brown broke down and cried.

A familiar annoyance twisted into a knot in Marshall's belly as he listened to the chauffeur, who was now devouring a greasy turkey wing, drone on and on about O. J. Simpson's problems.

In a circle around him, among the others, there was Aletha's producer, Mary Beth, hanging on to his every word as if she were a student enraptured by some new idea.

When Janeen arrived and sauntered, seductively, she thought, into the crowded living room, it seemed as if all the family looked away to avoid her. She felt like someone who was the last to know she'd been fired from a job.

What in the be-Jesus is going *on* here? she wondered. She snatched a glass of wine from a tray that someone had pushed in front of her. She looked around the room for Marshall, her future husband.

She had played too coy all these years with the men in her life. It was time to make amends by making demands. These guys seemed to want to just date you forever.

Well, Janeen Davis was tired of the silliness and wanted to get married and start a family. She didn't have forever! Her clock was ticking like a muthafucker! Marshall and she had good, solid businesses, and he seemed to have a good and stable family—despite the rumors about Aletha. But Aletha wasn't a major drawback considering the fact that she was a rich, powerful public figure, who would probably be able to direct all of those rich colleagues of hers in Janeen's direction as clients, as soon as she was part of the family.

Sometimes a woman just had to take control. That was her New Year's resolution. She was going to propose to Marshall and give him an ultimatum.

Oh, there he was!

She walked over to the group with the pontificating chauffeur in the center and kissed Marshall directly on the lips—leaving her mark.

Marshall kept moving away from the woman, but like iron filings to a magnet, she continued to cling.

The chauffeur winked at Janeen as he wiped some turkey grease from his mouth with the back of his hand. Noticing that she hadn't been paying any attention to his brilliant assessment of the O. J. case, he poked her playfully in the ribs and asked, "Don't you agree with me, sister?"

Janeen kept glaring at the white girl who glanced from time to time at Marshall, giving him the eye—or so Janeen thought. What was this white bitch looking for here in this house? Janeen reached over to take another drink.

Eric thought he was going to die when he watched Janeen walk into the room and prance her skinny ass directly over to Marshall to kiss him. He didn't miss the fact that her oily red lips lingered on his man's ear, as well.

"Why don't you go over and introduce yourself, Eric?" Desiree asked, noticing the agony in his sad, exotic green eyes.

"I think I'll just stand back and watch for a while," he said, taking another gulp of his drink while keeping his gaze on Marshall. "I want to see what Marshall is going to do."

"I'm with you, Eric," David agreed.

Eric walked away to the other side of the room in order to maintain a clear view of the group surrounding the chauffeur.

David was also curious about when Marshall was going to introduce Janeen to Eric. The suspense was just about killing him. David's writer's mind was aching to take control of the situation, but as a guest, he had to just stand next to his wife and wait for these characters to act out their own scene.

"Desiree, is it my imagination or do Eric and Janeen really share a very strong resemblance?"

"It is not your imagination at all. It's truly weird. It kind of makes you wonder."

"Wonder about what?"

"About the true nature of Marshall and Janeen's relationship. Why would Marshall's platonic female friend bear such a close resemblance to his lover?"

"Leave it alone, Dez. Don't start psychoanalyzing."

The chauffeur repeated his question to Janeen. "Don't you agree with me, sister, about—"

"I don't give a damn about O. J. Simpson's mess!" she snapped loudly, glancing hostilely at Mary Beth. "Frankly," she added, "I am sick and tired of hearing about filthy rich brothers who go with white women. I hope they all get what they deserve."

Marshall backed away slightly from the group as he stared at Janeen in disbelief and said, "Janeen, that's the sickest thing I've ever heard. What on earth is *wrong* with you, girl?"

Mary Beth was horrified. Not only was this black woman spouting the kind of racial rhetoric she'd hoped had ceased to exist, she was leveling a personal threat. And all because she mistakenly thought she had designs on Marshall Brown.

As much as everyone tried to make it seem like she was from some tiny hamlet in Jerkwater County, North Carolina, even Mary Beth Dean knew Marshall was a homosexual from the minute he stepped through the door. If this woman couldn't see that, she was the one who was going to get what she deserved.

Poor Janeen. What a circus, she thought, as she looked at Bruce, who was now approaching the group.

Bruce looked at Mary Beth and smiled with a drunken conspiratorial expression. He knew that *she* knew what was happening.

Mary Beth removed herself from the conversation and headed toward the couch. She had had her eye on Aletha's tall, fine cousin Elroy, who was standing across the room, glancing at her from time to time. She caught his eye and slid her tongue subtly over her bottom lip. She was kind of tipsy and hoped that she wasn't coming on too forward, or like a hoochie, as she had heard it called. Elroy sauntered over in her direction.

"Hi, I'm Aletha's cousin Elroy—"

"I know—" Flutter, flutter. "—I'm Aletha's producer, Mary Beth Dean." Flutter, flutter.

"That's a cute accent you got there, young lady. Where are you from?"

Those broad shoulders, narrow hips, and flashing dark eyes caused her to feel faint. If her parents were right about their warnings about black men, well, then go ahead, brother, do what comes naturally, she thought, giggling to herself and blushing at her outrageous fantasy. The feminist sisterhood would kick her butt to bloody hell if they knew what she was thinking.

"How did you know that I was Aletha's cousin?" he asked, putting down his glass on the end table next to where they were standing.

"I was talking to Aletha's aunt . . ."

"Agatha?"

"Yes. She told me who you were. In fact, I believe she gave me the run-down on almost everyone *in* this place—except for the help." She beamed and lightly touched his arm.

"That's definitely Agatha."

"Tell me something, Elroy."

"What's that, Mary . . . *Beth?*"

"Did *you* know that your cousin Marshall was gay?"

"The big secret was only a figment of his own imagination, honey." He laughed. "Can I get you a drink?"

"Yes, please."

"What can I get you?"

"Anything you want," she responded, staring meaningfully into his deep brown eyes.

Marshall wanted to go to see about his sister Aletha, who he presumed was still hiding in the kitchen for some reason. He still wanted to find out if she had really shot her boyfriend, and he also wanted both his sisters present for support when he introduced Eric to Janeen.

As he started to leave the room, Janeen, now slightly intoxicated from too much nervous drinking, grabbed Marshall's behind and said a bit too loudly, "Baby, *where* are you going? Why don't you stay right here and—"

"Lord, have *mercy*!" gasped Aunt Agatha.

Orgasmic squeals of delighted shock from the two waiters standing in the doorway pierced the room.

Everyone in the room stood stock-still, as if someone had pressed the pause button on their VCRs, as Eric stalked unsteadily across the room yelling out obscenities.

He firmly pushed Janeen away from Marshall. "What do you think you're *doing*, young lady? Get your filthy hands *off* my man!"

Janeen's look of utter disbelief froze on her face as she watched this male almost mirror image of herself fling back his long hair and put his arm around *her* Marshall's waist.

Both parents entered the room and stood like zombies as they watched this embarrassingly peculiar scene.

So *this* is how it goes, David thought as he and Desiree approached the group.

"*Tell* her, Marshall. Tell her *now*," Eric demanded, glaring with unbridled fury at Janeen. "Kick the woman to the *curb*, Marshall!"

"Janeen Davis, I'd like you to meet my friend—my live-in lover—Eric McPheerson."

At that moment Janeen wanted to throw herself from a forty-story window. She felt betrayed in a way she could never have imagined. How could she have been so *wrong* after all these years?

Mary Brown looked at her husband, who was staring at his son with an amused look on his face.

The whole family must take him for some kind of blind and ignorant fool, Eugene thought to himself, walking over to David and saying to him, "It's about time that old rusty Negro came out of the damned closet, don't you think, son?" and he walked past him toward Agatha without waiting for a response.

David was struck mute. The old man had *known* all these years, after all. What a useless charade it had all been!

Mary Brown went over to Janeen and said, "Honey, would you like another drink?"

Janeen spun on her heel, pushed her way through the accumulated guests. The loud slam of the bathroom door was as good as a do-not-disturb sign.

The family, David, Desiree, Marshall, and Eric, eventually removed themselves as gently as the situation allowed from the awkward tension in the room, and then went to see about Aletha and relay to her what had happened.

As they passed Mary Beth, Desiree heard the producer say to their cousin Elroy, "I would *love* to have dinner with you tomorrow evening. I'll give you my number . . ."

Desiree looked at David, who had heard it, too, and they both chuckled.

Aletha confessed to them all that she *had* in fact shot Reggie. No one was surprised by the revelation.

Some curious guests attempted to enter the kitchen to see what was going on. Eric quickly went over to the entrance and stated with haughty authority, "Now, now, you all go on back to the party. This is *family* business," then slammed the door in their faces, not really caring whether those people were family or not.

"Aletha," Marshall asked, leaning against the kitchen table opposite her, "what made you carry a gun to Reggie's apartment? Did you suspect him of something, or are you just going stark-raving mad?"

"Marshall, I always carry a gun. It's dangerous on these mean streets for a famous person like myself." Then, turning to Desiree's husband, she said, "You know that, right, David?"

"I don't carry a gun, Aletha." David grinned at her as he squatted on the floor next to his wife, who was sitting at the table, staring at her sister. "And considering what has transpired, I suggest that you stop. You could end up in jail."

"Girl, I would have done exactly the same thing as you did, if I had caught Marshall in bed with another man." Then shooting Marshall a quick, wicked look, Eric added, "Or another *woman*, for that matter."

David laughed and said, "Marshall, you'd better watch yourself. You have been *warned*."

"Eric and I live together, David; but, I'd never break into someone's home and—"

"Speak for yourself, baby," Eric stated, helping himself to the bottle of wine that Aletha had in front of her.

"I *loved* Reggie. I gave him *everything* I could, and I never even looked at another man . . . not really. As far as I'm concerned, he deserved to die!" Aletha hissed, banging her fist on the counter.

The room fell silent.

"Honey, I understand what you mean. If I had done what you had done to my last lover, Chester, and had blown him to hell where he belongs, I wouldn't have had to face him in that room tonight. No offense, Aletha," Eric said, and took another gulp of his wine.

"Umm-hmm." Aletha smiled at her brother's pretty lover. She couldn't believe that she had never even suspected that Marshall was gay. It was probably because she had never had the time to think at all about the private lives of her siblings. She realized that she liked this exotic assortment of family that she had. Maybe she'll just have to find the time and become more involved in their lives. It isn't as if she really had a life of her own anyway anymore.

Perhaps it would be a good idea to open herself up to them; everyone needed someone they could talk to, and these people seemed to be accessible and loving her.

She then decided to finally recount to them the tale of her disastrous affair with the man in Miami and the fact that he had recently burned her house down.

"Girl, I'll help you hunt him down like the wild, killer animal that he is!" Eric said with sympathetic outrage.

"Eric, chill out," Marshall said, looking over at Aletha, who had cracked up laughing so hard that she was now gasping and grabbing hold of her stomach.

Desiree and David suggested that she quit the show at the end of her contract and take some time with them in Maui to recuperate and rethink her life.

Aletha appreciated the offer, but she knew she could never stay with them. Watching their relationship together would only send her plunging into a greater depression.

She'd just have to work things out alone. Maybe she'd just leave the show and go live in her new house in the Bahamas. She had only three more months to go.

"You know, I've been thinking about taking a break, like you and David, Desiree. I have a beautiful place in the Bahamas, in Nassau. I bought it for me and Reggie . . ."

Eric looked over at Marshall.

Marshall laughed at the greedy look in his lover's eyes, which reminded him so much of his sister Aletha's way of approaching everything, and said, "Don't even think about it, Eric. I can't afford to buy you a house in the Islands. We'll just have to go down to Aletha's place, or—" He looked over at David. "—wherever those two are planning to play in the sun!"

"But since Reggie is no longer by my side—" Aletha sighed dramatically, lifting her glass and taking another gulp of wine. "—I'll just go there alone. I—I need to g-get away."

Oh, oh, thought David, knowing that when Aletha started stuttering, things took a strange turn.

"I n-need to go s-somewhere far away from man-st-stealing w-white women!" she snapped angrily, grabbing the bottle of wine in front of her.

Marshall tried to take it from her, but he wasn't quick enough. She refilled her glass.

Eric shot Aletha a mean look, which Aletha caught but didn't understand.

Desiree got up quickly from her chair and said, "I'm going to make some coffee."

"I don't want any damned coffee, Deth-er-ee," Aletha slurred. "I'm f-fine!"

David decided to play devil's advocate. He laughed and said, "You can't get away from white people, Aletha. Especially any place where there's a warm sunny climate. We're *everywhere*!"

"David, come over here and get the coffeepot from up in the cabinet," Desiree interjected, annoyed that David had decided to encourage a twisted dialogue with her now inebriated sister.

Aletha jumped up from the table, walked over to David, jabbed her index finger into his chest, and shouted, "*We?* Who's *we*?"

She walked back to the counter, sat down, and continued, "Deth-er-ee told me th-that Jews aren't white people. And she *knows*—" Aletha lifted her arms in the air, fanned them out, and wiggled her fingers. "—b-because *she's* been w-with *everybody*!"

They all stared at Aletha in silence.

David was sorry he had gotten her started. At that moment he wanted to gag Aletha, toss her into a closet, lock the door, and throw away the key. But then, he thought, smiling to himself as he went over to help his wife make coffee, he'd only end up on one of Aletha's shows, probably called "Abusive In-Laws."

Eric drained his wineglass, walked unsteadily over to David, and grabbed his hand to shake it.

"Welcome to the club, David. A white woman gave birth to me, and I'm not white either!"

"Come back over here, Eric," Marshall demanded. "You're just as drunk as Aletha!"

Aletha, realizing that she had offended Eric with her man-stealing white women comment, gasped and said, "Oh, my God. I—I'm thorry, Eric. I didn't mean—" She made a gesture with her hand, causing her to knock her glass and the wine bottle onto the floor. The crash startled everyone.

Mary Brown burst into the room and hissed, "What is *wrong* with you all? Why are you people holed up in here messing up my kitchen when we have guests out there?"

She looked at Marshall with an angry scowl and continued. "I want you, boy, to get out of here and take care of your business! You can't just leave Janeen out there like that. And as for the rest of you drunks, sober up and come back to the party like decent folks!"

"I'm not drunk, Mother," both Marshall and Desiree said at the same time.

"Well, I'm not talking to *you*, then, am I? I'm talking to the drunks in this room!" she snapped, looking directly at Aletha. "And Desiree, clean up this mess!" she said, pointing at the broken glass and puddle of wine on the floor.

"Mother, why am I always the one to clean up everyone's—"

Mary Brown sucked her teeth in annoyance, turned on her heel, and left the kitchen before Desiree could finish her sentence.

"Detheree, go on in the living room. I—I'll clean up the m-mesh. I'm the one who knocked the—"

"Aletha, listen to yourself. You can hardly talk. You're in no condition to clean up any broken glass. You'd only just end up getting cut. But you can help by bringing me a mop and broom."

"Pain means nothing to me anymore, Detheree. Reggie has made me impervious to—"

"Oh, shut up, Aletha!" Marshall snapped. "You shot a hole in the man and—"

"I *told* you, the bullet just *grazed* the sucker!" Aletha shouted. "Anyway, why don't *you* go out there, Marshall, and talk to Janeen? You a coward or something? Take care of your business like Mom told you to do!"

"Take care of *my* business? You needed to hire a date to come to your own mother's house, and you call me a coward? Why don't you go in there and get that gigolo escort of yours out of our parents' house?"

Eric, who had been sitting with his head down on the counter trying to concentrate on sobering up, moaned in agony and said, "Yes, Lord, please get th-that gigolo out of here, away from me! I can't take it. I justh can't take it."

"Shut up, Eric! I'm going to bring you some coffee," Marshall said, walking past David and Desiree, who were cleaning up the mess on the floor.

"I'm not going out there. Maybe he'll just go away," Aletha said, looking nervously toward the door.

"I'm not going out there either," Marshall said, returning to Eric with a cup of coffee.

"The people out there will end up asking me about Reggie, and I *know* that Mom wants me to explain Chester. I can't deal with that shit. Not today!"

"So what are you all going to do? Leave the house through the back door? How are you going to get your coats?" Desiree asked sarcastically, setting a cup of coffee in front of her sister. She leaned against the sink across from them.

Marshall and Aletha looked at each other with eyebrows raised in an expression that seemed to Desiree to say "not a bad idea."

"I was being sarcastic, you two! God! What's wrong with you?"

Marshall and Aletha ignored Desiree's reproach.

"Mar-thall," Aletha slurred.

"What?"

"W-when did you find out that you were a gay? When doesth one know something like that?"

"What do you mean?"

"Answer your sister, Marshall," Eric snapped impatiently. "You know what thee wants to know! When was the first time you slept with a boy?"

David and Desiree both regarded Marshall with looks of curious apprehension.

"In boarding school."

"How old were you?" Aletha asked, looking at her brother as if she now no longer recognized him.

"Thirteen . . . fourteen . . . I don't remember."

"Sure you do, Marshall," Eric said sternly, taking a gulp of coffee. "We always remember the year, day, and time of our *first*, right, Aletha?"

"*I'm* the one asking the q-questhions, now, Eric!"

"Speak for yourself, Eric. I've been gay all of my life. How's *that*?"

"Wow." Aletha sighed with amazement. "Do you think that if I had gone away to an all-thirls b-boarding school that I could have become a gay?"

"It's not 'a gay,' Aletha, it's just *gay*," Marshall said, snickering at the strange expression.

"Whatever . . ."

"Don't be ridiculous, Aletha." Desiree took away Aletha's wineglass and then sat in a chair near the counter. "You went to an all-girls prep school, and you are definitely not gay."

"Shit, Detheree, maybe I would be better off today if I was!"

Eric, who had placed his head back down on the counter, popped up and said, "Girrrrl, an athhole is an athhole!"

"David, this is getting ridiculous. Go out there and get these jokers some food."

"I am *not* a joker," Marshall huffed, indignant.

"Then I am not talking to *you*, then, am I?" Desiree grinned, winking at her brother.

David left the kitchen.

"Drink your coffee, Aletha," Desiree said, getting up to make some for herself.

"Did *you* know, Desiree, that Marshall was a gay?" Aletha asked, as if her brother weren't even in the room.

"What difference does it make?"

"What *difference*? You people are all friggin' crazy!" Aletha began to raise her voice, then looked over at Eric, who was leaning on his elbows staring at her. She dropped her voice and continued. "Tell me then, what does that Janeen girl out there have to do with the two of you guys?" she asked, pointing two fingers toward Eric and Marshall. "Is that what you call a ménage à trois or something?"

"It is most certainly *not*, Aletha," Eric snapped, glaring at Marshall. "Today is the first time I ever met the bitch. And it had better be the last."

"Let's drop all of this talk, which isn't going to go anywhere anyway. Marshall, you're going to have to go out there and talk to Janeen, apologize or whatever it is that people do in situations like these," Desiree said, sitting back down in her chair with her cup of coffee.

"Drop the talk?" Aletha said. "You can't tell me to *drop* anything, Desiree! Why don't you just go in there with your husband, Miss No-Skeletons-in-the-Closest, Miss Goody-Two-Shoes, M-miss . . ."

Marshall and Eric helped David carry a large platter of turkey, bowls of stuffing, cranberry sauce, some corn bread squares, and greens and set them on the kitchen counter.

"Now that that's taken care of, let's all have a bite to eat, say our good nights, and go home," David said, placing the platter down on the counter. "Marshall, you and Eric can stay over at our house tonight if you like."

Eric was elated with the idea.

He knew that he was going to *like* being a part of *this* family. David and Desiree were fabulous, and Aletha wasn't so bad. As an ambitious, famous person, she had simply had her share of life's troubles.

Desiree set plates and silverware on the counter, and everyone began to dig into the food.

"What's going on out there, David?" Marshall asked.

"When we finish eating, why don't we all go in and find out?" David replied. He looked over at Marshall, and asked, "What are you going to do about Janeen?"

An uncomfortable yet amused silence filled the room. None of them really knew anything much about Janeen Davis.

"Nothing!" snapped Eric, stabbing a slice of turkey.

Eugene opened the door to the kitchen and stood staring at his strange family.

"Want some food, Pops?" Aletha said, waving a turkey wing at him.

He shook his head, mystified by it all. What did these three children of his think they were doing anyway, hiding in his kitchen like refugees, leaving him and his wife to contend with their peculiar entourages? It was obvious that he and Mary had raised a pack of self-centered nuts!

He turned away, slowly closed the door behind him, and went back to the living room.

Gradually sobering up, they ended up enjoying a lively conversation about their jobs, David and Desiree's plans, Aletha's new house, and Marshall and Eric's relationship.

After a while, they realized it was getting late.

"You'd better go in there, Marshall, and talk to Janeen. We'll wait for you," Desiree said to her brother, patting him on the shoulder with a kind of empathy she hoped that she'd never have to experience again.

CHAPTER TWENTY-THREE

Marshall found himself back again in his mother's peculiar little room by the bathroom for the second time that day.

Janeen stood in front of him looking as if she were about to stab him with a dagger.

"How could you do this to me, Marshall? I just don't understand you at all. All these years we have been friends—or supposed to have been anyway— and you run a game on me like *this*? In front of the entire free world! You are a sick, fucking puppy! What is with this Eric crap?" Her head felt that it was about to burst wide open.

"Eric is my lover, has been for some time now."

"Are you insane or what? In all the years I've known you, you never once told me that you were gay. What are you, some kind of a freak?" She leaned forward with her hands on her hips.

"Have you ever met any female lover of mine, Janeen?" he asked, and leaned against a table overflowing with a pile of his mother's strange stuff.

"I thought we were—"

"Friends, right? That's what we *were*—platonic friends! Think about it. Have I ever made a pass at you?"

"A pass? I thought you respected our friendship and didn't want to risk jeopardizing it with a sexual relationship."

"Maybe you are the one who's a freak, Janeen. I'm a man. Why do you think I never even tried to make a pass at you in the almost twenty years of knowing you?"

"I never made a pass at you either—*freak*!"

"And *I* figured that that was because you knew I was a homosexual. You have to admit that you and I have had a strange relationship all these years. And it's not entirely my fault. Do you realize that you told me all about the men in your life, yet I never told you anything about *my* personal life? Weren't you even curious? Or is it that you are just a self-centered *freak* yourself?"

She felt that she had died and returned smack in the middle of someone else's life. Maybe she had slipped into madness without knowing it, she thought, breaking into an angry sweat.

"Well, what was that dinner about, that you made with all the champagne and stuff, when you returned from France this summer?"

"What did you *think* it was about?" Marshall suddenly felt quite ashamed, realizing that he had actually been enjoying this showdown. After all, she had never cared enough about him to find out who he really *was*!

"Well, it felt to me that you were thinking of taking our relationship to a new level. I guess I was dead wrong!"

"You got *that* right! Actually, my intention was to break the news to you about Eric."

"Oh . . . I see," she said calmly, yet at the same time feeling a hatred for the man that she had never felt toward anyone in her entire life.

"It was the first time I had ever invited you to my town house, right?"

"Umm-hmm," She felt like ducking in order to avoid the next blow.

"Did you ever wonder why?"

"I—I don't know, Marshall. Get to the point!"

"When you entered the foyer, didn't you even notice the huge framed poster of RuPaul on the wall?"

"Yes, Marshall." She sighed, wanting to slap him clear off the face of the earth and into the depths of hell.

"What did you think about that?"

What a small-minded, petty faggot, she thought, completely devastated that she had never known anything about that side of Marshall's personality in all the years she'd known him. "I just figured you liked RuPaul."

"A six-foot-by-four-foot poster of RuPaul didn't clue you in at all, Janeen?"

"You sick, sadistic, cowardly mutant of a homosexual! Actually, at this moment, I feel that your existence gives other homosexuals a bad name. If you are so in love with RuPaul, why wasn't *he* here at this dinner party instead of your little Eric?"

Eric had been listening by the door. He kicked it open and said, "I've had enough of this. Let's go, Marshall. Your brother-in-law and sister are waiting for us."

Eric couldn't imagine for the life of him why she was still here, among *his* family.

"Goodbye, Janeen. I'm sorry for . . . everything," Marshall said, moving forward to shake her hand. She backed away.

She started to look away, but then locked eyes with Eric, who was still a bit tipsy. With a smirk, he snapped his fingers at her quickly, three times, creating a Z formation—the gay man's universal sign of dismissal.

Eric and Marshall left to return to the kitchen.

Convinced that Aletha would be all right for the rest of the evening, the four of them kissed her good night and left her behind so she could figure out how and when she was going to get rid of Chester that evening.

They walked through the living room, waving good night to the roomful of remaining guests.

The parents were standing on the other side of the room. Mary Brown looked over at her silly children, sighed, grabbed her husband by the elbow, and left the room. In her opinion, they didn't deserve any parting words. They had ruined her party, although there probably hadn't been a single guest that evening who would have shared her sentiment.

In the background, Chester covered his mouth, stifling a snicker.

Eric grabbed Marshall possessively by the arm and strolled victoriously out of the house with the Simons.

Mary Beth watched Janeen's eyes follow Marshall's departure, and her heart went out to her.

She couldn't blame her, though, for having been so infatuated with Marshall. He was quite a stunning man. She wouldn't have minded running her fingers through that thick, woolly hair herself.

She'd never touched hair like that before, and she decided on the spot, to not deprive herself of the experience, she thought, glancing over across the room at Elroy. He smiled back at her.

Her folks could call her a nigger lover if they wished, she reflected as she looked around the room at this seductive group of dark people. Her folks seemed like Ma and Pa Kettle in comparison. Mary Beth Dean was going to find herself a handsome, *heterosexual* Marshall for herself.

Janeen sat slumped in one of the couches. A plateful of food, a consolation prize of sorts, sat untouched in front of her.

Mary Beth walked over to her and said, "I can imagine how you feel. Something like this happened to me once—"

Janeen got up from her seat and walked away from the presumptuous white woman. How could *she* ever understand *anything* about her? Sometimes, even girls like this Mary Beth Dean were the friggin' problem.

Janeen hated the Brown family! They were nothing but a bunch of cold, manipulative, and clannish snobs. She couldn't believe how Marshall, his sisters, brother-in-law, and that vindictive faggot hid in the kitchen all night sharing secrets among themselves. Probably laughing their heads off about her. They probably felt that they were too good to mix with the rest of the guests. She also couldn't believe how those uppity, deceitful parents had always treated her as Marshall's girlfriend while knowing all along that their son was a homosexual! She was so humiliated. She had to figure out a way to leave this party discreetly and with dignity.

Tears of disillusionment poured down Janeen's carefully rouged cheeks as she drove alone back to her rented hotel room.

Maybe her instincts were failing her. Maybe it was all the booze.

She just couldn't believe that this nigger had so cruelly and openly dumped her for another *man*!

And Janeen Davis was *still* famished.

SNAP SIX

CHAPTER TWENTY-FOUR

*L*ouise Washington turned the key and opened the door to her apartment. She looked about and reflected on the vast but uninteresting layout of her place. Now that her book, *Black Men: How to Find One, How to Get One, How to Keep One. The Twelve-Step Program*, was selling like hotcakes, she had begun to think about moving out of this so-called luxury housing complex in Harlem. Maybe she'd buy a house, perhaps up in Mount Vernon or some suburb like that, where she could find a neighborhood of well-educated, progressive, and politically correct black folks like herself.

She noticed that her son had returned home. He had thrown his duffel bag in the corner of the foyer and his Adidas were thrown on the floor of the living room, in her way. She knew exactly where she'd find him.

He stood in the kitchen, staring into the refrigerator, not quite able to make up his mind.

This boy, Brian, was getting on her last nerve. She couldn't believe it when she saw him on *The Aletha Brown Show* having a reunion with his long-lost father. She could have died from embarrassment. Friends she hadn't heard from in years made it their business to call her about this silliness. She didn't know a single black woman who didn't religiously watch *The Aletha Brown Show*. That's why she didn't hesitate for a minute to accept a booking on it in order to further promote her book. Now her son had created for her a difficult situation.

Then he had the *nerve* to go off and spend Christmas in Puerto Rico with his damned father, a man she hardly knew, who never spent a penny to help raise him. He said that he wanted to meet his half sister. He had even had the big-time Dr. Morgan call her house to invite her out to dinner, where he confronted her about the story of their relationship. Well, she had certainly succeeded in putting the man in his place. Who did he think he *was* anyway?

With the popularity of this book of hers and now her son's crazy tomfoolery, her life story was now all out in the streets. If her boy hadn't already been good and grown, she would have taken a strap to his narrow behind.

She sat down at the kitchen table.

"Brian, I want to talk to you. Sit down."

He knew what was coming. He had left rather quickly for Puerto Rico, before his mother could gather herself together from shock to talk to him about his *Aletha Brown Show* folly.

"Yeah, Mom, what's up?" He sat down across from her and bit into his apple.

"*What* on earth ever possessed you, boy, to go looking for your father on a damned *talk show*? And on top of it all, the very one I am scheduled to appear on. What is *wrong* with you? You've *got* to be one of the most simpleminded future doctors I ever heard of!" She banged her fist on the table. "Explain yourself, Brian!"

Brian Washington wanted to put it all out of his mind. He had been duped, just like his father had been, and it had been a chilling experience. He never wanted to even *see* a TV set again for the rest of his life.

How could he tell his mother what had actually happened? How could he tell her that he saw an ad in the paper that stated that for *free* for the Christmas season some detective agency was willing to help certain selected people find missing relatives?

He should have known better than to sign some papers with a joint called the A to Z Detective Agency. How could he have known that the outfit worked for *The Aletha Brown Show*? The next thing he knew, he found himself obligated to appear on some weird-assed TV program. It was as if he had gotten caught up in some black widow spider's web.

Brian had never watched any talk shows, so he had no idea of the kinds of pranks they pulled in order to get people to watch them.

He just wanted to bury it all behind him.

"I don't want to talk about it now, okay?"

"No! It's not *okay*," she yelled at her son, her hard eyes staring through angry slits at him. "Well, then, tell me *this*! Why would you spend the holidays with a man you never knew, who played absolutely no part in raising you?"

"Look, you've deprived me of a father all these years. Now I found him, and he seems to be interested in me and my life. *That's* why. Plus, after this long backbreaking school year, which is not even over yet, I thought correctly that I could have used some time away lying in the sun."

Louise just stared at her son. Often she'd wished that she had had a girl instead. She would probably understand a daughter better. Yet, it was kind of funny; every one of her girlfriends, who were single parents, had only boys, too. They were at a total loss as to how to help one another through this "growing manhood" stuff.

"Mom, I need to know something," Brian said.

"What's that, son?" Louise asked. She eyed him suspiciously while smoothing back her hair.

"Why would you write an advice book about men, when you have never even been married?"

Louise laughed and said, "Because I felt like it. It's obvious that books like mine sell quite well, no matter who writes them. Besides, you shouldn't have any complaints about it. My book put you in that cute little sports car of yours."

"I didn't want a sports car, if you remember. I wanted a Harley."

"Too dangerous, boy. I know what's best for you. You show absolutely no gratitude for my generous gift," she said, fanning her hands at him with a gesture of dismissal.

"But that book of yours—"

"What about it? It's number one on the nonfiction bestseller list—"

"Look, Mom, I *read* your book. I hear people talking about it. Some of them don't sound too pleased with it. Aren't you worried that some whacked-out woman might come after you?"

"Of course not!" She laughed but stopped herself when she noticed the look of genuine concern on her son's face.

"In your chapter about finding a black man, you tell women to look for their men in bars and clubs. You say that that's how you can find out whether a man is cheap or not. Aren't there better places to meet men? I mean, shouldn't you go someplace where you'll have more in common with people than just drinking?"

"You go to clubs, don't you?"

"Sure, to listen to the music and look at pretty women, but—"

"Well, there you *are*." She pointed at him with an air of satisfaction.

"But, Mom." He leaned over and touched her arm. "You advocate spying, lying, manipulating, and—"

"A woman's got to do what a woman's got to do to get her man, Brian." Louise grinned slyly at her son.

Brian shook his head. How could a mother of a son advocate such behavior for women? With his mother's book in circulation all over the country like it was, he realized that he was probably in for some pretty bizarre dating experiences.

He decided not to explore the issue any further. There was nothing anyone could do about the situation anyway. Her advice was now engraved in stone.

"Why don't you go and get ready, Mom. Don't you have a date? I know *I* do. And by the way, I think you should give second thoughts to going on that *Aletha Brown Show*. Those folks are demented. I'm afraid something bad might happen to you."

"Like what?" Louise was amused by her son's concerned expression.

"That some enraged woman will—"

Louise cut him off, with a flick of her wrist. "I'm not afraid of any women, boy. Don't worry about me. I've always been able to take care of myself."

"Whatever." Brian shrugged his shoulders in resignation.

He got up from the table to go take a shower. Brian hoped that his mother would fall in love, get married, and stop trying to control his life. It would be about *time*. She was almost fifty and had never been married. He could hardly believe that the public could take that ridiculous book of hers seriously, considering the circumstances.

As for *him*, he had a date with Helena Rodriguez, a girl he met on the beach in San Juan during the holidays. It turned out that she not only lived in New York City, but would also be attending the same medical school as he, in California, this September.

Maybe he'd marry a Hispanic woman, like his father had. He certainly didn't want to get tied up with one of those domineering black widow spiders he had been surrounded by all his life. Love his mother though he may, he had no intention of marrying someone like her.

Louise Washington was excited about her date with Congressman Patterson. She couldn't believe it when he tracked her down from seeing her on some television show promoting her book. He had told her that she was beautiful and that he liked the way she handled herself before the public.

Her girlfriends were green with envy over her newfound success. Too bad for them.

Wait until they started seeing pictures in the newspapers of her with her new man at all those fancy functions that politicians had to attend.

She put on a tight, red wool dress with a plunging neckline that showed off her large full bosoms. This getup should set their first date on a rolling boil.

The brother was handsome in that razzle-dazzle show business kind of way some men of his generation had. He *had* to be in his mid-sixties. He had that good hair that he slicked back and curled over his ears. She'd observed him on television interview shows and liked the classy way in which he talked, using his cigar as a prop in order to make a point. He had a raspy, attention-commanding voice.

Louise tied her hair in a sparkly black and red turban, which elegantly framed her youthful, round face.

She went in her closet and pulled out her long red fox coat.

She pulled tight, strappy, spike-heeled shoes onto her chubby feet and tipped into the living room, where she fixed herself a gin and tonic.

When Congressman Morris Patterson arrived, she noticed with slight disappointment that he was shorter than she had imagined. He was darker skinned than she had thought, too. She wasn't all that crazy about dark-skinned men. But then, she instantly reminded herself that this was hardly of any importance anymore, especially since he was a big-shot politician.

Her whole game plan had been to elevate her status in life, and dating a congressman, she was certain, would definitely help to ease her up the ladder toward that goal. No more office jobs for *her*! Louise smirked to herself with satisfaction.

Morris glanced around at the crowded room of Italian provincial-style furniture and had instantly recognized that the furnishings in the room had been exclusively purchased at the furniture store chain called the Furniture King. It was amusing how things sometimes seemed to all come together. That furniture chain was owned by the McPheersons from Queens who had been making big fat donations to his campaigns over the years.

He also noticed that she was a pretty woman, yet there was something amiss about the outfit she was wearing. That low neckline on those huge boobs revealed too obviously her intentions.

Oh well, he *well* knew how images on television could sometimes be deceiving. Perhaps she'd turn out to be a terrific woman underneath that getup.

He had liked the way she presented herself on those interview programs. She had become a bestselling writer and was hugely popular in the black community. Elections were coming up soon, and he thought it might boost his popularity even more if he were to have this Louise Washington on his arm.

"Would you like a drink, Morris?"

"I'll just have a Perrier with a twist."

"I only have club soda."

"That's fine. I'll have that." He sat down awkwardly on one of her overstuffed sofas.

Louise decided that she'd have the same thing. She wouldn't want the congressman to think that she was a lush.

"So where would you like to have dinner, Louise?" They both had been so busy that they had decided to pick the restaurant tonight. "I've made reservations at Chez Josette and at Winterhaven, if you'd like to go to one of those places."

Louise was disappointed. She didn't like strange foreign food. She always ended up hungry an hour later. And she never enjoyed those trendy downtown places; the tables were generally too small and uncomfortable.

He noted her disappointment.

"Well, you choose the place, *dear*."

She noticed with some alarm a subtle condescension in his voice.

"I'd love to go to Alphonse's Louisiana Garden."

Oh. That was the hottest place uptown in Harlem. He hid his disappointment at concluding that she'd rather dine up here, where the black folks would know who she was, than go downtown, to one of the best restaurants in the world.

"I'm *dying* to have some of their catfish."

Morris Patterson tried to suppress a cough, but couldn't. He hadn't eaten catfish since he'd fled Mississippi over forty years ago. He had no intention of having any tonight either, but he would, like the true gentleman he tried to be, indulge her in her request.

As they prepared to leave, he panicked as he watched her put on a fox fur coat.

He would be in big trouble if any of those animal-rights people caught him going out with a woman dressed like *this*!

"Please, Louise, don't wear that coat. Don't you have something else—a cloth coat, maybe?"

He was trying to tell *Louise Washington* how to dress. She was ticked off. Who in the hell did he think he *was*?

Morris Patterson was aghast. She ate like a horse! He couldn't believe that she wasn't as fat as a blimp. She kept chattering on and on about her book tours, never asking him a single question about himself.

So, *this* was the celebrated woman who wrote a book called *Black Men: How to Find One, How to Get One, and How to Keep One. The Twelve-Step Program.* The title was definitely catchy, but he had never read the thing. Damn, Morris thought, looking at this self-absorbed woman in disbelief. She'd never get past the "Find One" part with *him*. Her program was unreal.

"That's a really nice tie, Morris." She finally indicated that she had noticed anything at all about him.

"Thank you, Louise. I bought it in Italy. Have you ever been to Italy?"

"Oh, no, not *me*! I didn't lose anything over in that white man's country. I vacation in the Caribbean. One day I intend to visit the motherland." She laughed prettily.

What plebeian pretensions, he thought, glancing at his watch. Which country in Africa did she think was her mother's land?

When he dropped her off at her building, Louise invited him up for a nightcap.

He politely declined.

It was unbelievable, he thought, that a person could spend an entire evening with a politician without asking anything about his political agenda! The true irony of the situation was that she would remain ignorant of the fact that the hard-earned money she had spent—and would probably continue to spend—on major purchases for her home, went in part to campaign contributions for his elections. Instead, she had chosen to spend hours talking about that blatantly counterfeit self-help book of hers.

"Good night, Louise," he said, looking regretfully at this attractive yet naive and pompous lady.

"Pity," he sighed to himself, walking away toward his car.

What a fine gentleman, she thought to herself. Most of the men she'd known would have jumped at the offer of a nightcap just to try to climb into her bed.

She had had a wonderful evening. She enjoyed the intelligent conversation and the terrific food.

Now, with her new status, she was *finally* dating the kind of man she had always wanted to be with.

She smiled with satisfaction as she watched Congressman Morris Patterson's sleek, black limousine speed away into the night.

CHAPTER TWENTY-FIVE

*N*othing Mary Beth had learned in her radio and television classes could have prepared her for the world of television talk shows. But in less than two years, she'd gone from being a lowly production assistant making sure that the coffeepot in the green room was kept full to the producer of one of the most talked-about talkies.

She'd made it a point to study videotapes of every talk show, from the major syndicated hotshots to the insomniac specials. Her nearly total recall of every topic ever done in the last seven years qualified her for a Ph.D. in Voyeuristic Studies.

Mary Beth had decided that the surest method to earn her way into Elroy's good graces and broach the subject of Elroy with her family was by doing a show on interracial dating. She was also pleased that a side benefit of this show was that it might help drag Aletha's show out of its ratings doldrums and increase her own personal approval rating with her boss. This ratings booster was called "Brothers Who Prefer Others."

Aletha had been kind of nervous about it, but curiosity had gotten the best of her. Despite what her sister, Desiree, had said on the matter, Aletha still believed that most black men lusted after white women. Look at her cousin Elroy, for instance, she thought, glancing over at her producer. She figured that maybe the show could give her some insights on the issue. At the least, it probably would boost her ailing ratings.

Mary Beth wanted to do the show because she needed some tips on the issue. She had invited the writer Louise Washington to be on the panel with her book on how to find, get, and keep a black man. Mary Beth certainly felt she needed *this* kind of information, because she hadn't a clue as to how to keep her newfound one. She had also invited the nationally renowned black psychologist who specialized in interracial family therapy, her notes had said, Dr. Hubert S. Freeman, to be on the panel, along with four interracial couples.

Dinner and dessert with Aletha's cousin Elroy had certainly rocked her world, she remembered, smiling smugly to herself.

Aletha's sister and brother-in-law, the Simons, were an intriguing and glamorous couple. Mary Beth felt that she'd like their kind of situation for herself. She had become tired of the boring, high-handed white men she'd been dating lately. Most of them had been either obsessed with their careers or intimidated by hers. Indeed, most of the men in New York City, in her experience, were nearly completely asexual.

Not Aletha's cousin Elroy, though. He appeared to enjoy a healthy balance between his career—designing computer programs—and his personal life. He quite obviously enjoyed the company of an intelligent woman and was romantic, gallant, and ardent in his lovemaking.

It all had convinced her that it was time for a change in her lifestyle.

Aletha was momentarily stunned when she noticed the headlines of the tabloid newspaper that some jerk employee had conspicuously left on her desk.

"ALETHA BROWN'S DARK FAMILY SECRET!!" it screamed in letters spreading across the entire front page.

What "dark family secret"?

Someone had obviously sold the story about Marshall's homosexuality to the paper. As she skimmed the article, Aletha figured that it was either that gigolo Chester Lockwood or the goddamned chauffeur, who had recounted the scene that had taken place at her folks' Christmas dinner party.

Everyone, it seemed to Aletha, was suing her now, from Veronica McPheerson to that hot-looking brother, Dr. Brian Morgan.

It really didn't matter, because Aletha Brown could fix *anything*! She had access to the best lawyers in America.

On the other hand, Aletha was content to have found that she could again do something constructive for another member of her family. Through her contacts at Big Apple Escort Service, she had heard about a wealthy woman who had a penchant for well-built black men. Her brother's lover, Eric, had been exceedingly grateful when she told him that they had found a woman who lived all the way down in Mexico, who was willing to pay a man $250,000 a year to take care of her personal needs. It worked out well that both the woman and Chester found one another mutually suitable.

Eric was ecstatic that Chester had been removed from the country, and Aletha felt that she had, in some small way, made up for the selfish firing of his cousin, Veronica McPheerson.

She and Desiree called each other often now. Aletha found that she really enjoyed the company of her sister and her brother-in-law. She regretted having allowed her competitive nature to interfere with the relationship between her and the one person who understood her best. Aletha had every intention of making up for the squandered years of reckless self-absorption.

Things were beginning to look better. Aletha was going to make a brand-new life for herself with her family.

So why did she feel a peculiar gnawing sensation in her gut as the office around her seemed to shift momentarily out of focus?

In makeup, Bruce was attending to two of the guests, Dr. Hubert S. Freeman and the bestselling author Louise Washington.

Bruce didn't see any wedding band on the woman's finger. On what basis did some publisher decide to validate this woman's credibility, he wondered.

As he buffed a shine from the doctor's forehead, he wondered why on *earth* anyone would care why black men preferred "others." What was everybody talking about anyway? Most of the black heterosexual men that Bruce knew were married to black women. In fact, according to *his* observations, most people seemed to choose people from their own racial groups. This was obviously going to be another one of Aletha's Looney Tunes shows dictated by her sagging ratings. Where did they find these people anyway, who voluntarily go on television programs in order to expose themselves and their private lives to the wrath of the masses?

Louise Washington was in no mood to be on a panel of black men with their "others," she thought, looking in the mirror and admiring Bruce's masterful workmanship. "No wonder Aletha Brown always looks so divine on her show," she said to herself.

Nevertheless, she realized too late that she should have taken her son's advice.

Those people hadn't told her the topic, leading her to believe it was a show about relationships between black men and black women and that she would be the guest authority on the matter because of her book. Instead, sitting next to her was some joker who they said called himself an authority on interracial relationships.

Please!

Sometimes she'd get a nervous rush before going on one of these television programs, hoping that no one asked her why *she* wasn't married.

She leaned back in the makeup chair and closed her eyes, remembering that it had been months since her date with the congressman. He had never called her again.

He could promise a tax-free four years for all she cared. She'd be damned if she'd vote for *that* nigger.

Dr. Freeman was nervous.

This would be his first time on television. Although he had been hesitant to appear on a talk show, his wife had convinced him to do it, saying that it might increase his number of patients and make an even bigger name for him. Yet, he couldn't for the life of him figure out where those *Aletha Brown Show* people had gotten the idea that he specialized in *interracial* family therapy! He was simply a family therapist, who had never been with anyone but black women, including his wife.

Debra Parker looked around at the audience. The energy in the room was electrifying. She'd never thought to get a ticket to a talk show, especially *this* one, but someone had told her that the writer Louise Washington was to be on. Debra Parker had become her number one fan. She had read her book three times and wanted to see what the woman was really like. From her photo on the dust jacket she could tell that Louise Washington was a woman who knew what was what. She looked like a totally together sister.

Debra almost fainted when the panel of guests assembled on the stage. A bunch of black men with some *white women*! What did *this* have to do with her girl Louise Washington's book?

She wanted to run, but it was too late. The cameras were rolling.

Aletha began nervously, "Today's show is called 'Brothers who prefer others.'"

Frightened, she glanced over at security as an outraged roar soared toward her from the audience.

When Aletha looked up at the monitor, sweat balls jumped from her forehead as she noticed with horror that some asshole assistant had written "Black Men Who *Hate* Black Women" and now it was being displayed under the unsuspecting faces of her guests.

She felt detached through the taping, as if she was having an out-of-body experience. She watched her audience of angry black women irately shake balled fists at her guests with evil twisted expressions around their mouths, some yelling cruel obscenities. This was madness!

Aletha's mind flashed back to the evil, project-dwelling skeezer children who used to taunt her and Desiree when they were kids.

She then heard Louise Washington say to one of the men married to a white woman on the panel, "*Of course*, as black women, we have the right to criticize. We *own* you, brother!"

Aletha shuddered as she recalled the day she had uttered those very same words to Reggie then shot him. Shot him in his very own home.

"We are your mothers, your sisters," Louise continued.

The man interrupted her, "I love my mother and my sisters, but I feel that I'm healthy because I *don't* want to *sleep* with them!"

"What kind of a black man in his right mind would give up on spare ribs and neck bones just for some chicken pot pie and fish sticks?" an incensed sister from the audience yelled.

"*Tell* it, girl!"

Mary Beth stood off camera, twisting the cord on her headset while she puzzled over that last statement. She had grown up on all the food that the woman had mentioned, and yet her folks were as white as Wonder bread. She shrugged her shoulders and then looked anxiously over at Aletha, who was looking over at security.

"If God had meant for people to be racially mixed, we would have been all *born* that way like a pack of zebras!" an elderly black woman wearing what looked like a man's fedora festooned with pansies shouted. She eased herself back into her chair barely acknowledging the cheers and hisses that fell like rain.

Then, a young black woman wearing waist-length, braided, blond extensions and blue contact lenses stood up. She snapped the tips of her four-inch scarlet acrylic nails on her thumb and forefinger of her left hand and shouted, "I *know* why black men like you all go off and marry white chicks! It's because those bitches will let you get away with the kind of shit that the sisters would shoot you for!"

Aletha almost fainted to the floor.

Dr. Freemen started to say something when Debra Parker suddenly stood up.

She just *couldn't* believe it! Debra Parker felt an atrocious balloon of betrayal swelling in her breast.

Why was *her* therapist, Dr. Freeman, on the panel with these nuts? Her ex-doctor, Desiree Simon, had given her referrals of black doctors who were married to black people, or so she had *said*.

How could she have spilled out her secrets all those months to that lying, twisted, fake, black sister of Aletha Brown!

"How can you help black patients, Dr. Freeman, when you're married to a white woman?" she yelled, obviously confused.

The doctor's mouth slammed shut. That was his patient, Debra Parker, he thought. What was she *talking* about? A rush of fear silenced the already shy doctor.

One of the white wives, disgusted and tired of the insulting circus around her, glared at Debra Parker and said, "Maybe black men go to white women because they are sick and tired of loud, rude, confrontational, controlling women who—"

"Slut!" a black voice screeched.

"Straggly haired, tired, beat-up, white trash!" thundered another.

The white people in the audience, who for the most part had been eerily nonparticipatory, started to leave their seats and move toward the back of the studio.

Things were happening too fast. Aletha, having lost control, glanced again over at security.

A chair flew across the room.

Pandemonium reigned.

The black men fled from the studio with their white women.

Louise Washington ran to a corner and watched the insanity. She couldn't think of anything else to do.

Over the outbreak of mob hysteria, Aletha heard Mary Beth yell, in a voice filled with horror, "He's *dead*! They've *killed* the doctor! Oh, my God, they've killed him."

Upon hearing the sounds of bedlam in the studio and then hearing the tragic news, Bruce decided to quit the show on the spot.

* * *

"That sucker died for his sins," Debra Parker muttered to herself, her horrified facial expression belying her smug satisfaction.

Then she fainted.

Ms. Parker was convinced that this mayhem was all her fault.

CHAPTER TWENTY-SIX

"So, how are you today, Ms. Moskowitz?" Desiree asked, motioning for Rachel to sit.

"As a matter of fact, Doctor, I am terrific! I am here to tell you that I will not be returning for any more sessions."

"Oh? Why didn't you just call? You didn't have to make a special trip all the way—"

"You don't understand, Dr. Simon. I am here to thank you in person."

"You don't have to—"

"Yes, I do. I wanted you to know that I took your advice and wrote a letter, on my legal stationery, to the people who work for that nanny show. And you were *right*. It was amazing. Within only a few weeks or so, I have noticed they have taken an entirely different approach. It's like magic! I have no idea how they did it, but they *did*. And again, I want to thank you." Rachel Moskowitz handed Desiree a small gift box.

"I'm glad I could help. But I can't accept this." She pushed the box back toward her now ex-patient, making a mental note to tune into the program later in the week, or have David remember to tape it.

"Yes, you *can*. It has the same dollar value as this hour that you would bill me for. Since I won't be staying for this session, I feel that this is the least I could do to show my appreciation, for *everything*."

Desiree opened the box to find a gold and topaz butterfly lapel pin.

"It's lovely, Ms. Moskowitz," she gasped with delight.

"I noticed that you like jewelry."

Desiree absentmindedly touched her earlobe and realized that she had been wearing her favorite pair of gold and topaz earrings that day.

"Also, Dr. Simon, I had noticed a few months ago that you had some birthday cards on your desk, and since it had been late in November, I figured you to be a Sagittarian, meaning that your birthstone would be topaz. Am I correct?"

"Why, yes. I'm flattered that you—"

"You're welcome." Her ex-patient smiled, holding up her hand to stop her from saying anything further.

Desiree was amazed to find that there were still people in the world—especially during this mean-spirited nineties decade—who thought about other people. Maybe there was hope for humanity after all.

Suddenly, all the buttons on her telephone lit up. She tried to reach her receptionist on the intercom, but there was no response.

"Please excuse me, Ms. Moskowitz. There seems to be a problem with the phones." Desiree excused herself and rushed to the reception area.

Ms. Moskowitz followed.

As she approached the room, she heard her assistant yelling her name, her voice quavering in panic.

Desiree noticed that the small television set that she had allowed in the area was on, and that her assistant was staring at it in shock, holding the receiver to her ear.

"Dr. Simon. They've killed Dr. Freeman!"

"What?"

"On your sister's show! He was a guest and they killed him!" she shrieked.

"Oh my God." Desiree's head began to pound. How was it possible? she thought, walking over to stand in front of the TV set. She stared, watching the special bulletin.

Upon giving notice that she was closing her practice, she had referred a number of her patients to her colleague Dr. Freeman. What on *earth* had happened? And what in God's name was she going to do *now*? she wondered, her well-laid plans now exploding in her face.

Rachel, her face drained pale with astonishment, tapped her on the shoulder and said, "Dr. Simon, I am sure that your sister probably has the best legal representation there *is*, but just in case, here is my card."

She pressed her business card into Desiree's limp hand and fled the office.

Desiree turned to her receptionist and asked, "What was the show about?"

"Black men who prefer white women, Doc."

"What?" Desiree shouted, still staring at the reporters on the television. What did a show like that have to do with her friend Dr. Freeman? Why would Aletha even *do* such a show?

Suddenly her mind leaped to Aletha's new producer, their cousin Elroy's new girlfriend, Mary Beth Dean.

"Shit!" she uttered out loud. Desiree didn't know whether she should shit, go blind, or just go over to Mary Beth's apartment and slap her silly for her outrageously irresponsible behavior. She'd have to read Aletha the riot act, as well. What in the world had those two ninnies been thinking of, planning a show like that?

Damn!

"Dr. Simon?"

"What?" She was instantly sorry that she had snapped so rudely at her receptionist like that. After all, the woman had had nothing to do with this mess.

"Dr. Annunciata DaSilva, on line three."

Desiree reached over for the receiver, and the receptionist pressed down on the button.

"Yes, I *heard*! Umm-hmm. . . . I'm watching it on the news right now. . . .No, I have no idea what Aletha was thinking."

She thought of her poor patients, as Annunciata relayed what she had seen and heard, then thought of the poor Dr. Freeman and his widow. Then in a flash, she realized what she had to do. She had to ask Annunciata if she could possibly take on some of Dr. Freeman's patients.

"Annunciata, can you possibly meet me at Gleason's?

"You can? How about in an hour? Okay, in two hours. I need your help."

CHAPTER TWENTY-SEVEN

She had fled *The Aletha Brown Show* studio the first chance she could after the ambulance had arrived to take the poor doctor away.

Preoccupied with her thoughts, Louise Washington stepped from the cab and closed the door before realizing that she had left an inappropriately large tip. When she turned around, the cab driver had already sped away.

"I guess it's just payback time," she muttered to herself as she slid her purse back into her coat pocket.

Life had been good to her because she had decided, the day she left the convent, to paint each event and chapter in her life with the colors that she alone felt were fitting. She had found herself partial to bold, flat, primary colors. She had lived a pop art kind of life. She'd had a lot of fun and had been successful despite her somewhat deprived beginnings.

Never having had a traditional family, she had decided as an adult to leave the religious cloister of the alternative family she had inherited in order to live a life of worldly adventure and sensuality. Her survival tools had been meager, but she had managed to carve out a rewarding life through will, determination, and a hell of a lot of innovation.

Looking at the ledger of her life, she could check off a nice home, a healthy and successful son, some good friends, good health, and now a very comfortable living. She had even learned to live with the companionship of the nagging aching hole in her heart that nothing and no one person could ever fill . . . even her beautiful and talented young son, Brian.

Yet, through recent events, she had begun to detect that something had gone wrong a long time ago. Something she had begun to suspect that might have had to do with *accountability*. Things were—in some vague way that she couldn't put her finger on—slipping into small, thin cracks.

She had decided that she needed to seek guidance if she really wanted to get her life back on track before it was too late.

Louise Washington walked through the entrance of the huge cathedral.

She genuflected and crossed herself with holy water. Louise genuflected again and then, moving forward in a trancelike state which contained flashes of memory both beautiful and painful, she proceeded down the long aisle.

She found herself sitting in the confessional booth nervously clutching her rosary beads.

"Father, forgive me, for I have sinned."

"When was the last time you came to confession, Child?"

"Nineteen sixty-four, Father."

CHAPTER TWENTY-EIGHT

Down in Miami, Dr. Brian Morgan was sitting with his wife, Marta, watching the six o'clock news. His wife reached over and touched his hand protectively as the reporters recounted the events of the *The Aletha Brown Show* fiasco.

"You could have been killed on that television program, honey," his wife said incredulously, hitting the remote control to turn off the set.

Dr. Morgan had been relieved that his wife hadn't yet connected the dots that joined the Louise Washington on the panel with the how-to book to the woman who was the mother of his son whom she had met for the first time that past Christmas.

He figured that this would be the perfect time to tell her.

CHAPTER TWENTY-NINE

*V*eronica McPherson's eyes had been glued to the television set and the evening news.

"*This* would have never happened if *I* were still the producer, would it, my little man?" She walked over to pick up Derrick Junior from the floor. He had already started crawling all over the place, yet his first birthday was still months away.

"Holy shit!" her cousin Eric exclaimed from the sofa next to her. "Marshall! Come in here and look at *this*—on the news! Somebody was killed today on your sister's program."

Marshall and Clarisse ran in from the kitchen where they had been preparing dinner.

"What happened?" Clarisse asked, wiping her hands on her apron.

"Somebody died on Aletha's show?" Marshall asked incredulously, about to sit down in front of the television.

Veronica aimed the remote control and abruptly turned off the set.

"This would have never happened if I were still the producer!" she snapped.

Holding little Derrick tightly in her arms, she looked at each of the people in her den. She called them her New Age American Clan. There they were: her best friend, Clarisse, over forty and still single and now the baby's godmother; her cousin, Eric, a homosexual model and the baby's godfather; and the strangest twist of all, Aletha's brother, Marshall, her cousin's significant other. Just when she thought she had put her Aletha Brown–dominated life behind her, the woman's presence came back to haunt her.

News was always slow to reach the Betty Ford Clinic. At least, it had for Janeen Davis during her first month in captivity.

Okay, maybe it wasn't all that easy anymore to distinguish between a faggot and a straight, she thought, as she savored her lentils and rice.

The fact that she had allowed herself to believe Marshall Brown was her best friend all those years made her realize that this little vacation was necessary to evaluate and eliminate the glitches in her personal life.

Anyone like Marshall who could maintain a relationship with someone while withholding such fundamental details about their personal life must be some kind of a sadomasochist, a danger to himself and others, and certainly not any kind of friend, she had concluded.

Nevertheless, pushing all of that permanently behind her, she recalled last year's prediction about meeting rich clients in an isolated place.

Janeen looked around her and smiled at all the millionaire celebrities and other assorted hotshots and could see, in her mind's eye, her client list swell. As her eyes swept from the fifties' superstar actress to the billion-dollar rap star, she realized that she was content in the knowledge that even though she would probably never land a husband, she, Janeen Davis, would be as rich as Croesus as a result of her sojourn at this detox center.

She had made a note in her calendar to make another appointment with that psychic, Dr. Annunciata DaSilva, as soon as she completed her treatment.

"Hello, Ms. Davis. I understand that you are a decorator. I'd like to talk to you about my new place in Malibu. May I sit down?"

"Why, yes. Of course," she said breathlessly starstruck, toward the face of the celebrated woman whose packed-to-the-rafters concert she had attended only two months ago.

"I am—"

"Yes, yes," she interrupted. The introduction was completely unnecessary. Probably everyone in the world knew who the woman was, she thought, shaking the singer's hand.

CHAPTER THIRTY

"*A*nd the winner is . . ."

She wasn't all that optimistic, but Aletha was feeling fantastic in that snugly, giddy kind of way as she leaned into the crook of the elbow of her new man.

He had her roving fingers firmly locked between his hands, which he pressed steadfastly onto her lap, in order to discourage that reprehensible tendency she had, he'd discovered, to stroke her companion's cheek in public.

She thought she *owned* people and seemed to want everyone else in the free world to know it.

He couldn't figure why that Geraldo character kept glancing over at them. He was going to get to the bottom of this, later.

He had dated a couple of American women before and had found them to be the most aggressive women he had ever met. Aletha was definitely no exception. His weakness was that she had legs and thighs that made him want to slay dragons for her, and it was obvious that she had unfulfilled desires that he felt challenged to satisfy.

He glanced over next to him at Mary Beth Dean and her escort for the evening—Aletha's cousin Elroy. Ms. Dean was sitting up straight and tensely biting her already almost nonexistent fingernails.

"*The Aletha Brown Show*, Mary Beth Dean, Producer!"

Mary Beth shot up from her seat and screamed with what could be considered no less than rapture. In the process, one of Mary Beth's gaudy rhinestone rings brushed past and ripped the bodice of Aletha's brand-new Byron Lars matte jersey evening gown.

Aletha was unperturbed.

Her mind wandered back to the day when the interracial family therapist, Dr. Freeman, was murdered on her show. She made a mental note to light a candle in his memory when she got home.

There was thunderous applause.

Aletha rose from her seat to accept the long overdue acknowledgment.

CHAPTER THIRTY-ONE

"*THE END*," typed Reggie. *Finally* after six whole years of hard work and painful distractions he was on the final page of his novel. He had decided that the title would be part of a quote from the New Testament: *He Who Is Without Guilt*.

He stood up and stretched his arms, looking about at his relatively new and nurturing environment.

It had been over a year since Aletha had chased him away from New York with her inappropriate suspicions and her gun.

With the help of his agent, he had found a new apartment and a new life on the West Coast. She had not only landed him a lucrative book deal, but he was now working on his first movie contract, a screenplay for Seaside Productions. He walked down the steps of his sunken living room and pulled open the terrace doors of his Malibu apartment, which overlooked the undulating waves of the Pacific. He was the happiest he'd been in years because he was now completely on his own.

It was a beautiful evening, and he had absolutely nothing to do, no plans at all, because he didn't know a soul in Los Angeles.

He turned from the glittering Pacific seascape to return to the comfort of his living room. He flicked on the remote.

Aletha was up on some stage in New York accepting the TV talk show award. He was happy for her.

He started laughing when he noticed that someone had ripped the bodice of her evening gown. He wondered who that man could be and how he'd gotten trapped in her emotionally exhausting web.

"Good luck, gorgeous lady," he said out loud, clicking off the TV set.

CHAPTER THIRTY-TWO

*T*he following Christmas Aletha, looking radiant and rested, sat by the pool at the Simons' sunny, lovely, and peaceful rental in Maui. She had been nominated again this year and finally, after six nominations, *The Aletha Brown Show* had won. The statue for best talk show was finally living with its rightful owner. Of course, as had been predicted by Desiree's friend Annunciata, it had not been exactly the happy victory that she had expected. She knew why they had decided to give it to her this year. It was nothing she wanted to dwell on at this particular time.

In the garden, Sparky and Hemingway were playfully teasing some tropical birds.

Desiree and David were running about preparing their particular version of a luau. It was superb. They had invited over some of their new Hawaiian friends. Aletha looked over at her brother, Marshall, sitting in a chaise longue, his eyes tenderly following his lover Eric's long, bronzed body as he gracefully swam his laps across the pool.

"I love you, Aletha," her man whispered.

Aletha had decided to try something different this time. And so far she was quite content.

Massaging oil, with blissfully gifted hands, onto her silky thighs was her handsome and attentive lover.

When Desiree's ex-boyfriend Philip Akai had made a trip to the East Coast, she had suggested he call Aletha. While there, he had introduced her to Kevin, his friend from Hawaii.

"Do you think Aletha's 'Samurai Lover' will keep her in check?" David lightheartedly asked Desiree, pointing to the cozy couple.

"We can only hope," responded Desiree, looking over at Aletha and her latest paramour, Kevin.

Kevin Yamamoto.

EPILOGUE

Back in the forest—Central Park, rather—the van containing the six women, their hunger for revenge momentarily satisfied, sped away.

Under the serene blanket of winking stars a branch snapped, followed by the sound of a soft thud. The brother's raucous laughter was a mixture of relief and childlike glee. Those crazed, misguided wenches had hung him from a dead branch, and he had landed on a cushiony pile of pine needles. He worked himself out of the ropes that held his hands behind his back. As he lifted his hand to remove the rope around his neck, the black hoot owl flew back to help him.

He looked up at the owl and said, "You know, it's something, isn't it? Out of six women, not a damned one had any idea how to tie a knot! I told you not to panic, owl. Those broads didn't have a clue about what the hell they were doing."

He stood up to brush himself off and noticed that the owl was trying to tell him something. The owl swooped in a circle around him, flying away westward, returning to his shoulder and then taking off again.

He felt compelled to follow.

Glancing back to make sure that there was no one watching him, he started running as the owl picked up speed.

Where on earth was this bird leading him, he wondered, wiping away a thin line of sweat from behind his ear.

His feet propelled him through the park onto West Seventy-second Street, onto Riverside Drive, past those stately prewar apartment buildings. He arrived at the Seventy-ninth Street Boat Basin at the edge of the shore.

In the distance he saw a dimly lit sailboat swaying on the shoreline. As he approached, he noticed six male figures on deck waving at him, one shining a flashlight in his direction.

"We've been expecting you, brother," one of them said.

"Who the *hell* are you guys?"

"My name is Reggie," said the tall, light-skinned one. "And these are my friends!"

"Hop on in," said the tall, dark-skinned, bearded one.

The brother hesitated.

"Aw, come on, man. Don't worry. We're not going to serve you any catfish or nothing," bellowed the man puffing on a cigar, with a laugh that caused the others to join in.

"Where are we going?"

"Outta *here*, that's for sure," one of them muttered, shaking the brother's hand as he climbed onboard. The newly rescued brother looked out at the vast expanse of river before them.

Having been shot at, manipulated, insulted, and downright disrespected, the men sailed away.

Not too far in the distance, several beautiful mermaids with long, flowing locks and full, pink-nippled breasts emerged from the water.

The ladies winked, smiled, and swam ahead, seductively beckoning the men in their direction.

It looked like smooth sailing ahead.

David laughed and set down the final manuscript pages of Desiree's first novel.

"That was hysterical, honey."

"So, what did you think?"

"I think you have a pretty terrific sense of humor for a shrink."

"I guess I'm supposed to take that as a compliment, huh?"

"Absolutely. So, to whom are you going to dedicate this book?"

She stood up and stretched her arms over her head. She walked to the edge of the terrace and for a long moment, drank in their view of the glittering Mediterranean and the harbor of Saint-Tropez.

"I've decided to dedicate it to the sisters back in the States."

"A kind of cautionary tale for them, huh, honey?"

"I suppose."

"Nice." He slid his arm around Desiree's waist and embraced her.

. . . and they all lived happily ever after.

ACKNOWLEDGMENTS

A deeply heartfelt thank-you and love to my husband, Allan, for his love, support, and terrific sense of humor, which enabled him to patiently endure all of those 5 A.M. readings and those periodic anxiety attacks, which were definitely a large part of this writer's creative process.

Also, love and kisses to my mother, Eva, who insisted that I return to my writing, to my father, Henry, who taught me to look for the big picture, and to my grandmother Maggie, who has always been a staunch supporter of all my creative endeavors.

Hearts and flowers to my friends Camille Belcher, Denise Preston-Roussetzky, Helen Chu-Lapiroff, and her husband, Jerry, whose inspiration, keen, humorous insights, and suggestions concerning this novel were greatly appreciated.

A high five to my agent at William Morris, Matt Bialer, and his assistant, Maya Perez, for both recognizing a good thing and enthusiastically supporting it through its various incarnations.

I am grateful that fate has rewarded me for my first novel the opportunity to work with a talented editorial team, my editor, Cheryl Woodruff, and her associate editor, Gary Brozek. I enjoyed *their* wickedly funny wit as well.

By the way, Cheryl, thank you for keeping the hobbling to a minimum. Wink.

ABOUT THE AUTHOR

DELORYS WELCH-TYSON is a former gallery owner turned novelist. She lives in New York City and the south of France. *Gingersnaps* is her first novel.